THE OATH

*Also by John Lescroart
in Large Print:*

The Hearing
The Mercy Rule
A Certain Justice
The 13th Juror

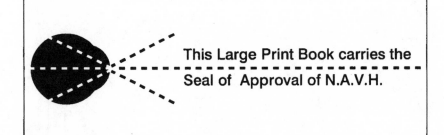

This Large Print Book carries the
Seal of Approval of N.A.V.H.

THE OATH

John Lescroart

Thorndike Press • Waterville, Maine

I 10.02

Published in 2002 by arrangement with Dutton, a member of Penguin Putnam Inc.

Thorndike Press Large Print Core Series.

The tree indicium is a trademark of Thorndike Press.

The text of this Large Print edition is unabridged. Other aspects of the book may vary from the original edition.

Set in 16 pt. Plantin by Rick Gundberg.

Printed in the United States on permanent paper.

I05

LP
F
Les
0

Library of Congress Cataloging-in-Publication Data

Lescroart, John T.
   The oath / John Lescroart.
    p. cm.
   ISBN 0-7862-4193-4 (lg. print : hc : alk. paper)
   ISBN 0-7862-4194-2 (lg. print : sc : alk. paper)
   1. Hardy, Dismas (Fictitious character) — Fiction.
2. Hospital patients — Mortality — Fiction. 3. San Francisco (Calif.) — Fiction. 4. Hospitals — Fiction. 5. Large type books.
I. Title.
PS3562.E78 O28 2002b
   813'.54—dc21   2002020721

This one's to Pete Dietrich,
Bob Zaro,
and, as always, to Lisa —
Doctor, Lawyer, Indian Chief

Acknowledgments

At the beginning of this effort, my knowledge of medicine and the medical establishment was limited, to say the least. I'd especially like to thank Marcy St. John, senior counsel with Blue Shield of California, and Pat Fry, chief operating officer of Sutter Health, for the insights and information that helped somewhat bridge this gap in my education and knowledge. Also, thanks to two nurses for their help: my sister Pat Barile, and Cheri Van Hoover.

In the legal realm, as always I depend most heavily on the expertise of my great friend and collaborator Alfred F. Giannini of the San Francisco District Attorney's office. Inspector Joe Toomey of the San Francisco Police Department has also been most generous with his time and expertise.

My day-to-day life is enhanced considerably by the competency and wonderful personality of my phenomenal assistant, Anita Boone. She is a treasure to work with and a joy to know.

No less heartfelt thanks — for a variety of other reasons — go to Tom Hedtke; Poppy Gilman; Jesse Tepper, president and founder of the San Francisco Little League; Peter J. Diedrich; and Dee Scocos. Richard Herman is a terrific author himself — go read him — and he supplied an important epiphany.

The names of three characters in this novel were supplied by the winners in charitable auctions; I would like to acknowledge the generous contributions of Margie Krystofiak to Serra High School of San Mateo, California; Frank Husic to *Imagine*; and Catherine Treinen to Cal-State Fullerton.

I am deeply indebted to all the people at Dutton for their tremendous support and commitment; in particular, I would like to single out Glenn Timony, Lisa Johnson, Kathleen Matthews-Schmidt, Susan Schwartz, and Kim Hadney for their yeoman efforts. Carole Baron has been and continues to be a terrific publisher, cheerleader, and friend; our regular discussions on book and other matters are a source of great pleasure, and have helped to sharply focus and improve the narrative of this novel. Mitch Hoffman is a great guy and superb editor; the book's final shape owes much to his suggestions and good taste.

Barney Karpfinger remains the best agent an author could ever have, and a true friend as well. His artistic encouragement, level head, business acumen, and sense of humor are each as important as they are rare. Barney, you're a true mensch, and I can't thank you enough for everything.

Closer to home, perennial best man Don Matheson just keeps those good times coming; and Frank Seidl remains the king of wine and laughter. Finally, my two children, Justine and Jack, continue to enrich my life on a daily basis.

My borrowings of their concerns and life events continue to inform and hopefully enrich these novels and my life, both of which would be empty without them.

PART ONE

I will follow that method of treatment which
. . . I consider for the benefit of my patients,
and abstain from whatever is deleterious and
mischievous. I will give no deadly medicine
to anyone if asked, nor suggest any such
counsel . . .

The Hippocratic Oath

The love of money is the root of all evil.

Timothy 6:10

Her stupid, old American car wasn't working again. So now Luz Lopez was sitting on the bus with her sick son, Ramiro, dozing beside her. This time of day, midmorning, the streetcar wasn't crowded, and she was glad of that. Ramiro, small for eleven years old, had room to curl up with his head on her lap. She stroked his cheek gently with the back of her hand. He opened his eyes and smiled at her weakly.

His skin was warm to her touch, but not really burning. She was more concerned about the cut on his lip than the sore throat. There was something about the look of it that bothered her. He'd banged it on some playground bars on Monday and today, Thursday, it was swollen, puffy, yellowish at the edges. But when the sore throat had come on yesterday, Ramiro had complained not about the cut lip, but the throat. Luz knew her boy wouldn't make a fuss unless there was real pain. He was up half the night with gargling and Tylenol. But this morning, he told her it wasn't any better.

She had to take the day off so he could see a doctor. Time off was always a risk. Though she'd been halfway to her business degree when she'd left home, now she worked as a maid at the Osaka Hotel in Japantown, and they

13

were strict about attendance. Even if the reason was good, Luz knew that every day she missed work counted against her. The clinic said they could see him before noon — a miracle — so maybe she could get his prescription and have Ramiro back at school by lunchtime, then she could still put in a half day back at the Osaka.

She had lived in San Francisco for over ten years now, though she would never call the place home. After the opponents of land reform in El Salvador had killed her father, a newspaper publisher, and then her brother Alberto, a doctor who had never cared about politics, she had fled north with her baby inside her. It had taken her husband, José, almost three years to follow her here, and then last year La Migra had sent him back. Now, unable to find work back home, he lived with her mother.

She shifted on her seat on her way to the Judah Clinic, which was not on Judah Street at all, but two blocks before Judah began, where the same street was called Parnassus. Why did they not call it the Parnassus Clinic, then? She shook her head, these small things keeping her mind from what it wanted to settle on, which was the health of her son.

And of course the money. Always money.

Ramiro's tiny hand lay like a dead bird in hers as they walked from the streetcar stop to the clinic, a converted two-story Victorian house. When she opened the front door, she abandoned all hope that they'd get to her quickly. Folding chairs lined the walls of the waiting room. More were scattered randomly in the

14

open space in the middle, and every seat was taken. On the floor itself, a half dozen kids played with ancient plastic blocks, or little metal cars and trucks that didn't have all the wheels on them.

Behind the reception window, four women sat at computer terminals. Luz waited, then cleared her throat. One of the women looked up. "Be just a minute," she said, and went back to whatever she was doing. There was a bell on the counter, with instructions to ring it for service, but the computer woman already had told Luz she'd just be a minute (although now it had been more like five), and Luz didn't want to risk getting anyone mad at her. They would just go more slowly. But she was angry, and sorely tempted.

At last the woman sighed and came to the window. She fixed Luz with an expression of perfect boredom and held out her hand. "Health card, please." She entered some information into her computer, didn't look up. "Ten dollars," she said. After she'd taken it and put it in a drawer, the woman continued. "Your son's primary care doctor is Dr. Whitson, but he's unavailable today. Do you have another preference?"

Luz wanted to ask why Dr. Whitson was unavailable, but knew that there would be no point in complaining. If Dr. Whitson wasn't here, he wasn't here. Asking about him wouldn't bring him back. "No." She smiled, trying to establish some connection. "Sooner would be better, though."

The woman consulted her computer screen, punched a few more keys. "Dr. Jadra can see Ramiro in twenty-five minutes. Just have a seat and we'll call you."

The words just popped out. "But there are no seats."

The woman flicked a look to the waiting room over Luz's shoulder. "One'll turn up any second." She looked over her shoulder. "Next."

While Ramiro dozed fitfully, Luz picked up a copy of the latest edition of *San Francisco* magazine. There were many of them in the room, all with the same cover photo of a strong Anglo businessman's face. Luz read English well and soon realized the reason for the multiple copies. The story was about the director of Parnassus Health — her insurance company. The man's name was Tim Markham. He had a pretty wife, three nice-looking children, and a dog. He lived in a big house in Seacliff and in all the pictures they took, he was smiling.

Luz cast a glance around the waiting room. No one was smiling here.

She stared at the face for another minute, then looked down at her sick boy, then up at the wall clock. She went back to Mr. Markham's smiling face, then read some more. Things were good in his life. His company was experiencing some growing pains, yes, but Markham was on top of them. And in the meantime, his patients continued to receive excellent medical care, and that was the most important

16

thing. That was what he really cared about. It was his lifelong passion.

Finally, finally, a nurse called Ramiro's name. Luz folded the magazine over and put it in her purse. Then they walked down a long hallway to a tiny windowless room with a paper-covered examining table, a sink and counter, a small bookcase and shelves. Posters of California mountain and beach scenes, perhaps once vibrantly colored, now hung faded and peeling from the walls.

Ramiro laid himself down on the table and told his mom he was cold, so she covered him with her coat. Luz sat in an orange plastic molded chair, took out her magazine, and waited again.

At 12:22, Jadra knocked once on the door, then opened it and came in. Small and precise, completely bald, the doctor introduced himself as he perused the chart. "Busy day today," he said by way of apology. "I hope you haven't had to wait too long."

Luz put on a pleasant expression. "Not too bad."

"We're a little shorthanded today. Twenty doctors and something like eight have this virus going around." He shook his head wearily. "And you're Ramiro?"

"*Sí.*" Her boy had opened his eyes again and gotten himself upright.

"How are you feeling?"

"Not so good. My throat . . ."

Jadra pulled a wooden stick from a container on the counter. "Well, let's take a look at it. Can

17

you stick out your tongue as far as you can and say 'ahh'?"

That examination took about ten seconds. When it was over, Jadra placed a hand on the boy's neck and prodded around gently. "Does that hurt? How about that?"

"Just when I swallow."

Five minutes later, Luz and Ramiro were back outside. They'd been at the clinic for over two hours. It had cost Luz ten dollars, more than she made in an hour, plus a full day's wages. Dr. Jadra had examined Ramiro for less than one minute and had diagnosed his sore throat as a virus. He should take Children's Tylenol and an over-the-counter throat medication. He explained that the way viruses work, symptoms go away by themselves within about fourteen days or two weeks, whichever came first.

A joke, Luz supposed, though it didn't make her laugh.

Two days later, Ramiro was worse, but Luz had to go to work. Last time they'd warned her about her absences. There were a lot of others who would be happy to take her job if she didn't want to work at the hotel anymore. So she had to take Ramiro into urgent care at night, after she got off.

On the bus, she gathered him in next to her, wrapped her own coat over his shivering little body. He curled up and immediately fell asleep. His breathing sounded like someone crinkling a paper bag inside his lungs. His cough was the bark of a seal.

This night, the clinic was less crowded. Luz paid her ten dollars and within a half hour, full dark outside now, she heard Ramiro's name called. She woke her boy and followed a stout man back into another tiny office, similar to Dr. Jadra's except there was no art, even faded.

Ramiro didn't notice. He climbed onto the paper-covered examining table, curled his knees up to his chest, and closed his eyes. Again she covered him with her jacket, and again she waited. Until she was startled awake by a knock at the door.

"I could use a nap myself," the woman said gently in good Spanish. She wore a badge that said DR. JUDITH COHN. She studied the folder, then brought her attention back to Luz. "So. Tell me about Ramiro. Where did he get this cut?"

"At school. He fell down. But he complains of his throat."

The doctor frowned deeply, reached for a tongue depressor. After a longer look than Dr. Jadra had taken, Dr. Cohn turned to Luz. "The throat doesn't look good, but I really don't like the look of this cut," she said in Spanish. "I'd like to take a culture. Meanwhile, in case it isn't a virus, I'll prescribe an antibiotic."

"But the other doctor . . ."

"Yes?" She reached out a hand reassuringly. "It's okay. What's your question?"

"The other doctor said it was a virus. Now it might not be. I don't understand."

Dr. Cohn, about the same age as Luz, was sympathetic. "Sometimes a virus will bring on a

19

secondary infection that will respond to anti-biotics. The cut looks infected to me."

"And the drug will take care of that?"

The doctor, nodding, already had the prescription pad out. "Does Ramiro have any allergies? Good, then. Now, if for some reason the cut doesn't clear up, I might want to prescribe a stronger antibiotic, but I'll let you know when I get the results of the test."

"When will that be? The results?"

"Usually two to three days."

"Three more days? Couldn't we just start with the stronger antibiotic now? Then I would not have to come back for another appointment."

The doctor shook her head. "You won't have to come here again. I can call in the other prescription if we need it."

Luz waited, then whispered, "There is also the expense, the two prescriptions."

Dr. Cohn clucked sadly. "I'm sorry about that, but we really don't want to prescribe a stronger antibiotic than Ramiro needs." She touched Luz on the forearm. "He'll be fine. You don't need to worry."

Luz tried to smile. She couldn't help but worry. Ramiro was no better. In fact, she knew that he was worse. Despite her resolve, a tear broke and rolled over her cheek. She quickly, angrily, wiped it away, but the doctor had seen it. "Are you really so worried?"

A mute nod. Then, "I'm afraid . . ."

The doctor sat down slowly and leaned in toward her. She spoke in an urgent whisper. "Everything will be all right. Really. He's got an

20

infection, that's all. The antibiotics will clear it up in a few days."

"But I feel . . . in my heart . . ." She stopped.

Dr. Cohn straightened up, but still spoke gently. "You're both very tired. The best thing you can do now is go home and get some sleep. Things will look better after that."

Luz felt she had no choice but to accept this. She met the doctor's eyes for a long moment, then nodded mechanically and thanked her. Then she and her bundled-up and shivering son were back out in the cold and terrible night.

1

At around 6:20 on the morning of Tuesday, April 10, a forty-seven-year-old businessman named Tim Markham was on the last leg of his customary jog. Every weekday when he wasn't traveling, Markham would run out the driveway of his mansion on McLaren within minutes on either side of 5:45. He would turn right and then right again on Twenty-eighth Avenue, jog down to Geary, go left nearly a mile to Park Presidio, then left again back up to Lake. At Twenty-fifth, he'd jog a block right to Scenic Way, cut down Twenty-sixth, and finally turn back home on Seacliff where it ran above Phelan Beach.

In almost no other ways was Markham a creature of habit, but he rarely varied either the route of his run or the time he took it. This morning — garbage day in the neighborhood — he was struck by a car in the intersection just after he left the sidewalk making the turn from Scenic to Twenty-sixth. The impact threw him against one of the trash receptacles at the curb and covered him in refuse.

Markham had been jogging without his wallet and hence without benefit of identification. Although he was a white man in physically good health, he hadn't yet shaved this morning. The combination of the garbage surrounding him with his one-day growth of beard, his worn-down running shoes, and the old sweats and ski cap he wore made it possible to conclude that he was a homeless man who'd wandered into the upscale neighborhood.

When the paramedics arrived from the nearby fire station, they went right to work on him. Markham was bleeding from severe head trauma, maybe had punctured and collapsed a lung. He'd obviously broken several bones including his femur. If this break had cut an artery, it was a life-threatening injury all by itself. He would clearly need some blood transfusions and other serious trauma intervention immediately if he were going to have a chance to survive.

The ambulance driver, Adam Lipinski, was a longtime veteran of similar scenes. Although the nearest emergency room was at Portola Hospital, twenty blocks away in the inner Richmond District, he knew both from rumor and personal experience that Portola was in an embattled financial state right now. Because it was forbidden by law to do otherwise, any hospital would have to take this victim into the ER and try to stabilize him somewhat. But if he was in fact homeless and uninsured, as Lipinski suspected, there was no way that Portola would then admit him into the hospital proper.

Lipinski wasn't a doctor, but he'd seen a lot of death and knew what the approach of it could look like, and he was thinking that this was one of those cases. After whatever treatment he got in the ER, this guy was going to need a stretch in

23

intensive care, but if he didn't have insurance, Lipinski was all but certain that Portola would find a way to declare him fit to move and turf him out to County.

Last month, the hospital had rather notoriously transferred a day-old baby — *a baby!* — to County General after she'd been delivered by emergency C-section in the ER at Portola in the middle of the night, six weeks premature and addicted to crack cocaine. The mother, of course, had no insurance at all. Though some saint of a doctor, taking advantage of the administration's beauty sleep, had simply ordered the baby admitted to Portola's ICU, by the next day someone had decided that the mother and child couldn't pay and therefore had to go to County.

Some Portola doctors made a stink, arguing that they couldn't transfer the mother so soon after the difficult surgery and birth — she was still in grave condition and transporting her might kill her, and the administration had backed down. But it countered that the baby, Emily, crack addiction and all, would clearly survive the trip across town. She would be transferred out. Separated from her mother within a day of her birth.

At County General, Emily had barely held on to life for a day in the overcrowded special unit for preemies. Then Jeff Elliot's *CityTalk* column in the *Chronicle* had gotten wind of the outrage and embarrassed Portola into relenting. If not for that, Lipinski knew that the poor little girl probably wouldn't have made it through her first week. As it was, she got readmitted to Portola's

ICU, where she stayed until her mother left ten days later, and where the two of them ran up a bill of something like seventy thousand dollars. And all the while politicoes, newspaper people, and half the occupants of their housing project — whom the administration accused of stealing drugs and anything else that wasn't tied down — generally disrupted the order and harmony of the hospital.

In the wake of that, Portola put the word out — this kind of admitting mistake wasn't going to happen again. Lipinski knew beyond a doubt that once today's victim was minimally stabilized, Portola would pack him back up in an ambulance and have him taken to County, where they had to admit everybody, even and especially the uninsured. Lipinski wasn't sure that the victim here would survive that second trip and even if he did, the ICU at County was a disaster area, with no beds for half the people who needed them, with gurneys lining the halls.

But there was still time before he had to make that decision. The paramedics were trying to get his patient on a backboard, and the police had several officers knocking on doors and talking to people in the crowd that had gathered to see if anyone could identify the victim. Even rich people, snug in their castles, unknown to their neighbors, might recognize the neighborhood bum.

Because the body was so broken, it took longer than he'd originally estimated, but eventually they got the victim hooked up and into the back. In the meantime, Lipinski had decided that he was going directly to County. Portola would just screw around too much with this guy, and Lipinski didn't think he'd survive it. He'd just shifted into gear and was preparing to pull out when he noticed a couple of cops running up with a distraught woman in tow.

He knew what this was. Shifting back into park, he left the motor running, opened his door, and stepped out into the street. As the cops got to him, he was ready at the back door, pulling it open. Half walking, half running, the woman was a few steps behind them. She stepped up inside and Lipinski saw her body stiffen, her hands come up to cover her mouth. "Oh God," he heard. "Oh God."

He couldn't wait any longer. Slamming the door shut behind her, he ran back and hopped into his seat. They had their identification. And he was going to Portola.

2

In the days long ago before he'd hit the big four-oh, Dismas Hardy used to jog regularly. His course ran from his house on Thirty-fourth Avenue out to the beach, then south on the hard sand to Lincoln Way, where he'd turn east and pound the sidewalk until he got to Ninth and the bar he co-owned, the Little Shamrock. If it was a weekend or early evening, he'd often stop here to drink a beer before age wised him up and slowed him down. Later on, the beverage tended to be a glass of water. He'd finish his drink and conclude the four-mile circuit through Golden Gate Park and back up to his house.

The last time he'd gotten committed to an exercise program, maybe three years ago, he'd made it the first week and then about halfway through the second before he gave up, telling himself that two miles wasn't bad for a forty-seven-year-old. He'd put on a mere eight pounds this past decade, much less than many of his colleagues. He wasn't going to punish himself about his body, the shape he was in.

But then last year, his best friend Abe Glitsky had a heart attack that turned out to be a very near thing. Glitsky was the elder of the two men by a couple of years, but still, until it happened, Hardy had never considered either he or Abe anywhere near old enough to have heart trouble. The two men had been best friends since they'd walked a beat together as cops just after Hardy's return from Vietnam.

Now Glitsky was the chief of San Francisco's homicide detail. Half-black and half-Jewish, Glitsky was a former college tight end. No one among his colleagues would ever have thought of describing the lieutenant as anything but a hard-ass. His looks contributed to the rep as well — a thick scar coursed his lips top to bottom under a hatchet nose; he cultivated a fiercely unpleasant gaze. A buzz-cut fringe of gray bounded a wide, intelligent forehead. Glitsky didn't drink, smoke, or use profanity. He would only break out his smile to terrify staff (or small children for fun). Six months ago, when he'd married Treya Ghent, the administrative assistant to the new district attorney, several of his inspectors had bet that the new lifestyle would mellow him out considerably. They were still paying the installments.

Hardy was a successful defense attorney. Though he and Glitsky were on opposite sides of the fence professionally, there was also most of a lifetime of history between them. When Glitsky's first wife, Flo, had died some years before, Hardy and his wife, Frannie, had taken his three boys in to live with them until Abe could work his way through some of the emotional and logistical upheaval. Last fall, Hardy had been the best man at Abe's wedding.

They didn't talk about it — they were guys after all — but each was a fixed point of reference in the other's life.

The heart attack got their attention.

Since a month or so after Abe's marriage, they'd fallen into some semblance of a regular exercise program, where a couple of days a week one would goad or abuse the other into agreeing to do something physical. After the macho need to demonstrate their awesome strength and breathtaking endurance to each other in the first few weeks had almost made them quit the whole thing because of all the aches and pains, they finally had arrived at a brisk walk a couple of times a week, or perhaps throw some kind of ball on the weekend.

This morning they were eating up maybe three miles an hour walking on the path around Stow Lake in Golden Gate Park. It was a cool and clear morning, the sun visible in the treetops. A mist hung over the water, and out of it at the near shore a swan with her brood of cygnets appeared.

Glitsky was talking work, as usual, complaining about the politics surrounding the appointment of two inexperienced inspectors to his detail of elite investigators in reaction to the unexplainable renaissance of hit-and-run accidents in the City by the Bay. In the past twelve months, Glitsky was saying, ninety-three persons had been struck by motor vehicles within the city and county. Of these, twenty-seven had died. Of the sixty-six injury accidents that didn't result in deaths, fourteen were hit and runs.

"I love it how you rattle off all those numbers," Hardy said. "Anybody would swear you knew what you were talking about."

"Those are the real stats."

"I'm sure they are. Which is why I'm glad we're on this path and not the street where we could be senselessly run down at any moment. But how do these numbers affect your department? I thought hit and runs weren't homicides."

Glitsky glanced sideways at him. "Technically, they are when somebody dies."

"Well, there you go. That's why they come to you. You're the homicide detail."

"But we don't investigate them. We have never investigated them. You want to know why? First, because there's a separate detail cleverly named 'hit and run.' "

"That's a good name if they do what I think," Hardy said.

"It's a fine name," Glitsky agreed. He knew, although the police department would deny it as a matter of course, that no hit-and-run incidents — even the homicides — were more than cursorily investigated by inspectors. What usually happened was that a couple of members of the hit-and-run detail would take the paperwork at the Hall of Justice the day after the incident. Maybe they would go to the scene of an accident and see if they could find a witness to provide a description or license number of the vehicle. If that failed, and there were no good eyewitnesses in the report, that was essentially the end of the investigation. If they had a license number, they punched it into their computers to see if they had a street address associated with the vehicle. Sometimes, if the accident got a lot of press and they had a vehicle description, they would call a body shop or two and see if any cars matching the hit-and-run vehicle had surfaced. Usually the answer was no. "It's a fine department, even. But it doesn't do what we do, which is investigate murders."

"In spite of your detail's name, which indicates an interest in all homicides."

"Hence the confusion," Glitsky said. "Some of our civic leaders remain unclear on the concept."

They walked in silence for another moment. "What's second?" Hardy asked.

"What's second what?"

"You said you don't investigate hit-and-run homicides, first, because there's a separate hit-and-run detail. When you say first, it implies there's a second."

Glitsky's pace slackened, then both men stopped. "Second is that hit-and-run homicides tend not to be murders. In fact, they're *never murders.*"

"Never say never."

"This time you can. You want to know why?"

"It's hard to ditch the murder weapon?"

"That's one reason. Another is that it's tough to convince your intended victim to stand in front of your car when there are no witnesses around so you can run him over. Most people just plain won't do it."

"So what's the problem?"

"The problem," Glitsky said, "is that with twenty-seven dead people in twelve months, the citizenry is apparently alarmed."

"I know I am," Hardy commented. "Perpetually."

"Yeah, well, as you may have read, our illustrious Board of Supes has authorized special funding for witness rewards and to beef up the investigation of all vehicular homicides."

"And a good idea it is."

"Wrong. It's a bad idea," Glitsky said. "There's no special investigation of vehicular homicides to begin with, not even in hit and run. Ninety percent of 'em, you got a drunk behind the wheel. The other ten percent, somebody's driving along minding their own business and somebody runs out from between two cars in front of them — *blam!* Then they freak and split. They probably weren't even doing anything wrong before they left the scene. These are felony homicides, okay, because the driver is supposed to stick around, but they are not murders."

"And this concerns you because . . . ?"

"Because now and for the past two months I've had these two new politically connected clowns — excuse me, inspectors — in my detail that I've been telling you about, and they seem to be having trouble finding meaningful work. And let's say that this hasn't gone exactly unnoticed among the rest of my crack staff, who by the way refer to them as the 'car police.' "

"Maybe they mean it as a compliment," Hardy said.

Glitsky shook his head in disgust, then checked his watch. "Let's walk."

Hardy could imagine the plight of the new inspectors, and knew that their treatment at the hands of the veteran homicide cops wouldn't be pretty. Despite all the scandal and controversy that had ravaged the self-esteem of other details in the police department over the past few years, the twelve men and women inspectors who served in homicide considered themselves the elite. They'd worked their way up to this eminence, and their jobs mattered to them. They took pride in what they did, and the new guys would not fit in. "So abuse is being taken?" Hardy asked.

"Somebody painted 'Car Fifty-Four' on their city issue. Then you know the full-size streetlight we've had in the detail for years? Somehow it's gotten plugged in and set between the two guys' desks, so they can't see each other when they sit down? Oh, and those little metal cars kids play with? Six or eight new ones every day on their desks, in their drawers, everywhere."

"I guess we're moving into the abuse realm."

Glitsky nodded. "That would be fair to say."

At a little after nine o'clock, Glitsky sat behind his desk in his small office on the fourth floor of the Hall of Justice. The door was closed. His two new men — Harlen Fisk and Darrel Bracco — had so far been called out on injury hit and runs about ten times in their two months here, and in theory they should have been rolling already on this morning's accident involving Tim Markham. But this time, they were seeking their lieutenant's guidance before they moved.

Glitsky blamed neither Fisk nor Bracco for being upset with the conditions they'd endured to date in the detail, but until this morning, he couldn't say he'd lost any sleep thinking about it. They were political appointees and they deserved what they got in their brief stops up the promotion ladder, hopscotching over other inspectors who were smarter, more qualified, and worked harder.

Harlen Fisk was the nephew of City Supervisor Kathy West. He went about six three, two fifty, and was self-effacing almost to the point of meekness. Darrel Bracco was trim, crisp, clean, ex-army, the terrier to Fisk's Saint Bernard. His political juice was a little more obscure than his partner's, but just as potent. His father, Angelo Bracco, had worn a uniform for thirty years, and now was Mayor Washington's personal driver — Bracco would have the mayor's ear whenever he wanted.

So these men could just as easily have gone whining to their supporters and Glitsky could right at this moment be getting a formal reprimand from Chief Rigby, who'd heard from the mayor and a supervisor that he was running his detail in an unprofessional manner. But they hadn't gone over his head. Instead, they were both here in his office, coming to him with their problem. The situation gave him pause and inclined him to listen to what they were saying, if not with sympathy, then at least with some respect for their position.

Bracco was standing at attention, and Glitsky had been talking for a while now, reprising many of the salient points of his earlier discussion with

34

Dismas Hardy. "That's why our office here in homicide is on the fourth floor," he concluded, "with the lovely view of the roof of the coroner's office, whereas hit and run has a back door that opens into the alley where the waste from the jail's kitchen comes. Murderers are bad people. Hit-and-run drivers have made an unfortunate life choice. There's a difference."

Bracco sighed. "So there's no real job here, is there?"

Glitsky came forward in his chair, brought his hands together on the desk before him. "I'm sorry, but that's how it is."

The young man's face clouded over. "So then why were we brought onboard?"

This called for a careful response. "I understand both of you know some people. Maybe they don't really understand some technical matters."

Fisk was frowning. "What about the man who was hit this morning? Markham."

"What about him?" Glitsky asked.

"He wasn't dead at the scene, but if he does die, then what?"

"Then, as I understand it, you get the case from H and R."

"And do what with it?" Bracco asked.

"Try to find the driver? I don't know." Glitsky — nothing he could do — spread his palms, shrugged. "Look, guys," he said, "maybe I could talk to the chief and see if he can arrange some kind of move. You both might want to think about transferring to gangs or robbery or someplace. Do some good work on some real cases, work your way back up to here, where you'll get some real murders, which this is not."

Bracco, still in the at-ease position, wanted to know his assignment. "In the meanwhile, we're here. What do you want us to do, sir? On this morning's accident?"

The entire situation was stupid, but in Glitsky's experience, stupidity was about the most common result of political solutions. Maybe these boys would learn some lesson. "You want my advice? Go out there yourselves. Look a little harder than H and R would. Maybe you'll find something they missed."

They weren't happy about it, but Bracco and Fisk thoroughly canvased the immediate neighborhood. Although they found no witnesses to the event itself, they did not come up completely empty-handed.

At very near to the time of the accident, a forty-five-year-old stockbroker named John Bandolino had come out of his house on Seacliff just west around the corner from Twenty-sixth to pick up his newspaper. He was on his way back inside when suddenly he heard a car with a bad muffler accelerate rapidly, then squeal around the corner. Since this was normally a serene neighborhood, Bandolino ran back down to the street to see if he could identify the troublemaker who was making so much noise so early in the morning. But the car was by then too far away to read the license plate. It was green, though, probably American made. Not a new car, certainly.

The other corroborating witnesses on the car were George and Ruth Callihan Brown, both retired and on their way to their regular Tuesday breakfast with some friends. They had just turned off Seacliff onto Twenty-sixth, Warren driving, when Ruth saw Markham lying sprawled in the garbage up ahead. After the initial shock, both of them realized that some kind of a medium-size green car had passed them in the other lane as they were coming up. They both turned to see it disappear around the corner, heard the muffler noise, the acceleration. But they didn't even think to pursue it — Markham was unconscious, and bleeding where he lay. They had their cell phone and he needed an ambulance.

The crime scene reconstruction expert had trouble pinpointing the exact location on Twenty-sixth where Markham had been struck. The force of the impact had evidently thrown him some distance through the air, and there were no skid marks to indicate that the driver had slammed on the brakes in panic, or, indeed, applied the brakes at all.

3

Lunchtime, and Lou the Greek's was hopping.

Without any plan or marketing campaign, and in apparent defiance of common sense or good taste, Lou's had carved its unlikely niche and had remained an institution for a generation. Maybe it was the location, directly across the street from the Hall of Justice, but there wasn't any shortage of other bars and restaurants in the neighborhood, and none of them did as well or had hung on as long as the Greek's. People from all walks of life just seemed to feel comfortable there, in spite of some fairly obvious drawbacks if one chose to view the place critically.

The entrance was through a frankly urine-stained bail bondsman's corridor, which led to an unlit stairway — six steps to a set of leatherette double doors. The floor of the restaurant was five feet below ground level, so it was dark even on the brightest day and never smelled particularly, or even remotely, appealing. A row of small windows along one wall was set at eye level indoors, though at ground level out. This afforded the only meager natural light. Unfortunately, it also provided a shoe's-eye view of the alley outside, which was always lined with garbage Dumpsters and other assorted urban debris, and often the cardboard lean-tos and other artifacts of the homeless who slept there. The walls had originally been done in a bordello-style maroon-and-gold velveteen wallpaper, but now were essentially black.

The bar opened at 6:00 for the alcohol crowd, and did a booming if quiet business for a couple of hours. There'd be a lull when the workday began across the street, but at 11:00 the kitchen opened and the place would fill up fast. Every day Lou's wife, Chui, would recombine an endless variety of Chinese and Greek ingredients for her daily special, which was the only item on the menu. Lou (or one of the morning drinkers) would give it a name like Kung-Pao Chicken Pita or Yeanling Happy Family, and customers couldn't seem to get enough. Given the quality of the food (no one would call it cuisine) and the choices available, Lou's popularity as a lunch spot was a continuing mystery even for those who frequently ate there themselves.

The party at the large round table by the door to the kitchen fit in this category. For several months now, in an unspoken and informal arrangement, a floating group of professionals had been meeting here on most Tuesdays for lunch. It began just after the mayor appointed Clarence Jackman the district attorney. At the time, Jackman had been in private practice as the managing partner of Rand & Jackman, one of the city's premier law firms, and the previous DA, Sharron Pratt, had just resigned in disgrace.

Jackman viewed himself mostly as a businessman, not a politician. The mayor had asked him to step in to the normally bitterly contested political office and get the organization back on course, prosecuting crimes, staying on budget, litigating the city's business problems. Jackman, seeking different perspectives on his new job, asked some colleagues from different disciplines — but mostly law — for a low-profile lunch at Lou's. This move was startling enough in itself. Even more so was everyone's discretion. Lunch at Lou's wasn't so much a secret as a nonevent. If anyone noticed that the same people were showing up at the same table every week, they weren't talking. It never made the news.

Jackman faced the kitchen door. The coat of his tailored pinstriped suit hung over the back of his chair. His white dress shirt, heavily starched, fit tightly over the highly developed muscles in his back. His face was darkly hued, almost blue-black, and his huge head was perched directly on his shoulders, apparently without benefit of a neck.

Lou the Greek must have gotten a good deal on a containerload or so of fortune cookies, because for the past couple of weeks a bowl of them, incredibly stale, was on every table for every meal. The DA's lunch today had been consumed with the serious topic of the city's contract for its health insurance, and when Jackman cracked one of the cookies open and broke into his deep, rolling laughter, it cut some of the tension. "I love this," he said. "This is perfect, and right on point: 'Don't get sick.' " He took in his tablemates. "Who writes these things? Did one of you pay Lou to slip it in here?"

"I think when they run out of license plate blanks at San Quentin . . ." This was Gina Roake, a longtime public defender now in private practice. Despite the thirty-year age gap, she was rumored to be romantically linked to David Freeman, another of the table guests.

"No way." Marlene Ash was an assistant DA on Jackman's staff. She'd taken her jacket off when she sat down, too, revealing a substantial bosom under a maroon sweater. Chestnut shoulder-length hair framed a frankly cherubic face, marred only by a slight droop in her right eye. "No way a convict writes 'Don't get sick.' It'd be more like 'Die, muthuh.' "

"That'd be an unusually polite convict, wouldn't it?" Treya Ghent asked.

"Unprecedented," Glitsky agreed. "And it's not a fortune anyway." The lieutenant was two seats away from the DA and next to his wife, who held his hand on top of the table. "A fortune's got to be about the future."

Dismas Hardy spoke up. "It's in a fortune cookie, Abe. Therefore, by definition, it's a fortune."

"How about if there was a bug in it, would that make the bug a fortune?"

"Guys, guys." San Francisco's coroner, John Strout, held up a restraining hand and adjusted his glasses. A thin and courtly Southern gentleman, Strout had crushed his own cookie into powder and was looking at the white slip in his hand. "Now this here's a fortune: 'You will be successful in your chosen field.' " He looked

41

around the table. "I wonder what that's goin' to turn out to be."

"I thought you were already in your chosen field," Roake said.

"I did, too." Strout paused. "Shee-it. Now what?"

Everybody enjoyed a little laugh. A silence settled for a second or two, and Jackman spoke into it. "That's my question, too, John. Now what?"

He surveyed the group gathered around him. Only two of the other people at the table hadn't spoken during the fortune cookie debate: David Freeman, seventy-something, Hardy's landlord and the most well-known and flamboyant lawyer in the city; and Jeff Elliot, in his early forties and confined to a wheelchair due to MS, the writer of the *CityTalk* column for the *Chronicle*.

It was Freeman who spoke. "There's no question here, Clarence. You got Parnassus sending the city a bill for almost thirteen million dollars and change for services they didn't render over the last four years. They're demanding full payment, with interest, within sixty days or, so they say, they're belly up. It's nothing but extortion, plain and simple. Even if you owed them the money."

"Which is not established," Marlene Ash said.

Freeman shrugged. "Okay, even better. You charge their greedy asses with fraud and shut 'em down."

"Can't do that." Jackman was using a toothpick. "Shut 'em down, I mean. Not fast anyway, although I'm already testing the waters with

42

some other providers. But it's not quick. Certainly not this year. And the Parnassus contract runs two more years after that."

"And whoever you're talking to isn't much better anyway, am I right?" Hardy asked.

"Define 'much.' " Jackman made a face. "Hopefully there'd be some improvements."

Treya put a hand on her boss's arm. "Why don't we let them go bankrupt? Just not pay them?"

"We're not going to pay them in any case," Marlene Ash answered. "But we can't let them go bankrupt, either. Then who takes care of everybody?"

"Who's taking care of them now?" Roake asked, and the table went silent.

The way it worked in San Francisco, city employees had several medical insurance options, depending on the level of health care each individual wanted. It seemed straightforward enough. People willing to spend more of their own money on their health got better choices and more options. In theory, the system worked because even the lowest-cost medical care — provided in this case by Parnassus — was adequate. But no surprise to anybody, that wasn't so.

"Couldn't Parnassus borrow enough to stay afloat?" Glitsky asked Jackman.

The DA shook his head. "They say not."

Gina Roake almost choked on her coffee. "They can get a loan, trust me," she said. "Maybe not a great rate, but a couple of mil, prime plus something, no problem."

"What I've heard," Jackman said, "their story

is that they can't repay it, whatever it is. They're losing money right and left every day as it is. And, our original problem, they don't need a loan anyway if the city just pays them what it owes."

"Which it doesn't," Marlene Ash repeated. "Owe, I mean."

"Can you prove that?" Glitsky the cop wanted to see the evidence.

"I intend to," Ash said. "Go back to the original invoices."

"Grand jury." Hardy cracked a fortune cookie.

Ash nodded grimly. "That's what I'm thinking."

"How can they say they'd run up thirteen million *extra* dollars and never saw it coming?" Roake asked. "That's what I'd like to know."

Jackman turned to her. "Actually, that was fairly clever. They say their contract with the city covers outpatient AIDS treatment, mental health and drug abuse counseling, and physical therapy, and they've been providing it all along without being reimbursed. The key word is 'outpatient.' They're out the money, they've already provided the service, we owe it to them." He shrugged. "They distort the hell out of the contract to get to that position, but all the unions want to read *their* contracts to cover those services, so Parnassus has some political support."

"So it's a contract language dispute," Freeman said. "Tell them to sue you in civil court."

"We would," Jackman said, "except that we're starting to think —"

"We *know*," Ash interrupted.

"We're starting to think," Jackman repeated, giving his ADA a reproachful glare, "that they didn't provide the care they allege. It was all outpatient stuff, after all. The record keeping appears to be uneven, to say the least."

"Grand jury," Hardy repeated.

Jackman broke a professional smile. "I heard you the first time, Diz. Maybe. But I'm also thinking about freezing their accounts and appointing a receiver to keep 'em running, which is the last thing Parnassus wants, but if they think it might get them paid . . . and they do need the money."

"You're sure of that?" Freeman asked.

Jackman nodded. "They're not paying their doctors. I'm taking that as a clue. We've received a couple of dozen complaints in the last six months. So finally we wrote a letter, told them to straighten up, pay their people or maybe we'd need to get involved, and sent a copy to each of their board members, still being paid, by the way, at an average of three hundred fifty thousand dollars a year."

"A year?" Glitsky asked. "Every year?"

"A little more, I think," Jeff Elliot said.

"Every year?" The lieutenant couldn't get over it. "I'm definitely in the wrong business."

"No you're not, dear," Treya told him. "You're perfect where you are."

Hardy blew Glitsky a kiss across the table.

"Anyway," Jackman forged ahead, "the threat got their attention. In fact, if you want my opinion, that was the proximate cause of this de-

45

mand for the thirteen mil."

"So what happens if we let them go bankrupt?" Glitsky asked. "How bad could it be?"

Freeman chuckled. "May I, Clarence?" he asked the DA, then proceeded without waiting for any response. "Let me count the ways, Lieutenant. The first thing that happens is that every city employee, and that includes you, loses their health insurance. So instead of paying ten dollars to see your doctor, now you're paying sixty, eighty, a hundred and fifty. That's per-office visit. Full price for prescriptions. So every union in town sues the city because you're guaranteed insurance as part of your employment contract. Then the city sues Parnassus for not providing the service, then Parnassus countersues the city for not paying for the service. So now everybody in town has to go to County General for everything and there's no room for anyone this side of multiple gunshot wounds. If you only have cancer, take two aspirin and call me in the morning. Bottom line is, if it turns out to be a bad year for the flu or AIDS or earthquakes, letting Parnassus go bankrupt could bring the city right along with it." Freeman smiled around the table. Bad news always seemed to stoke him up. "Did I leave anything out?"

"That was pretty succinct, David, thank you." Jackman pushed the remains of his fortune cookie around on the table. "In any event, Parnassus must be close to broke if it's resorting to this."

"We've got to charge them with something," Ash said.

46

Freeman had another idea. "I like bringing an action to freeze their accounts and appoint a receiver to investigate their books and keep the business going." The old man gave the impression he wouldn't mind taking on the job himself.

Jackman shook his head. "We'd have to go a long way to proving the fraud, David. We can't just walk in and take over."

"Even if they haven't paid their doctors?" Roake asked. "I'd call that a triggering event."

"It might be," Jackman agreed. From his expression, he found the idea potentially interesting. "Well," he said, "thanks to you all for the discussion. I'm sure I'll come to some decision. Jeff," he said across the table, "you've been unusually quiet today. I seem to remember you've written Parnassus up for a few items recently. Don't you have some advice you'd like to offer on this topic?"

The reporter broke a cynical smile under his thick beard. "You've already heard it, sir. Don't get sick."

4

Though he was nearly fifty years old, Rajan Bhutan had only been a nurse for about ten years. He'd arrived with his wife in the United States in his mid-twenties. For some time, he had made do with a succession of retail jobs, selling women's shoes and men's clothes in chain stores. This was the same type of work he'd done in Calcutta, although it didn't suit his personality very well. Small of stature, moody, and somewhat introspective by nature, he had to force himself to smile and be pleasant to customers. But he was efficient, honest, intelligent. He showed up for work every day and would stay late or come in early without complaint, so while he wasn't much of a salesman, he tended to keep his jobs — his first one at Macy's Herald Square, where he stayed six years. Then at Nordstrom for five more.

His wife had augmented their income by giving piano lessons and for about ten years they had been reasonably happy in their little apartment in the Haight, the only major disappointment in their lives the fact that Chatterjee was unable to get pregnant. Then, finally, when they were both thirty-five, she thought that the miracle had occurred, but it turned out that the something growing in her womb was not a baby, but a tumor.

After Chatterjee died, Rajan no longer found smiling, or sales, to be tolerable. During the months he'd nursed his wife, though, he'd discovered that giving physical care appealed to him in some important way. Over the next four years, he used up most of his savings going to nursing school full-time, until he finally received his RN from St. Mary's, and took a full-time job at Portola.

And true to form, he stayed. The doctors and administration liked him for the same reasons his bosses in retail had always kept him on. But he had few if any friends among the nurses. Dark and brooding now to an even greater degree than he'd been before when he'd worked in sales, he made little effort to be personable. But he was good at giving care. Over time, to his shift partners he became almost invisible — competent and polite, albeit distant and with his hooded demeanor, somewhat ominous.

Now he stood over the bed of James Lector. After checking the connections on all the monitors, he smoothed the blanket over the old man's chest, and turned to look behind him, across the room, where Dr. Kensing was with his partner today, Nurse Rowe, adjusting the IV drip on Mr. Markham, who'd only just been wheeled in from post-op.

Rajan looked back down at Lector, on life support now for these past couple of weeks. He had recently stabilized but who knew for how long? Looking at the old man's gray, inanimate face, he wondered again — as he often did — about the so-called wonder of modern medicine. The memory came back fresh again — in the last days, they had kept Chatterjee alive and supposedly free from pain with life support and narcotics. But as the years had passed, he'd come to believe that this had really been a needless cruelty — both to him for the false hope and to her for the denial of peace.

He believed in helping the sick, in easing pain. This was his mission, after all, after Chatterjee. But the needless prolongation of life, this was what bothered him now, as it always did when he worked the ICU.

He looked down again at Mr. Lector's face, then back over to Dr. Kensing and Nurse Rowe, working to save another person who might be permanently brain-damaged at best, should he survive at all.

Folly, he thought, so much of it was folly.

Shaking his head with regret, he sighed deeply and went to the next bed.

Dr. Malachi Ross stopped at the door to the intensive care unit and took a last look to make sure everything was as it should be. The large, circular room had seven individual bed stations for critical cases, and all of them were filled, as they were at all times every day of the year. The odds said that five of the patients in them, and possibly all seven, would not live. Ross knew that this was not for lack of expertise or expense; indeed, the expense factor had become the dominating element of his life over the past years. He was the chief medical director and CFO of the Parnassus Medical Group and keeping costs under control while still providing adequate care (which he defined as the minimum necessary to avoid malpractice lawsuits) was his ever more impossible job.

And which was, he knew, about to enter another period of crisis. In the short term at least. For occupying one of the beds here today was his colleague and chief executive officer, Tim Markham, struck down on his morning run, an exercise he practiced with religious zeal in an effort to stay vigorous and healthy to a ripe old age. Ross supposed there was irony in this, but he had lost his taste for irony years ago.

The monitors beeped with regularity and the other machines hummed. All around the room, white shades had been pulled over the windows against the feeble spring sun.

Markham was in the first bed on the left, all hooked up. He'd been up here for three hours already, the fact that he'd lived this long with such serious injuries some kind of a miracle. Ross took a step back toward the bed, then stopped himself. He was a doctor, yes, but hadn't practiced in ten years. He did know that the bag for the next transfusion hung from its steel hook next to the bed, where it ought to be. The other IV was still half-full. He had to assume everything was in order.

Exhausted, he rubbed his hands over his face, then found himself looking down at them. His surgeon's hands, his mother used to say. His face felt hot, yet his hands told him he wasn't sweating.

Drawing a deep breath, he turned and opened the door to get out.

He stepped out into the hallway where three more ICU candidates, postsurgery or post-ER, lay on their own gurneys attached to monitors and drips. They'd arrived since Markham had been admitted; now, as the beds in the ICU became available, these patients would be transferred inside for theoretically "better" intensive care.

Dr. Eric Kensing was supervising the unit this morning, and now he stood over one of the beds in the hallway, giving orders to a male nurse. Ross had no desire to speak to Kensing, so he crossed to the far side of the hall and continued unmolested the short way down to the ICU's special waiting room. Distinguished by its amenities from the other spaces that served the same basic purpose, the intensive care waiting room featured comfortable couches and chairs, reasonably pleasant art, tasteful wallpaper, shuttered windows, and noise-killing rugs. This was because a vast majority of the people waiting here were going to hear bad news, and the original architects had obviously thought the surroundings would help. Ross didn't think they did.

It was just another waste of money.

At the entrance, he looked in, noting with some satisfaction that at least Brendan Driscoll had left the immediate area for the time being and he wouldn't have to endure his reactions and listen to his accusations anymore. Driscoll was Markham's executive assistant and sometimes seemed to be under the impression that he, not his boss, was the actual CEO of Parnassus.

He gave orders, even to Ross, as though he were. As soon as he'd heard about the accident, Driscoll had evidently left the corporate offices at the Embarcadero to come and keep the vigil at Markham's side. He'd even beaten Ross himself down here. But now, thankfully, he was gone, banished by an enraged Dr. Kensing for entering the ICU for God knew what reason, probably just because he wanted to and thought he could.

But, disturbing though he could be, Driscoll was nowhere near as serious a problem to Ross as Carla Markham, Tim's wife. Sitting at one end of the deep couch as though in a trance, she looked up at him and her mouth formed a gash of hostility and sorrow, both instantly extinguished into a mask of feigned neutrality.

"He's all right," Ross said. Then, quickly amending it. "The same."

She took the news without so much as a nod.

He remained immobile, but his eyes kept coming back to her. She sat stiffly, her knees pressed together, her body in profile. Suddenly, she looked straight at him as though she'd only then become aware of his presence. "The same is not all right. The same means he is near death, and that is not all right. And if he does die . . ."

Ross stepped into the waiting room and put up a hand as though physically to stop her. "He's not going to die," he said.

"You'd better hope that's true, Malachi."

"We don't have to talk about that. I've heard what you said and you're right, there were troubles. But no crisis. When Tim comes out of this, we'll talk it out, make some adjustments, like we

53

have with a thousand other issues."

"This is not like any of them."

His mouth began to form a knowing smile. She was so wrong. Instead he cocked his head and spoke with all the conviction of his heart. "Don't kid yourself," he said. "They've all been like this." He stared down at her, watching for any sign of capitulation.

But she wouldn't hold his gaze. Instead, shaking her head once quickly from side to side, she reached some conclusion. "He wasn't going to make adjustments this time. The adjustments were what kept tearing him apart. If he doesn't live, I won't, either."

He couldn't be sure if she was referring to living herself — she'd threatened suicide the last time Markham had left her — or to making the kind of adjustments her husband had learned to live with. "Carla," he began softly, "don't be —"

But she wasn't listening. Suddenly, she was standing up in front of him, the semblance of neutrality dropped for now. "I can't talk to you anymore. Don't you understand that? Not here, maybe never. There's nothing to say until we know about Tim. Now excuse me, I've got to call the children." She walked by without glancing at him on her way out of the room.

Ross sat in one of the leather settees and pushed himself back into the chair. He gripped the edges of the armrests to keep his surgeon's hands from shaking.

Ross heard first the monitor alarm, then the code blue for the ICU. For twenty minutes, the

54

commotion nearly reached the level of bedlam even out in the hallway, when almost as abruptly as it had begun all the activity and noise came to a halt.

And then, suddenly, Tim Markham was dead.

Ross had gotten up out of his chair and was waiting outside the ICU, standing there when Doctor Kensing appeared from inside, his handsome face stricken and drawn. He met Ross's eye for a moment, finally looking down and away. "I don't know what happened," he said. "I thought we might have got him out of the woods, but . . ." The words trailed off and the doctor shook his head in defeat and misery.

If he was looking for commiseration, Ross thought, he was barking up the wrong tree. In fact, Ross found himself fighting the urge to say something spiteful, even accusatory. The time would come for that. Kensing had been Ross's particular nemesis for a couple of years, questioning his medical and business decisions, defying his edicts, crusading against his policies with the rest of the medical staff. Kensing's presence on the floor now, in the ICU directing Markham's ultimately failed care, was from Ross's perspective a bitter but not unwelcome act of fate that he would exploit if he could after the initial impact of the tragedy had passed. But it would have to wait.

Now, Ross had business to which he must attend. He didn't wait for Kensing to reappear in the hallway with his no doubt self-serving post-mortem analysis of what had gone wrong, as if he could know by now. He had no stomach for the

55

condolences, hand-holding and -wringing that he knew would attend the next hours at the hospital. Instead, he left the floor by elevator and got out in the basement parking garage, where he got in his Lexus and contacted his secretary, Joanne, on his cell phone. "Tim didn't make it," he said simply. "I'll be there in ten minutes."

5

David Freeman and Gina Roake, straight-faced, told Dismas Hardy that they were going to continue their walk from Lou's up to Freeman's apartment on Mason to look over some documents. Freeman would be back in the office later, if Hardy would be so kind as to tell Phyllis.

"I'd be delighted, David. Any excuse just to hear her sweet voice."

So, coming into the lobby alone, Hardy was congratulating himself for his restraint in not commenting on David and Gina's lame document-perusal excuse, when the dulcet-toned Phyllis stopped him. "Mr. Elliot from the *Chronicle* would like you to call him as soon as you can."

"Thank you. Did he say it was important?"

"Not specifically, but I assume so."

Hardy walked up and leaned against the top of the receptionist's partition. Phyllis hated when he did that. But then, she hated when he did anything. He smiled at her. "Why?"

"Why what?" Obviously thinking evil thoughts, Phyllis stared at his arms, crossed there on her shelf.

"Why do you assume it's important?"

To Phyllis, trained by Freeman, everything to do with the law was intrinsically important.

Hardy was untrainable, and try as she might to remain the complete professional, she couldn't seem to maintain her composure when he started in on her. She sighed in exasperation, tried to smile politely but didn't entirely succeed. "I assume all calls to your office are important, Mr. Hardy. Mr. Elliot took time out in the middle of his workday to call you in the middle of yours. He asked you to call as soon as you could. It must have been something important."

"He might have just wanted to talk. That happens, you know."

Clearly, Phyllis believed it was not something that *should* happen. "Would you like me to call him and ask?"

"Why, Phyllis." Hardy stepped back, took his arms off the shelf, looked at her approvingly. "I think you've just told a joke. And during business hours when you should have been working. I won't tell David." She remained silent as he turned and got to the stairway up to his office. "Oh, and speaking of David, he won't be in for a while. He's with Ms. Roake working on some documents, though I've never called it that before."

"Called what?" Phyllis asked.

Suddenly he decided he'd abused her enough, or almost enough. He pointed up the stairs. "Nothing. Listen, I've enjoyed our little chat, but now I've got to run and call Mr. Elliot. It could be important."

Hardy worked in stark, monklike, even industrial surroundings. Gray metal filing cabinets hunched on a gray berber wall-to-wall carpet.

The two windows facing Sutter Street featured old-fashioned venetian blinds, which worked imperfectly at best — normally he simply left them either up or down. Rebecca and Vincent, his two children, had painted most of his wall art, although there was also a poster of the Giants' new home, Pac Bell Park, and a Sierra Club calendar. His blond wooden desk was the standard size, its surface cleared except for his phone, a photo of Frannie, an Office Max blotter, a sweet potato plant that reached the floor, and his green banker's lamp. Under four shelves of law books and binders, the dried blowfish and ship in a bottle he'd brought from home livened up a Formica counter with its faucet, its paper towel roll on the wall, and several glasses, upside down, by the sink. The couch and chairs were functional Sears faux leather, and the coffee table came from the same shopping trip about six years before. His dartboard hung next to the door across from his desk — a piece of silver duct tape on the rug marked the throw line at eight feet. His tungsten blue-flight customs were stuck, two bulls-eyes and a twenty, where he'd last thrown them.

The phone was ringing as he opened the door, and he reached over the desk, punching his speakerphone button. "Yo," he said.

Phyllis's voice again, but giving him no time to reply. "Lieutenant Glitsky for you."

And then Abe was on. "Guess what I just heard. You're going to like it."

"The Giants got Piazza."

"In the real world, Diz."

59

"That's the real world, and I'd like it."

"How about Tim Markham?"

"How about him? Is he a catcher? I've never heard of him." Hardy had gotten around his desk to his chair and picked up the receiver.

"He's the CEO of Parnassus Health," Glitsky said.

A jolt of adrenaline chased away the final traces of any lunch lethargy. Glitsky usually didn't call Hardy to keep him up on the day's news, unless homicide was in the picture, so he put it together right away. "And he's dead."

"Yes he is. Isn't that interesting?"

Hardy admitted that it was, especially after all the talk at Lou's. But more than that, "Did somebody kill him?"

"Yes, but probably not on purpose. You remember our discussion this morning about hit and runs?"

"You're kidding me."

"Nope."

"Let's remember not to talk about nuclear holocaust on our next walk. Somebody really ran him over?"

"More like plowed into him. They kept him alive at Portola until a half hour ago, then lost him."

"They lost him at his own hospital? I bet that was a special moment."

"It was another thing I thought you'd like. But evidently they couldn't do much. He was critical on admit and never pulled out."

"And it was an accident?"

"I already said that."

"Twice now," Hardy said. "You believe it?"

"So far."

Hardy listened to the hum on the line. "The same week he tries to shake down the city? His company's threatening to go bankrupt? They're not paying their doctors and they're screwing around with their patients, and suddenly the architect of all this winds up dead?"

"Yep."

"And it's a coincidence? That's your professional take on it?"

"Probably. It often is, as I mentioned this morning."

"Except when it isn't. Lots of things happen that never happened before."

"Not as often as you'd think," Glitsky replied. This time, the pause was lengthy. "But you've answered my question. I just wanted an opinion from the average man on the street."

"You'll have to call somebody a little dumber than me, then," Hardy said, "but I'll send you a bill anyway."

Jeff Elliot's call turned out to be about the same thing, but he wasn't interested in Hardy's coincidence theory, dismissing it even more definitively than Glitsky had with one line. "You don't murder somebody with a car, Diz, not when guns cost a buck and a half and knives are free."

"I'd bet it's been known to happen, although Glitsky says not, too."

"See? And even if it has, it also has been known to snow in the Sahara."

61

"Is that true? I don't think so. But if it is, it proves my point."

A sigh. "Diz? Can we leave it?"

Hardy was thinking that all of his friends had lost their senses of humor. He didn't really think it was probably a murder, either, but it was interesting to talk about, and so much else wasn't. "Okay, Jeff, okay. So how can I help you?"

"Actually, you can't. This is just a mercy call, see if you'd like to take the rest of the day off, which I noticed at lunch you might be in the mood for."

"That obvious, huh?"

"I'm a reporter, Diz. Nothing escapes."

Hardy looked down at the massive pile of paperwork on his desk — his own and other lawyers' briefs, which were anything but. Memoranda. Administrative work that he'd been neglecting. Billing. A couple of police incident reports from prospective clients. The latest updates of the Evidence Code, which it was bad luck not to know. He had an extremely full workload at the moment. He was sure he ought to be glad about this, although the why of it sometimes eluded him.

Elliot was going on. "I'm thinking the shit's got to be hitting the fan over at Parnassus. It might be instructive to swing over and check things out. See if anybody'll talk to me and maybe I'll get a column or two out of it. So what do you say? You want to play some hooky?"

"More than anything," Hardy said. "But not today, I'm afraid."

"Is that your final answer?"

He pulled some of the papers over in front of him, desultorily flipped through the stack of them. A trained reporter like Elliot, if he'd been in the room, would have recognized some signs of weariness, even malaise. Certainly a lack of sense of humor. Hardy let out a heavy breath. "Write a great column, Jeff. Make me feel like I was there."

It wasn't the kind of thing Glitsky was going to talk about with any of his regular professional associates, but he couldn't keep from sharing his concerns with his wife.

Jackman let Treya take a formal fifteen-minute break sometimes if she asked, and now she and Abe stood in the outside stairway on the Seventh Street side of the building, sipping their respective teas out of paper cups. An early afternoon wind had come up and they were forced to stand with their backs against the building, the view limited to the freeway and Twin Peaks out beyond it.

"And here I thought you brought me to this romantic spot so we could make out in the middle of the day."

"We could do that if you want," Glitsky told her. "I'm pretty easy that way."

She kissed him. "I've noticed. But you were really thinking of something else?"

He told her about Markham, how intensely uncomfortable he was with coincidences, and Markham's death fell squarely into that category. "But I wasn't lying when I told Diz that probably it wasn't an intentional homicide. That was the voice of thirty years' experience whispering in my ear."

"But what?"

"But my other guardian angel, the bad one, keeps on with this endless, 'Maybe, what if, how about . . .' "

"You mean if somebody ran him down on purpose?"

He nodded. "I'm trying to imagine an early-morning, just-after-light, lying-in-wait scenario, but I can't convince myself. It just couldn't have happened in real life. Well, maybe it *could* have, but I don't think it did."

"Why not?"

She was about the only person he ever smiled at, and he did now. "How good of you to ask. I'll tell you. The first and most obvious reason is that the driver didn't finish the job. Markham lived nearly four hours after the accident, and if he hadn't been thrown into the garbage can, he might have pulled through it. The driver couldn't have known he'd killed him. If he'd planned to, he would either have backed up over him or stopped, got out of the car, and whacked Markham's head a few times with a blunt object he'd been carrying for just that reason."

"Sweet," Treya said.

"But true." He went on to give her the second reason, the one he'd given Hardy. A car was a stupid and awkward choice as a murder weapon. If someone were going to take the time to plan a murder and then lie in wait to execute it, with all the forethought that entailed, Abe thought even a moron would simply buy a gun, which was as

64

easy if not easier to purchase, far more deadly, and simpler to get rid of than any vehicle would be.

"Okay, I'm convinced. He probably wasn't murdered."

"I know. That's what I said. But . . ."

"But you want to keep your options open."

"Correct. Which leads me to my real problem. Did you get the impression at lunch today that my friend and your boss Clarence Jackman is going to get considerable political heat around anything to do with Parnassus? The death of its CEO isn't going to hide out in the *Chronicle*'s back pages and then disappear in a couple of days when it isn't solved."

"No, I don't think so," Treya agreed.

"So who gets the case, which is definitely a homicide and might conceivably be, but probably isn't, a murder?"

Treya had been living with the problems within the homicide detail and had a good sense of the dilemma. In the normal course of events, Abe would never have anything to do with this case. It was a hit and run. Someone from that detail would be assigned to locate the vehicle, they probably wouldn't, and that would be the end of it. Now, because he had Fisk and Bracco, he'd have to give the case to them — in fact, he already had. If he tried to pass it to one of his veteran inspectors, first his guy would be insulted and laugh at him, then the mayor and the supervisor would demand his head, and probably get it.

And then if — wonder of wonders — it turned

out to be a real-live, politically charged, high-profile murder after all, he'd have given it to his two rawest players, who would probably screw it all up, and that would not only infuriate Jackman, it might harm the district attorney's relations with the police department for a good portion of this administration.

"I'd say you've got to let the new boys keep it."

"That's what I've come to myself. But it's lose-lose."

"Luckily," she said, touching his cheek gently, "with all the practice, you've gotten so good at those."

But he had Fisk and Bracco back in his office at the end of the day and gave them the best spin he could put on it. ". . . an opportunity to give you guys some quality time. You do good on this, people here might be inclined to think you might turn into good cops after all." He paused, and purposefully did *not* add "and not just political stooges."

Darrel Bracco was as he'd been this morning, and as he always was in here — standing almost at attention behind the chair where his partner sat. "We never asked to get moved in here, Lieutenant. Neither one of us. But we did jump at the chance. Who wouldn't?"

"Okay." Glitsky could accept that. "Here's your chance to make it work."

A few minutes later, he was reading from a notepad he'd been filling with ideas as they struck him on and off for most of the afternoon. ". . . girlfriends? And if so, did they just break up? Then his children. How did he get along with them?"

"Excuse me." Fisk had a hand up like a third grader.

Glitsky looked over his notepad. "Yes?" With exaggerated patience. "Harlen?"

"I thought this was about all the problems Markham was having with his business? And now you're talking about his family?"

Glitsky pulled himself up to his desk and placed his pad flat upon it. His blue eyes showed little expression. "I want you both to understand something. The odds that Mr. Markham was killed on purpose, and hence this is a murder investigation at all, are not large. Harlen, you and I and Inspector Bracco were talking this morning about the fact that you didn't have much to do here in the detail. I thought you might enjoy taking a look at this thing from the ground up. And the ground is a victim's family."

"It's got nothing to do with the car, you're saying?"

The lieutenant kept his impatience in check. "No, I'm not saying that. The car is what hit him. And if somebody he knew was driving it, then it starts to look a lot more like a murder. Which, I repeat, and you should, too, it probably isn't."

"But it will keep us out of the detail," Bracco said. "Is that what you're saying?"

Glitsky nodded. "It might do that. And that is to the good, I think you'll agree."

When the inspectors had returned from their morning's exertions, they discovered a Tom

Terrific beanie on the center of each of their desks. The detail didn't appear to be moving toward acceptance, or even tolerance, of the new crew. It was a drag to have to deal with, Glitsky thought, but he wasn't going to get involved in disciplining the hazing activities. That wasn't his job, and if he tried to move in that direction, he'd lose whatever authority he did have before he knew it.

So, yes, it would keep Fisk and Bracco out of the office. A good thing. Glitsky picked up the notepad again and read from it. "Do any of his children have friends with a green car? What about the wife's social life, if any? Beyond that, everybody you talk to needs an alibi, and remember the accident happened at six or so in the morning, so anybody who says they weren't sleeping should be interesting."

"What about his work?" Fisk asked. "Parnassus?"

"We'll get there. It's a process," Glitsky said evasively. This was, after all, mostly a charity mission for his new inspectors, and he wasn't inclined to let them get in the way and muddy the waters in case Jackman did decide to convene a grand jury over business irregularities at Parnassus, which may or may not have involved Markham. "Let's see where it takes us," he said. But then he did remember a detail. "You'd better take a look at the autopsy, too."

The guys eyed each other, and Bracco cleared his throat. "He died in the hospital, sir," he said. "We know what he died of."

"We do?" Glitsky replied. "What was that?"

"He got run over. Thrown about thirty yards. Smashed into a garbage can."

"And your point is? Look, let's assume we find somebody who wanted to run over Mr. Markham and in fact did a pretty good job of it. So we arrest our suspect and somehow we've never looked at the autopsy. You know what happens? It turns out he died of a heart attack unrelated to his injuries in the accident. Or maybe somebody entirely different from our suspect stuck an ice pick in his ear, or poisoned his ice water. Maybe he was a spy for the Russians and the CIA took him out. The point is, somebody's dead, we check the autopsy first. Every time, *capisce?*"

He looked up and gave them his terrible smile. "Welcome to homicide, boys, where the good times just keep on comin'."

6

Eric Kensing still wore his blood-spattered green scrubs. He was slumped nearly horizontal in a chair in the doctor's lounge on the ground floor, his long legs stretched straight out before him, his feet crossed at the ankles. The room was otherwise empty. A lock of gray-specked black hair hung over his forehead, which he seemed to be holding up with the heel of his right hand.

He heard the door open and someone flicked on the overhead lights. He opened his eyes. It was his soon-to-be ex-wife Ann. "They said I'd find you here." Her voice at whisper pitch, under tight control.

"Looks like they were right."

She started right in. "At least you could have called me, Eric. That's what I don't understand. Instead I find it out on the goddamn radio. And with the kids in tow," she added, "thank you very much."

He got to his feet quickly, not wanting to give her the edge. "Where are they now? Are they okay?"

"Of course they're okay. What do you think? I left them at Janey's. They're fine."

"Well, good." He waited, forcing her.

"So why didn't you call me?"

He backed up a step, crossed his arms. He had

70

an open, almost boyish face in spite of the worry lines, the bags under his eyes, a puffiness at his once-proud jawline. But around his wife he'd learned, especially in the past year or two, to suppress any animation in his face. Not that he felt any conscious need to do that now anyway, but he was resolved to give Ann nothing. He might have been molded from wax, and could easily have passed for someone in his early fifties, though he was fifteen years short of that. "Why would I call you? His wife was here, his family. Besides, the last I heard you'd broken up again. For good."

She set her mouth, drew a determined breath. "I want to see him," she said.

"Help yourself. As long as Carla and his kids are gone. I'd ask you to try and be sensitive if they're still around."

"Oh, yes. Mr. Sensitive. That's your role, isn't it? Bedside manner, comforting the bereaved?"

"Sometimes." He shrugged. "I don't care. You do what you want. You will anyway."

"That's right. I intend to." Her nostrils flared. "How did he die here? How could that happen?"

"He got smashed up, Ann. Badly."

"People get smashed up all the time. They don't die."

"Well, Tim did."

"And you don't care, do you?"

"What does that mean? I don't like to lose a patient, but he wasn't —"

Her voice took on a hysterical edge. *"He wasn't just a patient, Eric."* She glared at him.

71

"Don't give me that doctorspeak. I know what you really think."

"Oh, you do? What's that?"

"You're glad he's dead, aren't you? You wanted him to be dead for a long time."

He had no ready response. Finally, he shook his head in resignation and disgust. "Well, it's been nice talking to you. Now excuse me — " He started to walk by her.

But she moved in front of him. "Where are you going?"

"Back to work. I've got nothing more to say to you. You came here to see Tim? You found me easy enough. You won't have any problem. Now please get out of my way. I've got work to do."

She held her ground. "Oh yes, the busy doctor." Then, taking another tack. "They said you were on the floor."

"What floor?"

"You know what one."

He backed up a step. "What are you talking about?"

"When he died."

"That's right," he said warily. "What about it?"

He'd had long experience with her when her emotions took over, with the sometimes astounding leaps of logic of which she was capable. Now he saw something familiar in her eyes, a kind of wild lucidity that he found deeply unsettling. "I should tell somebody," she said. "I'll bet I know what really happened up there."

"I don't know what you're talking about."

"Yes you do, Eric. I'm the only one who

knows what you're really capable of. How unfeeling you can be. How you *are*."

"Oh please, Ann, don't start."

"I *will* start. You killed him, didn't you?"

He thought she'd been going there, and now that she had, the depth of his rage allowed for nothing but pure reaction. Summoning all of his control, he turned to make sure no one else was within earshot, then leaned in toward her, inches from her face. He forced a brutal smile. "Absolutely," he said with all the cold conviction he could muster. "I pumped his IV full of shit as soon as I could get away with it."

She backed away and froze.

He had her. Her delicious panic impelled him to continue striking. "I kill people here all the time. It's one of the unsung perks of the job."

She stared at him with real fear for a long moment. But he'd shocked her back to herself. Her shoulders relaxed; she gulped a few breaths. "You think that's funny?" she asked. "You think it's something to joke about?"

"You think I'm joking? Were you joking when you asked me?" But then, suddenly, it had gone far enough. "Get a grip, Ann. Did I kill him? Jesus."

"You were there and you hated him."

"So what? Maybe you didn't understand the message. He got run over."

"And brought here."

"It was the closest ER, Ann. I didn't somehow arrange it."

"You should have taken yourself off his case."

"And why is that? So I wouldn't have a chance to kill him? Maybe you don't get it — how about if I wanted to kill him? How about that?" He stared at the total stranger with whom he'd lived a dozen years, who'd borne him three children. For an instant, he wanted to get another rise out of her.

But that gambit had played itself out. She shook her head finally. "You didn't kill him," she said. "You don't have the guts."

"You said it, not me. But whether I did or not, he's gone, isn't he? That's going to be tough on little Annie, isn't it?"

He'd hit her again where it hurt. She set her jaw, then suddenly reached out and pulled violently at a sleeve of his scrubs. "You son of a bitch. What am I supposed to do now, Eric? Tell me that. What am I supposed to do?"

"Whatever you were going to do, Ann. I don't really care. He wasn't coming back anyway." Then, a last thrust. "Don't tell me you don't have a fallback boyfriend?"

She came forward now in a wild fury, her fists flailing at him. "You bastard!" She kept coming, pounding at him, spewing obscenities, until finally he'd gotten ahold of both of her wrists. He gripped them tightly in front of him.

"Ow! Let me go. You're hurting me."

"Good."

"Let me go, damn you!"

"Don't you dare swing at me again. You hear me?" He held on for one more moment, squeezing with all of his strength. She continued to struggle against him, making little inhuman cries

74

with the exertion, trying to pull her arms away, to twist her body, but he had her and wasn't letting her go. Finally, he pulled her close in to him and locked her in his gaze. She wasn't ready to give it up, not yet, but he kept her in an iron grip, until at last he felt the fight go out of her. *"Do you hear me,* goddamnit?" he whispered.

"Yes. Let me go."

He stepped back and pushed her away as he released her. "I'm leaving," he said. "Get out of my way."

She was rubbing her arms, then holding them out. "Look what you've done," she said. "You've hurt me."

"You'll live," he said.

She stepped in front of him, all but daring him to go another round.

But leached out of the hurt and rage, he had no more stomach for fighting her. "Why don't you go home, Ann? Back to the kids. You don't belong here."

But she stared obstinately up at him. "I need to see *him.* Where is he now?"

He knew what she meant. She wanted to view Markham's body. But *fuck that,* he thought. "Best guess right this minute," he said. "Somewhere close to the center of hell."

Then he pushed past her and made it out of the room.

Little League was playing havoc with the Hardys' schedule. Vincent practiced on Mondays and Wednesdays, and Hardy was coaching.

So he and Frannie had had to change their sacred date night to Tuesdays for the duration of the season. Tonight, at a little after 7:00, Hardy pushed open the door of the Little Shamrock where they were supposed to rendezvous, but she hadn't yet arrived.

Her brother, Moses McGuire, though, was behind the rail, talking to a young couple who were decked out in a lot of black leather. In one of his manic phases, McGuire's voice boomed enough to drown out Sting on the jukebox, who wasn't exactly whispering himself.

Hardy pulled up a stool by the front window, half turned so he could watch the cypresses bend in the stiff wind at the edge of Golden Gate Park across the street. Moses glanced at him and began to pull his Guinness — an automatic call for Hardy nine times out of ten. The foam in the stout would take several minutes to fall out, and this way Moses could keep talking until it had. No point in breaking up a good story.

Which continued. ". . . so the guy'd had a stomachache for like nine months, they'd already taken out first his appendix — wrong — then his gall bladder — whoops, wrong again. Nothing helps. And they don't find anything and finally send him on his way, telling him he's stressed out. Well, no shit. So he starts doing acupuncture, seeing a chiropractor, taking herbs, getting massages, nothing helps. And meanwhile," here McGuire turned to Hardy, pointed at his pint, almost ready, "meanwhile, the guy's trying to go on with his life, he's supposed to be getting married in a few months."

The couple asked almost in unison, "So what happened?"

"So two weeks ago, he wakes up doubled over. Can't even get out of bed. They cut him open again, but this time close him back up and say they're sorry. He's got a month. They must have missed it."

"A month to live?" the girl asked. "Is that what they meant?"

"Yeah, but it wasn't a month, either," Moses concluded. "Turns out. It was five days."

The guy was staring through his drink, shaking his head. "Five days?"

McGuire nodded in disgust. "I served him a drink in here three weeks ago and went to his funeral on Monday." He grabbed Hardy's pint and walked it down the bar.

Hardy drank off a mouthful. "That was a fun story. Who were you talking about?"

"Shane Mackey. You didn't know?"

From his own days as a bartender, Hardy had known Mackey when he'd played on the Shamrock's softball team for a couple of years. He couldn't have been much beyond forty years old. Hardy remembered buying him and his fiancée a drink at the New Year's party here, four months ago. He carefully put his glass on the bar and swirled it. "Was that a true story?"

"The good parts, anyway. The wedding was going to be next month. Susan and I had already bought them some dishes."

7

At 9:30, Malachi Ross was in his office, in his leather Eames chair, a cup of coffee grown cold on the glass table in front of him. Across from him, in his wheelchair, a yellow notepad on his lap and a tape recorder next to Ross's coffee, sat Jeff Elliot. Through the vertical blinds, Ross was looking past the reporter, out over downtown from the seventeenth floor. But he noticed neither the lights of North Beach dancing below him nor the stars clear in the wind-swept sky above. He hadn't eaten since breakfast, yet felt no hunger.

They'd been at it for almost a half hour, and Ross had brought the discussion around to himself, his background. How he'd joined the Parnassus board as a doctor whose original job was to provide medical legitimacy for the company's profit-driven business decisions. This was back in the first days of aggressive managed care, and Ross told Elliot that he had come on as the standard-bearer for designating a primary care physician, or PCP, for each patient as the gate-keeper of the medical fortress, a concept which by now had pretty much become the standard for HMOs everywhere in the country.

"But not a popular idea," Elliot observed.

Ross came forward in his chair and met the re-porter's eyes. "Give me a better road and I'm on it tomorrow," he said. "But basically it works."

"Although patients don't like it?"

A resigned shrug. "Let's face it, Mr. Elliot, people are hard to please. I think most patients appreciate the efficiency, and that translates to satisfaction." He wanted to add that in his opinion, people were overly concerned with all the touchy-feely junk. The body was a machine, and mechanics existed who knew how to fix it when it broke. The so-called human element was vastly overrated. But he couldn't say that to Elliot. "It's really better for the vast majority of patients."

"And why is that?" the reporter asked. "Doesn't it just remove them from any kind of decision loop?"

"Okay, that's a reasonable question, I suppose. But I've got one for you, although you won't like the sound of it. Why *should* they be in it?" Again, he held up his hand, stopping Elliot's response. "It's hard enough to keep this ship afloat with professionals who know the business. If patients had the final say, they'd sink it financially. Now I'm not saying we shouldn't keep patients informed and involved, but —"

"But people would demand all kinds of expensive tests they don't really need."

Ross smiled with apparent sincerity. "There you are. Healing takes time, Mr. Elliot, and you'd be surprised at how many health problems go away by themselves."

He stood up and went over to the small refrigerator at the corner of the room and got out a couple of bottled waters. He gave one to the reporter and sat back down.

"Look," he said, leaning forward and speaking, ostensibly, from the heart. "I know this must all sound pretty callous, but nobody's opposed to losing the money on tests if they're necessary. Hell, that's what insurance is all about, after all. But if *fifty* guys show up month after month, and each one gets his test when only five really need it, then instead of Parnassus losing twenty-five grand, which is covered by premiums, we lose a quarter mil. To cover that, we'd have to increase premiums and copays by a factor of ten, which nobody can afford. So the whole system falls apart, and no one gets any health care."

Elliot drank some water. "But let's say out of the forty-five guys who don't get their tests, ten in fact need them. Not five. What happens to them?"

"They get identified, Mr. Elliot. Maybe a little late, which is regrettable. Nobody denies that. They're tough choices, I admit. I personally wish nobody had to go through any pain ever, honest to God. That's why I became a doctor to begin with. But it's my job now to keep this ship afloat, and if we tested every patient for everything they wanted as opposed to everything they truly needed, we'd sink like a stone, and that's the cold, hard truth. Then nobody would get any tests because nobody could afford them. You think that would be better?"

"Let me ask you one," Elliot asked. "I've heard a rumor you haven't paid some of your doctors. Would you care to comment on that?"

80

Ross kept on his poker face, but Elliot's awareness of this fact startled and worried him. He also thought he knew the source of it — the always difficult Eric Kensing, who'd admitted Baby Emily and then, he suspected, been Elliot's source on the breaking story. But he only said, "I don't know where you would have heard that. It's not accurate."

This evidently amused the reporter. "Is that the same as not true?"

Ross sat back in an effort to appear casual. "What we did was ask our doctor group to loan a sum to the company, with interest, that would come out of the payroll reserve. It was entirely voluntary and we've paid back everyone who's asked."

Jeff Elliot had been sitting listening to Malachi Ross's apologies and explanations for over an hour. Now the chief medical director was talking, lecturing really, about the rationale for the Parnassus drug formulary, maybe hoping that Jeff would spin the self-serving chaff into gold in his column, get some PR points for the group in Ross's coming war with the city.

"Look," Ross said, "let's say the Genesis Corporation invented a cancer-curing drug called Nokance. The budget to research and develop the drug and then shepherd it through the zillions of clinical trials until it got FDA approval comes in at a billion dollars. But suddenly, it's curing cancer and everybody wants it. Sufferers are willing to pay almost anything, and Genesis needs to recoup its investment if it's going to

81

stay in business and invent other miracle drugs, so it charges a hundred bucks per prescription. And for a couple of years, while it's the only show in town, Nokance gets all the business.

"But eventually the other drug companies come out with their versions of Nokance, perhaps with minute variations to avoid patent disputes —"

"But some of which might cause side effects?"

A pained expression brought Ross's eyelids to half-mast. "Rarely, Mr. Elliot. Really. Very rarely. So look where we are. These drugs also cure cancer, but to get market share, they're priced at ten bucks. In response, Nokance lowers its price to, say, fifty dollars."

"That's a lot more than ten."

"Yes it is, and you'd think that once we educate people, tell them all the facts, everybody would stop using it and go for the cheap stuff, wouldn't you?"

"They don't?"

"Never. Or statistically never. Given the choice, the patients almost always choose Nokance. It's the brand name people recognize. There's confidence in the product."

"Like Bayer aspirin."

"Exactly!" Ross silently brought his hands together, as though he was applauding. "So — and here's the point — although it costs us forty dollars more *per scrip* to supply the Nokance, if we approve it and keep it on the formulary, it costs the patients the same amount it always has, which is ten bucks, the drug copay. So we delist it."

"The Nokance?"

"Right."

"But — this is still hypothetical now — you're saying it's good stuff and you don't let your patients get it."

"They can get it, but we won't pay for it. If we did, it would wipe us out. We're dealing with extremely small margins for the survival of the company here. You've got to understand that. The point is that Nokance isn't the only stuff that works. That's what I'm trying to get through to you. The generics do the job."

Elliot had his own very strongly developed ideas about drug formularies. He had been suffering from multiple sclerosis for over twenty years, and on the advice of his doctors, he sometimes thought that he'd tried all the various generics in the world for his different and changing symptoms. Not invariably, but several times — at least enough to have let him develop a healthy skepticism — he'd experienced side effects or discomfort with the generics. When he'd gone back to the brand name, the problems vanished. So Ross would never sell him on the universal benefit of generic drugs.

"So just to be clear on your position," Elliot said, "your view is that this gatekeeping and cost cutting, from managed care to generic drugs, is essentially consistent with your Hippocratic oath, for example. Where the emphasis is first to do no harm, then to heal."

"Basically, yes." Ross seemed pleased with this take on it, but Elliot knew he wouldn't be for long. "We're in medicine, Mr. Elliot," he continued. "The goal is maximum wellness for the most people."

"And there's no conflict between your business interests and the needs of your patients?"

"Of course there is." Ross was leaning back in his chair comfortably, his legs crossed. "But we try to minimize it. It's all a matter of degree. The company needs to sustain itself so it can continue doing its work."

"And also make a profit, let's not forget. You've got to show earnings, though — right? — to please your investors?"

Ross smiled and spread his hands in a self-deprecating way. "Well, we're not doing too well at that lately."

"So I hear." Elliot came forward in his wheelchair, spoke in a friendly tone. "Do your investors ever express displeasure with the salaries of your officers and directors?"

Ross blinked a few times, but if the question bothered him, he covered it quickly. "Not often. Our board members are skilled businesspeople. If the pay weren't competitive, they'd go elsewhere. Good help is hard to find, and when you find it, you pay top dollar for it."

"And this good help, what does it do exactly? Run the company?"

"That's right."

"And yet you're close to bankruptcy." It wasn't a question, but Elliot let it hang for a beat. "Which makes one wonder if lesser-paid help could do any worse, doesn't it?"

Fisk and Bracco may have come across as a matched pair to their fellow homicide inspectors, but they really couldn't have been much more different from each other as human beings. And this meant they were different kinds of cops, too.

When it got to be five o'clock, Harlen Fisk asked his partner if he'd drop him off at Tadich's, the city's oldest restaurant. In spite of his pregnant wife and baby boy waiting at home, he'd be meeting his aunt Kathy and several of her supporters for dinner and schmoozing well into the night. He didn't invite Bracco to join them, and there were no hard feelings either way. The fact was, Fisk was a political animal with his eye someday in the distant future on political rewards.

By contrast, Bracco was the son of a cop, but even so, until he got the promotion to homicide, he hadn't clearly understood how much his father's connection to the mayor was affecting his career, how much the regular guys resented him. And he'd never asked for special treatment — it had simply come with the territory. Political people in the department thought they could make the mayor happy by being nice to the Bracco boy, and they weren't all wrong.

But when Fisk had told him that he was thinking about going to his aunt, the city supervisor, to complain about their continued ill-treatment on the fourth floor, Bracco had talked his partner out of it. One thing he'd learned from his father was that cops didn't whine. Ever. The thing to do was talk to Glitsky, he'd said. Ask straight and deal with the answers, which was that there was probably no intentional homicide here with the hit and run, and hence nothing to look into.

85

Bracco believed that this was the truth. But what else was he doing with his time?

So after he dropped Harlen off downtown, he spent a few hours checking leads that they'd picked up on the car during the course of the day. He didn't expect any results, but you never knew. His experience in hit and run had taught him that most of the time, the drivers would wait until they thought nobody was looking for their car anymore. They'd park it out of sight, keep the garage door closed. After a month, they would take it to a car wash or body shop. And that would be the end of it.

But maybe this time — long odds, but possible — it would be different. They'd gotten eleven patrol call-ins during the day. These were vehicles fitting the description that were parked at the curb or in driveways around the city, reported by patrolling cops. Fisk hated this kind of legwork. Bracco, on the other hand, put in a couple of hours checking out each and every one. The impact that had thrown Markham would have left a sign even on an old, thick-skinned American car, and a quick walk around with a flashlight would tell him if he would need to come back with a warrant. But none of the cars had anything close.

Not exactly knowing why, he killed another half hour walking through the parking garage at Portola Hospital, but there wasn't one old green car. So, feeling like an idiot, he sat in his car and wrote some notes to jog his memory tomorrow — check the Rent-A-Wrecks, don't forget the call-ins to H&R from citizens interested in the reward from the supervisor's fund (ten thousand dollars for information leading to the arrest and conviction, et cetera).

Finally, on his way home after a piroshki gut-bomb he bought at a place on Nineteenth Avenue, he decided to head back up to Seacliff, to Markham's house. Start, as Glitsky said, with the family. Look at the cars parked outside. After all, he reminded himself wryly, he was the car police.

"Can I help you?"

Bracco straightened up abruptly and shone his flashlight across the hood of the white Toyota he was examining. It was the last one of what had been twenty-three cars parked on Markham's block. The beam revealed a man of above-average height, who brought a hand up against the glare, and spoke again in a harsh, strained voice. "What the hell are you doing?"

Bracco noted with alarm that he was reaching into his jacket pocket with his free hand. "Freeze. Police." It was all he could think to say. "Don't move." Bracco didn't know whether he ought to flash his badge or draw the gun from his shoulder holster. He decided on the latter and leveled it at the figure. "I'm coming around this car." His blood was racing. "Don't move one muscle," he repeated.

"I'm not moving."

"Okay, now slowly, the hand in your jacket, take it out where I can see it."

"This is ridiculous." But the man complied.

Bracco patted the jacket, reached inside and

removed a cell phone, then backed away a step.

"Look, I'm a doctor," the man said. "A patient of mine who lives here died today. So I come out after paying my condolences and somebody's at my car with a flashlight. I was just going to use the cell to call the police myself."

After a moment, Bracco handed the phone back to the doctor, and put his gun back where it belonged. If he'd felt like an idiot before walking the parking lot at the hospital, now he was mortified, although he wasn't going to show it. "Could I see some identification, please?"

The man turned to look toward the house for a moment, then came back to the inspector. "I don't see . . ." he began. "I'm . . ." Finally he sighed and reached for his wallet. "My name is Dr. Eric Kensing," he said. "I was the ICU supervisor today at Portola Hospital."

"Where Mr. Markham died?"

"Right. He was my . . . boss, I guess. Why are the police out here now?"

Bracco found himself coming out with the truth. "I'm looking for the hit-and-run vehicle."

Kensing blew out impatiently. "Could I please have my wallet back?" He slipped it into his pocket, then suddenly asked, "You're not saying you really think somebody Tim knew hit him on purpose, then came here to visit the family?"

"No. But we'd be pretty stupid not to look, wouldn't we?"

"It sounds a little far-fetched to me, but if that's what you guys do . . ." He let the thought go unfinished. "Listen, are we done? I'd like to go now. My car didn't hit him. You see any sign

88

that I hit him? You want to check again and make sure? I interrupted you in the middle of it."

Something about the man's tone — a mixture of arrogance and impatience — struck Bracco. He knew that people reacted to cops in all kinds of different ways. Every once in a while, though, he believed that the reaction revealed something unusual, perhaps a consciousness of guilt. Kensing was reaching for the door handle, but Bracco suddenly and instinctively wanted to keep him for a few more words.

"You say Mr. Markham was your boss? I didn't realize he was a doctor."

Kensing straightened up at the car door and sighed again. "He wasn't. He ran the company I work for. Parnassus Health."

"So you knew him well, did you?"

A pause. "Not really." He shifted his gaze back over Bracco's shoulder again. "Now if we're done here . . ."

"What's in the house?" Bracco asked.

"What do you mean? Nothing."

"You keep looking back at it."

"Do I?" He shrugged. "I wasn't aware of it. I suppose I'm worried about them. It's been a real tragedy. They're devastated in there."

Bracco was picking up an off note that might have been fatigue but might be something else. He could turn his questions into an interrogation of sorts if he could manage to keep the right tone. "I thought you said you didn't know him well."

"I didn't."

"Yet you're worried about his family?"

"Do you have some problem with that? Last time I checked, it wasn't a crime to care about a victim's family." Kensing swiped a hand across his forehead, cast a quick look up and down the street. "Look, Officer, are we going somewhere with this that I'm missing?"

Bracco didn't anwer. Instead, he asked one of his own. "So, you didn't have any strong feelings about him?"

The doctor cocked his head to one side. "What do you mean? As a boss?"

"Any way."

This time, the doctor paused for a long moment. "What's your name, Officer, if you don't mind? I like to know who I'm speaking with."

"Bracco. Sergeant Inspector Darrel Bracco. Homicide."

As soon as Bracco said it, he knew it was a mistake. Kensing nearly jumped at the word. "Homicide?"

"Yes, sir."

"And you're investigating Tim's death? Why? Does somebody think he was murdered?"

"Not necessarily. A hit and run that results in death is a homicide. This is just routine."

"Routine. Checking the cars coming to his house?"

"Right. And you just called him Tim."

"Does that mean something? His name was Tim."

"You didn't know him very well, and yet you called him by his first name?"

Kensing was silent, shaking his head. Finally, he let out a long breath. "Look, Inspector, I don't know what I'm supposed to say. The man died in my unit today, while he was under my care. I've known him for fifteen years, and I came by here to pay further condolences to his wife and family. It's almost ten o'clock and I've been up since six this morning and I'm the walking dead right now. I don't see where calling the man by his first name has any meaning, and if you don't mind, I've got an early call again tomorrow. I'd be happy to talk to you at the hospital if you want to make an appointment."

Bracco realized that maybe he'd pushed his spontaneous interrogation too far. Everything Kensing said, tone or no tone, made perfect sense. There was no real point in harassing this probably decent doctor who had, in fact, voluntarily opened the door to another interview tomorrow. The inspector knew he'd overreached.

"You're right. But I may call you in the next few days."

"That'd be fine," Kensing said. "I'm not going anywhere."

They both stood in the street for another beat, then Bracco told him good night and turned for the house. Glitsky had told him it started with the family, and maybe he'd find something inside, get some valuable first impressions. But he hadn't gone two steps when he heard Kensing's voice again. "You're not thinking about going up to the house, are you?"

He stopped and turned. "I thought I might."

The doctor hesitated, seemed to be considering whether to say anything. Finally, he spoke up. "Well, you'll do what you're going to do, Inspector, but you might want to consider giving them a break tonight and coming back tomorrow. They've had a bad day. They're wrung out. I guarantee none of them drove your hit-and-run car. What are you going to ask them that can't wait?"

Bracco had had a long day himself. He looked back at the house, still lit up. It struck him that his need to find something, anything, to do with Tim Markham's death, and thereby prove his worth to Glitsky, was pushing him too far too fast. He'd invented phantoms and made some interrogation mistakes here with Kensing, just now.

And he was about to do it again with the family when he had no plan and there was really nothing to ask. He should leave them to their exhaustion and grief. Tomorrow was another day.

Bracco nodded. "That's a good call, but you and I might be talking again soon."

"I'll look forward to it," Kensing said, and opened the door to his car.

8

Glitsky had lived in the same upper duplex for twenty years and now, between the blessing of rent control and the latest surge in San Francisco real estate, he knew he would be living there when he died. Even if the owner sold it, a new owner could never make him leave unless he wanted to move in himself, and that would take forever and cost a fortune. Glitsky's rent could never go up beyond a piddling percentage. And with converted condo one-bedroom fixer-uppers now going for half a million dollars anywhere in the city, he knew he could never afford to buy something else. As it was, he paid rent of less than a thousand dollars a month for the place, which was on a quiet dead end, a really beautiful tree-lined block north of Lake. His backyard opened onto a greenbelt and running path at the border of the Presidio, so he often woke up to birds chirping rather than sirens wailing. Deer and raccoon sightings were common. He didn't kid himself — he knew he was one of the very fortunate.

Still, it wasn't as though he lived in ducal splendor. Ducal splendor, he felt, was hard to come by in thirteen hundred square feet, especially when that area was subdivided into three bedrooms, a kitchen, and a living room. Still, with Flo he'd raised his three boys here; the lack of room had never really been an issue then, and it wasn't now. For the past several years, a housekeeper named Rita Schultz had lived with him and Orel, and she had slept behind a screen in the living room. Rita was gone now, which made the living room seem gigantic. Treya's sixteen-year-old daughter, Raney, had taken over what had for a short while been the television room down the hallway behind the kitchen. They had plenty of room.

It was now 7:30 and both kids had gone off to school. Glitsky and Treya were both drinking tea, reading the newspaper at the kitchen table, which wasn't big enough to spread out the sections, so they played a quiet game, covering a portion of each other's pages whenever they turned their next one. When Treya had done this for the fourth time, covering the lengthy article Glitsky was reading about the latest news on the ancient water flows on Mars and what they all might mean, he put down his mug, reached over and, quite gently, ripped the offending page down the middle. He then dropped it on the floor.

"You are such a fun person," she said. "I don't care what everybody says."

"Are there people who don't think I'm fun?"

"Some, I think."

Glitsky shook his head. "This is very hard to believe. Hardy told me the same thing just last year." He made a caricature of a smile, which his scar rendered grotesque. "But put another page over mine before I finish this article and I'll rip your heart out. Okay?"

"We need a bigger table."

He was trying to get back to reading, but stopped again and looked across at her. "Yes, we do. But we'd need a bigger kitchen to hold it, and then where would we be?"

"Maybe we could knock down a wall here . . . no, I'm serious. And then —" The doorbell interrupted her and she looked at her watch. "Who could that be?"

"One of the kids forgot something." Abe was up and moving. "Nope," he said. "Business." He opened the door. "Good morning, Darrel. You're up early. Where's Harlen?" Then, "How'd you find out where I live?"

Harlen Fisk had known from somewhere, Darrel explained — politicians always knew — and had pointed the place out to him. So this morning, heading downtown from Seacliff, Bracco had to pass Glitsky's duplex and he decided to stop and maybe save themselves the trip back.

Now as they drove, his lieutenant sat beside him, clearly exercising his patience. "So let me get this straight. You were out in the street in front of Mr. Markham's house until nearly ten last night, then decided it was too late to go in and start asking questions. And why were you going to do that again? Ask questions?"

"You said it started with the family."

"That's true."

"So I was going to talk to them if I could. But a lot of people had come by for condolences and so on and I realized that the family must have had a long hard day, so I thought I'd let them get some rest. It could wait until today."

"And you were there again by when? Six thirty?"

"Closer to seven. I figured the kids would still have school and I wanted to catch them if I could. I didn't think any of them were going to sleep very well anyway."

"But nobody answered?"

Bracco flicked a glance across the car seat. "Nothing the first time when I just knocked, so I'm thinking they're still sleeping. So I gave it another twenty and rang four or five times and waited." He hesitated. "They were in the house when I left, Lieutenant. Dr. Kensing had just come out from visiting them. I'm ninety-nine percent sure that they went to sleep there. I don't know why they didn't answer. I think I would have woken them up at least."

Arms crossed, Glitsky merely nodded. He didn't know what if anything was going on at Tim Markham's house. He did consider it entirely possible that the household had slept through Bracco's knocking and ringing. He'd seen families of murder victims, physically exhausted and emotionally depleted, sleep around the clock and then some. Or they might have decided just not to answer the door to some unknown man at the crack of dawn.

But on another level, Glitsky was glad to see his inspector showing such initiative, even if it might turn out to have been misdirected. They'd know soon enough.

It was another clear, cold morning. They parked directly in front of the two-story mansion and walked to the front stoop, an expanse of flagstone broader and wider than Glitsky's living room. Bracco knocked, then pressed the bell, a booming three-tone gong easily audible outside the door. "I don't think they sleep through that, do you?"

Glitsky reached around, pressed the button again. And they waited. After one more try and another minute, Abe told Darrel to stay where he was and went to check around the house. The plantation shutters in the front windows were closed, but through the garage windows, he saw two cars parked where they should have been. Opening the gate through the fence to the back-yard, he was struck by the silence, and walked more briskly to the window in the back door. A large dog, apparently asleep on the floor, was visible at the far end of a kind of mud room, and Glitsky knocked forcefully several times. The dog didn't move.

Jogging now, coming back around to the front of the house, he saw that a woman had joined Bracco on the front porch. He checked his watch and saw that it was just eight o'clock. Slowing down now, walking back up to the stoop, he had his badge out and introduced himself. She was Anita Tong. As he'd guessed, the maid, arriving at work for the day.

"Were you expecting Mrs. Markham to be home this morning?"

Ms. Tong nodded. "Mr. Markham just died yesterday. Where would she go?"

"I don't know," Glitsky said. "I was asking you."

There was no answer.

"Do you have a house key? May I see it, please?"

Nervous now, nodding, she was biting her lower lip. She rummaged in her purse, extracted a set of keys, and dropped them onto the flagstone. "I'm sorry," she said, picking them up. "Here. This one."

Glitsky turned to his inspector. "Darrel, I want you to stay here. Ms. Tong, you should wait right here, too, with Inspector Bracco. Do you understand? Don't go inside."

Glitsky then opened the door and found himself in a large, bright, circular foyer. A spacious room opened off to his left and he walked a couple of steps into it and looked around. All seemed in order. Across the foyer, a dining room complete with formal table and chandelier was also as it should be, as was the breakfast nook beyond that.

Silence, though. Everywhere dead silence.

He went back through the dining room to the kitchen and hadn't gone a step into it when he saw the woman's body lying on its side, a gun on the floor by her head. Crossing to her in several long strides, he avoided the pool of drying blood and knelt by her for a second. He saw the source of the blood, a hole in the scalp low and behind the right ear. Although there was no doubt, he touched the cold skin of her neck, then pulled out his gun and started to check the rest of the house. Two minutes later, he walked to a wall phone upstairs in the master bedroom and punched in the number he knew best.

★ ★ ★

The crime scene investigation team had already been working the house for an hour and now its sergeant, Jack Langtry, was walking across the front lawn to where Glitsky stood with a small knot of coroner's people and police. The sun was out, but it hadn't warmed appreciably. Everyone standing around had their hands in their pockets.

Langtry hailed originally from Australia and was normally a hearty, rugby-type guy in his late thirties. Today his face looked somehow crooked and blotchy and he seemed to lurch from side to side as he walked, almost as if he were drunk. Glitsky separated himself from the general and subdued mass and met him in the middle of the lawn.

Langtry let out some air and squeezed at his temples with one hand. He kicked at the ground, raised his eyes, looked out at the horizon. "You know one of the things I loved most about this country when I first came here? No restrictions on who can own guns. But I think I'm getting to the point where I'm changing my mind. You put guns in a house with distraught people . . . I've just seen this too bloody often. Stupid sods."

Glitsky thought he understood what Langtry was implying, but this wasn't a time for guessing. He wanted to be clear on the crime scene investigation unit's position. "What do you think happened in there, Jack?"

Langtry scratched under the collar of his shirt, looked again at the bright blue sky. When his eyes got back to Glitsky, he was back in professional mode. "It was Markham's gun. We found the registration in the same drawer where he probably kept it, in his office off the kitchen. It was right by her hand."

"All right. It was his gun in her hand. What's that mean?"

"By itself, I don't know for sure. The lab might tell us something we don't know."

"Other than what?"

"Other than what it seems like."

Glitsky took a beat. "We playing twenty questions here, Jack, or what?"

"You were asking them, Abe. You want to know what I think, we can go straight to there. She did them all, then killed herself."

"Carla?"

"Was that her name?"

"Yeah. She killed her kids, too?"

Langtry seemed to get a little defensive. "You telling me you've never seen it?"

"I've seen it a lot, Jack. Maybe just not like this."

"Not like what?"

But Glitsky discovered he couldn't quite put his finger on what nagged at him about this theory. "I don't know, Jack. Maybe I'm whistling through my hat. Faro come up with anything?" Faro was Lennard Faro, the crime scene lab technician.

Langtry nodded. "He's still in there. You can talk to him. You wanted my take, it's probably what it looks like. Unless you know something I don't."

It was a question, and Glitsky shook his head.

"Just why? Why the whole family?"

But this wasn't a hard one for Langtry. "Her husband died yesterday, right? That's what I heard."

"Yeah. Hit and run."

"And maybe they were having problems before that?"

"I don't know. Did you hear that someplace?"

"No. But it's the profile. You know as well as me."

"Maybe not," Glitsky replied, though he thought he did. "Tell me."

Langtry squinted into the sky again, organizing his thoughts. "The world's too horrible to live in. There's too much pain and it all means nothing anyway. So she's sparing them from that. Doing them a favor, maybe."

Glitsky knew that this was the standard reading. In his career, he'd seen distraught women kill their families before. He'd read or heard about several others. It was always difficult to imagine or accept. But in his experience, those events — terrible though they had been — had a different quality to them, a more immediate and somehow more painful impetus than the simple death of the husband.

He remembered — years ago now — a family of five who'd escaped from Vietnam. The oldest boy, a young teenager, had died on the boat coming over, and then a few months after they'd arrived, they were packed into a one-bedroom place and one of the Chinatown gangs broke in, took some stuff, and then — possibly angry that the family didn't have more stuff to steal — shot

101

the husband dead. The next day, the mother had suffocated the two young kids, then cut her own wrists.

He'd seen another young woman in a so-called burning bed case. Her boyfriend had been beating her and finally she shot him in his sleep, then did the same with her baby and herself. About two years ago, a clinically depressed, suicidal woman named Gerry Patecik — for some reason, he remembered her name — overdosed herself and two out of her three kids with barbiturates in milk shakes after her husband walked out and filed for divorce.

So Glitsky had seen it — the bare fact of murder/suicide wasn't unknown or even terribly uncommon, given its heinous nature. But all the other cases he'd seen or heard about had a certain over-the-edge quality that seemed to be missing here. And he'd never before seen or heard of teenage victims — they'd always been younger children. This was an apparently comfortable family who'd simply lost their father. Tragic, yes — but could Carla Markham have been that close to the kind of complete and utter despair that would seem to be in evidence and still entertain a reasonable crowd here the night before? It was hard to imagine.

"Goddamnit, Abe," Langtry suddenly said. He turned back toward the house, as though looking to it for some answers. "Goddamn stupid stupid stupid."

Glitsky hated the profanity but he empathized with Langtry's fury. Four people were dead in the house, the woman and her three teenage children, shot in their beds upstairs. With the death of Tim Markham yesterday, this made an entire family wiped out in twenty-four hours. "I hear you, Jack," he said. "You got anything else I need to know?"

"Nah, it's all peaceful as a bloody tomb in there. It *is* a bloody tomb. Christ."

At that moment, a woman from the CSI team appeared in the doorway, carrying the rag doll body of the Markhams' dog, a large and beautiful golden retriever. Glitsky watched as, sagging under the weight, she crossed the flagstone stoop. Langtry took a step toward her, said "Carol," and got stopped by her glare. Crying silently, she didn't want any help. At the curb, she placed the lifeless form in the back of one of the ambulances still parked there, then walked over to one of the patrol cars and sat down inside, closing the door behind her.

Glitsky laid a quick fraternal hand on Langtry's shoulder as he passed him, then went up across the lawn and through the front door.

Inside, he found Lennard Faro, the crime scene lab specialist, standing by the sink in the kitchen. Dark and wiry, with a thin mustache and a tiny gold cross in his earlobe, he had his arms and legs crossed in an attitude of casual impatience. The photographer was taking pictures and he seemed to be waiting until he finished up.

Glitsky stopped for a second at the entrance to the kitchen, took another glance at Mrs. Markham's body, then joined Faro at the sink. "Jack Langtry tells me she shot the gun," he said.

Faro turned his head sideways. "Maybe. There it is. Close enough."

The gun lay on the floor, about a foot from Carla's right hand. "She right-handed?" Glitsky asked.

A mirthless chuckle. "You'll have to ask her."

Glitsky thought he deserved that. "Why don't you tell me what you know? Keep me from asking more stupid questions."

Faro took a beat, then straightened up. "You mind if we get out of here? The view pales after an hour or two." He crossed the kitchen, back out to the grand dining room, then into the foyer, where the front door was still open, fresh air coming in. "Okay. The gun's a twenty-two revolver, holds six slugs, although we've recovered only five casings, which fits. As I see it, she started upstairs with her son."

"Why do you say that?"

"It's the only one she tried to silence. The shot was through the pillow."

"Okay. Then what?"

Faro pointed upstairs. The dining room was expansive and open, its ceiling over twenty feet high, with a large skylight at the roof. Midway up, around the sides of the room, a banister marked the walkway to the rooms on the second story. "The next room over, at the end," Faro said, "is where the girls slept. Twins. It looks like she went in there next. No point in trying to silence the first shot, so she probably just did it quick."

"Then went downstairs and killed herself?"

Faro corrected him. "The dog first."

104

Suddenly the niggling detail he couldn't place earlier when he'd been talking with Langtry struck Glitsky. Even if Carla Markham thought the world too cruel for herself and her children, why would she shoot her dog? Certainly not to spare it the pain of going on. Much more typical would have been a note leaving the pet in the care of a relative or close friend.

"Sir?" Faro asked. "Did you say something?"

"Just talking to myself, Len. How about her own wound?"

"Back of the ear, right side, which fits again. But no exit wound, so I can't hypothesize about the trajectory. Strout ought to get all that."

"I'm sure he will," Abe said. "But let me ask you this, Len. You're going with Jack on murder/suicide, I take it?"

But the analyst shook his head. "We're not done here by a long shot, sir. I don't see anything that rules it out, let's put it like that. It looks like she fired the gun. No sign of any struggle any-where." He raised his shoulders, let them down. "But I don't know. You got a better idea, I'll look anyplace you want."

"I don't know if it's a better idea," Glitsky said, "but I'd ask Strout to double-check for the trajectory and find out if she was right-handed." With his own right hand, Glitsky pointed to a spot at the back of his right ear. "It seems a little awkward, don't you think?"

Harlen Fisk had been dispatched out from downtown and had joined his partner here at the house, where Glitsky had assigned to them the

105

task of interviewing Anita Tong. Now the lieutenant joined the three of them, who had gathered around the table in the breakfast nook.

The maid was still visibly shaken. When Glitsky had first come outside after discovering the bodies, she'd all but collapsed onto the stoop upon hearing the news, which had seemed incomprehensible to her. For the first several minutes, she kept returning to the same questions, then arguing with the answers.

What did he mean, *dead?* Glitsky must have been wrong. He didn't mean that they were *all* dead, did he? They couldn't all be dead, that wouldn't be possible. Not Ian, at seventeen the eldest child. He was too big, too strong and competent, almost a man now. Certainly, he would have heard someone coming into his room and woken up, wouldn't he? Was Glitsky sure he saw *both* of the girls, Chloe and Siggy? Maybe he hadn't. He might want to go back up and check again. Someone could still be alive.

Anita Tong was a petite and well-spoken woman. She'd been part of the Markhams' household for seven and a half years. They were her only employers. She lived a couple of miles south in the Sunset District, and worked in the house five days a week — Mondays and Tuesdays off — from 8:00 a.m. until 6:00 p.m.

Now, pulling up a chair, Glitsky straddled it backward. He picked up on Ms. Tong's story as she was telling the inspectors that she'd offered to stay on for the night — he assumed she meant last night — and thank God she hadn't. "But Carla — Mrs. Markham — said she and the kids

106

could handle things, I should go. They didn't expect many more people."

"How many were there when you left?" Bracco asked.

Ms. Tong considered a moment. "Her coffee group, mostly. Which is six other women. They meet every Friday morning. I think when they heard about Mr. Markham . . . anyway, they brought some casseroles and things like that, so I thought she might have wanted me to stay and heat them up and serve them. But no."

Fisk was nodding as though this was all somehow relevant. Bracco was taking notes on a yellow legal pad. At least, Glitsky noted with some surprise and relief, his new guys had put a tape recorder on the table. But he could see how they hadn't gotten very far if all of Tong's answers had gone this way. He decided to speak up, keep things on point, maybe give a little instruction while he was at it. "So, Ms. Tong," he said gently, "what time did you wind up leaving?"

"*Mrs.* Tong," she corrected him. "A little before seven."

"And there were only Mrs. Markham and her six friends in the house when you left? Nobody else?"

She turned to face him. "Well, the kids and a couple of their friends, too. Ian's, really, not the girls."

"Two of them?"

"I think so. Teenagers. They sat in here."

"Two of Ian's friends, then," Glitsky said. "Do you know their names?"

"One was Joel Burrill. He's here all the time.

107

The other one, I think Mark, but . . ." She shook her head.

"How about the names of the coffee group women?" Glitsky asked.

This was more promising, and Mrs. Tong brightened up slightly. "Well, there's Ruth Fitzpatrick, I know. And Jamie Rath. Oh, her daughter Lexi was here, too. She's in Chloe's grade. Jamie lives right around the corner. I could show you."

Glitsky made a little writing motion, signaling Bracco that he should be jotting down these names. To Mrs. Tong, he continued, "That would be good when we're finished here, if you don't mind. Now, as to the rest of the guests, was anyone else here when you left, or just the coffee group and Ian's friends? And Chloe's classmate."

"Well, of course Mr. Markham's assistant was here the whole time. Brendan, just crying and crying, worse than Mrs. Markham sometimes. Then there was Frank Husic next door. He's a very nice man. He heard about Mr. Markham on the radio and came right over to see if there was any way he could help." Mrs. Tong closed her eyes for a moment, then nodded to herself. "That's all when I was still here. After that I don't know."

"So you didn't see Dr. Kensing?" Glitsky asked.

Mrs. Tong's expression was instructive. She reacted visibly with recognition and, Glitsky thought, shock. "Dr. Kensing coming here surprises you?"

108

It took her a moment to phrase one syllable. "Well . . ." She stopped. The inspectors waited. Finally she shrugged. "Yes, I guess," she said.

"And why is that?"

Mrs. Tong was starting to close up. She drew her head down slightly between her shoulders.

Glitsky kept at her. "Did you know Dr. Kensing, Mrs. Tong? Was he a friend of the family?"

"Not exactly a friend, no. I didn't know him, but the name . . . the name is familiar."

Glitsky hadn't moved his chair, but he somehow seemed to have gotten closer to her. "And you wouldn't have expected him to come by? Why is that?"

Before Mrs. Tong could frame an answer, one of the inspectors interrupted. Bracco, eager to show off what he'd learned, pumped in, "He was on call at the ICU when Markham died. He probably felt he should."

Glitsky's gaze would have frozen flame. He turned mildly, though, back to his subject. "Mrs. Tong, I'm sorry. What were you going to say? Why you wouldn't have expected Dr. Kensing to come and visit?"

"I just . . ." She'd picked up the tension between Glitsky and his inspectors, and it didn't increase her comfort level. "I don't know," she said finally.

In some ways, Glitsky knew, this interview and their interruptions might someday prove instructive to Fisk and Bracco, but it wasn't any solace at the moment, as a willing and cooperative witness was clamming up before his eyes because he couldn't establish a rhythm, which was halfway to rapport.

But he wasn't through trying yet. She'd opened a different door a crack, and maybe he could get her to open that one. "All right," he said, "but you did say that Dr. Kensing wasn't exactly a friend. I believe those were your words. Didn't you say that?"

"I think so. Yes."

"Could you tell us what you meant by that?" He threw another, apparently benign look at his rookies, but it delivered the message loud and clear: Shut up and let her answer.

"Well, he worked for Mr. Markham."

"So you meant he wasn't exactly a friend because he was more an employee?" When she appeared to be considering that, Glitsky clarified it further. "As opposed to not exactly being a friend because he was more an enemy."

They waited, and this time Mrs. Tong's check around the table revealed a universal and hopeful expectation that prompted a more open response. "His name came up sometimes," she began, "with Carla and her friends. I couldn't help but hear, serving them, you know? Actually, not so much his name as his wife's." Suddenly another thought struck her, though. "Should I be saying any of this? Do I need to have a lawyer with me?"

Glitsky put his finger in that dike immediately. "I don't think so, ma'am. You haven't done anything wrong. You're not in any trouble." Having said that, he came right back at her, hoping a new question would trump the lawyer issue.

"Why did Dr. Kensing's wife come up at this coffee group?"

"She talked about divorcing him."

The antecedents hung in the air in an unidentifiable jumble. "Dr. Kensing's wife?" Glitsky asked. "Was divorcing him?"

"No." Mrs. Tong shook her head impatiently. "Carla. Mrs. Kensing was . . . I think everybody knows this . . . Mr. Markham had an affair with her."

Fisk brought his baby face forward. It was alight with excitement and possibility. "With Dr. Kensing's wife?" he asked avidly.

No, Glitsky wanted to say with his deepest sarcasm, with the golden retriever. But he bit it back. One more time, though, and he really was going to have to tell them to leave. He kept his own voice uninflected. "Are you saying that Dr. Kensing's wife —"

"Ann."

"Okay, Ann. She and Mr. Markham were having an affair? You mean it wasn't over?"

"It was supposed to be. When it all blew up —"

"When was that?"

"About five or six months ago, just before Thanksgiving. That's when Carla found out. She kicked him out for a couple of weeks then. I didn't think he was ever coming back. But he did. She asked him back. If it were me, I don't think I'd have forgiven . . . well, but that's me."

"But Mr. Markham did come back?"

Mrs. Tong nodded. "Swearing it was over, of course."

"But it wasn't?"

"I don't know." Now, a shrug. "Carla wasn't sure, I don't think. But she thought . . . She told the coffee group she was getting a private investigator, and if he was seeing her again, she was leaving him." A silence settled for a long moment, after which Mrs. Tong turned to Glitsky and picked up the thread. "So when I heard Dr. Kensing had been here last night, you're right, I was surprised."

Feigning a nonchalance he didn't feel, Glitsky leaned back and folded his arms over his chest. The information about Ann Kensing and Tim Markham made him reconsider two contradictory possibilities: first, that Mrs. Markham might have been depressed for a long while before last night, which would strengthen the argument for murder/suicide; but second, here was an apparent possible motive for a murder.

He would consider each more carefully when he got some time, but for now he had one more line of questioning for the maid. "As far as you know, Mrs. Tong, did Dr. Kensing know about the relationship between Mr. Markham and his wife?"

"I think so, yes. When Carla heard that they were getting divorced —"

"Kensing and Ann? They're divorced now, too? Over this?"

"I don't know if it's final yet, but I understood that they'd separated. At least when Carla heard they'd started the proceedings, she tried to make sure Mr. Markham wouldn't get named in any of the papers. So Dr. Kensing, he must have known, don't you think?"

9

Dismas Hardy was standing on the sidewalk on Irving Street talking with another lawyer named Wes Farrell. The two men had only met once or twice before, but the most recent time had been at Glitsky's wedding last September, where they'd independently and then together explored the limits of human tolerance for champagne. It was, it turned out for both of them, pretty high.

Last night, Frannie had eventually shown up at the Shamrock, and she and Hardy had gone on their date — Chinese food at the Purple Yet Wah. When they got home, he couldn't get McGuire's story about Shane Mackey out of his head. This morning, he'd called around and discovered that Mackey's family had indeed hired an attorney — Farrell — to explore malpractice issues surrounding his death. After all the medical talk recently, then Tim Markham's death yesterday, he was curious to know more. Farrell would be a good source of information. He could also, he knew, be a hell of a good time. So when Wes got to his office at a little after 8:30, Hardy was standing outside on the sidewalk, holding a bottle of bubbly with a ribbon around it.

Farrell greeted him like a long-lost brother, but then, seeing the offering, backed away in mock horror. "I don't think I've had a sip of that stuff since Abe's wedding, which is okay since I had about a year's worth that day if I recall, which I'm not sure I do."

"It's like riding a horse," Hardy said. "You've got to get right back on after it bucks you off. Churchill drank it every day, you know? For breakfast. And he won the Nobel Prize. Twice."

"For champagne drinking?"

"No. Peace and literature."

"Peace?" Farrell turned to let Hardy in past him. "I love how they wind up giving the Peace Prize to these world-class warriors. Henry Kissinger. Ho Chi Minh. Winston Churchill. These guys weren't exactly Gandhi, you know."

"Statesmen," Hardy said. "If you're a statesman you can kill as many people as you want as long as you're in a war, and then when you stop, everybody in Sweden is so grateful they give you the Peace Prize."

"I could be a statesman," Farrell said. "I'd like to kill lots of people." He was sitting now, re-arranging the pens on his blotter. "Maybe then I could defend myself, which would mean I had a client."

Hardy sat back and crossed an ankle over his knee. "Things a little slow lately?"

Farrell waved a hand vaguely at their surroundings. "Barely worth opening the office every day." He sighed. "If I didn't care so much about a couple of my clients . . ."

"The Mackeys, for example?"

Farrell's shoulders fell. He wagged his head back and forth a couple of times in despair, then

114

looked up through bassett eyes. "Don't tell me they came to you?"

Hardy barked a note of laughter, then checked it. Losing business wasn't a laughing matter. "No," he said. "I promise. I'm not stealing your clients, Wes. But it *is* about the Mackeys."

"What about them, besides that they've not only lost a son, but are screwed to boot?"

"Screwed how?"

"Because our great Supreme Court recently ruled, as you may have heard, that individuals can't sue their HMOs for medical malpractice because they don't practice medicine. They're business entities, not medical entities." He spread his palms, lifted then dropped them in frustration. "Unfortunately, Diz, this rejects more or less exactly the argument I'd filed in behalf of the Mackeys and my other five clients. And master of timing that I am, I hitched my wagon pretty much full-time to this issue, figuring it was the wave of the future. Anyway, so now I've got to rewrite all the pleading on some new cause of action. Failure to coordinate care, general negligence, the admin of the plan caused the P.I., like that. But meanwhile, there's no billings."

All the way back in his chair, Hardy sat with his arms crossed, halfway enjoying the rave. He knew the realities of billing. If you couldn't handle them, you didn't belong in the business. "So what happened with Shane?"

"Shane is like textbook." Farrell shot up and went to his file cabinet, from which he pulled a thick folder. "Look at this. Check this out."

Hardy stood and came over to the desk. Farrell had the medical records of everything that Moses McGuire had described in the Shamrock the previous night, but they went over it in a lot more detail, and with a final twist that made Shane Mackey's death even more tragic. One of Shane's doctors suggested that he might, possibly, have "something" that could respond to a new treatment being performed at Cedars-Sinai in L.A. But Shane's HMO had determined that this treatment was "experimental," so they would not cover him. Which meant the cost to Shane would be about three hundred thousand dollars out of pocket. "And after months of agony, trying to decide if he should incur the cost, he went for it. He and his parents sold their houses, basically cashed out, and he went down to L.A., where guess what?"

"He died," Hardy said soberly.

"He died," Farrell repeated. "But I've got a witness down there who says that if he would have come in three months earlier, they might have saved him."

Hardy whistled. "If he's credible, that could be worth a lot of money for you."

"Yeah, but it's not coming in tomorrow, let me tell you." Farrell closed the folder. "Anyway, the bad part for me is that it's all omission, very hard to prove. Stuff somebody might have or should have done, but didn't because Parnassus doesn't allow —"

Hardy straightened up, nearly jumped at the word. "Parnassus? That's the group here we're talking about?"

A nod. "Sure. Shane worked for the city, so they covered him."

"And what about your other clients? Were they with Parnassus, too?"

"Sure. They're the biggest show in town, after all."

"And with these other clients, somebody died every time?"

"Yep."

"Were they all omission cases, like with Shane?"

"Not all. There was one little girl — Susan Magers. She was allergic to sulfa drugs and the doctor she saw forgot to ask. I mean, can you believe that? You'd think they'd have allergies flagged in the computer when they call the patient's name up, but they elected not to load that software about five years ago, save a few bucks." He shook his head in disgust. "But let me ask you, Diz. If you don't have a client, what's your interest in all this?"

Hardy sat on the corner of the desk. "I'm not sure, to tell you the truth. I heard about Shane just last night and got to wondering if his fiancée or his family needed any help, which brought me to you. But when I hear it's all Parnassus . . ."

"What's all Parnassus?"

Hardy frowned, reluctant by habit to disclose information he'd been given in relative confidence. Instead, he temporized. "The name's just been coming up a lot lately. You heard about Tim Markham, didn't you?"

"What about him?"

Hardy looked a question — was Wes putting

117

him on? — but apparently not. "He got killed yesterday. Hit and run."

"You're kidding me!" Farrell's face went slack. "I've really got to start watching some nighttime television, reading the paper, something. When did it happen?"

"Yesterday morning. They got him over to Portola, where he died."

"God, in his own hospital. I love it. They must be shitting over there." Farrell broke a smile. "Maybe I could call his wife and see if she wants to sue them. Wouldn't that be sweet?"

"Sue who?"

"Portola, Parnassus, the usual suspects."

"Except that they didn't kill him, Wes. He got hit by a car."

Farrell sat forward, still grinning, his elbows on his desk. "Listen to me, Diz. Did you know Tim Markham? Well, I did. He gets admitted to a hospital filled with the doctors he's been screwing for fifteen years, he's not getting out alive no matter what. I guarantee it."

Hardy was smiling, too. "It's a good theory, Wes, but I don't think it happened."

Farrell pointed a finger. "You wait," he said.

Hardy sometimes wondered why he had a downtown office. He'd stopped in for an hour after seeing Farrell. Then he and Freeman had eaten a long lunch in Belden Alley. At a little after three o'clock, he had finally settled into the brief he was writing when he was interrupted by a call from his friend Pico Morales, who didn't want to bother him, but it was an emergency, having to do with one of his friends. He needed a criminal lawyer. Could Hardy please come down to the Steinhart Aquarium and talk to him? The guy, Pico said, was one of his walkers. Hardy knew what that meant. When Pico went on to say that the friend was a doctor named Kensing with Parnassus, that clinched it. Hardy was going for another drive, back to the Avenues.

As the curator of the Steinhart, Pico's long-standing ambition was to acquire a great white shark for the aquarium in Golden Gate Park. Four, six, nine times a year, some boat would haul up a shark and Pico would call his list of volunteers. A lifetime ago, Hardy had been one of the first. He would let himself in to the tanks in the bowels of the aquarium where, his mind a blank, he'd don a wetsuit and walk a shark for hours, round and round in the circular tank. In theory, the walking would keep water moving through the animals' gills until they could breathe on their own. It had never worked yet.

Half-hidden by shrubbery, the back entrance was all the way around behind the aquarium, down six concrete steps. In the dim hallway someone had left on a small industrial light. Hardy pushed at the wired glass door, which opened at his touch.

After all the years that had passed since he'd last been here, he was surprised at how familiar the place felt. The same green walls still sweated with, it seemed, the same humidity. The low concrete ceiling made him want to keep his head

119

down, although he knew he had clearance. He heard muffled voices, sounding as if they came from the inside of an oil drum. His footfalls echoed, too, and he became aware of the constant, almost inaudible hum — maybe generators or pumps for the tanks, Hardy had never really learned what caused it.

The hall curved left, then straightened, then curved again right. At last it opened into a round chamber dominated by a large above-ground pool filled with seawater, against the side of which leaned the substantial bulk of Pico Morales. Under an unruly mop of black hair, Pico's face was a weathered slab of dark granite, marginally softened by a large, drooping mustache and gentle eyes. He held an oversize, chipped coffee mug and wore the bottoms of a wetsuit, stretched to its limit by his protruding bare stomach.

In the tank itself, a man in a wetsuit was dealing with the shark, one of the largest Hardy had seen here — over six feet long. Its dorsal fin protruded from the water's surface and its tail fanned the water behind him. But Hardy had pretty well used up his fascination with sharks over the years.

The man who was walking the shark, however, was another matter.

"Ah," Pico said in greeting. "The cavalry arrives. Diz, Dr. Eric Kensing."

The man in the tank looked up and nodded. He was still working hard, and nearly grunting with the exertion, step by laborious step. Nevertheless, he was close to the edge of the tank him-

120

self, and he nodded. "You're Hardy?" he asked. "I'd shake hands, but . . ." Then, more seriously. "Thanks for coming."

"Hey, when Pico calls. He says you're in trouble."

"Not yet, maybe, but . . ." At that moment, as Hardy and Pico watched, the fish twitched and broke himself free from the man's grip, and he swore, then turned to go after it.

"Let it go," Pico snapped.

The man turned back toward the side, but paused for another look behind him. It was only an instant, but in that time the shark had crossed the tank, turned, and was heading back toward him, picking up speed. Pico never took his eyes off the shark and didn't miss the move. "Get out! Now! Look out!"

Kensing lunged for the side of the pool. Hardy and Pico had him, each by an arm, and hoisted him up, over, and out, just as the shark breached and took a snap at where he'd been.

"Offhand," Hardy said, "I'm thinking that's a healthy fish."

"Hungry, too," Kensing said. "Maybe he thought Pico was a walrus."

Hardy nodded, deadpan and thoughtful. "Honest mistake."

They were all standing at the edge of the tank, watching the shark swimming on its own.

Pico kept his eyes on the water, on the swimming fish. He'd had his hopes raised around the survival of one of his sharks before, and didn't want to have them dashed again. "You guys need to talk anyway. Why don't you get out of here?"

The Little Shamrock was less than a quarter mile from the aquarium. After the doctor had gotten into street clothes, they left Pico to his shark, still swimming on his own. Hardy drove the few hundred yards through a rapidly darkening afternoon. Now they had gotten something to drink — Hardy a black and tan and Kensing a plain coffee — and sat kitty-corner in front of the fire on some battered, sunken couches more suited to making out than strategizing legal defense.

"So," Hardy began, "how'd you get with Pico?"

A shrug, a sip of coffee. "His son is one of my patients. We got to talking about what he did and eventually he told me about his sharks. I thought it sounded like a cool thing to do. He invited me down one night and now, when I really can't spare the time, I still come when summoned. How about you? I heard you used to volunteer, too. I didn't think Pico allowed people to quit."

"I got a special dispensation." The answer seemed inadequate, so he added, "I got so I couldn't stand it when they all died."

A bitter chuckle. "Don't go into medicine."

"No," Hardy agreed. "I figured that one out a long time ago." He killed a moment sipping his pint. "But rumor has it you need a lawyer now." For the first time Hardy noticed a pallor under the ruddy complexion, the fatigue in the eyes.

122

"You know who Tim Markham is?"

Hardy nodded. "He got hit by a car yesterday, then died in the hospital."

"That's right. I was staff physician at the ICU when he died. And he was fucking my wife."

"So you're worried that the police might think you got an unexpected opportunity and killed him?"

"I don't think that's impossible."

"But you didn't?"

Kensing held Hardy's gaze. "No."

"Were you tempted?" Trying to lighten things up.

He almost broke a smile. "I used to fantasize about it all the time, except in my version, it was always much more painful. First I'd break his kneecaps, maybe slash an Achilles tendon, cut his balls off. Anything that would make him suffer more than he did." He shook his head in disappointment. "There really is no justice, you know that?"

Hardy thought he maybe knew it better than Dr. Kensing. "But justice or no," he said, "you're worried." It wasn't a question.

He nodded somberly. "If the police start asking about Tim. I can just hear me: 'Yeah, I hated him. You'd hate him, too. I'm glad he's dead.' I don't think so."

Hardy didn't think so, either, but all of this was really moot. "Let me put your mind to rest a little. It's my understanding that Markham died from his injuries, and if that's the case, you're not involved in any crime."

"What if somebody says I didn't do enough to save him? Is there such a thing as malicious malpractice or something like that? As a homicide issue?"

Hardy shook his head. "I've never heard of it. Why?"

"Because some homicide inspector named Bracco came by yesterday. And they're doing the autopsy today."

"I wouldn't worry about that. They autopsy everybody."

"No they don't. Especially if you die in the ICU after surgery. We did a PM at the hospital and I signed off on the death certificate — massive internal trauma from blunt force injury — but they hauled him off downtown anyway."

"He died of a hit and run," Hardy explained. "That's a homicide, so they do an autopsy. Every time."

But the doctor had another question. "Okay, but last night I met Bracco, checking out my car at Markham's place."

"Bracco?" Hardy shook his head, perplexed. "You sure he's San Francisco homicide, not hit and run? I don't know him."

"That's what he said. He had a badge."

"And he was checking out your car? Why were you at Markham's house anyway?"

"I knew Carla, his wife. I thought it would be appropriate to go by and give my condolences, to see if there was anything I could do." He let out a sigh. "You can't help it. You feel somehow responsible."

"So what was this cop doing with your car?"

Staring around the bar as though wondering how he got there, Kensing considered a moment, then came back to Hardy. "I think he was checking to see if it looked like my car had been in an accident, if I'd hit Markham. There were some other people there, too, before I left, visiting with Carla, other cars. I got the impression he had checked every one of them."

This seemed unlikely on its face. But then Hardy flashed back to the talk he'd had with Glitsky during their latest walk. The car police. This Bracco must have been one of the new clowns that was taking so much abuse in the homicide detail. "Well, in any event, from what I'm hearing, it doesn't sound like you've got any real problem here. You didn't kill him."

"But he died under my supervision, and it wasn't any secret I hated him."

"So, one more time, did you kill him?"

"No."

"He died of his injuries, right? Did you make them worse? No? So, look, you're fine." Clearly, the message still wasn't getting all the way through, so Hardy continued. "Let me ask you this. What were the odds Markham was going to die even if you did everything right?"

"Which I did."

"Granted, but not the question."

The doctor gave it some real thought. "Statistically, once you're in the ICU, only maybe two in ten get out alive."

Truly surprised by the figure, Hardy sat back on the couch. "That's all? Two in ten?"

Kensing shrugged. "Maybe three. I don't

125

know the exact number, but it's not as high as most people think."

"So the odds are, at best, you'd say thirty percent that Markham would have survived, even if you did everything that could have been done."

"Which I did. But yes, roughly thirty percent."

"So that leaves it as a seventy percent chance that the hit and run would have killed him, no matter what any doctor did or didn't do, am I right?" Hardy came forward on the couch. "Here's the good news. Even if you made a mistake — not saying you did, remember — whoever ran him down can't use malpractice as a defense in his trial. Someone charged with homicide is specifically excluded from using the defense that the doctor could have saved the victim."

Kensing's eyes briefly showed some life. "You'd think I would have heard that before. Why is that?"

"Because if it wasn't, every lawyer in the world would begin his defense by saying that it wasn't his client shooting his wife four times in the heart that killed her. It was the doctors who couldn't save her. It was their fault, not his client's."

Kensing accepted this information with, it seemed, a mixture of relief and disbelief. "But there wasn't any malpractice here." He spoke matter-of-factly. "Really," he added.

"I believe you. I'm just saying I can't see where you've got any kind of criminal charge looking at you. What put Markham there in the first place was someone running him down in a car. That's who this guy Bracco's looking for, the driver of the car." But an earlier phrase that had nagged suddenly surfaced. "Did you say you *knew* Mrs. Markham?"

Kensing's shoulders slumped visibly as the world seemed to settle on him. He looked down at the scarred hardwood floor, then back up. "You don't know? That's the other thing."

Hardy waited.

"Apparently something happened last night." He paused. "She's dead. And the rest of her family, too."

"Lord." Hardy suddenly felt pinned to the sofa.

Kensing continued. "It went around the offices sometime late this morning. I was seeing patients and didn't hear until about noon. Then, a little after that, Bracco called to make sure I'd be around. He wanted to come by and talk about it."

"So you talked to him today, too?"

Kensing shook his head. "It might have been a mistake, but I had my receptionist tell him I wasn't in. Pico called about the same time with his shark. I don't see patients Wednesday afternoon anyway, and I didn't want to talk to the police until I could sort some of this out. So I came over here, to the aquarium, and essentially hid out, walking Francis —"

"Francis?"

"The shark. Pico named it Francis. So I just hung out until I'd come up with a plan, which was get a lawyer. And Pico knew you." He made a face, apologetic and confused. "So here we are. And now what?"

Hardy nodded and sat back. Remembering his pint, he reached for it and took a drink. "Well, you're going to talk to the police, whether you want to or not."

"So what do I tell them about my wife if they ask?"

Hardy had already answered that, but this was the beginning of hand-holding time. "I'd just tell the truth and try not to panic. But if they look at all, they'll know about Markham and your wife, right? So be straightforward and deal with it. It doesn't mean you killed anybody."

Kensing let the reality sink in. "Okay. It's not going to matter if they're looking for the driver of the hit-and-run car anyway, right?"

"That's how I see it." Hardy looked across into Kensing's face. His eyes were hollow with fatigue. "Are you all right?"

He managed a weak chuckle. "I'm just tired, but then again, I'm always tired," he said. "I've been tired for fifteen years. If I wasn't exhausted beyond human endurance, I wouldn't recognize myself."

Hardy leaned back into the couch and realized he wasn't exactly in the mood for dancing, himself. "But still, you're out on your afternoon off walking sharks for Pico?"

"Yeah, I know," Kensing said. "It doesn't make any sense to me, either. I just do it."

"That was me, too." Hardy had walked his own sharks at the low point of his life, at the end of a decade of sleepwalk following the death of his son Michael, his divorce from Jane. It made no more sense to him then than it did to Kensing

128

now. But for some reason walking his sharks had seemed to mean *something*. And in a world otherwise full of nothing, that was something to cling to.

Both men stood up. Hardy gave Kensing his card and along with it a last bit of advice. "You know, they might just show up at work or your house. They might knock on your door with a warrant or a subpoena. If any of that happens, say nothing. Don't let them intimidate you. You get the phone call."

Kensing's mouth dropped a fraction of an inch. He blew out heavily, shaking his head. "This is starting to sound like serious hardball."

"No. Hardball's a game." Hardy might be all for client reassurance, but he didn't want Kensing to remain under the illusion that any part of a homicide investigation was going to be casual. "But from what I've heard, we're okay. You weren't driving the car, and that's what killed him. His wife has nothing to do with you, right? Right. So the main thing is tell the truth, except leave out the part about the kneecaps."

10

John Strout worked through his lunchtime conducting the autopsy on Tim Markham. The damage done to the body from its encounter with the hit-and-run vehicle and then the garbage can was substantial. The skull was fractured in two places and multiple lacerations scored what the coroner thought might have been an unusually handsome face in life — a broad brow, a strong jawline with a cleft chin.

Markham had been struck on the back left hip bone, which broke on the impact, along with its attached femur. Apparently, the body snapped back for an instant against the car's hood or windshield, and this might have accounted for one of the skull fractures. The other probably occurred, Strout surmised, when the body ended its short flight. The right shoulder had come out of its socket and three ribs on the right side were broken.

Among the internal organs, besides the digestive tract, only the heart, the left lobe of the lung, and the left kidney escaped injury. The right lung had collapsed, and the spleen, liver, and right kidney had all been damaged to greater or lesser degrees. Strout, with forty years of medical experience, was of the opinion that it was some kind of miracle that Markham had survived to make it to the emergency room. He thought that blood loss or any number of the internal injuries, or the shock of so many of them at once, should have been enough by themselves to cause death.

But Strout was a methodical and careful man. Even if Tim Markham hadn't been an important person, the coroner wasn't putting his signature on any formal document until he was satisfied that he'd as precisely as humanly possible identified the principle cause of death. To that end, he had ordered the standard battery of tests on blood and tissue samples. While he waited for those results, he began a more rigorous secondary examination of the injuries to the internal organs.

A particularly impressive hematoma on the back of the liver was commanding his complete attention, but he was subliminally aware of his assistant Joyce making her way back through the length of the morgue. When she stopped next to him and hovered, he continued with his examination for a moment, then drawled, "This here could'a done it by its lone self." Then, looking up and seeing her expression of worried concern, he pulled away from his work. "Is something wrong, darlin'?"

Joyce was new to the staff, but not as new as the equipment they'd recently bought to upgrade the lab. For the past few days, Strout had been supervising Joyce as she conducted tests to calibrate these machines, which ran sophisticated scans on blood and tissues. Since he had Tim Markham's body on the slab this afternoon, he'd given Joyce samples from his body.

Now she appeared extremely nervous, and for a moment Strout thought she must have broken one of the expensive new toys. "Whatever it is, it can't be that bad," he told her. "What's the problem?"

She held up a slip of paper, the results from the lab tests she'd been running. "I don't think I could have done this test right. I mean, the machine . . ." She let the thought hang.

Strout took the paper and squinted at the numbers, saw what she was showing him, and pulled off his sanitary gloves. "That the right number?"

"That's what I wanted to ask you. Could that be right? I ran it twice and I think I must have done something wrong."

His eyes went to her face, then back to the paper, which he now took in his hand and studied with great care. "This from Mr. Markham's blood?"

"Yes, sir."

"Dang," he whispered, mostly to himself.

From the morgue, Strout walked down the outside corridor that connected his office with the back door of the Hall of Justice. A biting afternoon breeze had come up, but he barely noted it. After passing through the guards and the metal detector, he decided to bypass the elevators. Instead, he turned directly right to the stairs, which he took two at a time. Glitsky wasn't in his office. As was the norm in the middle of the day, there were only a couple of inspectors pulling duty in the detail, and neither had seen the lieutenant all day. Strout hesitated a second, asked the inspectors to have Abe call him when he got in, then turned on his heel and hit the stairway again.

One floor down, he got admitted to the DA's sanctum — hell, he'd come all this way, he wanted to talk to *somebody* — and in another minute was standing in front of Treya Ghent's desk, asking if Clarence Jackman was available in his room next door. Somethin' pretty interestin' had come up. But even before she answered, her look told him he guessed it wasn't going to be his lucky day. "He's been at meetings all morning, John, and then scheduled at other ones all afternoon. That's what DAs really do, you know. They don't do law. They go to meetings." Strout considered Ms. Ghent — or was it Mrs. Glitsky? — a very handsome, dark-skinned mulatto woman with a few drops of Asian or Indian blood mixed in somewhere, and now she smiled at him helpfully. "Is there anything I can do for you?"

He thought a minute. "Do you know where Abe's got to?"

She shook her head no. "He left the house this morning with one of his inspectors. I haven't heard from him since. Why?" Although she knew the answer to that. Strout wanted to see her husband because he was head of homicide. There was no doubt that the "somethin' pretty interestin' " he'd referred to wasn't a hot stock tip.

The lanky gentleman sighed, then sidestepped

and, after asking her permission, let himself down onto the waiting chair by the side of the door. "Got to catch my breath a little. I come up by the stairs, which at my age ain't always recommended."

"It must have been important," Treya said, she hoped with some subtlety.

Not that Strout needed the prompt. He was fairly itching to get it out. "You recall the discussion we all had the other day over to Lou's about the Parnassus Group?" Of course she did. Mr. Jackman was still mulling over his options. "Well, you just watch. It's goin' to get a lot more interestin' in a New York minute."

In a few sentences, Strout had brought her to the crux of it. When he'd finished, she said, "Potassium? What does that mean?"

"It means the hit-and-run car didn't kill him, 'tho he might'a died from those injuries eventually if they'd just left him alone. But they didn't."

"It couldn't have been an accident? Somebody grabbing the wrong needle?"

He shrugged. "Anything's possible, I s'pose. But on purpose or not, he got loaded up full of potassium, and the thing is, that can look pretty natural even if someone does an autopsy. So I'm thinkin' you might know where your husband might be. He's goin' to want to know."

When Jackman got the news about the potassium, he asked Treya to patch Abe in his car and have him come to his office as soon as he arrived back downtown. Then he'd called Marlene Ash and John Strout, both of whom had replied to

134

the summons and were here now, too.

It was 6:45, and the freshening afternoon breeze had transformed itself into a freezing gale, the howl of which was easily audible even in the almost hermetically sealed DA's office.

As Jackman stood at his office window looking down at the still-congested traffic below him on Bryant Street, the first large drops of rain, flung with great force, seemed to explode onto the glass in front of him. Unconsciously, he backed a step away.

He was aware of the hum of urgent shoptalk behind him. The discovery about the potassium had been extraordinary enough, but when Glitsky had finally responded to Treya's call and told her where he'd been all day and what had happened to the Markham family, a sense of impending crisis seemed to wash through the Hall of Justice like a tsunami. At almost the same moment that Abe told Treya about the Markham family, word of the tragedy hit the streets and the calls started coming in to Jackman's office from all quarters — newspapers, television, radio, the mayor's office, the Board of Supervisors, the chief of police.

Just as Jackman turned away from the window, Glitsky appeared in his doorway. "Abe, good. Come on in."

The lieutenant touched Treya's arm, nodded around the room. Jackman sat on the front of his desk, facing them, and wasted no time on preliminaries. "So we got a whole prominent family dead in a twelve-hour period. The man's company has the city's contract for health care, and it's damn near broke. I'm predicting media madness short term, and long term? God knows what chaos if Parnassus can't recover. Anybody disagree with me?" He knew nobody would, and he clearly expected the same unanimity with his next question. "Does anybody here have any ideas about how we're going to characterize these developments? I'm going to need some good answers when people start asking."

The scar through Glitsky's frown was pronounced. He cleared his throat. "We say we're looking into it. No further comment."

"I thought that would be your position."

"It's the only position, Clarence." Glitsky, still slightly shell-shocked from his day at Markham's home, didn't know where the DA was going with this meeting, why it was being held at all. "It's also the truth," he added.

"As far as it goes, yes it is. But I'm thinking we might want to help people decide how they want to think about this. All of it. I think we want to say right up front that Tim Markham was murdered."

Glitsky glanced at the faces around the room. At this point, the conversation seemed to be about him and Jackman. "Do we know he was murdered?"

"We know what happened, Abe," Marlene interjected. "It's obvious."

"I hate obvious," Glitsky replied evenly. "Couldn't it have been an accidental overdose? Was he on potassium anyway for some reason?" He faced Strout. "Couldn't somebody have just made a mistake in the hospital?"

The coroner nodded. "Could've happened."

But Jackman didn't like that answer and he snorted. "Then why'd the wife kill herself?"

"Who said she killed herself?" Glitsky asked.

"That's the preliminary report I heard," Jackman said.

"You know why they call it 'preliminary,' Clarence? Because it's not final. It might not be true. We really don't know anything yet about the wife and kids, that whole situation —"

"Sergeant Langtry told me it was clearly a murder/suicide, Abe. Just like many he'd seen before. And you, too, isn't that right?"

"There might be some similarities, but there are also differences. It's just plain smarter if we don't say anything until we know."

But Jackman was pacing in front of his desk, commanding the room with his presence. "I may know what's plain smarter, too, Abe. I may even agree with you. But humor me. Other inquiring minds are going to want to know — the press, the mayor's office, you can guess — and they're going to ask me. I'm concerned that if we don't say anything, it looks like we don't know any-thing —"

"We *don't* know anything! It's okay if it looks like that."

Jackman ignored the interruption, repeating his earlier statement. "We know Markham was murdered. We believe his wife was a suicide."

"I don't know if I believe that at all, Clarence. John here hasn't even done an autopsy on her yet." Glitsky reined himself in a notch. Jackman was playing devil's advocate, he knew, but he would hate it if the DA committed his office to a public stance when it wasn't necessary. It would be more politics messing with his job. "All I'm saying is that it's possible somebody could have gone to a lot of trouble to make it look like a suicide. I know Langtry thinks it might be, but we haven't eliminated any possibilities yet, and I'd be more comfortable — *you'd* be more comfortable, Clarence — if we could eliminate a few before we start talking to the press."

Jackman frowned. "You're saying maybe somebody killed her and her family and tried to make it look like a suicide? They find anything at her place that supports that?"

"Not yet, no sir. But there's still a lot of lab work to be done." Glitsky pressed on. "I'll go with suicide the minute we can prove it, Clarence. I promise you. But for now we've got a theory that looks squirrelly to me, which is Markham gets to the hospital all banged up, nearly dead in fact, and somebody decides, spur of the moment, to take the opportunity and kill him?"

Jackman wasn't backing down. "I honestly believe it will look just precisely like that to some reporter somewhere."

"Okay, so tell him you've got a problem with that. Like why take the risk if he was probably going to die anyway?"

Jackman went back to Strout. "He wasn't necessarily going to die, was he, John?"

Conjecture wasn't Strout's long suit, but the DA had asked him a direct question and he felt he had to say something. "Maybe not. Especially once he's out of the ER." He stopped, lifted his

138

shoulders, let them drop. "He could have survived."

"So," Jackman took Strout's answer as a ringing endorsement, "somebody, maybe even his wife —"

"Maybe even the wife!" This was new and, to Glitsky's mind, completely bizarre. "You're saying Carla killed her husband at the hospital?"

Jackman backed off. "All right, maybe not. But somebody at the hospital came to the conclusion that Markham was going to pull through and, for some reason, couldn't have that."

"All I'm saying then, Clarence, is let's find the reason."

The exchange was threatening to grow heated and Treya stepped in. "Maybe there needn't be a rush on the wife, Clarence? You only need to make the point that *somebody* killed Mr. Markham. And I think we'll all agree," Treya added quickly, turning to her husband, "that the potassium points much more clearly to a murder than an accident at the hospital. Wouldn't that be true, Abe? Could you agree to that?"

Glitsky understood what she was asking him. More, what she was doing. And while now with the potassium overdose Glitsky believed it likely that Markham had indeed been murdered, belief wasn't certainty and never would be. "Okay," he said to his wife. "Let's for the moment agree Markham was murdered in the hospital. So you tell whoever asks that we're investigating. That's what we do. What's the rush to go public?"

From Treya's expression, Glitsky realized that finally he'd asked the right question. Jackman raised himself off his desk. "Just this, Abe. If Markham was murdered, it goes to the grand jury. I can legitimately use an investigation into his death as a way to get into its books and business practices at Parnassus. We've got every reason to look in his files, take the place apart, see if we can find out why. And who's gonna complain? Somebody killed their top guy. Why wouldn't they *want* to cooperate in every way?"

Jackman let his words hang in the air, then continued. "If we begin any kind of inquiry on the billings and their lawyers get into it, we're talking months, maybe years, delay on subpoenas, delay delivering records that they may have shredded by then anyway, or forged new ones. Plus all the public bickering, loss of faith in the city's institutions, blah blah blah. This way, we're in. It's a murder, Abe, and even in this town a solid majority of the voters oppose murder. Nobody will see it as more complicated than that, at least for now. The grand jury's looking into the murder of Tim Markham. There is every justification in the world to probe his relationships and even business practices. And since he was killed in Portola Hospital, there's a demonstrable link there."

But Glitsky was shifting in his seat again. It was a bad idea to get the DA's office involved in his investigations, particularly if Markham's murder was just the cover for a financial probe of Parnassus. "What if we find Markham's killer before you get finished?" he asked.

Marlene answered. "We'll leave the grand jury

impaneled. We just keep going on the financial stuff."

Abe frowned at this, but he knew that technically, Marlene could do just that. The grand jury was not crime specific — Jackman and Ash could simply use it to go fishing.

"But I'll still have your support for the murder investigation as the priority?" he asked. "I don't want to get a suspect close to the net and not be able to bring him in."

"That won't happen, Abe," Marlene said.

"Couldn't happen," Jackman repeated. "We're on the same team."

Glitsky smiled all around, fooling no one. "Well, with that assurance," he said as he stood up, "I'd better get to work."

PART TWO

11

Hardy hit the button shutting off the alarm. Throwing off the covers, he forced himself to sit up lest he give in to the urge to lay back down, just for a minute. Frannie murmured something from behind him, and he felt her hand brush against the small of his back. Reaching around, he squeezed it quickly, then let go and stood up.

The house *felt* dark. He stood a minute, summoning the will to move. Outside, a fresh gust rattled the windows. The storm, still blowing.

After he'd showered and shaved, he pulled on his pants and a shirt in the bathroom so he'd be as unobtrusive as possible. He didn't remember distinctly, but he must have had a rough night's sleep. He still hadn't quite gotten to fully awake. Frannie hadn't yet stirred, either — he thought he'd go downstairs and bring a cup of coffee up for her. That way they would get a few minutes of peace together before the daily marathon of getting the kids off to school.

In the kitchen, he turned on the light and fed his tropical fish. The long hallway to the front door seemed especially dark as well, but he'd already concluded that it was the weather, so he didn't give it any more thought. When he opened the door, he noted with satisfaction that the *Chronicle* had made it up onto the porch —

by no means a daily occurrence. Maybe it was a sign. He was in for a lucky day.

But God, he thought, it was dark.

He'd often expressed his belief that one of the greatest of modern inventions was the automatic coffee machine that began making your critical morning brew about the time that your alarm went off, so that when you got to it, it was ready for you. But when he got back to it, he stopped, frowning. The carafe was empty. Worse, the little green "program" light was still on — when it went into "run" mode, the light turned red. What was going on? He distinctly remembered preparing the coffee last night before he'd gone up to bed, and now he leaned down, squinting, and checked the clock.

4:45.

Turning around, he looked up at the large clock on the kitchen wall. Same time. Finally, he thought to consult his watch, and got the third corroboration. It was quarter to five on Thursday morning and he was wide awake, dressed up and nowhere to go. And for no particular reason other than that somebody had obviously reset his alarm. When he found out which kid it had been, there would be hell to pay. He had half a mind to wake both kids up now, identify the culprit, break out the thumb screws.

But so much for his run of good luck. And he still had to wait for his damn coffee to brew. With nothing to do now except kill time, he angrily opened the paper and threw it down on the dining room table. Sitting down, he noticed that yep, it was still dark.

At least now he knew why.

Then he noticed the headline: "HMO Chief's Death Called Murder." With the subhead about potassium, he had all he needed to know, although he read the whole article. His new client appeared only once, as the attending staff physician at the ICU, but once was enough. Hardy started to worry.

The accompanying article on Markham's family ratcheted his concern up even further. The paper characterized the event in ambiguous terms, hinting that the evidence seemed to implicate the wife in murder/suicide — another senseless American tragedy, the reason for which might never be known. But in his guts, Hardy felt that Markham's death being ruled a murder made any conclusion about the how and why of the family's slaughter decidedly premature.

When he finished the second article, he sat in contemplation for several minutes. Then he got up and poured a cup of coffee, came back to the table, and read Jeff Elliot's column.

CityTalk
BY JEFFREY ELLIOT

As medical director of Parnassus Health, the beleaguered HMO that is under contract to insure the city's employees, Dr. Malachi Ross has been under a lot of pressure over the past months. From his original and eventually overturned refusal to allow prescriptions of Viagra as a covered expense to the much more serious Baby Emily incident at Portola Hospital, his business decisions have come under almost continuous fire from any number of consumer, public interest and watch-keeping organizations, including this newspaper. Now, in the wake of the death on Tuesday of Parnassus' CEO Tim Markham, and Ross' election to that position by the Parnassus board, it looks as though his real troubles may have only just begun. (As this column goes to press, the *Chronicle* has learned that Mr. Markham's death has been called a murder by police investigators.)

Early last week, as one of his last official acts, Mr. Markham presented the city with a bill in excess of $13 million for previously undiscovered outpatient care at various neighborhood clinics. A source at the DA's office describes the paperwork on these billings as "at the least, irregular," and quite possibly "fraudulent." At the same time, Parnassus has applied for a rate increase of $23 per month for every covered city employee, which if approved represents an extra hit of nearly $700,000 a month to the city's budget.

At the same time, the woes of Parnassus and of its flagship hospital, Portola, continue to grow. In an interview on Tuesday evening, Dr. Ross admitted that the medical group is mired in a deep cash crisis, although he characterized the nonpayment of some Parnassus doctors as a voluntary loan program. Another source — a doctor within the group — had a slightly different take: "Sure," he said. "It's voluntary. You volunteer to loan your salary back to the group, or you're fired."

Nevertheless, Ross remained confident that Parnassus can weather this crisis. "The goal is maximum wellness for the most people," he said. When asked if he saw any conflict between the group's business interests and the needs of its patients, Ross replied, "The company needs to sustain itself so it can continue doing its work."

Because it conducts business with the city, Parnassus' finances are a matter of public record. Last year, the average staff physician with Parnassus had a salary of $98,000. The average executive board member, of which there are thirty, sustained itself to the tune of nearly $350,000 including bonuses, per person, for a total expense to the company of approximately $10.5 million. As CEO, the late Mr. Markham had the highest salary in the group — $1.4 million, and Dr. Ross was next, drawing $1.2 million in salary and performance bonuses.

Imagine how well he'd do if Parnassus was not going bankrupt.

Glitsky was in the elevator, and when the door opened on the fourth floor, he was looking at Dismas Hardy, who said, "I was just at your office. You weren't there."

"You're kidding." Glitsky stepped out into the lobby. "When?"

"Just now."

"I wasn't in my office?"

"No sign of you."

"One of the things I've always admired about you is that keen eye for detail."

The two men fell into step together, heading back toward the homicide detail. "What's another one?" Hardy asked.

"Another what?"

"Thing you've always admired about me. One implies there are more."

Glitsky glanced over at him, walked a few steps, shook his head. "On second thought, that's the only one. Keen eye for detail."

At homicide, inside Glitsky's office, Hardy took one of the fold-up chairs in front of the desk. He looked around critically. "You could use some art in here," he said. "It's a little depressing."

"I like it depressing," Glitsky said. "It keeps meetings short. Speaking of which," he pointed at his overflowing in-box, "that is today's workload and I'm behind already. What can I do for you?"

"My keen eye for detail tells me that you're not in much of a sociable mood this morning, so I'll get right to it. I take it Bracco is one of your car police."

"That would be accurate." He reached for his in-box. "Well, drop by anytime. It's been a real pleasure."

"I've got one more. What do you know about Tim Markham?"

Glitsky stopped fiddling with paper, cocked his head to one side, and frowned. "Who are you representing?"

"Eric Kensing."

"Swell. When did that happen?"

"Recently."

Glitsky sat forward in his chair and brushed a hand over his scar. "As I recall, the last time I talked to you about a case at this stage, I lost my job for a couple of weeks."

"True. But it was the right thing to do." A year before, Glitsky had been put on administrative leave after he'd shown Hardy a videotape of his client's questionable confession before the DA's office had cleared it for discovery purposes. "And you know what Davy Crockett always said? 'Be sure you're right, then go ahead.' "

"I always thought that was the stupidest thing I'd ever heard. The jails are full of people who think like old Davy. Genghis Khan, I believe, had the same motto."

"And a fine leader he was. I've just got a couple of quick questions. They won't get you fired. Promise."

"Ask one and let me decide. And quickly, if that's possible, though history argues that it isn't."

"Is Kensing in trouble?"

Glitsky nodded in appreciation. "That was pretty good for you." A shrug. "Well, no matter where we stand on charging Markham's murder, I'm betting your client is one guy who's definitely going to need a lawyer on the malpractice side alone. Aside from that . . ." Glitsky threw a glance over to the door — closed. He came back to Hardy. "I suppose he told you he's got a motive." He paused, then gave it up. "He was also the last person with the family."

151

"You mean Markham's family? The paper implied that it was the distraught wife."

"Yeah. I read it." Glitsky sat back. "I think you've had your question."

"You think it wasn't the wife? And if it wasn't, it was the same person who did the husband?"

"I don't think anything yet. I'm keeping an open mind."

"But if my client's a suspect for Markham, then he's —"

Glitsky stopped him. "We're not talking about this, Diz. You're way over your quota for questions. That's it."

"Okay. This isn't a question. I talked to Kensing this morning before I even left the house. He wants to talk to you."

"Sure he does. And I'm the queen of Bavaria. You're going to let him?"

"I told him it was a dumb idea. I was even a little adamant. But maybe you've heard, doctor knows best. He figures you'll hear his story and leave him alone. He's a witness, not a suspect."

"Is he talking immunity at this stage?"

"No, nothing like that. He didn't do anything wrong. He's a witness."

"And the best defense is a good offense."

Hardy shrugged. It wasn't his idea. He knew Glitsky might take it that way, but he thought that his job at this point was to mitigate Kensing's discomfort and arrange the talk on his schedule. "So how about my office, close of business?"

Glitsky considered, then nodded. "Okay. Doable."

"And he's a witness, not a suspect."

"I believe you've mentioned that a few times."

"Though you haven't said you're okay with it."

"There's that eye for detail again," Glitsky said. Then, sitting back. "He is what he is, Diz. I'm afraid we'll just have to see how it plays out."

After leaving homicide, he went down to Jackman's office to see if he could come upon any potentially helpful scrap of news regarding his new client. It wasn't likely, but the DA was relatively inexperienced in criminal matters and might inadvertently drop something if he and Hardy were simply two friends, casually schmoozing.

At Jackman's outer office, Hardy stopped in the doorway. Treya, on the telephone saying "Yes, sir" a lot to someone, smiled a greeting and held up a "just a sec" finger. Hardy came in, walked over, and kissed her on the cheek, then sat in the chair next to Jackman's door. Treya continued with her proper responses in her modulated, professional voice, but she rolled her eyes and made faces in the midst of them.

Watching her, Hardy broke a grin.

When Glitsky's first wife had died, Hardy would never have believed that anyone could have approached Flo as an equally compatible mate for his best friend. But in a little less than a year, Treya had won him and Frannie over. Not only competent and confident, Treya's sense of humor went a long way toward blunting Abe's razor edge.

153

At last she hung up. "The mayor," she explained. "Always wanting my opinions on the issues." Then, a questioning look. "Did you have an appointment? Is Clarence expecting you? I don't have you down."

"No. I'm just dropping by, see if he had a minute to chat."

"I don't think chat's on his agenda today. He just had me tell hizzoner he wasn't in." She smiled sweetly. "Maybe you would like to do it the normal way and schedule something?"

"I would, but I'm not sure when I'll be back at the hall."

"Here's an idea, Diz. You could *plan* to be. Others have been known to."

"But Clarence and I go way back. We're pals."

"He feels the same way."

"I just hate to see the spontaneity go out of our relationship."

Treya nodded sympathetically. "So does Clarence. He frets about it all the time. I'll put you down for tomorrow at three. You can talk about it then." The phone on her desk rang and, waving Hardy good-bye, she picked it up.

Back at his office, Hardy phoned the aquarium and discovered that Francis the shark was still alive and swimming under its own power. But Pico still wasn't admitting victory. "He hasn't eaten a damn thing. Swimming's one thing, but he's also got to eat."

"How do you know it's a he?"

"How do you think I got to be curator here? Could it be the Ph.D. in marine biology? The

154

ability to tell males from female fish? One of those?"

"I always figured it was affirmative action of some kind. What are you trying to feed it?"

"Fish food." Pico was clearly done with Hardy's input on the subject. "Can we talk about something else? How'd it go with Eric?"

Hardy's brow clouded, his tone grew serious. "I've got one for you. How well do you know him?"

"Pretty well. He's been our family doc for years. We used to be closer — socially, I mean — before he and Ann broke up. Why?"

"Do you think he could kill anybody?"

Pico snorted. "No way." A pause. "You want to hear a story, what he's like?"

"More than anything if it makes him look good."

"Okay, you remember when Danny first started having his problems?"

"Sure." Pico's eldest was seventeen now, but ten years before, he'd been diagnosed with leukemia. Hardy remembered some of the high drama surrounding the diagnosis and treatment, which had resulted in bone marrow transplants and, ultimately, remission. "Was that Kensing?"

"Yeah. But what maybe you don't know is that he made the tentative diagnosis long before some board would have approved the treatment he ordered. They said it was way too expensive. They wanted to wait, have him take more tests, like that. So what did Eric do?"

"Tell me."

"He didn't think we could wait. If we waited,

Danny might die. So he lied."

"To who?"

"The HMO. When's the last time you heard about a doctor risking his paycheck to save a patient? Well, Eric did. He made Danny's records appear that the leukemia was more advanced than it was. If he was wrong and it cost his HMO big bucks for nothing, sorry. But if he was right, Danny lives." Pico checked his voice back a notch. "Anyway, so that's who Eric is, Diz. Check it out. He does this kind of stuff all the time. Christ, he makes *house calls*. He walks my sharks. You ask my opinion, the guy's at the very least a saint, if not a certified hero."

But when Hardy hung up, a thought nagged at him. Pico's story had a down side. Kensing might be a saint and a hero, but a good cross-examiner could make the point that he had also proven himself capable of a sustained and elaborate fraud. He falsified medical records, possibly cheating his own employer out of maybe thousands of dollars. And if he did it once with Danny Morales, the odds were good that he'd done it with many other patients. And that at least some of those times, the odds were good that he'd been wrong.

David Freeman's enormous office was panelled in a burnished and ancient dark wood. Burgundy drapes framed the two windows, in the center of which presided the lion's claw-footed, leather-topped desk, most of its forty-eight square feet of surface cluttered with papers, files, ashtrays, in- and out-boxes, paperweights, celebrity photos, a couple of telephones. The fully stocked wet bar also featured a temperature-controlled wine cellar, Anchor Steam beer on tap, two cigar humidors, and an espresso machine. A couple of seating areas gave clients — and opposing attorneys — a choice between a formal or informal setting. On the floor, Persian rugs. On the various pedestals and tables, knickknacks from half a century of rich and grateful clients. A Bufano sculpture of St. Francis of Assisi blessed the room from one corner. A selection of original John Lennon erotic lithographs added a counternote. In a Byzantine-style glass case, a selection of alleged murder weapons ("alleged" because their respective owners all got acquitted) testified eloquently and mutely to Freeman's skill in the courtroom. The fact that David could acquire them from prosecutors and police after he'd won the case was further testament to his popularity.

Hardy crossed a leg over a knee and sipped from the demitasse of espresso, then put it back on the arm of the sofa. His landlord had brewed himself a cup, as well, and brought it over to his desk, where he blew on it once and, engrossed in some paperwork, drank it off in a gulp, replacing it carefully in the exact center of its little porcelain cup. For another full minute or more, Freeman didn't look up, but turned the pages in front of him, occasionally making a note, occasionally muttering a phrase or two to himself, arguing or agreeing with what he was reading.

As he watched him work, Hardy couldn't help but be struck again with the man's almost childish energy and enthusiasm. Freeman was seventy-six years old. He'd been practicing law for fifty years and though he'd seen it all, there was still precious little about it that didn't energize him. He came into his office every day of the week by about seven o'clock and when he didn't go to court, which he did as often as possible, he stayed at his desk until late dinnertime, then often returned for a nightcap or two while he whipped out a quick twenty pages of memos or correspondence.

It seemed to Hardy that the old man had shrunk three or four inches in the eight years they'd been associated, and put on fifteen pounds. He could almost braid his thin, long, white hair. If he let them grow, he could probably do the same with his eyebrows. A downright slovenly dresser — "juries don't trust good clothes" — he favored brown suits, many of them picked up in thrift stores, whether or not they fit perfectly. He never had them pressed. He smoked and/or chewed cigars constantly, and drank at least a bottle of wine, himself, every day at the office, and probably most of another for lunch and then again at dinner. He never exercised. The skin of his hands and face was mottled with liver spots. Today, he had bloodstains around his collar from where he'd cut himself shaving. Looking at him, Hardy thought he was the happiest, and possibly the healthiest, person on the planet.

And he didn't miss a trick. "You feeling all right, Diz? Getting enough sleep?"

Hardy thought he'd been looking right at him,

but he hadn't noticed him look up. There was no point in getting into it, the mistake with his alarm clock, the whole question of children in one's life. If Hardy started whining, Freeman would only say, "You made that bed. Get over it." So Hardy left it at, "Postlunch slump is all. Plus, I got up early."

"I hope it was billable," Freeman said. He pointed across to his bar area. "You want another cup, help yourself. Meanwhile, speaking of billable, I'm at your service, but talk fast. I'm due in federal court in forty minutes. The appeal on Latham, God bless his wealthy murdering heart. So what got you up?"

Hardy gave him an abridged version of his meeting with Dr. Kensing, and the old man clucked disapprovingly. "You talked to a new client for more than an hour, even *de facto* took his case, a possible *murder* suspect, and the subject of your fees never came up?"

In the world of criminal law, you collected your fees up front. Hardy had experimented a time or two with being less than rigorous on that score and had discovered that the conventional wisdom turned out to be true. If you were successful and got your clients off, they didn't need a lawyer anymore, and why should they pay you? On the other hand, if you failed and they went to jail, why should they pay you for that, either? So you usually wanted to casually mention the word "retainer" within about six sensitive minutes after saying hello.

Freeman the kind mentor was merely reminding him. "This is why, my son, I'm afraid you're

159

going to die impoverished and there is really no excuse for a good lawyer to die poor."

"Yes, sir. I believe you've mentioned something like that before. Anyway, I emphasized to Glitsky that he's a witness, not a suspect."

"Ah." Freeman nodded genially, sipped at his coffee. "The good lieutenant wants to get to know him a little better, is that it?" The old man pulled himself up straight behind the desk and summoned his courtroom bellow. "Are you out of your mind?" He got his voice back under control. "A witness, not a suspect? He's a prime suspect! And I'll tell you something else. Kensing sure as hell thinks he is. Why do you think he wanted to get a lawyer onboard? In fact, the more I think about it, the more I like him."

"You've never met him."

"So what? You've only met him once. Are you trying to tell me that you know he's not guilty of murder?"

"He injected Markham with potassium?"

"Or ran him over. Maybe both."

"David —"

"Why not? The dead guy was screwing his wife, which is the oldest motive in the world."

"So after waiting two years, he killed him?"

His worldview intact, Freeman sat back, serene as Buddha. "Happens every day. Seriously, Diz. What about this doesn't work for you? It looks pretty good to me. Solid enough, anyway, for an indictment, easily for an arrest. You know how that works."

Seeing it now through Freeman's eyes, he was forced to concede that his client in fact did have motive, means, and opportunity to have killed Tim Markham. In his day, Hardy had won many grand jury indictments with any two of them, occasionally with only one.

And now he'd brokered this stupid little meeting with the head of homicide in a few hours. Kensing might show up here in the office and if more evidence had come to light, Glitsky might serve him with a grand jury subpoena, or even arrest him on the spot.

And all Hardy had done for Kensing to date had been to send him off to work with some low-watt advice and a little kneecap humor. He realized now that the familiar settings of the aquarium and the Shamrock and the two men's mutual friendship with Pico Morales had gotten him off on the wrong foot here, temporarily blinding him to the realities Kensing faced. What had he been thinking?

Suddenly he was on his feet. "Excuse me, David," he said. "I've got to get out of here."

"I have this incredible sense of déjà vu," Glitsky said. "Didn't we already do this?"

"That was this morning," Hardy replied. "New opportunities abound if we but have the courage to face them."

The lieutenant leveled his eyes at his friend across his desk, then zipped open the side pocket of his all-weather jacket, pulled out a few disks of some kind of white stuff, broke off a piece, and popped it into his mouth. "Want some of this rice cake? It's awful." He looked at it for a long moment before he pitched it into the wastebasket.

"What happened to the peanuts?" Hardy asked. For years, one of Glitsky's desk drawers was the homicide detail's peanut receptacle and the lieutenant would often carry a few handfuls around with him. "I could eat a few peanuts."

"Too much cholesterol, or fat, or one of those. I forget which."

"So on top of the heart stuff, you got CRS, too?"

Glitsky sat back, folded his arms, and stared. "I'm not going to ask."

"Okay, fine. If you don't know, you don't know. And if you guessed wrong, you'd just say something negative anyway. But it's never too late to change, you know. Accentuate the positive."

"Latch on to the affirmative." Glitsky's voice was the essence of dry. "I've got another one for you. Let's call the whole thing off."

Hardy's brow clouded. "Different song. And notice, a negative theme again. But this time, as it turns out, precisely what I had in mind."

"What's that?"

"Well, I regret to inform you that my client will not be available for our interview this evening after all. This case is just too hot for me to let him talk. However, if you'd like to give me inquiries in writing, I'd be happy to try and get you any information you require."

Glitsky chortled. "And if you'd like to kiss my toes, perhaps I shall become a ballerina. It's been my dream."

The two men looked benignly at each other.

Glitsky finally broke the impasse. "All right," he said. "What's CRS?"

Hardy paused for dramatic effect. "Can't . . . remember . . . shit." He grinned. "One sad day, you won't ask."

12

Glitsky had made it clear that the respective performances of Bracco and Fisk yesterday during the interview of Anita Tong left something to be desired, so much so that he'd forbidden them to talk directly to any of the other witnesses Tong had mentioned. Specifically, they were not to approach Eric Kensing or anyone at Parnassus headquarters. If they developed new leads for themselves and found anyone else on their own, they could use their judgment. Provided they immediately reported back to homicide — daily — with any results.

The lieutenant had even suggested that, since it was their area of expertise, maybe it would be an effective use of their time to visit some body shops and car washes, follow up on patrol sightings of suspicious vehicles in the projects and neighborhoods. Fisk accepted this assignment with relative good humor, tinged possibly with acceptance and even relief, but after a couple of hours of it, driving around in a continuous steady rain, Bracco lost his patience.

"Goddamnit, this isn't a hit and run anymore, Harlen! Glitsky told us to build a case, and we're probably gonna break some eggs making any kind of decent omelette out of it. But I'm damned if I'm driving around anymore looking for a fucking car all this miserable day. That's not what killed him anyway."

They had come up from the Mission and now were stopped at a red light on Van Ness near city hall. Fisk, huddled down in the passenger seat with his arms crossed against the chill, was shaking his head. "Glitsky said look for the car. Don't mess with Kensing."

"Okay, but how about his wife? She's fucking Markham, you know she's in this somehow."

This made Fisk uncomfortable. "I don't know. That's pretty close to Kensing, don't you think? Besides, where is she?"

"Up on Anza, behind USF. I've got her address."

"How'd you find that?"

"I called information and asked." He grinned over at his partner. "Believe it or not, it works. She lives like four blocks from the Kaiser on Masonic. I played a hunch and called there. Sure enough. You ever notice how all doctors' wives are nurses? I say we go talk to her."

Fisk still didn't like it, but after a beat he brightened. "You know the other night you dropped me at Tadich's? I mentioned the case to my aunt Kathy, and she said the whole Parnassus mess had been really hard on Nancy Ross. She felt so sorry for her."

"Nancy Ross?"

"Malachi's wife."

"I don't know Malachi Ross," Bracco admitted.

Fisk allowed a small smile. "Parnassus," he said. "With Markham gone, he runs it now. You didn't read 'CityTalk' today? It was pretty interesting."

"Are you turning into a cop on me, Harlen? So your aunt knows his wife?"

"Pretty well, I think. She knows everybody."

"It's something." Bracco pointed. "And even as we speak, city hall looms on the right." Abruptly making up his mind, he pulled directly over to the curb. "Let's go say hi."

Kathy West showed no sign of sharing any of her nephew's genes. Maybe, Bracco thought, she was the wife of the blood relation to Harlen. In her mid-fifties, with a no-nonsense, stop-and-start demeanor and frail bone structure, her little bob of gray-peppered hair, she reminded Darrell Bracco of nothing so much as a sparrow. A friendly, really intelligent sparrow.

The office of the city supervisor on the second floor was small — tiny — but pleasant. There was an antique desk, built-in bookshelves, a row of windows along the west-facing wall. When her nephew and his partner showed up unexpectedly, they didn't appear to be interrupting anything. She greeted them both warmly, then sent her administrative aide, a well-dressed obsequious young man named Peter, for some coffee.

After a few minutes of small talk and a quick cook's tour of her workspace — three desks in an outer cubicle, a cramped library and file room — when the coffee arrived, she closed the door to her office behind them and they all sat. "So," she began, "I'm assuming you're here to talk about Parnassus. Wasn't that 'CityTalk' column devastating? I don't see how Malachi Ross will be able to face his employees today, to say nothing of his board. Well . . ." She stopped, expectant.

Bracco stepped into the breach. "Harlen said you knew Mrs. Ross. I wonder if you could tell us a little about her before we go and interview her."

"Why would you want to do that? Surely she isn't any kind of a suspect?"

Fisk's replied frankly, "We're on what you might call a short leash with Lieutenant Glitsky. This is our first real case and I think he wants us to work in from way outside. Not spook any important witnesses with naive questions."

"Parnassus may be part of the motive, if there is one." Bracco's tone was confident, as though he'd done this kind of thing a hundred times before.

"But Nancy Ross?" West asked. "Was she even there when Markham died? She would have had to be at the hospital, wouldn't she?"

"She's not a suspect," Fisk reiterated. "We're just interested in the personal side of Parnassus, if you will. The players. If there might be anything there."

"Well . . ." She put her cup down. "I really don't know Malachi Ross at all, although of course we've met several times. Nancy, on the other hand, I know fairly well. She is a lovely person. Very active, socially, I mean. She also volunteers with the Opera Board, the Kidney Foundation, several other charities, many of a medical nature." West narrowed her eyes slightly. "I may as well tell you that politically, as well, she's been a friend. So I'm afraid I'm not going to be a very good source of dirt."

"We're not looking for dirt," Bracco assured her. Though the idea that there might be some dirt was appealing, this wasn't the venue to pursue it. "Was she a nurse, by the way?"

West shook her head no. "I don't believe Nancy has ever worked for a living. I mean, at a real job. She's never needed to. She comes from money."

"But even when her husband was young? To help out?" Bracco asked.

West laughed. "When her husband was young, Inspector, Nancy was a baby. She's Mr. Ross's second wife. I'd be surprised if she's thirty-five." A cloud crossed her brow. "Her parents weren't altogether taken with the marriage. I remember hearing that the money from that source dried up. They didn't like the idea of Nancy being a trophy wife for an older man, and they cut her off entirely. I mean her money. Not that it mattered, as it turns out. Malachi does very well . . ." She shook her head in commiseration. ". . . as the entire city now knows."

Harlen finally thought of a question. "Does she do anything with her husband? For Parnassus?"

The supervisor shook her head. "I don't really think so, not specifically with the company. But she entertains all the time, and I suppose to some degree that's part of his business."

"All the time?" Bracco asked.

A nod. "I don't know how she does it with the small children — she's got her twin girls, I think they're about six — but I suppose with the nannies . . ." She collected her thoughts a moment. "But back to your question, I'd guess she throws a really lavish party once a month, with smaller affairs — charity do's — two or three times a week."

Bracco wasn't familiar with the lifestyle, and didn't seem to understand it. "This would be most weeks?"

"I'd say so. When she's in town."

"As opposed to where?"

"Well . . ." She smiled and opened her palms in front of her. "Wherever she wants to go, I'd suppose. They have a second place — really stunning, I've been there, seven or eight thousand square feet — right on the lake at Tahoe. And I know they — or she and the girls — they Christmas at Aspen or Park City. They have their own plane, I believe."

Darrel Bracco jogged through the rain with his partner, got to his car and into his seat. When Harlen was buckling up beside him, he caught his eye. "Wow."

"Real money," Fisk agreed. "Real live money."

"Their own airplane? I'd like my own airplane."

"How could you pay for the gas to go anywhere, though?"

"Yeah, there's that." Bracco pulled out into the traffic. The rain continued as though it would never end, drifting in sheets before them. It was nearly noon, and still dark as dusk, and after a bit, Bracco's expression closed down to

169

match it. "But we knew they were rich to begin with, didn't we? I don't see what else it gets us."

Fisk considered that. "It got us a better cup of coffee than Ed's body shop."

"At least that." The message, especially welcome coming from Fisk, was a good one. They were finally working a righteous homicide, not a variant of hit and run. And the truth was that it wasn't the same at all. Now, without any real guidance, the job was to follow where their intelligence and instincts led them. They were gathering random information, that was all. And by definition much of it would be irrelevant. But some of it might be important — you just didn't know until you knew.

Without any discussion, Bracco turned west, toward Kaiser and Ann Kensing's house. Fisk, concentrating, sat in a deep silence for a couple of blocks. Then. "Darrel."

"Yeah?"

"What does a plane cost, you think?"

"I think it's one of those things where if you've got to ask, you can't afford it."

But his partner was a ball of surprises today. Something had started his engine over this investigation, and now he was obviously pursuing a train of thought. "No, not that. I mean just the upkeep alone — the hangar, the gas, monthly payments, insurance?"

"I don't know. I suppose it would depend on where you keep it, the size of the plane, all that. Why?"

Fisk shrugged. "I'm thinking about a million two. How far it goes?"

This wasn't a hard one for Darrel. "If I had a million two, I'd be retired on the beach in Costa Rica. Where'd that figure come from?"

"That's what Ross makes a year." Bracco shot a glance of utter skepticism across the seat, and Fisk retorted. "Hey, that was the number in the paper — 'CityTalk.' It's got to be true. But my point isn't how much money it is. It's whether it's enough."

This made Bracco laugh. "It's enough, trust me."

"Is it? Two mansions, a past marriage, which means alimony and probably child support. A new, young, party-giving society wife, kids in private schools, servants, airplanes, vacations."

"A million two, though." For Darrel Bracco, son of a cop, a million dollars might as well be a trillion. They were both unfathomably large sums of money, a lifetime's worth of money.

Clearly, though, not so for Fisk. "You ever read a book called *Bonfire of the Vanities*?"

"Was that a book? I think I saw the movie."

"Yeah, well, the movie sucked, but it was a book first. Anyway, a cool thing in the book was this guy running down the list of his expenses, showing how impossible it was to get along on only a million dollars a year. And this was like ten years ago."

"He should have called me," Bracco said. "I could have helped him out."

"The point," Fisk pressed on, "is that maybe we just did learn something we can use from Aunt Kathy. Instead of concentrating on how rich Ross is, it might be smarter to think how

171

poor he is. I mean, face it, if your expenses are greater than your income, you're poor, right? No matter what you make."

They stopped at Kaiser first and discovered that Mrs. Kensing had called in sick.

The rain that had been falling steadily since last night had found a new life. Monsoonlike, driven nearly horizontal by strong winds off the ocean, the drops pelted both inspectors as they stood on her front stoop. She answered the door wearing heavy gray socks, designer jeans, and a red, cowl-neck pullover. Bracco's immediate impression was that she hadn't slept in a couple of days.

Her shoulder-length blond hair was a mess. Without makeup of any kind, she appeared drawn and gaunt. Still, there was no hiding her attractiveness. Her eyes, especially, were a deep-set, wide and compelling, almost electric blue. He'd never seen eyes quite like them.

Even after they'd introduced themselves, badges out, Mrs. Kensing simply stared at them until Bracco finally asked if they could come in. Nodding, she took a step back, opening the door as she withdrew. "I'm sorry," she said ambiguously, then waited another long moment before she brought the door closed behind them all.

The light was dim in the vestibule. They stood dripping on the woven cloth rug in the tiny area. "Maybe we should . . ." she said distractedly, and not finishing the sentence, led the way a few steps down a short hall, then to the right into the kitchen.

Overflowing onto the floor, a huge load of laundry lay piled on the table. Skirting that, she pulled out a stool. The counter still held dirty dishes from the morning — a milk and a juice carton, two boxes of cereal, some brown pear and banana slices on a cracked saucer. Finally she focused on them where they stood in the small humid room.

"All right. What?" The startling eyes flicked back and forth between the inspectors.

Bracco pulled out his tape recorder and put it on the counter in front of her. He cleared his throat and recited his name and the date, his badge number, the usual. He hadn't rehearsed what he was going to say, hadn't really considered what the woman's state of mind might be before she'd opened the door. But now he had to begin with something soon or, he sensed, she'd throw them both out. "Mrs. Kensing, Tim Markham and you were lovers, weren't you?"

She cleared her throat. "We used to be, but he broke it off. Twice."

"Why?"

"Because he was guilty about his family. Especially he didn't want to hurt his kids. But he didn't love his wife anymore. So he kept coming back to me."

"But he left you again, too? Isn't that right?" Bracco asked.

"Temporarily. He would have come back again."

"So why did he leave?"

"Because he had to try again with them. One more time, he said."

Fisk asked, "And when was that?"

"Last week. Late last week."

"And were you okay with that?" Bracco asked. "With his decision?"

"How could I be? I knew . . ." Her eyes were hard. "I knew he'd come back to me eventually, just like he always did. He loved me. I didn't see why he had to put everyone through it again. All the back and forth. I told him he should just separate. Make it clean."

"The way you did in your marriage?" Fisk asked.

If she took offense, she didn't show it. "Yeah, like I did. As soon as I realized I loved Tim and not Eric, I told him he had to move out. I mean, what was the point? I wasn't going to live a lie."

Fisk looked across at his partner. "And how did Carla take all this? His leaving her?"

"He never left her," she corrected him bitterly. "I was always on the side."

"But she knew about you? What then?"

"Well, she threatened him, of course. Said she'd leave him and take all his money. He wouldn't get visitation. That's why he went back."

"You mean this last time?"

But Fisk didn't wait for her to answer his partner's question. "You know that Carla and the children are dead, too?"

She went still for a beat. Then, "I saw that, but I turned it all off. I'm not interested in her. She doesn't have anything to do with me." She looked up at them in defiance. "I don't want to talk about this anymore. I don't care about her."

Fisk spoke up. "Maybe Carla didn't take him back? Maybe she was still mad at him?"

Suddenly she broke and raised her voice. "*Aren't you listening to me?!* It was done." The wind gusted and heavy drops pounded at the kitchen window. "He was going to tell her everything he'd done wrong in his life. Make a fresh start. What a fucking fool!"

"But did he in fact tell her?" Fisk asked.

"Who cares? What could it matter now? I never saw him again after he left me," she snapped. "I don't know what he did."

"And when was that?" Bracco asked more gently. "The last time you saw him?"

She slapped angrily at the counter. "*Goddamnit!* I don't care! Don't you hear me? What matters is I'm left here." She gestured despairingly around the cluttered, tiny kitchen. "Here. By myself."

Fisk asked abruptly, "Did you know that your husband treated Mr. Markham at Portola?"

"Yeah, I knew that. I saw him right after." Her gaze sharpened. "Why is that important?"

"Markham had broken up your marriage. Maybe he still hated him."

"Yeah, but so what?" She shook her head wearily. "This all shook out two years ago. It's ancient history."

The inspectors shared a glance. "You're saying he wasn't still bitter?" Fisk asked.

"Sure he was bitter. He made no bones about hating Tim. He always . . ." She hesitated. "Why?"

Fisk told her. "We're trying to find out who

killed him, Mrs. Kensing. I know you'll want to know that, too."

Her eyes narrowed. "What do you mean, *killed* him? He got hit by a car."

"No, ma'am, he was killed," Bracco said.

"You didn't know that?" Fisk asked harshly. "Didn't you read the paper this morning?"

"Yeah," she answered in a voice heavy with sarcasm. "I got my kids off to school, then had the maid bring in the paper with my coffee and bonbons. She hasn't gotten to the laundry or the dishes yet." Dismissing Fisk, she turned to Bracco. "You're saying somebody ran him over on purpose?"

Bracco nodded. "It wasn't the accident," he said. "He was killed at the hospital. Somebody shot him up with potassium."

Her eyes flashed with the onset of panic. "I don't know what you're saying."

Fisk took a step toward her. "You're a nurse and you don't know about potassium?"

"Of course I know that. What about it with Tim, though, with his dying?"

"It's what killed him," Bracco replied. "Really."

Slowly, the news seemed to register. "In the hospital?" Then slowly, as the thought congealed, her face changed by degrees until finally it was contorted with rage. "That son of a bitch. That miserable motherfucker." She looked from one inspector to the other, her rasping voice filled with conviction. "You can stop looking," she said. "I *know* who killed him."

13

Kensing was working at the Judah Clinic and didn't seem inclined to return calls, so Hardy decided that he'd simply show up, hoping that his unexpected appearance would help convey the air of urgency he was beginning to feel. So he ventured out into the teeth of the storm and made it to the clinic in time to spend another half hour in the crowded waiting room before Kensing, in his white smock and stethoscope, came out to see him. The doctor told him he couldn't get away, even for a few minutes.

His doctor work was more important. He was swamped here, as Hardy could see. And anyway, wasn't their appointment supposed to be for tonight?

Hardy tried to make him understand the reality they both faced, but the doctor couldn't seem to accept it.

"I don't see how it's any different than it was yesterday," Kensing replied. He made a helpless gesture with his hands.

"Everything about it is different," Hardy explained with a patience he didn't feel. "Yesterday, nobody thought Markham was murdered, so it didn't matter that you hated him. Now it does. A lot. So you've got motive, means, and opportunity. It's bad luck to have all three of these around a homicide, trust me."

But he dismissed Hardy's concerns with a shake of his head. "We covered all this on the phone this morning, didn't we?" He put an arm on Hardy's sleeve. "Look, I appreciate your concern, but I've got to keep things moving here at the clinic or we won't even get to talk tonight. Sorry you had to come all the way down, but this won't work."

Hardy closed some space between them and lowered his voice. "That's what I've been trying to tell you. We're not going to talk tonight, Doctor. At least not with the police. I canceled the interview."

Kensing showed a little pique. "Why'd you do that?"

"Because I'm your lawyer and it's my job to protect you."

"I don't need protection. Once they hear what I've got to say, especially if I give it to them voluntarily, they'll cross me off their list."

"Really? And you know this because of your vast experience in criminal law, is that it?" Hardy was right in his client's face. "Listen to me. I promise you — you have my solemn word — that they will *not* do that. Don't kid yourself. Like it or not, you are a murder suspect. They won't be looking for reasons to let you off. They'll be looking for reasons to bring you in. And I'm not going to give them a chance to do that. You and I need a lot more time together. A lot more. Like most of the weekend."

Kensing shook his head. "I don't know about that. I've got Giants tickets for Saturday. I've got my kids and I'm taking them."

"That's really swell," Hardy said, "but you're not taking anybody anywhere if you're in jail. The point is you and I need to block some time. This is serious stuff, okay?"

In the waiting room over Kensing's shoulder, a baby began to wail.

Kensing checked his watch, frowned, looked over at the crying infant. "All right," he said, gesturing toward the noise, "but this is serious, too. What I do." He offered a professional smile. "Maybe Sunday, though, how'd that be?" Giving Hardy a conspiratorial pat on the back, he turned and disappeared through the door that led to the doctors' offices.

Hardy, who had walked a block and a half from the parking lot, felt the squish in his soaking shoes, the chill in his pants, damp below the knee. After Kensing left, he sat down for a minute in one of the plastic chairs, then combed his wet hair with his fingers, stood up, and buttoned his raincoat for the walk through the squall back to his car.

"Just checking on my investment," Hardy said when Moses McGuire looked up in surprise from behind the Shamrock's bar. He was the only person in the place.

"What investment? I gave you your quarter in trade, in case your memory fails you, which it never does. You drinking?"

Hardy hadn't had a drink in the daytime in six months, but between his failure to talk with anybody at the hall, Freeman's attitude, the weather, and his recent debacle with Kensing, he was ready to try anything to change his luck or his timing. "You got any Sapphire behind the bar?"

Though McGuire disapproved of gin in any form, he didn't have to ask Hardy how he wanted it. Up, dry, chilled glass. As he was pouring, he asked, "You all right? Frannie okay?" He had pretty much raised his little sister, Hardy's wife, by himself, and he still felt protective.

"We're fine. I had an appointment near here that didn't work out. Nothing to do with Frannie." He sipped his martini, nodded appreciatively. "This," he said, "is perfect."

Moses, whose own Macallan scotch, neat, was a permanent fixture in the bar's gutter, lifted his own glass, clicked it against Hardy's, and raised it to his lips. "That," he replied, "is gin and dry vermouth and ice. *This*" — holding up his own glass — "is perfect. But I accept the compliment with grace and humility. Why didn't you have him come to your office?"

"Who?"

"Your appointment. I didn't know you made house calls."

"I don't. This one seemed important."

"Well, to one of you, at least."

At that truth, Hardy nodded ruefully. "Then again, maybe I just needed an excuse to break up the routine."

Moses pulled up the stool he kept behind the bar. "I hear you," he said. "You want to plan a road trip? We leave now, we could be in Mexico by nightfall."

"Don't tempt me." Hardy lifted his drink, sipped at it, spoke wistfully. "Maybe I could pull the kids out of school . . ."

"I wasn't thinking of bringing the offspring with us."

Hardy noted the tone, looked at the battered face across the bar. "You and Susan okay?"

"At least we're not getting divorced, I don't think." He drank some of his scotch. "But sometimes I'm sure it's only because we made a deal that the first one to mention the D word gets the kids. I hear Mexico's warm this time of year."

"It's always warmer than here."

They both looked out the picture window, where the rain continued in sheets. The cypress trees that bordered the park were bent over halfway in the wind.

Abruptly, Hardy stood up. He pushed his unfinished martini to the edge of the bar.

"You leaving so soon?" McGuire asked him. "You just got here."

Hardy pointed to his drink. "If I finish that, and I desperately want to, I'll never leave."

"Fortunately, you don't have to."

"No, I do have to. I've got work and the devil's trying to give me an excuse not to do it. But I've got an idea for you and Susan. Why don't you get somebody to cover for you here and bring the kids over tonight. We'll take 'em. You guys go out. How's that sound?"

"It could work," McGuire said. "Though it isn't Mexico."

"Yeah, but what is?" Hardy laid a friendly punch on McGuire's arm. "Think about it."

★ ★ ★

Standing in front of the grand jury after a working lunch with Clarence Jackman and Abe Glitsky, Marlene Ash was in her element. The twenty citizens gathered before her in the Police Commissioner's Hearing Room on the fifth floor of the Hall of Justice, one floor above Glitsky's office and two above Jackman's, cared mightily for justice to be done. They might appear to be a hodgepodge of humanity — certainly both genders and most of the ethnic populations in the city were represented here today — but Marlene knew that these people sitting now before her, and the others like them on juries (and not just grand juries) all over the country, were the backbone of the legal system she worked within. Without them, the "average" good citizen, justice would be an empty concept, the social fabric would tear.

So she played fair with them, respecting their intelligence and experience. "Ladies and gentlemen of the grand jury," she began. "On Tuesday, April 10, Timothy Markham began his customary, invariable morning jog. When he got to Twenty-sixth Avenue, here in the city, he was run down by a green, early model American car. The driver fled the scene in his vehicle.

"But the car accident is not what killed Mr. Markham.

"Instead, after he'd been somewhat stabilized in the emergency room at Portola Hospital, and as he lay helpless in his hospital bed, a person or persons as yet unknown injected his body with an overdose of potassium.

182

"Potassium is a common medication. It is readily available in emergency rooms and intensive care units. But potassium can kill when administered in large doses. And such a dose was given to Mr. Markham.

"That same night, his wife, Carla, and their three children died of gunshot wounds in their home. We have convened here today to take evidence to determine the identity of the killer or killers in this series of brutal deaths."

All eyes were glued on her. Most of the members had pads on the desks in front of them, ready to take notes. "The coroner has ruled that Carla Markham's death by gunshot is a possible suicide, but this is still a matter of uncertainty. Lieutenant Glitsky, the chief of the homicide detail, will be testifying here for you in a few moments. He will be conducting a parallel investigation into that aspect of the case, and he may decide to his satisfaction that in fact Mrs. Markham killed her family and herself, or he may arrest a suspect before you have gathered enough evidence to issue an indictment." She paused and met a few eyes among her jurors. "We'll cross that bridge when we come to it. In the meanwhile, the city has received a bill in the amount of thirteen million dollars for services . . ."

Hardy wasn't exactly sure what had brought him to Portola in the first place. He'd vaguely wanted to talk to someone in administration, he thought, but nobody would talk to him. He hadn't made an appointment — it was becoming his theme for the day. Everybody was busy, all the health care professionals and administrators were dealing with the fallout from the week's horrors within the hospital itself, to say nothing of the upheaval under the corporate umbrella. They had no time for impromptu meetings.

This whole day ought to teach him to rein in his boyish enthusiasm, he told himself as he squished down the hallway on his way to the lobby and out. He was just steeling himself for the dash outside when he noticed a sign that directed people to various locations, one of which read CAFETERIA. Realizing that if he didn't ask no one could say no, he turned back and followed the arrows. It was long past lunchtime, and the place, while not deserted, wasn't crowded, either. Hardy grabbed a muffin and a cup of coffee, paid the cashier, and stood waiting for his muse to speak. Alone, at a table by a window, a woman in a nurse's uniform sat reading a book, and he began to walk toward her.

Closer up, he pegged her as between thirty and thirty-five. Nice looking, light brown hair worn short, medium build. "Excuse me," he said.

She kept her eyes on her book and held up a finger. After finishing her paragraph, she looked up. "Yes? Can I help you?"

Welcome words. But Hardy didn't know what if anything he expected to discover here by talking to her. But he'd never know if he didn't start. "My name is Dismas Hardy. I'm Dr. Kensing's lawyer. Do you mind if I sit down for a minute?"

A flicker of distrust faded as quickly as it had appeared. She lifted her shoulders, dropped them, and said, "Sure, but why? Am I in trouble?"

Hardy pulled a chair around across from her. "I don't think so. Should you be?"

It flustered her. "No! I mean, you said you're a lawyer. Usually aren't people in trouble when lawyers come visit them?"

"Now that you mention it, I suppose they are. This isn't one of those times, though." He handed her a business card and while she looked at it, he asked her name.

"Rebecca," she said. "Rebecca Simms."

"That's my daughter's name. We call her 'the Beck.' "

She nodded, somehow reassured, and she looked down again at the card. "Dismas? Is that right?"

He nodded. "The good thief on Calvary. Also the patron saint of murderers. I often wonder what my parents were thinking."

"So is Dr. Kensing in trouble?" she asked.

Hardy temporized. He blew on his coffee, set it down untouched in front of him. "The short answer is yes."

"Because of Tim Markham? Them calling it a murder?"

Hardy was thinking he'd picked the right table. "Exactly."

She shook her head disgustedly. "But that is so ridiculous. Murder. Please."

"Ridiculous in what way?"

"Well, I'm not saying it must have been an accident. Someone could have deliberately given him the wrong dose, I suppose. But we use potassium all the time in the ER."

"Are you an ER nurse?"

"Sometimes," she said. "We rotate a lot. I've been in there my share of times."

"And is the potassium pretty readily available?"

"Sure, to any medical person. It's right there behind the nurses' station."

From Hardy's perspective, this was good news if only because it gave more people — besides his client — access to the drug. "So in your opinion, an overdose of potassium wouldn't have to be deliberate? Or malicious?"

"No. They're usually not, in fact."

"They happen a lot?"

"Sometimes." She didn't seem too worried about it. "I remember we had one on this Saturday night near the end of last summer, there were some shootings in the Addition, and I think a car crash or two. Anyway, the ER was a madhouse, you can imagine. The doctor's yelling out orders right and left. One of the shot guys was bleeding out, his heart was failing, and he needed fluids with potassium, so he got one dose and before the doctor came back to him, somebody had given him another one, thinking it was the first."

"So what happened? Did he die?"

"No. The doctor recognized what was happening immediately. So he shocked him, then pumped him with insulin and glucose, and he came out."

"So why, do you think, didn't they use that on Mr. Markham?"

"I don't know. I wasn't there. They'd have had to recognize the problem first, right? I mean, in my case with the shot guy, the doctor was right there, ordering potassium. Maybe Dr. Kensing didn't know. Or didn't put it together soon enough. What does he say?"

Hardy showed some frustration. "He's been busy. Until it made the news, he thought Markham had just died from the accident."

"People do, you know. Just die."

A curt nod. He knew. It was coming up on the birthday of his long-gone son, Michael. With an effort, he shook the clutch of the memory. "One of the reasons I came out here today was to get a sense of the place, of general conditions here. I've heard rumors that some doctors are unhappy with the administration. Patients are getting turned away. Then there was that whole Baby Emily thing."

Her eyes widened with recognition. "That was Dr. Kensing, too, wasn't it? He's the one who admitted her. I knew there was something I remembered when you first mentioned him. That was it."

Hardy played smart, as though he'd known this about Kensing all along, although it was the first he'd heard of it. "Did he get in a lot of trouble for that?" Suddenly, reflexively, Rebecca turned her head, focusing over Hardy's shoulders to the corners of the room behind him. With a little frisson of electricity, he realized that his questions had somehow put her on her guard. "What is it?" he asked.

She exhaled heavily, scanned the room again,

checked her watch and her book. Finally, she came back to him. "You never really know with these kinds of things, I mean what really happened. But you wouldn't have believed the memos, all the stupid . . ." She huffed another time, got herself back under control. "Anyway, everybody talked all about it for weeks, of course. All of us — the staff — even the doctors, you know, and it's not so common that we all agree on anything — we all thought he'd done absolutely the right thing. I mean, this was a *baby*. What was he supposed to do? Let them leave her over in County without her mother?"

"And I take it the administration didn't like it?"

She laughed harshly, then leaned across the table, and answered in a whisper, "I heard they actually fired him, which is when he went to the newspapers —"

"Excuse me." The laundry list of what Hardy didn't know about his client continued to grow, and to astound him. He and his client had to talk. Really. But he couldn't bother about that now. "You're telling me that Dr. Kensing broke the story, too? To the papers?"

She nodded. "He never admitted it, but everybody knows it was him. I think it's only a matter of time now before they really fire him, even if they have to make up a reason. Not that he's alone."

"What do you mean?"

She made sure again that no one had come within earshot. "I mean most people here are scared of losing their jobs, of either doing some-

thing or not doing it, either way. It's really bad."
She frowned. "So are they going to charge Dr.
Kensing with this murder? That would be awful."

"I don't know," Hardy said. "They might."

"Because Mr. Markham was going to fire
him?"

"That could be a motive, yes." Another one,
Hardy was thinking. But he asked, "You're sure
it was Markham who wanted to fire him?"

"Sure," she said. "He ran the whole show
here. Who else?"

14

"Glitsky, homicide."

"Who is this?"

"What did I just say? This is Abe Glitsky, San Francisco homicide. Who's this?"

"Jack Langtry. Abe? Is this really you?"

"Yeah, it's really me, Jack. What's going on?"

"This is really weird. I just hit redial on Carla Markham's cell phone. She called homicide before she died?"

"Where are you now?"

"Downstairs. Evidence lockup."

"Don't move. I'm on my way."

Langtry was waiting in his office in the bowels of the hall. With him was another of his crime scene investigators, Sgt. Carol Amano. He had put the phone on the middle of the desk all by itself, almost as though it were some kind of bomb. He'd already ordered complete phone records on the Markham house and on this cell phone. He'd also called Lennard Faro at the lab and requested that he join them ASAP.

Glitsky was down here with them, pacing as he talked, which was something he rarely did. Langtry realized that his adrenaline was way up. "Okay, but let's consider other possibilities," Glitsky was saying. "It was in her purse. Maybe one of our guys couldn't get to a phone and called back in here while we were doing the house."

"No way." Amano wouldn't even consider it.

Langtry, too, was shaking his head. "I agree. Not a chance, Abe. You saw who we had on the scene. Me, Len, Carol, the other guys, we're talking the 'A' team. Nobody's taking a phone out of a purse at a homicide scene and using it to call home. It just couldn't happen. But assuming we've got what it looks like here, she called homicide. So what does it mean?"

"It would be helpful to know when," Glitsky said.

"We could have that in a few hours if we're lucky," Langtry replied. "But I think we can assume it was after she left the hospital and before the crowd started showing up at her place."

"Probably while she was driving home," Amano added.

Glitsky processed that for a second. "Which was before anybody knew about the potassium. Before we knew it was a murder."

"Maybe *she* knew it was a murder," Amano said with a muted excitement. "Maybe she did the murder and was calling to confess, then changed her mind."

"Was she at the hospital, Abe? When he died?"

"Yeah," Glitsky answered distractedly.

"Okay, then," Langtry said. Catching Glitsky's expression, he asked, "Why not?"

"I don't know."

"Maybe he broke up with her again." Amano clearly liked the idea. "He was leaving her for good. She went into a jealous rage . . ."

Glitsky was shaking his head. "And then luckily he got hit by a random car, giving Carla the opportunity to ride in the ambulance with him and then kill him with potassium at the hospital? After which she went home and entertained all of her friends for six or seven hours before finally killing herself and her kids? This doesn't sing for me, people. It doesn't even hum."

The two CSI inspectors shared a glance. "Do you have another theory?" Langtry finally asked.

Glitsky's scar was tight through his lips. "No. I don't like theories. I don't know what time she made the call, or why she made it, or if anybody in the detail picked up. She might have seen the accident, for all I know."

Amano walked over to the door and looked out down the hallway. Then she turned. "Here comes Faro."

A few seconds later, the snappily dressed and diminutive forensics inspectors bopped into the office, said hi all around, asked what was up. When he heard about the cell phone, he nodded thoughtfully. Certainly, he thought, it was significant, but what it meant exactly he didn't want to hazard a guess. Like Glitsky, Faro liked it when evidence led to a theory, instead of vice versa. "But I do have some news."

"Hit me," Glitsky said.

"Well, two things. On the trajectory — we're talking Mrs. Markham here, the head wound — back to front."

Glitsky repeated the words, then asked, "So the gun was behind her ear, and the slug went

192

forward? Strout say how often he's seen that with self-inflicted wounds?"

Faro gestured ambiguously. "You know him better than me, sir. He said sometimes."

"Helpful."

"I thought so, too. But the other thing. She was left-handed."

"How'd Strout get to that?"

"He didn't. I got it. There was a collection of lefty coffee mugs at the house, you know the kind — 'Best Mom in the World,' 'Queen of the Southpaws' — that kind of thing. Also, she'd addressed some envelopes and the writing slants like a lefty."

"But the gun was in her right hand?"

"Near it," Faro corrected him. "But yeah. Anyway, the GSR" — gunshot residue — "results might give us a better hint if she in fact fired the thing, but they won't be in for a few more days."

"Okay, Len. Thanks." Glitsky's scowl was pronounced. "Well, thanks to all of you. Anything new comes up, I want to hear."

Glitsky wasn't about to join in the guessing games out loud, but this latest evidence all but convinced him of what he'd been tempted to believe from the start. Carla Markham's death hadn't been a suicide at all. She wouldn't have shot herself with the wrong hand and at an unusual angle. She wouldn't have shot the dog. Or her teenage children.

And this meant that someone had killed her. He didn't as yet know why, but the call to homicide on the day of her death made it likely that she'd seen or suspected the murderer of her husband.

Glitsky had the door to his office closed. He was drumming the fingers of both hands on his desk, trying to stop himself from this premature conjecture. He told himself that he didn't know enough yet to form any consistent theories, let alone any conclusions.

But one consideration wouldn't go away. If someone had in fact killed Carla, he was convinced that it was the same person that had killed her husband. He had no idea of the motive for the wife, but he didn't need that. He already had a suspect with a strong motive for the husband. And means. And opportunity.

It was time to squeeze him.

Kensing arrived home from work to find Inspector Glitsky waiting at his front door, tucked in out of the fall of rain. He greeted him politely, but seemed a little confused. "I thought Mr. Hardy had canceled this meeting."

Glitsky shrugged in a noncommittal way. "Sometimes lawyers don't want their clients to talk to the police. Usually it's when those clients are guilty. He told me you wanted to talk to us." Glitsky wasn't pushing. "I thought we might save each other some time, that's all."

After a moment's reflection, Kensing invited Glitsky up into his condo without ever thinking to ask him for a warrant. He lived in a two-bedroom converted condominium across from Alta Plaza, a park in the Upper Fillmore.

The unit took up the entire floor in a stately, older, three-story building. It sported classic high ceilings, exposed dark beams, hardwood floors. A huge bay window with three panes of watery ancient glass overlooked the park, and Glitsky stopped to look out of them for a moment, to comment on the rain.

A few minutes later, after he'd boiled some water for tea for the lieutenant, the doorbell rang again. It turned out to be the inspector he'd spoken with outside of the Markham house — Bracco — and another man who introduced himself as Fisk. He let them both in, too, and asked if they would like something to drink.

Glitsky had brought a portable video camera to go with the small tape recorder that he set on the kitchen table. When the audio tape was rolling, he told Kensing again for the record — as he'd mentioned on the stoop — that he understood from talking to Mr. Hardy that the doctor wanted to get the police interview out of the way. "You can, of course, decline to talk," he continued in a friendly manner, "or postpone the meeting until Mr. Hardy is available, but we know how busy you are. We all are, to tell the truth. As I said downstairs, we just thought it might be easier to get this done now, early in the process."

Kensing nodded. "That's what I told Mr. Hardy. I don't have anything to hide."

But the low-key, courteous lieutenant wanted to nail it down, and added, "You're sure you wouldn't prefer to have Mr. Hardy here?"

"No, it's fine. I think he's being a little over-protective anyway. It doesn't matter. Him being here or not isn't going to affect what I say. I don't mind."

"Thank you," Glitsky said with great sincerity. He knew that he was getting Kensing to talk without his attorney being present, and that this was legally proper. The right to remain silent belongs to the suspect, not to his lawyer. Kensing could remain silent if he so chose, but equally, he could decide to talk. "We appreciate it very much."

He seated Kensing in front of the camera, turned it on, and began: "All right, then, Doctor. Three two one. This is Lieutenant Abraham Glitsky, SFPD, badge number one one four four . . ." He continued the usual litany, identifying the case number, his witness, where they were, who else was present. Finally, Glitsky cast a quick glance at his two acolytes. He had a yellow pad out on the table in front of him, and he consulted it briefly, then got down to it. "Dr. Kensing," he began, "did you sign Mr. Markham's death certificate?"

Kensing adopted a rueful expression. He could see what was coming. "Yes, I did. Although in a situation like this one, my signature is provisional."

"Provisional. What does that mean?"

"It means in lieu of an autopsy. It can be overridden, as it was in this case, by the medical examiner." With no sign of emotion, he spelled it out. "Often, especially when a patient has been hospitalized, the cause of death is apparent, and there's no particular call for an autopsy. Although Mr. Hardy told me that hit-and-run homicides are always autopsied."

"He's right. But you didn't know that before he told you?"

"No."

"And Mr. Markham's cause of death was apparent to you, was it?"

"Yes. At the time. He'd been hit by a car and sustained major internal injuries with massive bleeding. It was a little surprising that he even made it to intensive care."

"So you did not expect an autopsy to be performed?"

"I never thought about it."

"All right. Doctor, are you familiar with the symptoms of potassium overdose?"

"Yes, of course. Basically, in layman's terms, your hearts stops beating effectively."

"And your treatment?"

He shrugged. "If we know it's potassium, we inject glucose and insulin, then defibrillation — shock — with CPR."

"And there was no way you could have recognized the true cause of Mr. Markham's problem, which was the potassium?"

"No. I don't see how."

"Okay." Glitsky consulted his notes, seemed to be gathering himself for another salvo. "Now, Doctor, you knew Mr. Markham well, isn't that true?"

"I knew him for a long time. He was my boss. How well I knew him is another question."

"Yet it's the one I asked. Isn't it true that he and your wife had a relationship that contributed to the breakup of your marriage?"

Kensing swallowed, but his mouth was dry as sand. He began to think that agreeing to this interview might have been a serious mistake.

Forty-five minutes later, they finally finished with the personal stuff. Glitsky didn't even pause a moment before moving on to a rather sharp grilling about Kensing's role in the Baby Emily matter, the Parnassus response.

"And Mr. Markham fired you?"

"Not really. He did warn me, though, that there would be serious repercussions if he found out that I'd been the leak to the press."

"And were you?"

Kensing tried to smile, but it came out crooked. "I'd rather not say, if that's all right."

Glitsky took that as a yes, and decided he didn't need the information.

"And where did that discussion with Mr. Markham take place?"

"He called me to his office. We talked there."

"And did he subsequently discover that you had been the leak?"

"I don't think so. I never heard that he did." Another weak and harmful attempt at levity. "He never fired me, so I guess not, huh?"

Glitsky, inexorable, moved on. Kensing had just admitted that, besides Baby Emily, there had been "a few" other issues with which he and Parnassus hadn't agreed. Kensing volunteered that he often prescribed drugs that were not on the formulary.

"In other words," Glitsky clarified, "drugs the company didn't approve."

"It wasn't that so much," Kensing explained. "The drugs I prescribed were fine. In fact, they were better." Kensing drew a paper towel, already damp with sweat, across his forehead. "The company's policy is that we physicians prescribe drugs from the formulary, that's all."

"And you made it a habit not to use this list?"

"Not a habit. When I thought it was appropriate." He felt he needed to explain. "The generics are not always *exactly* the same, chemically, as the proprietary, so they're not always as effective. Or they'll have other problems."

"Like what?"

"Any number of things. You'll have to take it twice as often, or it might have undesirable side effects, like indigestion. So in some cases, or when I'd had a bad experience with a certain generic on the formulary, I'd go with the proprietary."

"And Parnassus has a problem with this?"

He shrugged. "It costs them money."

"Could you explain that?"

"Well, the way it works at Parnassus is that most patients have the same copay, I think it's ten dollars, no matter what the drug costs. So if a proprietary costs thirty dollars and the formulary's generic costs ten, the company loses twenty dollars for every proprietary prescription that it fills."

"And you would prescribe these proprietary drugs regularly?"

"When it was appropriate, yes. My job is to save lives, not the company's money."

"And did you have more words with Mr.

Markham about this practice?"

By now, Kensing's hands were visibly shaking. He took them off the table, put them into his lap. For the past grueling hour or so, he wished that he'd listened to his lawyer and taken his advice not to talk to these men. But having started the interview, he didn't know how to go about trying to stop it. Finally, he tried. "If you don't mind, I'd like to be excused for a moment," he said.

But Glitsky wasn't inclined to let him go to the bathroom, even if only to gather himself. "In a bit," he said crisply. Then repeated his question. "Did you have words with Mr. Markham on this drug issue?"

"No, I did not. We did not speak."

"Since when?"

"About two years ago."

"Two years ago? And yet the Baby Emily affair was in the past few months and you said you spoke to him then."

Kensing wiped his whole face with the paper towel. "I thought you meant about this prescription issue. When we talked about that."

When the police finally packed up their equipment and left, Kensing sat shaking on his living room couch for a long while. Eventually, he decided he'd better call Hardy, see about some damage control. Outside, it had nearly come to night, and the rain continued to pour down his front window.

Hardy was still at his office, trying to catch up on his other clients' work. Kensing then told him what had happened, that the interview had been

200

really, really unpleasant, a mistake after all. "I think they must really believe I had something to do with this," he concluded.

There was a long silence, and when it ended, Kensing was completely unprepared for Hardy's fury. "Oh, you think so, Doc? The lieutenant in charge of homicide interrogates you for two hours about a murder that's on the front pages every day, that might be connected to a brutal murder of a whole family, and you've got motive, means, and opportunity and you think maybe, just maybe, they might think you're a righteous suspect. You studied anatomy, didn't you, Doc? Does everybody else have their head up their ass or is it just you?"

Kensing just sat there looking at the receiver in his hand. He felt a rush of blood to his head, and then physically sick. He thought he might throw up. His knuckles were white on the phone. His throat was a barren desert, constricted. After a few more seconds, unable to get a word out, he hung up.

When Hardy called Kensing back twenty minutes later to apologize for his outburst, he didn't find himself fired, as he'd half expected. Instead, his client apologized back to him, ending with his observation that Glitsky "might really think I killed Tim."

About time he got that message, Hardy thought. But he only said, "It'd be smart to assume that." But he had called his client back for another reason besides the apology. If he was still defending the good doctor, he had some pertinent questions to ask him. "Eric, I went by Portola today and talked to some nurses there. What do you think are the odds that the overdose was accidental?"

"Basically, in this case, zero. Why?"

Hardy ran down Rebecca Simms's theory about the occasional inadvertent overdose. When he'd finished, Kensing repeated what he'd said before. "No. It wasn't that."

"How do you know?"

"I was there. Markham wasn't even on potassium. He was stable. Relatively, anyway."

"So," Hardy asked simply, "what's that leave? Who else had access to him?"

"Carla, I suppose, technically. Maybe Brendan Driscoll earlier. Ross, a couple of other doctors. The nurses."

"How many nurses?"

"You'd have to check the records. I don't know. There's usually two, sometimes three. I think there were two." The enormity of it seemed to hit him for the first time. "You're saying one of those people killed him, aren't you?"

"That's what it looks like, Eric." He refrained from adding, "Either one of them or you."

"Jesus," Kensing said weakly. "So what do we do now?"

Hardy hesitated for just an instant. Trace awkwardness remained from the earlier outburst. But he went ahead. "This may seem a little prosaic after what you've been through tonight, Eric. But before things go any further, we've got to talk about my fees."

"Can't you just bill my insurance?"

Neither man laughed.

Hardy waited out a reasonable silence, then said, "You might want to get where you can be comfortable. This is going to take a while."

Glitsky wanted to debrief the car police after the Kensing interrogation at his condo, so although it was late, he drove back downtown. Now he was back at his desk, waiting for Fisk and Bracco so they could talk about what, if anything, they'd learned, how they were going to proceed on this investigation. Outside his door, five of his other inspectors were hanging around catching up on their paperwork. Someone had brought in a pizza, the smell of which was driving Glitsky crazy since he was supposed to go light on the food groups that used to be his favorites, which included cheese and grease.

What was keeping those guys? He'd thought they were right behind him. Finally he heard some laughter out in the detail and got up to check it out. He thought it entirely possible that somebody had Krazy Glued Fisk to his chair.

Glitsky gave up the good fight and grabbed a slice of pizza from Marcel Lanier's desk, and put half of it in his mouth before he could change his mind. When he had swallowed enough of it so that he could talk, he asked what was so funny.

Lanier was a veteran of the detail, and he leaned back in his chair with his feet crossed on his desk. His hands were linked behind his head. "Just the DA's office sent up another crazy today, and I finally figured out a way to help him without sending him to the FBI."

203

Glitsky knew that a regular feature of life in the city was the abundance of bona fide lunatics — folks who generally lived on the streets and heard voices, thought they were possessed, communicated with aliens. Occasionally, one of these people would take their concerns to the public defender's office, which would in turn direct him to the central police station downstairs in the hall. There, the desk would nod sympathetically and forward him to the DA's office, which always sent him to homicide. Most of the time, homicide turned him over to the FBI, where God knew what happened to him.

". . . but today I had this great idea," Marcel was saying, "and told this poor gentleman what he had to do was braid together a string of paper clips — I gave him a whole box, it took him like an hour — until it reached from his head to his feet. Then he had to attach it to his hair and let the other end drag on the floor, and that would stop the voices."

"And why would it do that, Marcel?" Although Glitsky wasn't sure he wanted to hear the answer.

"Because then he'd be grounded." He held up his right hand, laughing again with the other inspectors. "I swear to God, Abe. He walked out of here a cured man."

"You're a miracle worker, Marcel. That's a beautiful story. Can I have another slice of pizza?" Glitsky turned to go back to his office, but stopped as Bracco appeared in the detail's doorway. One of the guys behind him sang out, *"Car fifty-four, where are you?"* to the enjoyment

204

of the other inspectors.

Glitsky made a face of disapproval, pointed at his new young inspector and then to his office. When Bracco was inside, standing at-ease as he did, Glitsky waited at the door another minute. "You guys take the scenic route or what? Where's Harlen?"

"He's, uh, he's not here."

Glitsky brought the door to behind him. "I got that far on my own, Darrel. The question was where he *is*, not where he's not."

"I don't know exactly, sir. He had an appointment."

"He had an appointment?"

"Yes, sir. One of his aunt's fund-raising —"

Glitsky interrupted him. "Were you under the impression that you had an appointment here with me? Weren't my last words to you something very much like, 'See you back at the hall'? Did you think I meant like tomorrow morning?"

"No sir. He said he had to go and he'd already put in his hours for the day, sir."

Glitsky's scowl deepened for an instant and then, suddenly, he found himself chuckling. " 'His hours for the day.' I love that. What planet's that boy from? All right, sit down, Darrel, if you haven't got your hours quota filled up yet. I'll deal with Harlen tomorrow. Lord." After Bracco was seated, he pushed his own chair back from his desk, rested his hands over his belly, and put his feet up. "So what's your take on Dr. Kensing?"

Bracco sat the same way he stood, with a ram-rod-straight back. Using only the front half of the chair's seat, he kept his hands entwined on his lap. "I guess he's got motive to burn — and who else has any reason to kill Markham? — but without any hard evidence, no jury would convict him, I don't think."

"I agree."

"I think he sounded guilty, if that means anything," Bracco opined. "I think he thought he was smarter than us and could direct the way it would go tonight."

Glitsky allowed the trace of a smile. "I flatter myself I may have disappointed him."

"So what do we do?"

"For the moment, I'd be interested in a minute-by-minute account of how Dr. Kensing spent his day last Tuesday, and I mean from when he woke up."

"You think it's him?"

Glitsky nodded. "I'd like more physical evidence, but even without it, he was there, he hated and maybe feared Markham, he had every opportunity. Sometimes that's all we get."

Bracco seemed to be wrestling with something. Finally, he came out with it. "If he did kill Markham, are you thinking he also killed the wife?"

"I'm deeply skeptical of the notion that she killed herself. Let's put it that way." He told Bracco about the cell phone in her purse with its call to homicide, the back-to-front trajectory of the slug, the wrong-handedness with the gun.

"She called homicide? On her cell phone? When was that?"

"Six o'clock." Langtry had left the message on

Glitsky's voice mail. Information might be slow in coming, but it was showing up, and that's what counted.

"So while everybody was at her house . . . ?"

"Yep. And nobody was here in homicide. She didn't leave a message."

"Six o'clock was about when Kensing got there, wasn't it?"

Glitsky nodded. "From what I can tell. Pretty close."

A silence descended.

Again, Bracco hesitated, considering whether to talk. Again, he decided he must. "You know, we talked to Kensing's wife today and —"

Glitsky raised his eyebrows. "When was that, and why?"

"Well, remember you said you'd rather we didn't interview certain witnesses. We didn't want to get in your way, so we stayed around the edges. We went to see Harlen's aunt, then Ann Kensing."

The lieutenant brought his hands up and rubbed them over his eyes. Then he met Bracco's eyes over the desk. "I shouldn't have given you the impression that I didn't want you to talk to people, Darrel. You can talk to anybody you want. This is your case."

"Yes, sir. Thank you."

"But I want you to report to me every day. Before you go out, after you get back in."

"Yes, sir. But if I may —"

"You may. You don't have to ask that. What?"

"Are we still going on the assumption that the original hit and run was an accident? Harlen still wants to look for cars. I mean, somebody hit him. Maybe it was on purpose."

Glitsky's gaze was level, his voice reasoned and calm. "At this point, I'd be surprised if it wasn't an accident, but I wouldn't have predicted Markham's family would get shot, either. Why? You got some kind of lead on the car?"

"No, sir. I just wanted to be clear on whether we should drop it entirely or not."

"If that moment comes, Darrel, it will be clear to you. Until it is, keep your options open. Now can we go back to what you were going to say, about Mrs. Kensing?"

Bracco took a second or two dredging it up, and finally he spoke with a kind of reluctance. "Well, she sort of said she thought he admitted it, but Harlen and I didn't think she really meant that. She was very upset, pretty unaware of what she was saying."

Glitsky stopped chewing his pizza and took a long beat. "She said who admitted what?"

"Kensing. Killed Markham."

"She said he told her that?"

"Yeah, but really, I don't think . . . you had to have been there. She was just screaming, crazy upset."

Glitsky pulled at his ear, doubting what he'd just heard, wanting to be absolutely sure he was getting it right. "Are you telling me that Ann Kensing told you that her husband *said* he killed Mr. Markham? He said this to her face?"

"Yes, sir. That's what she said, but . . ."

"And you've not gotten around to telling me this before now?"

"You were already set up with the camera and ready to go, sir, and if you remember we didn't get any time alone together before you started. So we thought we'd wait until we —"

Glitsky seemed to be fighting for control. "Didn't this strike either of you as important information?"

Bracco shifted uncomfortably. "Well, my understanding was we weren't supposed to give much credit to hearsay, which was what it was, really. At least we thought."

Fingers templed at his lips, Glitsky lowered his voice to keep himself from raising it to a scream. "No, Darrel. Actually, that would be an eyewitness testimony to a confession, which is almost as good as admissible evidence gets. Did you by any chance have a tape running?"

Sure enough, on the tape, Ann Kensing came across as hysterical, even raving. The tirade was laced with obscenity, with crying jags and breakdowns, with a screaming keening and insane laughter. But there was no question about what she'd heard, what it meant. She'd told Bracco and Fisk that the only reason she hadn't gone to the police the day before is because she believed the hit-and-run accident had killed Tim Markham. As soon as she realized he'd been murdered, and *how* he'd been murdered . . .

"Listen to me! Listen to me! I'm telling you he told me he'd pumped him full of shit. That's exactly *what he said. Yeah, full of shit. Those words. Which means he killed him, didn't he? It couldn't mean anything else. I mean, nobody else knew then, did*

they? Not before the autopsy. Oh, you bastard, Eric!
You miserable, miserable . . ."

Glitsky heard it all out, then told Bracco to
take the tape directly to the DA's office for transcription. Somebody would still be there, and if
they weren't, call somebody at home and get
them down here working on it.

When Bracco had gone, Glitsky pulled an arrest warrant form out of his desk and started to
fill it out, but after the first few lines, his hands
stopped as though of their own accord. This was
new and unambiguous evidence — true — and
probably strong enough by itself to arrest Eric
Kensing. But given the overwhelming, multiple
motives and all the political repercussions of the
Parnassus question, Glitsky thought the better
part of valor would be to hold his horses until the
morning and go to Jackman to make the final
call.

The only remaining question in his mind was
whether he should include Carla's name — and
the kids' — on the warrant.

15

When Hardy dragged himself through the front door of his dark and quiet house at 11:15, he wondered if he'd have the energy left to make it up the stairs to his bedroom. Maybe he should just let himself collapse on the couch here in the living room.

There was still a glow from the embers in the fireplace. He put down his briefcase, hit the wall switch for the dim overheads, then shrugged himself out of his raincoat and suit coat and crossed the room. On the mantel, Frannie's new-since-the-fire collection of glass elephants caravanned around several potted cacti. He'd gotten into the habit of rearranging them almost every day — it was a chess game without rules or a board that served as some kind of connection between him and his wife. Nonverbal, somehow positive, and every little bit helped. Between the kids, her school, and his work, he sometimes thought they almost needed to make an appointment to say hello. Without their formal date nights, they would lose track of each other completely. So he made a few moves with the elephants.

The embers collapsed in a small shower of sparks. Hardy put an arm up against the mantel, rested his head on it. After a minute, he found himself on the ottoman, his elbows on his knees, staring blankly into the last of the glow.

"I thought I heard the door." Frannie was wrapped in a white turkish towel bathrobe they'd bought in Napa on their last getaway weekend almost a year before. She came across to where he made a space for her, squeezed in next to him, rubbed her hand over his back.

"What are you doing up?" he asked.

"Moses and Susan only left a few minutes ago," she said. "I was awake."

"Moses and Susan? What were they doing here?"

"And Colleen and Holly. Evidently you told him we'd baby-sit for them tonight so they could go out." It was half a question. "Which was a nice thing for them, but next time you might want to let me know. Especially if you're not going to be here."

He hung his head, shook it wearily. "What can I say? I'm an idiot. I'm sorry."

"Sorry's good." Her hand kept moving across his back. She wasn't mad, though perhaps would prefer if he could remember commitments he'd made that involved her. "But it's all right," she continued. "It went fine. It was lucky I was home, that's all. Abe called, by the way. And some woman named Rebecca, who said it might be important."

Earlier in the day, he might have felt some spark of interest. At the moment, it only felt like more work. "She's a nurse at Portola I talked with today. This new case." He was still furious that Glitsky had gone behind his back to inter-

212

view his client. He tried to keep the anger out of his voice. "What did Abe want?"

"He said you'd know."

Hardy gave it a second. "He lied." Did he want to get into a long explanation? But her hand felt good on him. They were together. He leaned slightly into her. "He took a statement from my client after I told him not to. Full court press, guns blazing. Maybe he found out my guy didn't do it and wants to say he's sorry. But I doubt it."

"He must think your client did something." This was always an issue. Since Hardy had begun working as a defense attorney, she remained uncomfortable with the fact that her husband consorted not only with people accused of crimes, but often with those who had actually committed them. When the charge was something like a DUI or some kind of thievery or fraud, it wasn't so bad. But when it was murder, Frannie tended to worry on the not unreasonable theory that anyone who had killed once might get angry with somebody else — say, their attorney — and do it again. "So did your client do it after all?"

"He says not," Hardy said simply. "But who doesn't?"

"And you believe him?"

"Always." He faced her. "My problem is Abe. I've got no idea what he's doing."

"That's probably what he called about. To explain."

"I'm sure." Not, Hardy thought. He glanced at his watch. "I'm tempted to call him right now and wake up his sorry ass." He sighed wearily. "What was the other call? Rebecca? The nurse? She said it might be important?"

He could see that Frannie hated to admit it again — she'd already done her duty by telling him once. Clearly, she hoped he'd forget. But no. Hardy didn't forget much about his work — only baby-sitting deals he'd made with relatives. It was Frannie's turn to sigh. "She said no matter what time it was."

"I guess that would include now, huh?"

"I thought you might want to come to bed sometime."

"I'll try to keep it short."

He felt something go out of her. "I left her number by the phone," she said, standing up. "Have you had anything at all to eat?"

He shook his head. "My client's finally started to figure out he's in trouble, but it was all I could do to get him to talk to me on the phone. It was originally supposed to be his night for his kids. He thought the thing with Glitsky was going to take like a half hour. I asked him when he thought we could get a few minutes, maybe talk about some things so I didn't have to find them all out from third parties. So he says he doesn't know — he's got his kids this weekend, too. He works a million hours a day. But I had him with me on the phone. There wasn't going to be any other time. So I told him to call his ex-wife, change his plans, tell her not tonight. We had to talk."

Frannie was just looking down at him. She'd crossed her arms over her chest, her body language expressing it all — disappointment, disapproval. Sadness. "There's leftover spaghetti in the refrigerator," she said.

"I don't know if it's anything," Rebecca Simms said.

"That's all right," Hardy said. "If it's keeping you up, it's probably worth talking about." He sat at his dining room table, his yellow legal pad in front of him, the portable phone at his ear. He'd poured himself a glass of orange juice and drank half of it off in a gulp. "Did you remember something about Dr. Kensing?"

"No, not exactly that. Not that at all, really."

Hardy waited.

"I've been thinking about how I should say this, since I don't really know anything specific, not for sure. I just went back on the floor after we talked and I guess the whole discussion we had — you know? The general conditions here?"

"Sure. I remember."

The line hummed empty for another few seconds. Then Rebecca blurted it out. "The thing is, everybody on the staff knows something is really wrong here. The nurses, I mean. Probably some of the doctors, too. But nobody really talks about it. It's more a feeling, like a ghost is hovering over the place or something."

Hardy closed his heavy eyes. She sounded like she meant it literally. Terrific, he thought. The woman he picked at random in the hospital cafeteria, although she'd seemed like an intelligent person by the light of day, was in fact a nut case and now she had his home phone number.

215

Frannie was right — he shouldn't have it on his business card.

"Well." Hardy was ready to end the conversation. "I don't know if a feeling —"

"No, no." She cut him off. "That's not it. It's . . . what I'm saying is that people are dying here."

Hardy had picked up his juice glass and now he put it down. His fatigue was suddenly gone. "What do you mean, people?"

"Patients. People who shouldn't die."

"What kind of patients?"

"Mostly old, I think. Mostly in the ICU."

"But you're not sure?"

"No, not a hundred percent." He could hear the exasperation in her voice. "That's what I said at the beginning. I'm not sure."

"Okay," he said, hoping to keep her moving along this trail. "That's all right. I'm interested."

"But nobody's really sure of anything, or saying if they are . . ."

"Right. But I'm more interested in general conditions there anyway. It doesn't have to be specific — the low morale and so on . . ."

"Well, all of that's true, too, the tight money, the job insecurity, all that. But really, when we were talking I couldn't put my finger on exactly what it was, until tonight when I got home and it hit me . . ."

"What did, though?" This was pulling teeth, but they seemed to be loosening.

She paused a moment. "It sounds stupid to even say."

"Can you try? I won't think it's stupid, no matter what. Promise."

A longer pause. "Well," she said, "if people keep dying when they shouldn't . . ."

Hardy finished for her. "Maybe somebody's killing them."

"Yes." The relief in her voice was palpable. "That's what I was trying to get at. That's what it is."

"Do you have any idea who it might be?"

"No. Well, maybe, I don't know. As I said, I don't even know if it's true. But the first one I heard about was maybe a year ago, a man had had a stroke, but it was one of those situations, you know, where the family was hoping he'd recover, the prognosis was okay if he came out of his coma, and they didn't want to pull the plug. So they were waiting. Everybody thought he'd be long term, but then two days into it, he suddenly died."

"Okay," Hardy said. "But doesn't that happen?"

"Sometimes. Sure."

"It doesn't necessarily mean somebody killed him."

"No, of course not." She went silent again for a long beat. "If it was that one man, everybody would have probably forgotten about it by now. But he was something like the third patient to die in as many months. So one of the ICU nurses mentioned it in the nurses' lounge. There's this one weird little guy who works up there, a nurse actually. Rajan Bhutan is his name. He was on duty for all of them."

"Somebody thinks he might be killing patients?"

217

"No, not really. I don't even know why I mentioned that. I mean, nobody thought about it at the time, but then . . . it kept happening."

"It kept happening," Hardy repeated. "How often?"

"I don't know. I really don't know. But often enough." He heard her breathe out heavily, the load off.

But Hardy put another one right on. "Do you know if anyone's gone to the police about this? About this man Rajan?"

"No. I don't know. If someone had, wouldn't we have heard?"

"You'd think so."

"And . . ." She chopped off the thought.

And Hardy jumped on it. "What?"

"Nothing." A pause. "Really, nothing."

"Rebecca, please. You were going to say something."

The decision took a while. "Well . . . let's just say that it would be hard to keep working if anybody went to the police or the newspaper or anything. I mean, look at Dr. Kensing and Baby Emily. Imagine if it got out that Portola was killing its patients. There's a culture there that's" — she sought the word — "self-protective, I guess."

"Most cultures are," he said. "But I don't know if I can believe it about this. You're saying the administration wouldn't want to know if one of their staff is killing patients?"

"Oh, they'd want to know, all right. They just wouldn't want anybody else to know. It's like bad doctors."

"What's like bad doctors?"

A little laugh. "Well, basically, there are none."

"What does that mean?"

"It means every doctor on the staff is great until they're transferred to, say, Illinois. They get great references, maybe even a raise and moving expenses. Why? Because there are no bad doctors."

"And no whistle-blowers."

This was a sobering statement, and Rebecca Simms reacted to it. Her voice went hollow, nearly inaudible. "And I'm not being one now, Mr. Hardy. I've got three children and my husband and they all need me to keep this job. I don't know anything for certain. I just thought it might help you to know the general conditions, as you called them. We know Mr. Markham was killed, don't we? Maybe that changes something."

"Maybe somebody could go to the police."

"I don't think that's going to happen. I mean, what would they say?"

"They'd say what you just said to me."

"But it's all so nebulous. There isn't any . . . there's no real proof. . . ."

"There would be bodies." Hardy refuted her in his calmest voice. "They could autopsy the bodies. Haven't they done postmortems anyway? At least on one or two of them?"

"I don't know. I don't think the families usually . . ." She trailed off, repeated that she just didn't know. "Anyway, you're not part of this. I mean here at the hospital. Maybe you can do something."

Hardy realized that this was as good as it was going to get, at least for tonight. "Maybe I can," he said. "I'll try, anyway." He thanked Rebecca for the call. "You were right. It was important. And I don't think there's really any reason for you to be afraid. I'll keep you out of whatever I do. You were brave to call me."

He heard the gratitude in her voice. "Thank you," she said. "You're a good man. I'm sorry it was so late."

When he hung up, he remained at the table, unmoving, for a long while. He hadn't been able to keep the phone call very short after all, and no doubt Frannie was by now asleep. Even if she wasn't, the mood would have passed, had already passed by the time she went upstairs. Rebecca Simms had called him a good man, but he wasn't feeling much like one at the moment.

Eventually, he finished his juice, got up, and took the glass into the kitchen, where he rinsed it in the sink. He was drying it when he heard a recognizable something behind him. He turned to see his son, one foot resting on the other one, squinting at him in the doorway. "Hey, bud," he said quietly. "Whatcha doin'?"

Vincent wasn't quite a teenager yet, but most of the little boy in him was recently gone. Now his hair was buzzed short and his ears stuck out, while the frame that had tended to a round softness had become lanky, nearly skinny. "I couldn't get to sleep."

Hardy came over, went down to him. "You haven't been asleep yet all night?"

220

The boy sat on his knee, threw an arm around his neck. "No. I'm having bad dreams."

"What about?"

"Where you keep disappearing. We're all in this forest and you're just going off for a minute to do something, and then we wait and wait until Mom says she's going to go looking for you, but we beg her not to go because then she won't come back, either, but then she goes and the Beck and I are left there, and we start calling after her, which is when I wake up."

Hardy didn't have to use much imagination to come up with the underpinnings of this scenario, although Vincent certainly wasn't using it as a guilt trip. He hoped he wasn't that sophisticated, yet. If it was his sister, Hardy wouldn't have been so sure. He pulled him closer, which at this time of night his son would still accept. "Well, I'm here," he said comfortingly, "and if you woke up, that means you were asleep, doesn't it? Which means you could get to sleep after all, couldn't you?" The lawyer, arguing, making his point.

"I guess so," Vincent said.

"Come on, I'll tuck you back in."

But Vincent's bed, in the room behind the kitchen, hadn't been slept in at all. He pointed to the back of the house, Hardy's old office. "I'm in the Beck's room. Mom said it was okay."

They got to the connecting door and Hardy noted the heap of blankets next to his daughter's bed. "Why are you in here?" Hardy thinking it was no wonder his son wasn't sleeping soundly on the hardwood floor.

"You know the Beck. She gets scared," Vincent whispered.

Hardy knew. Fanned by her school's various "awareness" programs, Rebecca's profound and random fears — about death, teen suicide, stranger abduction, AIDS, drug addiction, and so many more — had reached crisis proportions about a year before. "I thought we'd worked most of those out. What's she still afraid of?"

"Just the dark, mostly. And being alone sometimes." Interpreting his father's heavy sigh, Vincent hastened to add, protecting her, "It's not every night. She's way better than she was."

"Good. I thought so. Do you have a futon or anything to lay on under those blankets?"

"No. I sleep good just on the floor."

"I see that," Hardy said. "Except for the bad dreams and being awake at twelve thirty." But Hardy spoke in a conspiratorial, not critical, tone. The two guys in the house had their own relationship — they had to stick together. "Let's get you something, though, okay?"

So they grabbed cushions from the chairs in Vincent's room and put them on the floor. As he got settled, Hardy pulled the blankets over him. "You could probably get in your own bed now and the Beck wouldn't notice."

But he shook his head, happy to be important. "That's okay. She needs me here sometimes. Girls do, you know, Dad."

Hardy rubbed his hand over his son's buzz cut. Vincent wasn't meaning to twist the knife in his heart — he was honing his little man chops, which hopefully someday he would put to better use than his father did. "I know," Hardy said. His hand rubbed the bristly head again. "Are we still not kissing each other good night?" This nightly ritual had ended only a couple of months before, just after Christmas, but occasionally when Vincent's guard was down, or nobody else in the family was around, he'd forget that it wasn't cool to kiss Dad anymore. Tonight Hardy got lucky, and figuring it was going to have to be one of the very last times, held onto the hug an extra millisecond. "Okay, get some sleep, Vin."

"I will now. Thanks, Dad."

"You're welcome."

"Want to hear a joke?"

Hardy, halfway to his feet, summoned his last unit of patience. "One," he said.

"What do you get when you turn an elephant into a cat?"

"I don't know."

"No, you've got to try."

"Okay, I'm trying. Watch. My eyes are closed." He silently counted to three. "Okay, I give up. What?"

"You really don't know? An elephant into a cat? Think."

"Vin . . ." He stood up.

"A cat," Vincent said. "You turn an elephant into a cat, you get a cat. Get it?"

"Good one," Hardy said. "You ought to tell it to Uncle Abe. He'd love it."

For reasons that eluded him, he stalked the house front to back several times, rearranged the elephants yet again. Then he sat for a while in

223

the living room, until he was fairly certain that Vincent had dozed off. He came all the way into the Beck's room again, leaning down over the cushions and then the bed to make out the dim outlines of his children's faces, calm and peaceful now in sleep.

He eventually, finally, made it up to the master bedroom. There he double-checked the alarm to find that it was still — again? — set for 4:30. He would have to issue a home edict making his alarm clock off limits except for him and Frannie. He moved it ahead two hours.

In bed, with his wife breathing regularly beside him, he wondered briefly about all the subliminal communication going on in his house, among his family. He and Frannie with the elephants, the Beck's now unspoken but still clearly upsetting fears, Vincent's last joke an obvious attempt to keep his father in the room another few seconds, although he would never simply ask. The dynamic, suddenly, seemed to have shifted and Hardy, at least, felt adrift, moving among the rest of them with a kind of gravitational connection, but nothing really solid, holding them together.

He lay awake now, echoes of his son, unable to sleep despite his exhaustion. His memory had dredged up a contradiction that now gnawed at him. Earlier in the day, Rebecca Simms had derided the idea that someone had killed Tim Markham in the hospital. It was ridiculous, she'd said. It must have been an accident.

Or he'd simply just died, which, she'd reminded him, "people do." But by tonight, such

224

deaths — unexplained possible homicides — had become common, a regular feature during the past year or more at Portola. He wanted to call her back and clarify her position — maybe he'd broken through the culture barrier at the hospital where criticism wasn't tolerated and then forced her to consider the unthinkable with Markham, and it had awakened other ghosts.

But the facts of the deaths alone — if they were facts, if they could be proven — were staggering in their implications, and not just for his client, although Kensing was going to be in the middle of whatever transpired. For Hardy, it would mean more hours, greater commitment, escalated involvement; less time with his wife, less connection with his children, less interest in the daily rhythms of his home.

It also meant that he was truly putting himself in harm's way. If someone, whether it was this Rajan Bhutan or someone else at Portola, had in fact killed again and again and if Hardy was going to be involved in exposing those crimes, then he was going to be in that person's sights.

He turned again onto his side, and might even have drifted off into a semblance of a dream state, where he was swimming in turbulent waters with some of Pico's sharks circling, snapping at him, closing in. Then something — some settling of his house, a random noise outside — sent a surge of adrenaline through him and he threw his covers off and sat bolt upright in bed. His breath came in ragged surges.

It woke Frannie up. "Dismas, are you all right? What time is it?"

225

"I'm okay. I'm okay." But he really wasn't. That largely unacknowledged yet pervasive fear that Rebecca Simms had described at Portola seemed to be stalking him, as well. Even the familiar darkness in his own bedroom felt somehow sinister, as though something terrible lurked hidden just at the edge of it.

He tried to laugh off the imaginings for what he told himself they were — irrational terrors in the wake of a nightmare. But they held their grip. Finally, feeling foolish, he switched on his bedlight for a moment.

Nothing, of course. Nothing.

Still, it took a long while before his breathing became normal. Eventually, he let himself back down and pulled the covers over him. After a minute, he turned and settled spoon fashion against his wife.

Before his brain could start running again, sleep mercifully claimed him.

16

Kensing finished his morning rounds at Portola's ICU and walked out to the nurses' station. Waiting for him there was the tall and thin figure of Portola's administrator, Michael Andreotti, who wanted a private word with him. They walked silently together down one long hallway, then took the elevator to the ground floor, where Andreotti led the way into an empty conference room next to his own office in the admin wing, and then closed the door behind them.

By this time, Kensing had a good idea of what was coming, but he asked anyway. "So what's this about?"

There was no love lost between the two men, and the administrator wasted no time on niceties. "I'm afraid that the board has decided to place you on leave for the time being."

"I don't think so. They can't do that. I've got a contract."

Andreotti more or less expected this response. He had the paperwork on him, and he handed over the letter. "It's not my decision, Doctor. As I said, the board has decided."

Kensing snorted derisively. "The board. You mean Ross. Finally seeing his chance."

Andreotti felt no need to respond.

"What's his excuse this time?"

"It's clearly explained in the letter, but there seem to be too many questions involving you related to Mr. Markham's death."

"That's bullshit. I didn't have anything to do with that."

Andreotti's mouth turned down at Kensing's unfortunate use of profanity. "That's not the board's point. There is the appearance." Andreotti was in bureaucrat mode. He might as well have been a mannequin. He was only there to deliver the letter and the message, and to see that the board's will was implemented.

"What appearance? There's no appearance."

Andreotti spread his hands. "It's really out of my control, Doctor. If you want to appeal the decision, I suggest you call Dr. Ross. In the meantime, you're not to practice either here or at the clinic."

"What about my patients? I've got to see them."

"We've scheduled other physicians to cover your caseload."

"Starting when?"

"Immediately, I'm afraid."

"You're afraid. I bet you are." Kensing's temper flared for an instant. "You ought to be."

Andreotti backed up a step. "Are you threatening me?"

Kensing was tempted to run with it, put some real fear into this stooge, but starting with Glitsky's visit last night, he was beginning to get a sense of how bad things could really get with this murder investigation, this suspicion over him. Some reserve of self-protectiveness kicked in. "This is wrong," was all he said. Glancing down at the papers in his hand, he turned on his heel and walked out.

It wasn't yet 9:00 in the morning. The storm had finally blown over. The sky was washed clean, deep blue and cloudless.

Kensing was back at his home, in the living room of his condominium. He moved forward and forced open one of the windows, letting in some fresh air. Then he walked back to his kitchen, where Glitsky had skewered him last night. The lieutenant's teacup was still in the sink. It was one of a set he'd inherited from his parents after his dad had died, and now he abstactedly turned on the water to wash it, then lifted the dainty thing carefully. There was a window over the sink, as well, and Kensing simply stopped all movement suddenly, staring out over the western edge of the city, seeing none of it.

The cup exploded in his hand, shattering from the force of his grip.

He looked down in a cold, distracted fury. The blood where the shards had cut him ran over his hand and pooled in the white porcelain saucer amid the broken fragments in the bottom of the sink.

Jeff Elliot had his home number from the Baby Emily days, and called him twenty minutes later. He'd been hounding Parnassus for stories lately, and he'd heard the news about the administrative leave this morning, probably not too long after Kensing had gotten it himself. Elliot offered to let him tell his side to a sympathetic reporter who was covering the whole story soup to nuts. He could come right by if Kensing could spare an hour or so.

When he arrived, Elliot wheeled himself into the kitchen. He'd been here before during Baby Emily, and knew his way around. After he sat, his first comment was about the several Band-Aids on Kensing's hand.

"I was trying to slash my wrists in despair. I guess I aimed wrong." The doctor laughed perfunctorily and offered an explanation. "Don't pick up a butcher knife by the blade. You'd think I'd have learned that by now somewhere along the way." Deftly, he changed the subject. "Hey, I loved your article on Ross, by the way. You captured him perfectly."

Elliot nodded in acknowledgment. "What motivated that guy to become a doctor in the first place I'll never know. He seems to care about patients like the lumber companies care about the rain forests." But then he got down to business. "So they finally laid you off?"

Eventually, they got around to personalities at Parnassus, the players. Elliot said he'd been talking a lot with Tim Markham's executive assistant, a bitter, apparently soon-to-be-jobless young man named Brendan Driscoll.

"Sure, I know Brendan. Everybody knows Brendan."

"Apparently he knows you, too. You had heated words in the hospital?"

230

Kensing shrugged. "He wouldn't leave the ICU when Markham was there. I had to kick him out. He wasn't very happy about it."

"Why was he even there if he's just a secretary?"

"Bite your tongue, Jeff. Brendan's an executive assistant and don't you forget it."

"So what's his story? Why's he so down on you?"

"It must be a virus that's going around. I'm surprised you haven't caught it. But the real answer is that Brendan's one of those hyperefficient secretaries, that's all. His job is his whole life. He'd been with Markham since before he came on with Parnassus. Anyway, he scheduled every aspect of Markham's life. Including Ann, although let's leave that off the record."

"Your wife, Ann?"

He nodded. "*She* . . . now she really doesn't like him. But Brendan's one of those people who identifies so completely with their boss that they really come to believe they can do no wrong themselves. I'd take him and anything he says with a grain of salt."

"Well, I did for my purposes. But he could hurt you. He wants everybody to know how close Markham was to firing you, how you were true enemies."

"Well, he's half-right there," Kensing replied. "We didn't get along. But he wasn't going to fire me. In fact, if anything, he was on my side. He knew what he'd done to me with Ann. If he fires me, what's it going to look like? I'd sue him and the company for a billion dollars, and I'd win. And he knew it."

"So what were all the reprimand letters about?"

A shrug. "Markham covering his ass with the board, that's all. He's trying to keep costs down, get those uppity doctors like me in line, but they just won't listen. Especially me, I'm afraid. I've got a bad attitude. I'm not a team player. But Tim couldn't touch me."

"But that's changed now? With Ross at the helm?"

Kensing's expression grew more serious. "Ross is a big problem. In fact, I should tell my lawyer there's a good argument to be made that killing Markham was the worst thing I could do if I wanted to keep my job. The truth is that Markham was the only thing that stood between me and Ross. Now he's gone. If I listen real carefully, I can even now hear the ice beginning to crack under me."

There was the faint sound of a key turning in a lock, and a door slammed behind them. Kensing was halfway to standing up when they heard a woman's voice echoing out of the hallway. "Somebody could sure use a good fuck about now. Oh!"

A mid-thirties Modigliani woman with frizzy hair was standing in the entrance to the kitchen. Seeing Elliot at the table, she brought her hand to her mouth in a cliché of surprise. "Oh shit." She turned to Kensing with a "what can you do" look and threw her hands up theatrically.

"Well, this might be a good time for introductions." Kensing was up now, and moving toward the woman. "Judith, this is Jeff Elliot, from the *Chronicle*. Jeff, meet Judith Cohn."

"Sorry," she said to the room. "I'll just sink through the floor now."

"I'll get over it," Elliot said. "Occasionally I could use one myself."

It turned out that Cohn wasn't Ross's biggest fan, either.

"That son of a bitch. He can't just lay you off," she said, fuming. "You should've just stayed there working."

Kensing was standing by the sink again and he shook his head. "Andreotti had a call in to security. They showed every inclination to escort me out if I didn't want to go alone."

Cohn stood up in the kitchen, walked to its entrance, slapped the wall, and turned back to face the men. "Those fucking idiots! They can't —"

Elliot suddenly snapped his fingers and interrupted her. "Judith Cohn? You're *the* Judith Cohn?"

She stopped, her eyes glaring in anger and caution. "I must be, I guess. Is there another one?"

But Elliot didn't shrink. As a reporter, he was used to asking questions that made people uncomfortable. "You're Judith Cohn from the Lopez case?"

"That's me," she answered in cold fury. "Infamously bad diagnostician. Perhaps child killer."

Kensing came forward. "Judith," he said with sympathy. "Come on."

Suddenly, the spunk seemed to go out of her. She came back to the kitchen table, pulled out a chair, and sat on it. "That's not going to go away, is it? And I guess you're right, maybe it shouldn't."

"It wasn't you," Kensing said. "It wasn't your fault."

"Whoa up," Elliot said. "Wait a minute!" He was leaning back in his wheelchair, focusing on first one of the doctors, then the other. Finally he settled on Cohn. "Look, I'm sorry, your name just clicked. I wasn't trying to be accusatory."

Cohn's face was hard and bitter. "But the name clicks, doesn't it?"

"It wasn't that long ago," Elliot said apologetically. "I'm a newspaperman. I remember names." He scratched at his beard. "And the kid's name was Ramiro, right?"

"We're not opening this can of worms again, Jeff. The topic's not on the table."

But Cohn raised her hand to stop him. "It's all right, Eric. It's past now."

"Not so long past. Markham sure wasn't over it."

"He is now." Cohn obviously took some comfort in the thought. "Actually, this might be a good time to tell somebody the facts." She turned to Elliot. "You know the basic story, right? This kid goes to urgent care with his mom. He's got a fever, sore throat, funky-looking cut on his lip."

Elliot nodded, recalling. "Some other doc had seen him a couple of days before and told him he had a virus."

234

Kensing spoke up. "Right. So this night, Judith is at the clinic, swamped. Overwhelmed, really. She sees Ramiro and sends him home with some amoxicillin and Tylenol."

"And two days later," Elliot concluded, "he's in the ICU with the flesh-eating disease."

Kensing nodded. "Necrotizing fasciitis."

Elliot remembered it all clearly now. The flesh-eating disease was always news, and when there was a local angle, it tended to get everybody worked up. So he'd heard of it, and had even heard the rumors about Judith Cohn's — among many others' — alleged part in the tragedy. The official story didn't include her by name, however, and Elliot's own follow-up inquiries at the hospital were met with what he'd come to expect — the typically evasive Parnassus administrative fandango that left all doctors infallible, all administrative decisions without flaw. He'd never gone to press because he'd never felt he had it exactly right.

But Cohn was telling him now in a voice heavy with regret. "They're right. I should have recognized it."

Kensing shrugged. "Maybe the first doc who saw him could have, too. But neither of your diagnoses are what killed him."

"What do you mean, Eric?" Elliot asked.

"I mean that at every step in the treatment, Parnassus took too long deciding what they could afford to do to save him. Ramiro didn't have the right insurance. There was a glitch on one of the forms in his file. Was this test covered? Was the oxygen covered? Who was going to

235

pay?" He angrily shook his head. "Long story short, they were counting pennies all the way, and it compromised his care. Fatally."

Cohn's eyes had gone glassy, the memory still painful to her. Elliot asked her gently, "You didn't treat him at all after his initial visit to the clinic?"

"No. I never saw him again. Except at his funeral."

Kensing took it up. "But did that stop Markham from singling her out within the physicians' group as the primary point of failed care?"

"That's the impression I got," Elliot admitted. "But nobody would go on the record."

"Everybody got that impression," Kensing said. "Of course, what it really was, was Markham looking for a scapegoat. He himself had been the point man for the lame explanations of what we were not doing and why. Judith was his way to take the heat off him. Fortunately, the physicians' group went to bat for her."

"At least enough so I wouldn't lose my job," she added with real bitterness. "The only consolation is that I saw Luz — the mother? — at the funeral. She seemed to understand. She didn't blame me. She blamed Markham."

"Markham?" Elliot asked. "How did she know Markham even existed?"

Cohn obviously thought it was a good question. "You remember that puff piece they did on him in *San Francisco* magazine? It was lying out everywhere in the system that that poor woman went with her sick boy. Markham's happy face and how he cared so deeply for his patients. She still had the cover with her at the funeral. She showed me."

"And you want to know the supreme irony there?" Kensing asked. "It wasn't Markham either. In fact, they'd all been Ross's decisions. Ross is the chief medical director. He makes those calls. The truth is that Ross lost that kid single-handedly, and nobody seems to have a clue."

A silence settled. After a minute, Elliot spoke. "Do you live here, Judith?"

"She stays over sometimes," Kensing answered quickly, then added, "Why?"

"I was wondering if she was here last Tuesday morning."

It was Judith's turn to ask. "Why?"

Elliot felt he had to tell them that in talking with the hospital staff, checking the records, he had discovered that Eric had been well over an hour late for work on the morning Markham had been hit.

Kensing closed his eyes, squeezed his temples with one hand, looked across at Elliot. "I don't even remember that. Was I? And what would it mean if I was?"

"It would mean you didn't have an alibi for the time of the hit-and-run accident." Elliot turned to Judith. "And you could corroborate the time he left for work."

"That's the most ridiculous thing I've ever heard!" she said. "Now someone thinks Eric drove the hit-and-run car, too?"

"No one necessarily thinks it," Elliot said. "I've just heard the question, that's all."

"What idiots," Judith said.

"Well, idiots or no," Elliot said, "you ought to appreciate what other people might be saying."

"I think I'm getting a feel for it," Eric answered wearily.

"Tuesday night I was here," Judith said. "Does that help?"

"Yeah," Kensing said, "but that was midnight." He turned to Jeff. "I stopped by the Markhams'. Judith was asleep when I got home."

Cohn gave the subject a minute's more reflection, then shook her head. "Come on. You're in the hospital, working your normal job, which means you're not some criminal. You're a regular person with a decent career. Suddenly an accident victim comes in and there's a good chance he's going to die. Now it turns out that *you know this person.* Not only that, but he's somebody you hate enough to want to kill. *To kill!* And just like that he's delivered to you and you decide on the spur of the moment to take this tremendous and probably unnecessary risk and make sure he dies where they might be able to trace it back to you." Judith sat straight up, dripping ridicule. "Please."

"Except that from what I hear, that's essentially what happened," Elliot said soberly.

Hardy's morning had been awful. He'd slept fitfully with Rebecca Simms's news percolating somewhere in his unconscious. Unknown dead people featured in several half-remembered dreams, and he was up and out of bed before 6:00. After the kids were off at school, damned if he'd call Glitsky for the company. He'd walked briskly alone for an hour, to the beach and back, but he hadn't warmed up first so the exercise had left him feeling tight and old. One of Freeman's clients had parked in his space under the building, and by the time he went to get his car back from where he'd parked it on the street, he'd gotten a ticket. Finally, just before lunchtime, after a morning of reviewing bills and other mail he'd ignored for the past week, and before he left the office to go to the *Chronicle* building, he placed a call to homicide when he was fairly sure the lieutenant would be at lunch. And sure enough — his first stroke of luck the whole day — Glitsky had been out.

Now he sat on a low filing cabinet in the cubicle that was Elliot's office on the ground floor of the *Chronicle* building. His frustration with Kensing surfaced in an overformal tone. "I confess to being somewhat surprised to learn at this late date that he has a girlfriend. We talked last night on the phone for hours. I asked him to tell me everything important about his life he could think of, and he never mentioned her."

"Judith," Elliot said. "Really pretty. But maybe it's not an important relationship. Maybe it's one of those modern things where they just have incredible sex every couple of hours, but otherwise don't even like each other. Wouldn't that be horrible?"

"Awful." Hardy remained somewhat distracted. "Do you know when they got together?"

"No. Why?"

"Because it'd be nice to know if she was in the

239

picture while he and Ann were still married. Maybe his wife leaving didn't break his heart after all."

"You should ask him."

"I will, but it'd be swell if he volunteered some of this stuff. I didn't even know he was the leak on Baby Emily."

"Was he?" Jeff's open face was the picture of innocence.

But Hardy hadn't stopped by the *Chronicle* to talk about his client. He wanted to know if Elliot had heard any rumors about a rash of unexplained and unexpected deaths at Portola.

"No." But the thought of it, of the story in it, lit up the reporter's eyes. "How big a rash?"

"I don't really know. My source wasn't sure of the details, or really even of the bare facts. But she seemed pretty levelheaded, and she was definitely scared."

"So what did she say?"

Hardy gave him a fairly accurate recounting of his talk with Rebecca Simms. About halfway through, Elliot pulled a pad around and began taking a few notes. When Hardy had finished, Elliot said he'd like to talk to her.

"I can ask her," Hardy replied, "but I got the feeling that even talking to me made her nervous. Evidently the administration at Portola likes to keep a tight lid on their internal affairs. People who talk become unemployed pretty quick."

"Okay, so help me. Where do I look?"

They both came up with it at the same time. "Kensing."

Jeff closed the door to his cubicle and put on the speakerphone. Kensing told him that yes, Judith was still there, but she'd worked the night shift at the clinic and had gone in to bed. He was just hanging out, he said, windows open, reading a book. It was the first one he'd read in maybe a year. Max Byrd's *Grant*. Fantastic. The best first sentence he could remember reading anywhere. " 'Start with his horrible mother.' Isn't that great?"

Elliot agreed that it was a fine line. But he'd called because Dismas Hardy was here with him in his office and they wanted to ask him about something. When Hardy had finished with Rebecca Simms's story of unexplained deaths at Portola, Kensing was silent long enough for Elliot to ask him if he was still there.

"Yeah. I'm thinking." Then, "I can't say the idea hasn't crossed my mind. But people are *always* dying in the ICU. I mean, they don't get in there until they're critical to begin with. So what you're asking, I take it, is whether people died who shouldn't have died, right? Are we off the record here, Jeff? I don't need any more bad press right now."

"Okay. Sure." Jeff wasn't crazy about agreeing, but under the circumstances there was nothing else he could do.

"While we're being formal," and Hardy no longer had any intention of being anything but formal in his relations with this client, "this conversation isn't privileged, either. Just so you know."

"All right. So what are you suggesting? Some

kind of rampant malpractice? Or something more serious."

"I'm not suggesting anything," Hardy said. "I'm asking if anything has struck you."

"Well, I'd be surprised if we've filed many eight-oh-fives. I'll go that far."

"What are those?" Hardy asked.

"Reports to the state medical board. When a doctor screws up seriously enough for the administration to suspend his clinical privileges for more than thirty days, then the hospital's supposed to file an eight-oh-five with the state. They're also supposed to forward it to the National Practitioner Data Bank, which is federal — and never goes away. You get listed in the data bank, your career is toast."

"So why don't these things get turned in?" Hardy asked.

"You're a lawyer and you're asking me that? You're a doctor and some hospital writes you up, what do you do? You sue the bastards, of course. You're a patient who finds out your hospital hired a bad doc, you sue the hospital. Everybody sues everybody."

Elliot couldn't resist. "I always assumed you lawyers loved that part," he said to Hardy.

But Hardy was hearing something else altogether. "Are you telling me, Eric, that Portola's got these doctors, *and knows it,* and they're not filing these reports?"

"Let me answer that by saying that we have people on the staff whom I would not personally choose as my own physician."

"So what really happens when some doctor

242

messes up?" Hardy asked.

"Couple of things. First, you notice I mentioned the magic thirty-day suspension from clinical privileges. So instead you get grounded for twenty-nine days. Ergo no eight-oh-five, right? You're within the guidelines. And no national database."

"Are there any Portola doctors on this database?" Jeff was always chasing the story. "How can I find out?"

"You can't." Kensing's voice was firm. "The public can't get access to it, for obvious reasons. Although prospective employers can. In any event, there's another way reporting doesn't happen. It's probably more common."

"And what's that?" Hardy asked.

"Well, the eight-oh-fives are based on peer reviews."

"Other doctors," Elliot said.

"Right. And there's some feeling among doctors, especially now at Portola, that we're all in this shit storm together, so we better protect one another. If one of our colleagues isn't making the right medical decisions, okay, you go have an informal discussion, mention the standard of care we all strive for. But we're all under this intense financial pressure, we're all working too hard all the time, the bottom line is we're not ratting one another out."

"Never?" Hardy asked.

"Maybe with some egregious lapse — I'm talking inexcusably gross fatal error — and maybe even more than one. But anything less, you're not going to get a peer review at Portola that recommends an eight-oh-five. Most hospitals in the country, I'd bet it's close to the same story."

In the cubicle, Elliot and Hardy looked at each other. "What about other causes of death?" Hardy asked. "Maybe intentional deaths?"

This gave Kensing pause. "What do you mean, intentional?"

"Maybe pulling the plug early, something like that." Hardy considered, then added, "Maybe something like this potassium."

"You're talking murder, aren't you?" No answer was called for. "Do I think that's been going on at Portola?"

"Do you?" Hardy asked.

"Only in my most paranoid moments."

Elliot jumped in. "Do you have many of those, Eric?"

Kensing sighed audibly. "There was another patient in the ICU at the same time as Markham. Did you both know that?"

"I thought there were several," Hardy said.

"That's true. What I meant was that there was another patient who died."

"Who was that?" Hardy's every instinct knew that he was on to something, and that this was part of it.

"His name was James Lector. Seventy-one, never smoked. He'd developed some complications after open-heart surgery and we had him on life support for a couple of weeks, but he was off that and responding to treatment. His vital signs had been improving. I was thinking of moving him out in a few days."

"And he died?" Hardy said.

244

"Just like that. No reason I could see. Just . . . stopped."

"I would never reveal a source," Elliot said. "I'd take your name to my grave."

Hardy ignored him. "So besides this man Lector," he asked, "how many would you estimate? Deaths you couldn't explain?"

"Actually, I started keeping track last November. This little log book I have."

They waited.

He continued. "I thought I'd go back and see if there was a pattern. Maybe something to get them off my back."

Elliot asked him why he started keeping track. "I don't know exactly. I guess now that you ask, I wanted my own ammunition for when they finally got around to firing me. I didn't think anybody was killing patients on purpose, but we were losing patients we shouldn't have — like the Lopez boy, Jeff. So if fiscal policies were affecting medical care, I wanted to come back at them with that. I more or less just thought the place was going to shit and I wanted some record of specifics."

This time, the silence hung for a while. Finally, Hardy asked, "How many, Eric?"

"Not including Tuesday," Kensing said. "Eleven."

17

Whatever the special at Lou the Greek's would turn out to be today, Hardy didn't have a taste for it. He was hoping he could just stick his head through the door and survey the room to see if it contained Wes Farrell.

But no such luck.

Smack in the middle of the lunch hour, the place was wall to wall, three deep ordering drinks. The law continued to be thirst-making work, Hardy noted. He pushed himself into the crowd, got through the crush by the bar, and made a quick tour of the room, exchanging the occasional pleasantry with a familiar face, but mostly moving. If Farrell wasn't here, he didn't want to be, either. Not least because he didn't want to run into Glitsky.

He was still pissed off.

Hardy's call to Farrell's part-time secretary had luckily caught her at her desk and she'd told him her boss was scheduled to be in court all day. She wasn't sure if it was muni, superior, or federal, but she'd guess muni, which meant the Hall of Justice. So Hardy's hunch was lunch at the Greek's, and it turned out he was right. Wes had scored a back booth, invisible from the front door. He shared it with a large, nearly full pitcher of beer and a couple of guys who, in jeans

246

and work shirts, were not dressed to impress any judge Hardy had ever heard of.

Sliding in next to Farrell, Hardy asked how he was doing. "So good I ought to be twins." Wes introduced everybody around the table. It turned out that his two companions — Jason and Jake — were father and son, which Hardy had guessed as soon as he'd sat down. The boy, Jake, maybe twenty years old, was Farrell's client. They were celebrating (hence the beer) because Jake's arresting officer hadn't shown up at his preliminary hearing this morning. Since he was the state's chief witness, the prosecution had dismissed all charges. Hardy had better manners than to ask what those had been.

So, they both insisted, Wes was a hero.

"He's always been one of mine," Hardy agreed. "In fact, that's why I'm here now." He turned to Wes. "Something important's come up. Can I steal you away for a few minutes? You guys mind?"

Just so long as he left the beer, everything was cool.

They worked their way to the side door — less crowd to get through — and out into the alley where now, just past noon, cans of garbage basked, baked, and from the smell, ripened in warm sunshine. Farrell blinked in the brightness, took a deep breath, and frowned. "I think somebody must have died near here. What's up?"

Hardy was ready, reaching for his inside coat pocket as they walked up toward Bryant and some good air. "I've got a list of names here and

I was curious if any of them looked familiar to you."

Farrell took the piece of paper, glanced down at it. "What's this about?"

"Your favorite hospital."

A quick look up, then back at the list. Hardy saw his eyes narrow. He stopped and came up again. "Okay. I give up."

"Anybody you know?"

"One of 'em. Marjorie Loring."

"She's one of your clients with the Parnassus lawsuit you're filing, isn't she?"

"Not exactly. Her kids are. She's dead herself."

"I know. So's everybody else on that list. Did they do a postmortem on her?"

They'd stopped in some shade in front of the bail bondsman's office at the entrance to Lou's. Farrell squinted into some middle distance, trying to remember. Then he shook his head. "They always do. But they probably didn't spend much time on it. They knew what she died of."

"And what was that?"

"The big C. She was another one of those 'whoops' cases, as in, 'Whoops, we should have really got around to looking at that a little bit sooner.'"

"But when she died? Was it before her kids expected her to go?"

"They didn't know how long it would be exactly." But he pursed his lips, a muscle worked in his jawline. Hardy let him dredge it up. "Although it was, yeah, pretty quick if I recall. One of those, 'You've got maybe three months, unless it turns out to be three days.' "

"Three days?"

"No, no, figure of speech, one of my few flaws. I exaggerate. I think it was like a week, two weeks, something like that."

"And it was supposed to be three months?"

Farrell shook his head. "But you know how that works, Diz. It was three months outside, maybe as much as six. The reality turned out to be less. It happens all the time. It might even have been a blessing."

Hardy could accept that on its face. But not if somebody hurried the process along. "Do you think Mrs. Loring's family would agree to ask for an exhumation?"

Even with the preamble, the question shocked him. "What for?"

"A full autopsy."

"Why? You think somebody killed her?"

"I think it's possible."

Suddenly Farrell's gaze focused down tightly. A few years older than Hardy, a little softer in the middle, Wes usually affected an air of casual befuddlement. Some might even have read this as incompetence, but Hardy knew he was nobody's fool. A couple of years before, he'd electrified the city's legal community with his defense of another lawyer, a personal friend accused of murdering his wife. The case was considered unwinnable even by such an eminence as David Freeman. But Farrell had gotten his client off with a clean acquittal. Now he was giving Hardy his complete attention. "What about the other ten people on your list? Same thing?"

Hardy didn't want to exaggerate. "Let's say there are similar questions. I want to talk to my client before we go any further, of course, but after I do. . . ." He let it hang.

Farrell backed into the last wedge of shade. "Last time we talked you didn't have a client," he said.

"I've got one now. You know Eric Kensing?"

"And you want to call him before I talk to the Lorings because . . . ?"

"Because for some of these names," Hardy indicated the list, "he was on duty in the hospital when they died. Before we exhume Mrs. Loring and find out she didn't die of cancer, I'd be happier knowing Dr. Kensing wasn't on the floor taking her pulse at the time."

Farrell admitted that that would be bad luck. "So they haven't arrested him yet, I gather?"

"At least not as of a half hour ago, but things could change even as we speak."

Farrell narrowed his eyes. "You're talking Abe?"

Hardy nodded, spoke curtly. "He seems a little fixated."

"Abe's not dumb."

"No, he's not, but he took Kensing's statement last night, then left. No arrest. I guess what I'm trying to do is buy my client some time. Abe might get carried away in his enthusiasm. If Kensing gets arrested or indicted, he's never going to work again. And I've got friends who think he's a hero."

Wes chuckled, jerked a thumb toward Lou's.

"Those two yahoos at the booth in there think *I'm* a hero. That doesn't mean anything." Then. "Did your boy do it?"

"Early on, he said not." Hardy left it at that.

Farrell's eyes shifted from side to side. This turn in the conversation — the objective fact of the guilt or innocence of a client — threatened to breach a largely unspoken rule among defense attorneys. But suddenly Hardy knew why Farrell had brought it up. The friend of his, for whom he'd won such a stunning acquittal, in whose innocence Wes had believed with his whole heart, turned out to have been guilty after all. "If you want to be sure," he said, "you'd damn well better find somebody else who did it."

Hardy cracked a tiny smile. "Okay, then, that's who I'm looking for. But my first line of defense is to find out if these Portola patients who are dying before they should are any part of this Markham thing."

"How do you propose to do that?" Farrell's expression reflected his deep skepticism. "Certainly Marjorie Loring couldn't . . ." He stopped, softened his look. "Maybe I just don't get it," he offered. "Let's pretend her kids let us dig her up in the first place, which is a wild assumption, by the way. So Strout agrees to do an autopsy, also not a sure thing. So then they find, say, that potassium killed her. How in the world does that help your client?"

"Well, right off, if he wasn't there . . ."

Farrell waved that off. "Okay. He wasn't there when Lincoln was shot, either. But it doesn't mean squat about Markham. And then what if it wasn't potassium?"

Hardy had admitted these problems to himself, and had gotten to a marginally satisfying answer. "If some other patient at Portola, unconnected to Markham, is another murder — especially if Kensing wasn't around when it happened — it might make somebody like Glitsky think he's missing something. He might want to fill in more blanks before they arrest Kensing. At this point, it's mostly delay, frankly, but I'm out of other great ideas."

"Well, delay's always a fine tactic, if it works." Farrell, clearly, still wasn't convinced. "But if your man thought these were questionable deaths, why didn't he ask for full autopsies originally?"

"I asked him the same question."

"That's 'cause you're a smart fellow. And what'd he say?"

"Basically, that all the deaths were expected anyway, and from expected reasons. It wasn't like these were people in the prime of health who suddenly died. They were dying people who died. Just a little early. The hospital ran postmortems. Sure enough, they were all dead." Hardy shrugged. "Essentially he put it down to just a general degradation in care at Portola." He moved closer and whispered conspiratorially, "But listen up, Wes. The point is that if anybody at Portola killed Marjorie Loring, you win no matter what."

"And that's because . . . ?" He stopped because he suddenly understood. He could bring a slam dunk lawsuit on behalf of Marjorie Loring's children. There would be no need to prove general negligence or some other malpractice issue. He could begin billing immediately again. If Marjorie Loring didn't die of natural causes, but was a homicide committed in the hospital, Wes stood to make a pile in a very short time by doing comparatively very little. "I'll talk to her kids," he said. "See what we can do."

Treya looked up from her desk to the wall clock. She broke a genuine smile and rose from the chair. "Dismas Hardy, Esquire, three o'clock, right on the button. Clarence is expecting you, he'll be right with you, but he's got someone in with him for just another minute. Are you coming from upstairs?" she asked. Meaning Glitsky's detail.

"No."

"So you haven't talked to Abe?"

"Not yet. Frannie told me he called last night, but I got home late."

"He really wants to talk to you."

"And I him, of course. Maybe you could make us an appointment?"

"Isn't he coming down for this one? I know Clarence asked him."

This didn't strike Hardy as good news, but he covered his reaction with a smile. "Good. Maybe we can chat afterwards."

He sat and waited, aware of his nerves and his still-smoldering anger. He'd spent countless hours here in the DA's office — from back when he'd been a young assistant DA himself through his recent trials as a defense attorney. In well over ninety percent of those hours, there'd been conflict between himself and the person on the other side of that door. Since Jackman's appointment as DA, that had changed. Now in a few minutes, he knew he was about to go back where he belonged, on the defense side. It was perhaps going to be a subtle shift, and hopefully cordial, but a real one nonetheless.

Jackman's door opened. Marlene Ash was inside. Now that he thought of it, he should have expected that Jackman would have asked her, too. She was, after all, going to prosecute Parnassus and, in all likelihood, his client.

"Diz, how you doin'?" Jackman boomed. "Come on in, come on in. Sorry we're running a little late."

He came through the door, smiling and smiling. "If you and Marlene aren't finished," he began, giving them every chance, "I don't mean to rush you. I'm sure Treya and I can find some way to pass a few more pleasant minutes."

Jackman smiled back at him. Everybody was still friends. "Marlene thought she might want to stay a while, if you don't mind. There were a couple of things she wanted to run by you. Did Treya tell you I've asked Abe to stop by? And here he is."

Glitsky and Hardy sat on either end of the couch — neither words nor eye contact between them. Marlene still sat in her chair, Jackman pulled another one up. A nice little circle of friends around the coffee table.

Hardy got right down to it. "I understand that

in the wake of Mr. Markham becoming a potential murder victim, you've decided to convene a grand jury. I hear that they are investigating not just Markham's death, but the whole Parnassus business situation. In fact, I think it was even my idea, originally, before anybody died. I just wanted you all to know that I really don't expect any huge public display to recognize my contribution here, although a tasteful bust in the lobby downstairs or a small commemorative plaque in the corner at Lou's might be nice."

Glitsky's scar was an unbroken line through his lips. "The man could talk the ears off a water jug."

Sitting back, Hardy extended an arm out along the top of the couch, affecting a relaxed pose that he didn't feel. "As my friend Abe points out, I'm a believer in communicating." He directed a pointed glance at Glitsky, then came forward on the couch. "I understand what some of you would like to happen next. I talked to Dr. Kensing about an hour ago. He told me that his wife now claims he admitted killing Markham." Hardy finally faced Abe. "I figure that's what you must have called me about, to give me a heads-up that you were bringing him in."

Glitsky said nothing.

Hardy continued. "But of course, since you interviewed my client despite my explicit request that you not do so, perhaps you were prepared to dispense with a courtesy call, too."

A muscle worked in Glitsky's jaw. The scar stood out in clear relief.

He went on. "I think the only reason he's not already in jail is because you decided to wait until Clarence was ready to sign the warrant." The expressions around the room told Hardy that he'd pegged it exactly. "But that's not why I'm here," he said. "I'm here to keep my client out of jail."

Glitsky snorted. "Good luck."

"I'm not going to need luck. If all you've got is the wife's story, you don't have any case that'll fly in front of a jury. You must know that."

Marlene took this moment to get on the boards. "According to Abe, we've got plenty to go with, Dismas. If the man's killed five people, he shouldn't be on the streets."

"Marlene, please. Let's not insult each other's intelligence. Dr. Kensing had no motive in the world to harm the family."

"That you know," Glitsky said.

Again, Hardy turned directly to face him. "Am I to assume that means that you have discovered one?"

Jackman cleared his throat and answered for Glitsky. "We assume, Diz, that the murders of Markham and his family are related. I think you would agree with that as a working hypothesis, wouldn't you? But that's really not germaine. Dr. Kensing has plenty of motive for Markham. Plus means and opportunity."

"But no evidence, Clarence. No real evidence. It's mostly some motive."

"Don't shit a shitter, Diz," Marlene said. "First, we don't have *some* motive, we've got a *ton* of motive and nobody else has any. Second,

256

we know when Markham was killed and Dr. Kensing was right there. Moreover," she went on calmly, "Markham got killed by drugs administered through an IV, and your client is not exactly a janitor. He's got access. So we've got motive, means, and opportunity and not the slightest doubt about these facts."

Hardy repeated his mantra. "But no physical evidence. No direct evidence. Nobody saw him do it and no physical evidence shows he did it. You can prove that *maybe* he did it, but maybe he didn't, and that, I need hardly remind you, is reasonable doubt."

"His wife says he admitted it," Glitsky growled. "That's evidence. Kensing told her he pumped him full of shit a day before the autopsy, before anybody knew he was murdered. Oh, you didn't catch that detail yet?" Glitsky cleared his throat. "I called you last night. I thought maybe we could talk about that. Maybe you didn't get the message."

"I told you not to interview my client," Hardy shot back. "Maybe you didn't get *my* message." Hardy fought to control his temper. This wasn't the way to get what he wanted. He turned to Ash. "So his wife, who hates him, says he killed her lover. That's it? You'll never convict on that."

But Ash remained calm. "I believe, with the rest of the evidence, that in fact I might, Dismas."

" 'Might' is not particularly strong, Marlene."

"You want to help us do better, is that it?" Glitsky's tone was glacial.

"As a matter of fact, I have a suggestion that might have that effect," Hardy said. "I won't pretend that Dr. Kensing isn't my main concern. I know you're about to arrest him. Hell, maybe you've already got your warrant." Hardy waited, but no one admitted that. Which meant maybe it wasn't too late. He sucked in a breath. It was party time. "I'm going to do a little preamble," he began.

"Surprise!"

Hardy ignored Glitsky, made his pitch directly to Jackman. "Look. Let's say you bring in Kensing and charge him with murder. Abe could arrest him today. I'll even grant you that the wife's statement would almost certainly get you an indictment if you put her before the grand jury. In either case, you'd have to give me discovery, of course."

Discovery included everything about the prosecution — physical evidence, exhibits, testimony, police reports, and so on. The defense had the absolute right to the prosecution's case. This was Law 1A, but Hardy didn't think it was a bad idea to remind everybody that one way or the other he was going to see all the evidence they had anyway. It was automatic.

"But you haven't arrested him yet," he continued, "or brought him before the grand jury. So he's not been charged, and therefore there's no compulsion for you to share anything with me yet."

"Is the preamble over?" Glitsky asked.

Hardy didn't even acknowledge the interruption. He kept his eyes on Jackman. "What I pro-

258

pose is a horse trade." He pressed ahead quickly. "What you really want is Parnassus, Clarence. You know it, I know it, everybody here knows it. You want to find out where the rot is and cut it out, but you've got to be careful you don't cut it so badly that you kill it. If Parnassus goes belly up, the people who'll take the biggest hit by far are the city employees. Now this would be legitimate bad news for a lot of good people, but it's the worst possible political scenario for you, Clarence, if you want to keep this job and continue the good work you've started."

Jackman's mouth turned down slightly in distaste. Hardy didn't think it was only over his brownnosing. He'd hit a nerve, as he hoped he would.

"All right. So how does your client fit in?" Jackman asked.

"He fits because everything's mellow over at Parnassus only so long as you're looking for whoever killed their CEO. They're all expecting you to do that. So the corporate types won't see your people showing up and go rushing out to shred their files, and whatever other obstructions they'll come up with. But once you arrest Kensing, you've got no pretext."

He stopped to let the notion sink in, but Marlene didn't have to wait. "With all respect, Diz, that's bullshit. The grand jury can look anywhere they want, anytime they want. It's got nothing to do with your client."

"I'm not arguing with that, Marlene. You can arrest him and continue to investigate at Parnassus. You have every right. Still . . ." He went

259

back to Jackman. "Here's the city's health care provider, already reeling from near bankruptcy, terrible cash flow problems, subzero morale, and now the loss of its chief executive. If word gets out that you're trying to shut the place down —"

"That's not our intention," Marlene said.

But Hardy shook his head. "It doesn't matter. If you arrest Kensing and then continue poking around, that's what it's going to look like. Which means the shit's going to hit the fan. You all know this town. Everything gets exaggerated. Everything's an issue. What's going to happen when it looks like lots of city workers aren't going to have medical care? It will not be pretty."

All this was well and good and possibly true, but Glitsky wasn't buying it at all. "And the way we avoid this potential catastrophe is we don't arrest your client?"

"Only until the grand jury can do its job. Say thirty days."

"Thirty days!" Glitsky was apoplectic. "Are you out of your mind? If he killed Markham, and my evidence says he did, he likely killed his whole family, too. I don't care if it brings down the whole federal government, the man belongs in jail."

Hardy turned to Ash. "The case sucks, Marlene. You arrest him and you know what's going to happen. Parnassus goes in the toilet and after it does, if Kensing beats the case at trial, you guys all go with it."

But with all the arguing, Jackman still hadn't lost the thread. "You mentioned trading, Diz. You're asking us to give you thirty days . . ."

"And your discovery," Hardy added.

Glitsky threw up his hands and stood up. "How 'bout a chauffeur, too? Maybe some massage therapy?"

Hardy kept ignoring him.

The DA's face was lost in concentration. "All right, for purposes of this discussion, and your discovery —"

"Not a chance! No way we do this, Clarence. I'll go bring him in on a no-warrant before that happens."

Jackman filled his large chest with air. He had Glitsky by an inch or two and thirty pounds and all of it was never more visible than it was now, when it was clearly so tightly controlled. His voice, when it came, was a deep bassoon of authority. "That you will *not* do, Lieutenant!" He took another slow breath, then continued in a conversational tone. "You've had ample time before this to arrest Dr. Kensing without a warrant, Abe. But you're the one who brought me into this decision loop, and now it's mine to make. I hope that's abundantly clear."

Glitsky couldn't find his voice. He stared around the room in open disbelief if not downright hostility. Jackman ignored him and turned to Hardy. "Thirty days and discovery in return for what?"

"In return for his testimony in front of the grand jury."

The sense of anticlimax was palpable. Glitsky was shaking his head in bewilderment that Hardy had wasted all of their time and effort for so little. Marlene's face reflected a similar reaction. Even Jackman folded his arms over his chest and cocked his head to one side. But his eyes, at least, still probed.

Hardy felt the topic wasn't closed. "Look, Clarence, as it stands now, when you get Kensing in front of the grand jury, I'm going to tell him to take the Fifth. You'll be lucky if you get his name. This way, you've got Marlene here —" He turned to her. "Imagine this. You've got your primary murder suspect answering any question you might have without his lawyer there. It's a prosecutor's dream."

But she was unconvinced. "It's not my dream, Diz. You'll just have more time to give him a story, which he'll stick to." She looked to her boss. "This won't work, sir. He's not offering anything, really."

"But I am, Marlene. Think about this. I'm offering an insider's look inside Parnassus, exactly what you all need."

"We can get that anyway, Diz."

"Where? From who? Everybody else who works there is going to be covering for themselves or their employer. Even the other doctors."

"That's not true. The grand jury will protect them, no matter what they say in there. That's exactly what it's for, Dismas. So people can talk freely."

"It's what it's *designed* to do, right, Marlene. But it doesn't always work that way. You won't find too many doctors who are going to want to help you in your efforts to cut off the source of their paychecks. But even if all you want is to go after my client on Markham, you've got him all to yourself for as long as you want. No relevance issues, no inadmissibility, no defense objections, total open season."

Marlene's stare was unyielding.

Glitsky had moved over to the doorsill and was leaning against it, a sullen statue. "What if he kills again?" he asked. "His own wife, for example. I'd feel pretty bad if she died. Wouldn't you?"

Jackman broke in between them. "It seems to me he's had ample opportunity to kill his wife if he wanted to, Abe."

"But now, with her statement, he's got a better reason to."

"So we protect her," Jackman said. "Or move her. Or both. And it seems to me that Dismas has a point. If only out of self-preservation, Kensing isn't going to do anything while he knows that he is our chief suspect in another murder."

Hardy knew that in some ways, Jackman's inexperience was showing. Murderers rarely acted rationally. But, he thought cynically, that's what politics was about. The inexperienced taking control. He'd take some self-serving self-deception if it kept his client out of jail.

Jackman turned again to Glitsky.

"Marlene and I were talking about these very issues before Dismas got here, Abe. We agreed then that the Parnassus investigation will take on a very different cast as soon as we make an arrest on Markham. And we were trying to strategize to address the problem. It seems to me now that Diz's solution might have merit."

Glitsky's scar was a tight, thick rope now through his lips. "The man's a murderer, Clarence."

Jackman wasn't going to fight about it. If anything, he was judicious and calm, nodding patiently. "He may be, of course. But as we've said here, I really don't believe he's a danger to the community. Now I don't want to close the door to revisiting that assessment. Daily, if need be. But in the meanwhile" — he turned to Hardy — "I'm inclined, Diz, to accept your assessment on Parnassus. I don't want them spooked. I don't —"

The concession speech was interrupted by the door slamming — hard — behind Glitsky as he stormed out.

Beyond his client's freedom and the prosecution's discovery, Hardy had originally intended to make yet another request to the DA. It was normally supposed to be Jackman's call, and by asking his permission, Hardy might continue to succeed in his little charade that cooperation was, in fact, his middle name. But Glitsky's abrupt withdrawal had cast a pall over those who'd stayed, and he decided that to ask for more would be pushing things.

But the other item of business remained. And the more he thought about it, the less it seemed to matter if he asked Jackman's permission first. He needed an answer and needed it now. His client was still in big trouble. And he wasn't really going behind anybody's back by asking John Strout. If the coroner found anything as a result of Hardy's request, he would report it to Glitsky and Jackman anyway.

Hardy wasn't hiding anything — his motives or his actions. Or so he told himself.

He walked out the back door of the hall along the covered outdoor corridor that led to the jail on the left and the morgue on the right. The air smelled faintly of salt water, but he also caught the scent of flowers from the huge commercial market around the corner. He was feeling as though he'd accomplished quite a bit during the day. When he was done with Strout, he'd try to remember to buy a bouquet for his wife, even his daughter. It was Friday evening. The weekend loomed long and inviting, and maybe he and his family could fashion some quality time together if they worked at it.

It turned out that Strout was cutting up someone in the cold room at the moment, but the receptionist told Hardy he shouldn't be too long. Did he want to wait? He told her he thought he would.

The coroner's regular office — as opposed to the morgue — was a veritable museum of ancient and modern weapons and instruments of torture. Always an interesting place to visit, the room made no concession to safety. All of Strout's bizarre stuff was out in the open to admire and hold and, if you were foolhardy enough, to try out. If one of his city-worker assistants ever became disgruntled, Hardy thought, he could have a field day going postal here —

stab a few folks with switchblades or bowie knives, blow up others with hand grenades, shoot up the rest with any number of automatic weapons from the arsenal.

Hardy sat on the bench at the garrote — red silk kerchief and all — considering his victory upstairs and pondering both the wisdom and the odds for success of his next move. The important thing, he reminded himself again, was to keep his client out of jail. He knew that between Glitsky's constant press, Marlene's handling of the grand jury, and Kensing's difficult and unpredictable behavior, the thirty days Jackman had promised him could evaporate like the morning fog. Hardy had to have something more, in spite of the risk that what he was about to suggest might in fact strengthen the case against his client.

He realized that it came down to a gamble, and this made him uncomfortable. But he didn't feel he had a choice. The noose was tightening around his client's neck. His guts told him that it was worth the risk. But if he was wrong. . . .

"You want, I can get that snot rag around your throat and tighten it down just a little bit. I'm told it's quite effective for the libido." Strout was referring to the garrote, and even more grimly to erotic asphyxia, the heightened orgasm which occurred during hanging and some other forms of strangulation. "Seems to be all the rage these past few years, 'tho my own feelin' is that it just plain ain't worth the trouble. But maybe I'm wrong. Lots of folks seem to give it a try. Anyway, how y'all doing?"

The two men made small talk for a couple of minutes while Strout shuffled his messages. After he'd gotten behind his desk, and Hardy had moved to a different chair, they got down to it.

When Hardy finished, Strout scratched around his neck. "Let me get this straight," he said at last. "You're comin' in here as a private citizen askin' me to autopsy another Portola patient who died the same day as Mr. Markham?"

"If you haven't already done it."

"What's the subject's name?"

"James Lector."

Strout shook his head. "Nope, haven't done it. But they do an automatic PM at the hospital. You know that?"

"And they never miss anything, do they?"

This was a good point, and Strout acknowledged it with a small wave. "How close was the time of death to Markham's?"

"Within a few minutes, actually."

"If I take a look, what exactly would I be lookin' for?"

"That I don't know."

Strout took off his horn-rims, blew on them, put them back on. The coroner had a mobile, elastic face, and it seemed to stretch in several directions at once. "Maybe I don't see what you're gettin' at. If you're sayin' Glitsky thinks your client killed Mr. Markham, then how's it s'posed to help your client if another body turns up with potassium in it on the same day?"

"It won't," Hardy agreed. "I'm hoping it's not potassium." What he did hope was that James

Lector was unexplained death number twelve. It wouldn't clear Kensing, but it might take some of the onus off his client for Markham's death. "Either way," he continued, "isn't it better if we know for sure what Lector died of?"

"Always," Strout agreed. He thought another moment. "And why would I want to order this autopsy again?"

Hardy shrugged. "You decided that Lector was a suspicious death, dying as he did within minutes of another homicide in the same room at the same hospital."

The medical examiner's head bobbed up and down once or twice. He pulled a hand grenade that he used as a paperweight over and spun it thoughtfully a few times on his blotter. Hardy watched the deadly sphere spin and tried not to think about what might happen if the pin came out by mistake.

Finally, Strout put his hand on the grenade, stopping it midspin. His eyes skewered Hardy over his glasses. "You're leavin' somethin' out," he said.

"Not on purpose. Really."

"If I'm doin' this — which I'm not promisin' yet, mind you — then I want to know what you're lookin' for, and why."

Hardy spread his hands, hiding nothing. "I think there's some small but real chance that James Lector is the latest in a series of homicides at Portola." This made Strout sit up, and Hardy went on. "So Lector's death may or may not have been natural, and may or may not have been related to Tim Markham's," he concluded.

"But certainly if Lector was murdered and died from a *different* drug than Markham, then there's a lot more going on at Portola than meets the eye at this stage."

"But again, it wouldn't do much for your client."

"Maybe not, John, but I need to find some evidence of other foul play where I can make an argument that my client wasn't involved. And don't tell me — I realize that doesn't prove he didn't kill Markham. At least it's somewhere to start, and I need something."

Strout was considering it all very carefully. "You got the Lector family's permission?" he asked. "When's the funeral scheduled?"

"No and I don't know. If you ordered an autopsy, we wouldn't need the family to . . ." This wasn't flying and he stopped talking. "What?"

"I believe I mentioned that there's already been a PM. If they got a cause of death they're happy with and I say I want another look at the body, it's goin' to ruffle feathers, both at the hospital and with the family. 'Specially if like the funeral's tomorrow or, say, this mornin' and we got to dig him back up." But something about the idea obviously had caught Strout's interest. If somebody was getting away with multiple homicides in a San Francisco hospital, it was his business to know about it. "What I'm sayin' is o' course we could do it without anybody's permission if I got a good enough reason, which I'm not sure I do. But any way we do it, it'd be cleaner if we asked nice and got an okay from the family."

"I'll talk to them," Hardy said.

"Then I'll make a gentlemen's deal with you, Diz. If it gets so it doesn't make anybody too unhappy, we'll do this. But if the family makes a stink, you're gonna have to go to court and convince a judge to sign an order. I'm not gonna do it on my own."

Hardy figured this was as good as it was going to get. He didn't hesitate for an instant. "Done," he said. "You'll be glad you did this, John. Ten to one you're going to find something."

Strout's expression grew shrewd. "Ten to one, eh? How much you puttin' up?"

Hardy gave it some thought. "I'll go a yard," he said.

"A hundred bucks? You lose and you'll owe me a grand?"

"That's it."

"You're on." Strout stuck out his hand and Hardy hesitated one last second, then took it.

18

It was Friday afternoon, the best time to do it.

Joanne announced his appointment in her pleasant, professional voice. She, of course, knew all about it, having typed the termination papers, but she would do nothing to give it away. Also present, kitty-corner from his desk at the small conference table, was Costanza Eu, Cozzie for short, the Human Relations director at Parnassus. This was going to be, had to be, strictly by the book. Malachi Ross, behind his desk when Driscoll came in, didn't get up.

"Brendan." He didn't bother with much of a welcoming smile. "Have a seat."

Driscoll was within a spit either way of forty. Meticulously groomed, he sported a carefully trimmed mustache in an unusually attractive, somehow asymmetrical face. With his powerful physique and his short dark hair dyed a discreet blond at the tips, he could have been sent from central casting to play a young, slightly sinister CEO in any daytime soap opera. From his carriage, no one would surmise he was a mere secretary or — as Markham had always called him — an executive assistant. Today he wore a muted blue tie and a black pinstriped business suit, and he wasn't a step inside Ross's door when he cast a quick eye at Cozzie and knew what was up.

271

He didn't take the proffered seat. Instead, he approached it and put his hands on the back rest. "I was hoping I'd have the opportunity to clean up Tim's files before we got to this," he said. "Though of course I understand. But I'll do what I can in the next two weeks."

Ross made an elaborate expression of disappointment. "I don't think that will be necessary, Brendan. I've decided, and the board has agreed, that you won't be required to stay on after today." He had the thick envelope on the desk in front of him, and he picked it up. "We've included a check in lieu of your two weeks' notice, and on top of that what I think you'll find to be a very reasonable severance. Due to your long tenure with the company, as well as Mr. Markham's high regard for your services, the board has approved seven months of your full salary and five more months at half, as well as of course your fully vested pension, and letters of recommendation from myself and several other members of the board. You'll also have the option to remain enrolled in the employee health plan."

Driscoll stood rooted, his mixed emotions playing on his face. Eventually, he nodded and swallowed, accepting the fait accompli. "Thank you, Doctor. That's very generous. I assume you'll be wanting my keys and parking pass and so on."

Even as he said it, he had his wallet out, then reached into his pockets. After he'd placed all the required items on Ross's desk, he stood at attention in front of it for another long moment.

Finally, he cleared his throat. "I kept his calendar mostly on the computer at my desk, although there's an incomplete hard copy in my top right drawer. I haven't gotten around to calling all of his appointments yet. There's also some unsent correspondence and I believe a few internal memos. If you'd like to send someone back with me, I'd be happy to print out . . ."

But Ross threw a glance, prompting Cozzie to speak up. "That won't be necessary, Brendan. We'll be going through all that material in the coming weeks. Standard procedure is we'd prefer to have you escorted from the building directly when you leave this meeting." She smiled with all the warmth of a cobra. "We understand that this can be a little disconcerting, but I'm sure you understand that it's nothing personal. Some people . . ." She let it hang, then shook her head and continued. "The contents of the closet by your desk, including your sweater and other personal goods, are boxed up just outside. Security will help you with them."

Some of the starch had gone out of Driscoll's bearing. He turned back to Ross. "What are you going to do about Mr. Markham's personal files? He left very specific instructions that I should . . . well, of what I should do if . . ."

"We'll take care of them," Ross said reassuringly. "Don't you worry. As you know, Mr. Markham left descriptions of his projects and detailed instructions for the board against just such a tragic event as this." Ross rose halfway out of his chair and smiled perfunctorily. "I did want to thank you again for your loyalty and discretion. And now, for your cooperation."

It was a dismissal, and at Ross's invisible sign, Cozzie was on her feet, coming around the table with a line of inane chatter, guiding the clearly shell-shocked Driscoll back toward the door. "You've got a beautiful day to start your new life, I must say that. Look at that blue out the windows. I don't remember the last time I've seen the sky so clear. And to think after the storm the last few days. . . ."

Firing Brendan Driscoll, that officious little mouse, had been the first, albeit tiny, ray of sunshine in his life since Markham's death. No sooner had Cozzie left his office than he rose from his desk, went over to the wet bar, and poured himself a viscous shot of frozen vodka from the bottle of Skyy he kept in his freezer. The no doubt heart-wrenching departure scene with Driscoll in his reception area played itself out in about ten minutes while he savored his drink. Joanne buzzed him to say it was over. Driscoll was out of the building.

Ross strode from his office, made some lame joke to Joanne, and turned right down the carpeted hallway. Floor-to-ceiling glass on his left made him feel almost as if he were walking in the air — the bay sparkled below him, while the Bay Bridge, already jammed up with traffic, seemed close enough to touch. Sitting at Driscoll's former desk, out in Markham's reception area now, he experienced a strange and momentary sense of dislocation. In a couple of weeks, he realized, Joanne would be sitting out here and he would have moved to the gorgeous suite behind him. It was the very pinnacle of the greasy pole he'd been climbing for what seemed all of his adult life.

At every step, he'd done what he had to do to get here. There was no question — as the board had affirmed — that he was the best equipped to handle the job. And now, with Markham's micromeddling and needless hypocrisy a thing of the past, he believed he could turn the business side around in a matter of months. If only he could keep the company afloat until then.

He thought it was eminently doable. He had ideas. Sending the city that $13 million bill for its past outpatient copays had been one of them, although admittedly merely a stopgap measure. Short term, he had the city over a barrel. And long term, his plans would stop the bleeding and get Parnassus back to financial health.

While he waited for the screen to come up on the computer, he pulled out the drawers of Driscoll's desk one by one and nodded in satisfaction. They'd done a good job cleaning them all out. He fully expected to find the hard files behind the locked door of Markham's old office. Ross intended to come in over the weekend and review every page of that material. But in the meantime, he had an hour before close of business, and another hour after that before his dinner appointment, and he wanted to make sure that Driscoll's computer contained nothing of an embarrassing nature.

Long ago, before cash had been such a problem, Ross had purchased a state-of-the-art computer system that he still considered one of his most astute investments. The customized business program he'd ordered allowed unlimited access to all files from certain employees, such as Cozzie and himself, who were given what they called "operator privileges." This allowed Ross's Human Relations department to keep tabs on nearly everything that went on. The system's security programs could count actual keystrokes per hour so the department could know which secretaries were underutilized or, more typically, just plain lazy. Likewise, if an employee spent too much time on the Internet, or wrote a screenplay or love letter on the company's time, Cozzie would know about it by the end of the week, when the reports came out. She would then review these reports with Ross, and together they would decide which person they would discipline, for everyone was guilty of something. It was, Ross believed, a beautiful thing — make laws governing all behavior, then enforce them selectively against people you don't like.

Only Brendan Driscoll, perhaps the worst offender in the company, had managed to thwart the system. He wrote love letters, short stories, and poetry on his computer, he visited porn sites on the Internet. When Markham was traveling, he would sometimes talk to his friends on the telephone for half the day (for of course the phones were integrated to the computer system, as well). But Driscoll got away with it all because Markham wouldn't let him go.

But now Ross sat at his terminal. Driscoll had

a password for his personal files, but Ross had his own "operator privilege" password, and it trumped Driscoll's. He typed in his own initials and password, a secondary directory came up, and Ross involuntarily, unconsciously broke a tight smile.

The Mandarin Oriental Hotel, one of the crown jewels of San Francisco, presented a look and feel of restrained opulence that Malachi Ross found appealing. It was also within easy walking distance of his office, and taking the leisurely stroll on this glorious evening was even more pleasurable than usual. After the grueling few days he'd just spent — not only in the immediate wash of Markham's death, but dealing with fallout from the *CityTalk* broadside — he'd take any comfort he could, wherever he could get it.

There had been some comfort back at Parnassus — more on Eric Kensing in Driscoll's computer files than he would have thought possible. There was correspondence about his wife, Ann, Markham's responses to what appeared to be intimations of a kind of (at least) emotional blackmail that Kensing had used to keep his job, memos to file, references to cash payoffs, private reprimands, ultimatums. Amazing! He'd printed it all out and told Joanne to deliver it to the district attorney by messenger.

He printed out a few other files, as well. These he put in his own briefcase, then deleted the originals from the computer.

Nancy and the girls were up at Lake Tahoe for the weekend. He'd told her she ought to have their pilot Darren fly them on up without him. He'd been working around the clock all week as it was, and in all likelihood that schedule would continue through the weekend and for the foreseeable future.

He'd told her on Wednesday night. They were in their bedroom getting ready to go out to dinner. The door was open to the hallway. They could hear the girls just outside, playing with Bette, their nanny. Nancy gave him a quick pout. She would miss him terribly, especially *that way*. Glancing at the open door, the voices twenty feet away, she unzipped her skirt and stepping out of it, dropped it to the floor. Turning her back to him, she leaned over and rested her elbows on the antique Italian writing desk by the end of their bed. Over her shoulder, she smiled in that "I dare you, we've got maybe two minutes" way she had, and whispered urgently, "It would be easier to go if you gave me something to remember you by."

"Good evening, Mr. Ross, and welcome again to Silks. You look like you're enjoying a particularly pleasant memory."

He snapped out of his reverie, smiled perfunctorily. "Hello, Victor. Nice to be here again."

"Right this way," the maître d' intoned. "Your guest has already been here for a few minutes."

His guest was Ron Medras, a very well put together, athletic, mid-forties senior vice president with Biosynth, which until about eight years ago had been a small drug manufacturing firm. It had carved out a nice, survivable niche producing generic, mostly over-the-counter knockoffs of aspirin, Tylenol, baby's cold and flu formula, and anti-inflammatories. At about that time, caught up in the feeding frenzy for mega-earnings and exploding stock prices that were overtaking the Silicon Valley, Medras and several other like-minded executives at Biosynth decided that three-bedroom homes in Mountain View or Gilroy were all well and good, but six-bedroom mansions in Atherton or Los Altos Hills, all in all, were better.

Biosynth knew it could easily produce equivalent, or near-equivalent, product of the stuff that was making billions and billions of dollars for Merck, Bristol-Myers Squibb, Pfizer. What it didn't have was marketing, *aggressive* marketing to big clients — hospitals and HMOs. Instead, it merely worked the chain drugstores that comprised the bulk of its sales. That would change.

Tonight, Medras was on a typical sales call. Ross was not his biggest client by a long shot, but he remained an important one. This was because there was often resistance when a new drug of any kind came on the market, and Ross had been willing over and over again to list Biosynth's new products on the Parnassus formulary nearly as soon as they were in production. This often had a snowball effect. San Francisco wasn't a huge market, but it had very high visibility. That made it plenty big enough for Biosynth's purposes. When Medras went to companies ten or twenty times the size of Parnassus, he'd be able to say to them: "This stuff is so good the main health care provider in San Francisco has listed it on its formulary." And, either impressed or reassured, the other medical directors would buy.

A couple of preprandial drinks accompanied ten or fifteen minutes of expressions of regret and sympathy from both men over the loss of Tim Markham, remembrances of good moments with him, praise for his vision, leadership, personality. But in this phenomenal setting, with an hors d'oeuvres plate of perhaps the best sashimi in the Western Hemisphere, it was difficult to sustain a somber mood. By the time the wine steward offered Medras a tasting sip from the bottle of '89 Latour that they'd ordered to go with their Asian lamb chops, they'd moved along to more enjoyable topics. They passed a pleasant hour discussing their golf games, new toys (Medras had just leased a new Saratoga aircraft), investment tips and opportunities.

Ross had developed a taste for hazelnut in the form of Frangelico liqueur, and he was enjoying his second snifter with his coffee when Medras finally got around to what they'd both come to talk about. Biosynth had been developing a new product for the past year or so. Top secret up until now, it had been waiting for FDA approval, and Medras had it on good authority that the good word would be coming down in the next month or so. The company had gotten ahold of a process that enabled them to make insulin at one-fifth of what it now cost to produce.

Ross put down his snifter. "Are you talking one-fifth as in twenty percent?"

Medras nodded, avarice lighting his eyes.

"And we would pass the savings along directly to you."

Ross quickly did the math in his head. "A dollar a dose? Copays would cover that by themselves. It would move the whole item from the red to the black."

"Yes. We believe it would. Although, of course, there are some issues."

"There always are." But Ross knew that if a company such as Parnassus came onboard in a big way, many of these problems could be mitigated. Complaints about possible rare side effects, for example, might not be forwarded to the government. And if the new insulin made it to his formulary, its credibility could be nearly instantaneous.

"I wanted to let you know about this," Medras went on, "because the sales force will be calling on your medical staff over the next couple of weeks. We'd like to have enough samples out there, with enough history, so that when we go on sale for real, people feel comfortable with the product, doctors and patients alike. This is really an incredible breakthrough, Malachi. It could really make a difference."

Ross believed him, although he didn't have to. The FDA would make sure. And if somehow it failed anyway, Ross didn't consider it his job to be the FDA's watchdog.

He had his own mission, which was demonstrating that good medicine and profit were not incompatible. The relationships that he and other like-minded medical executives forged with Biosynth and other similar companies were helping to make universal health care a reality. Lower-cost insulin was but one example of hundreds. Someone had to ram it down people's throats, if need be. There really was no other way, and simply no such thing as a free lunch.

Reassured that his new product would appear on the Parnassus formulary as soon as the FDA approved it, Medras payed the bill, finished his own coffee, and said good-bye. After he'd gone, Ross stayed at the table to finish his Frangelico. The room was coming alive now with well-dressed couples and foursomes and he sat back for a last moment to enjoy this perk of his position. Then he reached down by his right foot and picked up the thin leather briefcase that Medras had left for him. He pushed his chair back a few inches, enough so that he could open the briefcase on his lap. Inside were three wrapped bundles of hundred-dollar bills, a credit card–style room key, and a page of Biosynth letterhead on which Medras had written a room number.

Five minutes later and forty-two floors above the city, Ross carried the briefcase with him as he exited the elevator and crossed the enclosed glass walkway that joined the two towers of the Mandarin Oriental. It was full dark now and the city lights glittered far below him. He always stopped here, enjoying the sense of vertigo, of floating above it all.

When he got to his door, he inserted the card, knocked, and pushed the door open.

"Mr. Ross?" A voice sweet as music, cultured and mellifluous. Naked, she appeared from the bedroom around the corner, a young and very pretty Japanese woman. Ross's eyes fastened on a small tattoo of a dagger over her right breast. It pointed straight down and ended with its tip at her nipple, which was pierced by a tiny gold ring. "Hello," she said, with a respectful bow. "I am Kumiko. Come. Let me help you with your clothes."

19

Something weird was happening with the weather again — the night had become nearly balmy.

Bracco and Fisk were parked in the street in front of Glitsky's. Bracco was behind the wheel; his window was down and he rested his elbow on it. He was chewing a toothpick that he'd picked up from the counter at the sandwich shop on Clement where they'd bought their Reubens and Dr Peppers.

Fisk had his window down, too, and fidgeted in his seat. He slurped the last of his drink. "He's not coming. This is stupid."

Bracco turned his head. "You don't have to stay. I'll just tell him you had someplace to go. You can take the car. I'll get home somehow. You've got a family, Harlen. So does he. He'll understand."

"He didn't seem all that understanding this morning."

This was true. Glitsky had come to Harlen's desk first thing and loudly offered to transfer him to any other department immediately if he didn't want to be in homicide anymore. Homicide inspectors didn't cut out early. Did Inspector Fisk understand?

Although now, Fisk thought, it wasn't early. It was nine damn o'clock. "He's not expecting us,

Darrel, I don't care what he told you. He left work early and pissed off and now he's out for the night, maybe the weekend."

"So go." Darrel took the keys from the ignition and flipped them into his partner's lap. "But I'm staying."

Fisk slammed his hand on the outside of the door. "I can't go alone, is my point. If we both go, okay, we say we tried. But if it's just me and you're still here . . ."

Bracco still had a lot of his Dr Pepper left, and he put the straw to his mouth. When he took it out, he swallowed and said, "He told me to report every day. In person."

"Yeah? Well, he's not here, if you haven't noticed. He wasn't in the detail when we checked in. He doesn't expect you to hunt him down to report. He obviously forgot all about us."

A shrug. "Maybe."

But Fisk continued to rave. "What if he died, then what? Would you go report at his gravesite? There's exceptions to things, you know."

"This is the first day, Harlen. You don't make exceptions on the first day you're doing something. That makes them the rule." He looked up in his rearview mirror, saw some headlights turn into the street. "Here comes somebody."

Fisk turned all the way around in his seat. "It's not him."

"Five bucks says it is."

"You're on."

Furious at what he had taken to be Jackman's and Ash's usurpation of his arrest prerogative, as well as Hardy's scheming lawyer games at his expense, Glitsky hadn't been in the mood for any more work today. They could all go to hell.

By the time he got home, he'd decided to take the whole weekend off as well. He pitched his beeper and cell phone into the dresser next to his bed, then saw Orel's note reminding him that he and Raney had both left directly after school with their snowboard club for one last chance to maim themselves before the summer. So no kids for the weekend. He really was taking it off.

When Treya got home, he asked her if she was up for a night on the town. He didn't have to ask twice. They went to a Moroccan place on Balboa, where they sat on the floor and ate with their fingers, washing everything down with sweet, hot tea that the waiter poured from the height of his waist down to the cups on the floor, never spilling a drop. Good theater.

The night was so beautiful that they decided to walk to Ocean Beach. On the way back, something about their hips remaining in contact made them decide to head back home.

A free spot at the curb just four driveways from their place had them both thinking it was their lucky night, all the stars aligning to give them some privacy and peace. Glitsky's arm was over Treya's shoulder, hers around his waist.

"Don't look now," Treya said. Two men had just stepped out of their car and were walking toward them. She whispered, "Let's hope they're punks thinking about mugging us. We can kill them quick and get inside."

"They're punks, all right," Glitsky answered

sotto voce. Then a little louder. "Gentlemen. Out for an evening stroll?"

"You said to report every day, sir," Bracco explained.

"If this isn't a good time . . ." Fisk made it clear he didn't think it was, either.

"No, this is a great time, Harlen."

"A great time," Treya agreed, nodding at Fisk. "A terrific time."

Glitsky touched her arm. "I don't believe either of you know my wife. Treya. Inspectors Fisk and Bracco."

"*Enchanté,*" she said in a passable French accent. Her smile possibly appeared sincere. "I've heard so much about you both."

On the one hand, Glitsky was marginally happy that Darrel Bracco took him so literally. On the other, he didn't want his men getting into the habit of dropping by his place. But now it was a done deal. His romantic night with his wife continued as she sat next to him on the couch. Bracco and Fisk were on chairs they'd carried from the small, small kitchen.

"This is Parnassus then?" she asked sweetly. "Does anybody mind if I stay?"

There were no objections.

Bracco had placed his little notepad out on the coffee table in front of him. He regularly checked his notes. "We began at the hospital, first thing. Did you know Kensing was late for work Tuesday morning? An hour late."

"No," Glitsky said. "I don't know anything about what Kensing did that day. But why do you think that's worth mentioning, if he was?"

"The car," Fisk replied. "Where was he at the time of the accident?"

"The original accident?" Glitsky asked. "With Markham?"

"Are you still considering that part of the murder?" Treya asked. "I thought once they found the potassium, you pretty much ruled that out."

Actually, Glitsky had given it short shrift from the outset, and still did. But he realized that these guys had a bias and didn't want to dampen their newfound enthusiasm. "We're keeping an open mind on all theories at this point," he told her in their secret code. He came back to the inspectors. "So did you ask Kensing where he'd been?"

"No, sir," Bracco replied. "We haven't talked to him again ourselves, but last night he never mentioned it when you were questioning him. It seems like it might have crossed his mind."

"He told people that morning that he'd had car trouble."

Cars again. Glitsky nodded, noncommittal, but privately convinced that they could bark under this tree forever and it wouldn't get them a thing. "How about after Markham got to the ER? What was it like there? Busy? What?"

Bracco was ready with his answer. "Actually, it was a pretty slow morning. They had a kid who needed stitches in his head and a lady who'd fallen down and broken her hip. But they had already been brought into the back when the ambulance pulled up."

"The back?" Glitsky asked.

288

"Yeah. There's a waiting area when you first come in, then when they see you, they take you back to this big open room with lots of portable beds and a medical station — where the nurses and doctors hang out, in the middle. That's where they brought Markham as soon as he got there, then into surgery, which is down the hall a ways."

"There's a half-dozen surgery rooms on that floor," Fisk added. "Every one of them has a supply of potassium and other emergency drugs."

"There's also potassium at the station near the portable beds."

"Okay." This was nice, but Glitsky had already deduced that there must have been some potassium around someplace. As before, these two inspectors had no doubt gathered a lot of information. Their problem was in recognizing which of it was useful. If he wanted to get it, he realized he'd have to ask the right questions. "When they let Markham in, was his wife with him?"

They looked at each other, as if for confirmation. "Yeah. Outside and then while they prepped the operating room for surgery. Maybe ten minutes."

"Then what? When he went to the operating room?"

Another shared look, and Bracco answered. "She was in the waiting room when he got out, then she moved up to ICU's waiting room."

"Okay," Glitsky said. "But was she alone by the central nurses' station by the portable beds at any time? Is what I'm getting at." There was no way, he realized, that they would have pursued that question, so he went right to another. "How was she taking it? Did anybody say?"

Fisk took the lead. "I talked to both of the nurses that had been there —"

"How many are on the shift usually?" Glitsky interrupted.

"Two at night, which is ten to six. Then four during the day."

"So there were four on duty? Where were the other two?"

Bracco came to his partner's rescue. "With the other two patients, sir. Because one of the ER docs had been late that day, they were short a doc at the start of the shift. They'd prepped one of the other ORs for the hip, and one nurse was waiting for the surgeon with the lady there. The other one stayed with the kid and his mom and the doc sewing his head."

"Okay." Glitsky thought he had the picture finally. Two doctors, four nurses, three patients, two visitors. He turned to Fisk. "So you talked to Markham's nurses about how the wife seemed? Male or female, by the way? The nurses?"

"Both women," Fisk replied. "And yes, sir, I asked them both how she was." Glitsky was still waiting.

Treya read her husband's impatience and asked nicely, "And how was that, Inspector?"

"Distraught," Fisk answered. "Very upset. Almost unable to talk."

"They both said that?"

"Yes, sir. They agreed completely."

"Crying?"

"Yes, sir. I asked that specifically. She was cry-

290

ing quietly on and off."

Glitsky fell silent. Bracco had been listening intently to this exchange, and consulting his notes, decided to put in his own two cents' worth. "I talked to one of the nurses, too, sir, a Debra Muller. She walked with Mrs. Markham when they were bringing Markham into the OR and then back to the waiting room, where she — Muller — spent a few minutes holding her hand. Anyway, Muller, the word she used was 'shell-shocked.' Mrs. Markham kept repeating things like, 'They can't let him die. They won't let him die, will they?'"

Glitsky was thinking a couple of things: first, that of course Mrs. Markham could have been a good actress, but this didn't sound like a woman who was planning to kill her husband in the next couple of hours. Second, if Nurse Muller had accompanied her from the portable bed area to the surgery and back, then she hadn't been alone to pick up a vial of potassium from the medical station in the center of the room. But he wanted to be sure on that score. "So she didn't wait in the portable bed area?"

"No, sir. Outside in the waiting room, and then upstairs by the ICU."

"All right," Glitsky said. "Let's move along. How long was Markham in the OR?"

Fisk cast a grateful eye over to Bracco, who'd taken not only good notes, but some of the right ones. "A little under two hours," Darrel said, then volunteered some more. "And by the time he'd come out and gotten admitted to the ICU, some of the Parnassus executive staff were there.

Malachi Ross, the medical director. Also Markham's secretary, a guy named Brendan Driscoll, who evidently got in a bit of a discussion with Dr. Kensing."

"About what?"

"Access to his boss."

"Markham? He was unconscious, right? Did he ever regain consciousness?"

"No, sir."

"Then why did he want to see him? This Driscoll."

"Nobody seems to know." Bracco's disappointment over his failure to find out was apparent. "But he did get in, though."

Glitsky leaned forward. "Driscoll? Was in the ICU? For how long?"

"Again," Bracco answered, "nobody knows for sure. But when Kensing found him in there —"

"You're telling me he was alone?"

"Yes, sir. Evidently. And when Kensing found him in there, he went batshit and kicked his ass out."

Glitsky replied with an exaggerated calm. "I don't believe 'to go batshit' is a legitimate verb, Darrel. You're saying Kensing and Driscoll had an argument?"

"Short, but fairly violent. Kensing physically threw him out."

"Of the ICU? Of the hospital?"

"No. Just the unit. Intensive care. But Driscoll was still around when Markham died."

"People remember him?"

"Yep. He lost it entirely. Just sobbing like a baby."

"Okay. And what was your source for this later stuff? Did the OR nurses come up?"

"No," Fisk replied. "There's another nurses' station outside the ICU."

"I've got the names," Bracco added. "There are at least twelve regular ICU nurses, three shifts, two a shift, but they run two weeks on, then two off. It's pretty intense, evidently."

"Hence the name," Treya commented drily.

Glitsky squeezed her hand. He went on. "But you're telling me that even with all that help, sometimes the ICU is empty, right? Except for the patients?"

"Right." Bracco was off his notes and on memory again. "Everybody's on monitors for heartbeat and blood pressure and kidney function and who knows what else. The doctors and nurses go in regularly, but it's not like there's a nurse there in the station all day. They've got other jobs — keeping up supplies, paperwork, taking breaks."

Glitsky considered that. "Can they see anyone who goes in or comes out of the ICU from their station?"

"Sure, if they're at it. It's right there."

"So who came in and went out?"

Bracco turned a page or two of his notepad and read, "Besides Kensing, two other doctors, Cohn and Waltrip. Then both nurses — I've got their names somewhere back —"

"That's all right. Go ahead."

"Then Driscoll, Ross, three members of the family of another patient in there. They were there for morning visiting hours. I could get their names."

"Maybe later, Darrel, if we need them. What time did Markham die, did you get that?"

Again, Bracco was ready. "Twelve forty-five, give or take."

"So Markham was in the ICU maybe four hours?"

"That's about right. Maybe a little less."

Another thought occurred. "Ross went in, too? Why was that?"

"I don't know," Bracco said.

"But he's a doctor, you know," Fisk added. "He's got the run of the place. He was in there with Kensing right after they got him up from OR."

After a moment of silence, Glitsky finally nodded. "Okay. That it?"

Bracco flipped a page or two, then lifted his head and looked across at Glitsky and Treya. He brought his head back up and nodded. "For today, sir." Then he added, "I'm sorry we interrupted your night for you."

"Don't be silly," Treya said quickly, standing up. Then wagged a finger at them, joking. "Just don't do it again."

Glitsky took her lead and was on his feet. "Working late's part of the job." He had meant it sincerely as a simple statement of fact, but as soon as the words were out, he realized from Fisk's expression he took it as another Glitsky reminder of his failings as a cop.

Which wasn't fair. These two inexperienced inspectors had finally done some investigative work. They'd stayed late to make their report to him. They were trying hard. They had worked a

294

long day. Glitsky knew that a kind word to them wouldn't kill him. He tried to put some enthusiasm into his voice. "That's a good day's work, guys. Really. Keep at it," he said. "One thing, though. Tomorrow morning, make sure you get your tapes into transcription ASAP. I want to get all this into the record."

The two men froze, threw a concerned glance at each other.

Glitsky read it right. "You *did* tape all these interviews, didn't you?"

Hardy remembered to buy the flowers. Beautiful bouquets, too, both of them. Baby pink roses for his daughter, the Spring Extravaganza for his wife. They were next to him on the passenger seat of his car even as he drove around looking for a parking place in his neighborhood. He didn't think there was much chance that Frannie and the Beck would appreciate them much just now, since they were probably both asleep.

It was ten minutes until midnight.

He'd left Strout's office in high spirits. The warm night, the fragrant air, a true sense of accomplishment. He'd cut a great deal for his client with Jackman, convinced the coroner to autopsy James Lector as soon as he cleared the way for it with his family. He called Frannie on his cell phone and told her he didn't think that would take more than an hour, and then he'd be home. Maybe on the way he could also pick up some fresh salmon and they'd have the first barbecue of the season.

And back at his office the good luck had held. Lector's death notice was in yesterday's *Chronicle*, and it named the next of kin, who were listed in the phone book. Hardy called the eldest son, Clark, reached him at his home on Arguello, halfway out to Hardy's own. He made an appointment for when he got there. Perhaps most astoundingly, he only had one message on his answering machine — Pico with the sad news that Francis the shark finally hadn't made it. He just thought Hardy would want to know.

But even Pico's disappointing news couldn't bring him down. In fact, he was half tempted to call him back at the Steinhart and invite him and his family over at the last minute for the salmon barbecue, cheer them all right up. Then he remembered that he'd done pretty much the same thing with Moses and Susan the night before, and he reconsidered. Maybe it should just be his family, together, for tonight.

But after the first half hour with Clark and Patti Lector, and James's widow Ellen, he called Frannie again and told her he was sorry, but it might be a while. The Lectors were not in favor of an autopsy. It was going to be a long, hard sell. He'd try to get home as soon as he could, but she might want to go ahead with the kids and not wait on him for dinner. There was no anger, not even real disappointment in her voice when she'd told him it was all right. The only thing he thought he discerned was a bone weariness, and in some ways that bothered him more than if she'd thrown a fit.

He finally found a parking spot three long

blocks from his house. Bedraggled bouquets in hand, he undid the latch on his picket fence, closed it back behind him, then in five steps crossed the walk that bisected his tiny front lawn. At long last, he'd succeeded in getting the Lectors' permission, but only after tomorrow's service, which would not end with Mr. Lector's body in the ground at the family's burial plot in Colma, but rather on John Strout's metal table at the morgue.

Dragging himself up his front steps, he vowed that he had had enough of this getting home at all hours. He had to change something, not just for himself, but for his children, his wife, his marriage.

Of course, no light shone anywhere. He let himself in quietly, although the wood had swollen with the warm weather, and he had to push the door to get it closed. Tomorrow, he thought, he'd fix that — plane it true. Working with wood was something he'd once been good at, even passionate about. Then maybe he'd do some more household chores. Spring cleaning. They could open all the windows and let the air blow out the last of the winter's must, maybe put on some old Beach Boys, or the Eagles, and turn it up loud, get that peaceful easy feelin' going while they all worked together putting the house into summertime shape. Unplug all the telephones.

Flicking on the hall light, he stepped into the living room and dropped the flowers into his reading chair. Frannie's note was under one of the elephants on his mantel, just where she knew he'd see it when he got in.

"Dismas. Decided to take the kids to Monterey for the weekend. Back late Sunday afternoon. Fran."

No "dear," no "love," not even "Frannie."

He crumpled the note in one hand, leaned against the mantel with the other. His head dropped as though he'd been struck.

20

By 8:00 the next morning, Hardy was on the road.

He didn't know in which of the dozens if not hundreds of hotels and motels they'd be staying, but if Frannie and the kids were in Monterey, he considered it a dead lock that they'd hit the aquarium first.

The place wouldn't open for another fifteen minutes, but already a long line of visitors stretched up the hill from the entrance. He started there, got to the end, then found a low wall across the street on which he could sit, keeping an eye on the line as it grew while he waited.

He'd seen no coastal fog as he'd driven down Highway 1, and there was no sign of any now. Normally Monterey was as fog-bound as San Francisco, but clearly it was going to be a post-card day — soon he wouldn't even need the light jacket he was wearing.

They came around the corner two blocks up-hill. The kids were in the midst of some of their typical goofiness — even from this distance, Vincent's giggle carried down to him, then Rebecca's scream as she lunged back at him. Frannie walked a few steps behind them, head down, tolerant or uninvolved, her hands shoved into the pockets of a Stanford sweatshirt. She

299

was in shorts and running shoes, and with her long red hair down and loose, she could have easily passed for the other kids' older sister, maybe eighteen or twenty years old.

Hardy stood up by his low wall, continuing to watch their approach. The kids were playing like puppies, poking at each other, tickling and laughing. This silliness often if not always drove Hardy crazy at home, especially in the past few months. Suddenly, at this remove, he could view it a little more objectively. His children were doing exactly what they were supposed to be doing. They were good kids suddenly on a surprise vacation, and they were having a great, appropriate, carefree, and healthy time with each other.

What, Hardy wondered, was *his* problem that he couldn't enjoy them more?

Now Rebecca had her arm around Vincent's shoulder — they were almost exactly the same height. Suddenly Frannie skipped a couple of quick steps downhill and caught up with them with a joyous yell, a tickling goose under each of their ribs. "Gotcha!" More screams, more laughing, the kids turning back on their mother now, darting in and out of her reach while she parried and thrusted to keep them away. Hardy almost couldn't imagine the level of pure fun they all seemed to be having.

He started crossing the street as Vincent broke away after his latest raid. They'd now come down to about a block from Hardy, and his son stopped and stared down at him. After a beat, the recognition became certain, and he screamed in what seemed complete abandonment and happiness. "Dad!" Five seconds later, he plowed into Hardy at full speed, arms and legs all around him. Then a real hug before Hardy put him down. "I didn't think you were coming. Mom said you were too busy."

"I decided not to be."

Rebecca, too, ran down and threw her arms around him. "I'm so glad you're here, Daddy. It's such a perfect day, isn't it? I can't believe how beautiful it is here. I am *so* happy."

"Me, too." Hardy held her for a moment, then raised a hand, sheepishly greeting his wife. "Hi."

She had her arms crossed. "Hi."

Rebecca, who never missed a thing, asked, "Are you guys mad at each other? You're not getting divorced, are you?"

"Never," Hardy said, still holding his daughter. "Even if we were mad, we wouldn't get divorced."

"You're sure?"

"Jeez, Beck." Vincent didn't have much patience for his sister's paranoia. "How many times they got to tell you? They're not getting divorced." He whirled on his parents. "Right?"

"Right," Hardy said.

Frannie still hadn't ventured a word on the subject, but suddenly the expression of frustrated bemusement that she'd been holding shifted, and she walked the remaining few steps to where Hardy stood with his arms around the Beck. "I love your father very much," she said, planting a kiss on his cheek, "and we will never get divorced, ever." She gave him a long look. "Although someday I might have to kill him."

His daughter's jaw dropped, her eyes wide in terror. "Mom!"

"Joke, Beck. Joke." For his parents' benefit, Vincent rolled his own eyes at his sister's stupidity. "Like she's really going to kill Dad." Suddenly, then, seeing an opening, he poked at her with a finger again. Immediately, with a squeal of delight, she spun out from Hardy's embrace, after him down the hill.

Leaving Hardy and Frannie, standing there.

"Do you want me here?" he asked.

"Of course. Although I wish it didn't have to take kidnapping your children to get your attention."

"I wish that, too. But I guess sometimes it does."

"I don't think you're hardwired for that. Maybe you could work on it."

"That's what I'm doing, believe it or not. I'm trying. Even as we speak," he added. Then he shook his head. "I'm sorry."

She put an arm around his waist, started walking down the hill. "I'll get over it."

Bracco lived in three converted rooms over a stand-alone garage behind his father's house out in the Sunset District, on Pacheco Street.

He'd been pulling long hours this past week, so this morning he slept in. After an hour on free weights, he'd done some jogging and eaten five bananas with most of a box of Wheaties. Now, showered and dressed, Darrel sat with his father at a wooden table by an open window in the kitchen. The back of the house had a southern exposure and sunlight washed half the table. From time to time, a wisp of breeze would ruffle the lace curtains at the window.

Angelo Bracco had once looked a lot like his son, and there was still a resemblance in the face. But he'd lost his wife six years before — she'd cooked him healthy meals and also kept him interested in looking good. After she was gone, he went back to meat and potatoes. Then he started driving for the mayor, sitting all day. In these past few years he'd bulked up to where his five-foot, nine-inch frame carried around two hundred and twenty pounds. This morning he was wearing a form-fitting T-shirt. After they'd had their first sips of coffee, Darrel decided to say something. "You know, you wanted, you could use my weights sometimes. They're just sitting out there."

His father chose not to answer directly. "I saw you go out this morning. How far'd you run?"

A shrug. "I don't know. Five miles maybe. It was a good day for it."

"Couldn't resist, huh? Feel the burn, is that what they say?" Angelo sipped his coffee. "If I ran five miles, I'd drop dead."

"You probably would, but you don't start there. You work up to it."

He saw that his son meant well, and nodded in acceptance. "Well, maybe I will."

"I'd walk with you if you wanted. You got to start doing something, Dad. Lose a little of that." He pointed at the belly. "They say walking is as good as running."

"For what? You believe that?"

Darrel had to break a smile. "No. But it's a start. But the weights . . . I mean, there's lots of things nowadays. You could join a club, even."

This brought an outright laugh. "Maybe I'll walk, okay. Really. I'll think about it. But a club is out, okay? If I'm going to be in that much pain, I don't want anybody else to see it." He sat up straighter in his chair, sucked his gut in marginally, then let it back out. "So is that why you knocked at my door? To preach me the benefits of working out?"

"No," Darrel said soberly. "I just happen to notice my old man's put on some weight and it's probably not doing him a whole lot of good, that's all. Maybe I'd like him to stay around a while longer, okay?"

"Okay."

"So what I came over for is Harlen."

"What about him?"

"Well, here it is Saturday and we're both scheduled off, which I've got no problem with if nothing's happening. Except now we're in the middle of this homicide and we've got witnesses to interview if we're going to get anywhere, which it seems like we might if we keep at it. But he's got his family and it's Saturday . . . I only just now talked to him."

"So what's your problem?"

"My problem is we're partners and I don't want to cut him out, but I want to go talk to some people."

"So call him again, tell him what you're going to do, and go do it."

"That simple, huh?"

His father nodded. "It usually is."

"Today's date is April 14, 2000, Saturday. The time now is twelve twenty hours. This is Inspector Sergeant Darrel Bracco, star number one six eight nine. I am currently at a residence at 2555 Lake Boulevard. With me is Mrs. Jamie Rath, DOB 6/12/58. This interview is pursuant to an investigation of case number 002231977."

Q: Mrs. Rath, how well did you know Carla Markham?

A: She was my best friend. I've known her since our girls were in kindergarten together.

Q: And when was the last time you saw her?

A: Last Tuesday. I went to her house when I heard what happened to Tim.

Q: How late were you there?

A: I left around nine thirty, quarter to ten.

Q: And who outside of the Markham family was still there when you left?

A: Dr. Kensing was still in the living room. But the rest of us left in kind of a knot.

Q: Did you know Dr. Kensing before that night?

A: I knew of him, but we hadn't met. I know Carla seemed surprised when he arrived.

Q: Why was that?

A: Well . . . it was just awkward. He and Mr. Markham didn't get along, and then him being the doctor that day. Of course, this is before I knew that Dr. Kensing had killed Tim.

Q: I don't think we know yet that he killed Mr. Markham.

A: Well, I do. And I think he almost expected Carla to thank him for getting rid of him. Except what Dr. Kensing didn't know is that they'd patched it up.

Q: You're saying that prior to his death, Mr. and Mrs. Markham hadn't been getting along, is that it?

A: That's fair to say. But then, just this last weekend, Carla told me that they patched things up. Tim bared his poor little psyche — told her all about his affairs, his job problems, the incredible stress, the creep. So she was hopeful. Again. That's where they were on Tuesday, and it's why she couldn't believe he was gone, so suddenly. It was like whiplash.

Q: Did she appear depressed to you? Any suggestion she might commit suicide?

A: No way. I've known Carla for twelve years, Inspector. For the last three of those, she's been getting used to the idea of living without Tim. Why? Because she was going to leave him someday anyway. She knew that.

Q: But you just said they'd patched things up.

A: This time. But who knew for how long? Tim would fail again eventually — that's just who he was — and she'd wind up leaving him. She knew that, I'm sure, deep down. So it might have filled her with disappointment that he died, or even broken her heart at some level, but there had to be some relief there, too. And no way in the world would she kill herself over it.

Kensing walked up the six steps and pushed at the button next to the door of his old house on Anza Street. He still thought of it as his house and it made him sick to see how far Ann had let the place go. The once bright and appealing yellow paint had faded to a jaundiced pallor and was peeling everywhere. The white trim had gone gray. The shutter by the window nearest him hung at a cockeyed angle. The window boxes themselves had somehow misplaced even their dirt, to say nothing of the flowers he'd labored to establish in them. Back when he and Ann were good, they'd always kept the house up, even with all the hours they spent at their jobs. They'd found the time.

Now he looked down and saw that the corners of the stoop had collected six months' worth of debris — flattened soda cans, old newspapers and advertising supplements still soaked from the recent storm, candy wrappers, and enough dirt, he thought, to make a start of refilling the window boxes.

Where was Ann? Dammit, if she was still asleep, he was going to have to do something, although what that might be he didn't know. She should be awake at least to feed the kids. He pushed at the bell again, figured it must have stopped working, so he knocked. Hard. Three more times with his fist, shaking the door. He was turning to leave when he heard her voice.

"Who is it?"

"It's Eric, Ann. Open up."

"Didn't you get my call?" she asked. "I called two hours ago."

"Hi, Dad," his nine-year-old yelled from inside.

"Terry, you be quiet!"

"Hi, Ter. Hi, girls. You there?"

He heard sounds from both of them, Amber and Caitlin.

"Stop that!" his wife yelled at the girls, then talked again through the door. "I left a message telling you not to come." This was one of Ann's favorite tricks. Although she knew that Eric had a cell phone and beeper, she'd only call at his condo and leave a message he wouldn't get. Then she could be mad at him for being unreachable.

"Well, I never got it. Did you try the cell?"

"I didn't think of it. I thought you'd be home."

"Well, it was a nice morning. I went out for breakfast."

"With your girlfriend, I suppose."

He didn't feel the need to answer that. Instead, he tried the knob. "Come on, Ann. You want to open the door?"

"I don't think so. No."

"Well, that's going to make it a little tough for me to take the kids out to the ball game, isn't it?" His schedule allowed him only rare visits with his children during the week, so he made it a point to take them on weekends. Ann, burdened by her life, as well, had always before been happy to pass them off to him. Until now.

"Ann? What's this about?"

"You can't see them."

He kept his voice under control. "You want to open the door and we can talk about it?"

"There's nothing to talk about. You go away or I swear to God, Eric, I'll call the police."

"Ann, let's not do this in front of the kids. Just open up."

"No! You're not coming in. I'm not letting a murderer take my children."

The crying started. It sounded like Amber, the middle one, first. But the others immediately took the cue from her. Ann's voice, shrill and loud, cut through them all, though. "Stop that! Shut up, all of you! Stop it right now!"

"Ann!" Kensing pleaded through the door.

"Mom!" His son, Terry, hysterical. "I'm going out with Dad! You can't stop me."

"Oh, yes I can!"

Something slammed into the door.

"God, Ann! What are you . . . ?"

More sounds of manhandling. Then. "Terry, get upstairs, you hear me! You girls, too!"

Kensing grabbed the doorknob, shook it with both hands. "Ann, let me in! Now! Open up!"

She was herding all of them upstairs, to their rooms. He stood for another moment on the stoop, then ran down the steps and up the overgrown driveway on the side of the house. The back door was locked, too.

But unlike the front, it had six small glass panes in its upper panel.

Kensing wished it was the usual cold day and he had a jacket he could wrap around his hand, but all he wore was a collared golf shirt. Still, he had his fist clenched. He had to do it, padding or not. But then he remembered the man last year who'd died after slashing his arteries trying to do the same thing — bled out in six minutes. The instant's hesitation gave him time for another flash of insight that stopped him cold.

He was already a murder suspect. Even if he had every reason in the world, he'd better not break into his wife's house. But the kids — Ann had lost control, and though she'd never hit any of them before, she might be capable of anything right now.

He pulled out his cell phone and punched 911, then ran back up front. The dispatcher answered and he gave the address and briefly described the situation. "I'm outside now. I need some help immediately."

Back up on the stoop, he heard Ann, upstairs, still screaming at the kids. A door slammed up there. Finally, he heard her footsteps on the stairs inside, coming down. Now she was at the door. "Eric," she said. "Eric, are you still there?"

He didn't say anything. He was pressed against the wall, scrunched down under the sill of the stoop. He knew she wouldn't be able to see him even if she leaned out the front windows. His heart thrummed in his ears. In the distance, he heard the wail of a siren.

Then he heard the lock tumble, saw the door-knob begin to move. He grabbed and gave it a quick turn, then hit the door with his shoulder. Ann screamed as the force of it threw her backward.

But she didn't go down.

Instead, she gathered herself and charged at

him. "Get out of here! Get out of my house!"

He held her arms, but she kept kicking at him — at his legs, his groin. She connected and knocked the wind out of him. His grip went slack for a second. She ripped a hand free and swiped it across his face. He felt the hot flush of the impact and knew she'd scratched him. Raising his hand, he pulled it away and saw blood. "Jesus," he said.

"Daddy! Mommy!" From up the stairs.

"Don't!" Ann screamed. "Stay up there!" She never turned around, though, and came again at him. She kept coming, driving him back to the door, then out it onto the stoop. She kicked again at his groin, barely missing, but the kick spun him to one side. Now she charged full force, her fingernails out for his face.

Blocking her hands, he stepped back defensively. Her forward motion carried her by him. Her foot landed on one of the wet newspapers, which slipped out from under her. With another yell of anguish, she fell. Her head hit the concrete as her momentum carried her forward. She rolled down the steps all the way to the sidewalk, where she lay still.

The children flashed by Kensing and down the steps. They had just gotten to her, kneeling and keening around her, when a police car, its siren blaring, pulled up and skidded to a stop. Two patrolmen came out with their weapons drawn and leveled at Kensing.

"Don't make a move! Put your hands up!"

Glitsky and Treya had gotten out of bed late,

311

got a sense of the incredible day outside, and decided on the spur of the moment to drive up to Dylan's Beach, about forty miles north of the city. On the way up, they detoured over to Hog Island for an hour or so and ate oysters every way they could think of — raw, grilled on the barby with three different sauces, breaded and deep fried with tartar sauce. Fortified, even sated and happy, they took the long way north along the ocean — switchback one-lane roads that wound through the dairy farms, the redwood and eucalyptus groves, the timeless and seemingly forgotten settlements of western Marin county.

It was truly a different world here than anywhere else in the greater Bay Area, all the more magical because of its proximity to the kitschy tourist mecca of Sausalito, the tony, crowded anthill of yuppies that was Mill Valley. On this side of Tamalpais, clapboard main streets with a half dozen century-old buildings called themselves towns. The single sign of life would be twenty Harleys parked outside the only saloon — there was always a saloon. Along the road, they passed handmade signs nailed to ancient oaks advertising live chickens, pigs, sheep. Fresh eggs and milk every few miles.

Most of it looked slightly gone to seed, and Glitsky had been up here many times when, with the near-constant year-round fog and wind, it had seemed almost uninhabitable, a true wasteland. Today, in the warm sunlight — it would hit eighty degrees at the beach before they headed back home — the ramshackle and run-down landscape suddenly struck him as deliberate.

Lots of hippies from the sixties and drop- and burnouts from the seventies and eighties had set- tled out here and they didn't want it to change. They didn't want new cars and faux-mansions, but a slower pace, tolerant neighbors, privacy. Most of the time, Glitsky scoffed at that lifestyle — those people didn't have a clue, they weren't living in the real world.

But today at the beach he was watching what he would have normally called a cliché of an aging hippy. A man about his own age, early fif- ties, was weaving some spring flowers into his lit- tle girl's hair. Glitsky found himself almost envying him, the simplicity of this life. The woman with him — the girl's mother? — was another cliché. Her hair fell loose halfway down her back. She had let it go gray. She fingerpicked an acoustic guitar and would sing snippets of Joni Mitchell as the words occurred to her. It was possible, Glitsky the cop thought, that they were both stoned. But possibly not. Possibly they were blissed out on the day, very much like he and Treya.

"A chocolate chip cookie for your thoughts." She sat next to him, blocking the sun from his face.

He was stretched out on his side on their blan- ket in the warm sand. "Cookie first." He popped it whole into his mouth and chewed it up. "Thank you."

"Now thoughts," she said. "That was the deal."

"You don't want to hear my thoughts. They're scary."

"You're having scary thoughts *here?*"

"I like it here. I'm almost completely happy. That's scary."

"Comfort and happiness are scary?"

"They don't last. You don't want to get used to them."

"No, God forbid that." She reached a hand out and rubbed it over his arm. "Forgetting, of course, that you and I have had a pretty decent run together these past few months."

He put a hand over hers. "I haven't forgotten that for a second. I didn't mean us."

"Good. Because I'm planning on making this last a while."

"A while would be good. I'd vote for that."

"At least, say, another nineteen years."

"What's ninet . . . ?" Glitsky stopped and squinted a question up at her.

"Nineteen years." She spoke with an undertone of grave concern. With an age difference of nineteen years between them, the question of whether they should have their own child someday had nearly split them up before they'd gotten engaged. Glitsky had already done what he called "the kid thing" three times. He was finished with all that, he'd informed her.

It was one of the hardest things she'd ever done, but Treya told him if that were the case, they had to stop seeing each other. She wasn't going to use the issue in a power play to get or keep him. If parenthood wasn't something he wanted to go through again, she understood completely. He was still a fine man and she loved him, but she knew who she was, what she wanted.

For some time Glitsky had lived with her decision, and his own. Then one day he woke up and realized that he had changed his mind. Her presence in his life was more important than anything else. He could not lose her — nothing could make that happen.

But now that once-distant someday had arrived, and Treya was biting her lip with the tension of whether or not her husband would accept the reality. "I don't think children have as good a chance if they're raised in a home where the parents aren't comfortable and happy, so I think we really ought to keep that going at least until the baby's out of the house and on its own. Don't you?" Trying to smile, she gripped his hand tightly in both of hers and met his eyes. "I was going to tell you last night when we got home, but then your inspectors were there, and by the time they left it was so late. . . ." Her tremulous voice wound down to a stop.

He stared back at her for a long beat, his expression softening by degrees into something akin to wonder. "Why do you think it took us so long?" He brought her hands to his mouth and kissed them. "It sure wasn't for lack of trying."

21

Four hours later, Glitsky was sitting on his kitchen counter, trying to maintain a professional tone when he felt like screaming. He was talking on the wall phone to one of the deputy sheriffs from San Francisco General Hospital. The deputy had called homicide about this lady who'd been arrested and brought to the hospital earlier in the day with a broken ankle and a concussion. She couldn't seem to stop talking about her husband being the murderer in the family, so why was she the one who was in jail? The deputy figured that if anything about this woman involved murder, he ought to bring it to somebody's attention. But when he'd called homicide, nobody had any idea what he was talking about, so they gave him Glitsky's home number.

"What do you mean, they arrested her? They didn't arrest *him?*"

"The husband? No, sir. Not that I can tell. They didn't bring him here, but maybe he wasn't hurt." When healthy people got arrested in the city, they went to the jail behind the Hall of Justice. If they needed medical care of any kind, SFGH had a guarded lockup wing, and that's where her arresting officers had taken Ann Kensing.

In ten minutes, Glitsky had tracked down the

home numbers for both of these guys, and one of them — Officer Rick Page — had the bad luck to answer the phone. Even over the wire and without benefit of his terrible face, Glitsky's tone of voice, rank, and position conspired to reduce the young cop to a state of panic. He ran his words together staccato fashion, repeating half of what he was trying to say. "It was, it was a nine-one-one DD, domestic disturbance. When we got there, we got there and the woman was on the ground, surrounded by her kids. Her children."

"And the man?"

"Well, he, he was bleeding from his face, pretty bad where she cut, cut him."

"Cut him? With what, a knife?"

"No. Fingernails. Scratched, I meant scratched him, not cut. On his face. He was up some outside stairs when we got to the scene. Me and Jerry — my partner? — we pulled up and both drew down on him."

"On him?"

"Yes, sir."

"But then you arrested *her?* Even though she was the one more badly hurt, is that right? How did that happen?" Glitsky's anger and frustration were still fresh, but he had calmed enough to realize that he wasn't getting what he needed from Officer Page. He toned his voice down a notch or two. "You can slow down a little, Officer. Just tell me what happened."

"Yes, sir. First, he's — the guy, Kensing — we checked back with the dispatcher when he told us and it was true, he's the one who called in the nine-one-one. He was locked out of his house and was worried his wife was going to hurt his kids. He said he needed help."

"I'll bet." Glitsky was thinking that Ann Kensing was smart to lock him out. "But you got there and what?"

"Well, the first thing, she was on the ground, on the sidewalk at the bottom of the stoop. There were steps, you know, going up to the house. The husband was still at the top, just standing there. Three kids were down with her, screaming bloody murder. We didn't know — it could have gone any way from that situation, sir. So we both pulled our pieces and approached the suspect, who at that time we thought was the guy."

"And how was he?"

"Cooperative, scared. He wanted to go and see how his wife was, but we had him freeze. He had his hands up and didn't move a muscle, which was good. From what we see so far, we're taking him downtown at that point."

"Okay," Glitsky said. "What changed that?"

After a short hesitation, Page started again. "The main thing was, I talked to him. The first thing he said, I mean he's reaching for the sky and bleeding like a pig out of his face, and the first thing he does is *thank me* for getting there so fast."

"He thanked you?"

"Yes, sir, which makes it like the first time I've ever had that in a DD. You know what I'm saying?"

Glitsky did know. Usually, by the time the police got involved in a domestic dispute, the gentler social amenities, especially extended to the cops coming to break up the fight, weren't in the equation anymore. "Go on."

"Anyway. So Jerry was with the wife, trying to get the kids to calm down. He, the guy, Kensing, asked if he could sit down on the step and I said no way, turn around, the normal drill and go to cuff him. At which point, one of the kids, the boy, he starts coming up the stairs and he's going, 'What are you doin' to my dad? Leave my dad alone. It wasn't him. It was Mom.' "

"The kid's saying that?"

"Yeah. And Kensing's cool. He's going, 'It's all right, Terry.' The kid. 'He doesn't know what happened.' Meaning me, you know. But I'm not letting the kid get near him." This, of course, was standard procedure because irate parents — especially fathers — who see jail time in their immediate future have been known to take their own children hostage in an effort to avoid it. "So I get in front of him and call for Jerry, who's gone back to the unit to put in a call for the paramedics. By this time, the wife's sitting up, holding the two girls. There's some citizens — neighbors — coming out to look. Time to put up my piece, which I do."

"Okay."

"Okay, so it's all slowing down. Kensing's cuffed and he asks can he turn around, slow, and I let him, and he tells his kid just stay put, don't worry, it's all going to work out. He tells me, calm as can be, that he's a doctor. He can help

319

his wife. But I'm getting a funny feeling right about now anyway."

"About what?"

"About it's mostly always the guy, you know, sir. Doing damage."

"I know."

"But this guy. He's almost relaxed. Nowhere near the usual rage. He says she just slipped and I'm goin', 'Sure she did,' but he says, 'Look,' and nods down to this mark on the landing, where it's pretty obvious at least *somebody* slipped. A wet newspaper. And the kid goes, 'It's true. I saw her. She just slipped. He didn't touch her.'

"So I'm thinking, Shit, now what? I mean, we get to a DD and *somebody's* going downtown, right? I mean, usually the guy, but no way are we leaving without one of them. It's a real drag coming back two hours after everything was patched up fine with the lovebirds, except then one of them shoots the other one. You know what I mean?"

"I hear you," Glitsky said.

"But what am I going to do? I walk Kensing down the steps and put him in the back of the unit, locked up, and this time one of the neighbors comes up — I got her ID and everything, if you want to talk to her — and she tells me the same thing. She saw it all — Kensing was completely defensive, never hit her, she scratched him, came at him again and slipped." Page took a breath. "So Jerry and I have a little powwow and break up the two daughters and ask them about it — same story, it's the wife all the way. And by this time, the ambulance is here. The wife's groggy and can't walk on one foot. Plus she's going to need stitches in her head. So Jerry and I decide she goes, the guy stays home." In the course of the long telling, Page's voice had grown in confidence. Now he spoke matter-of-factly. "I don't know what else we could have done, Lieutenant. Four witnesses pegged the wife. The guy didn't do anything wrong."

Glitsky was tempted to ask Page if he realized that the man he hadn't arrested was the prime suspect in a homicide investigation, but why would the officer know that? And what point would it serve? And now for a while at least, Ann Kensing was safe. Unhappy and hurt, but safe. He'd take that. "So he's at her house now with the kids?"

"I don't know, sir. He might be at his home address, which I've got. Would you like to have that?"

"I've got it," Glitsky replied. "Maybe I'll go have a word with him."

"Sorry about not letting you in, Lieutenant, but I've got my children in here. They've seen enough cops for the day. One of 'em's already asleep and the rest of us are watching videos. It's been a long day."

"I just wanted to ask you a couple of questions. It won't take fifteen minutes."

"Fifteen minutes? It won't take any time if I don't let you in. It seemed to me we went over everything already the other night and according to my lawyer, I shouldn't have talked to you then."

"That was before today. Before the fight with your wife."

"We didn't have a fight. Fighting takes two people. She attacked me."

"Why were you over there in the first place?"

"It was my day for the kids. I had Giants tickets. Pretty simple. Look, this really isn't a good time, all right? Now I'm being a father to my children, who are traumatized and exhausted enough." Kensing shifted to his other foot, let out a heavy breath. "Look, I don't want to seem like a hard-ass, Lieutenant, but unless you have a warrant to come in here, good night."

In his Noe Street railroad-style duplex apartment, Brendan Driscoll worked at his computer in the tiny room behind the kitchen all the way at the back. In spite of the beautiful day, he'd remained in the shaded, musty, airless cubicle, completely engrossed in his work, since an hour after he'd woken up, at 10:30 in the morning, with the worst hangover of his adult life.

Now, nearly twelve hours later, he stretched, rubbed his hands over his face, and pushed his chair back away from the terminal. In a minute, he was in the kitchen popping four more aspirin and pouring himself an iced tea when Roger appeared in the doorway.

"It moves," Roger said.

Brendan looked over at him. "Barely."

"How's the head?"

"The head is awful. The head may never recover. The rest isn't really that great, either. What's in a Long Island iced tea, anyway? And how many of them did I have?"

Roger shrugged, then shook his head. "You told me to stop counting, remember? But I know that was after the third one, when I mentioned it might be smarter to stop."

"I should have listened to you."

"This is always the case. So," Roger inquired, "with all the hours you've spent atoning for your sins in your cave today, is your penance served?"

"It isn't penance I'm seeking," Brendan said. "It's revenge." He went over and pulled up a chair at the kitchen table. "I just feel so betrayed."

Roger sat down with him. "I know. I don't blame you."

"That's my problem. I don't know who to blame." He sighed deeply. "I mean, do I blame Kensing, or his stupid wife for making Tim feel like he had to jog every day. That's what created the opportunity in the first place."

"Well, the jogging didn't kill him, Brendan."

"I know. But if he hadn't gone out . . ."

"He wouldn't have been hit, and he wouldn't have been at the hospital . . . we've been through all this already."

They had, ad nauseam, Brendan realized. He sighed, then squeezed his temples, wincing from the hangover pain. "You're right, you're right. It staggers me, though, that Ross thought he could buy me off and purge my files. Could he really think that I couldn't see this coming, that I wouldn't be prepared?"

22

Jackman was as good as his word, and on Monday morning, Hardy had two more binders of discovery on the Markham case ready for him when he got to his office.

He got himself a cup of coffee, settled down at his desk, and opened the first folder. Someone had obviously lit a fire under the transcribers, because already several interviews had been typed up, including Glitsky's with Kensing, with Anita Tong the housekeeper, Bracco's with Ann Kensing. He flipped pages quickly. Nothing was tabbed yet — that would be one of his more tedious jobs — but he was satisfied to see much of what he'd hoped and expected: the original incident report at the hit and run; the hospital PM, performed immediately after Markham's death; Strout's autopsy findings and official death certificate; the first cut of the crime scene analysis of Markham's home.

He'd been at it for over an hour, unaware of the passing of time. His hand automatically went to his coffee mug and he brought it to his lips. The coffee had gone cold. Suddenly he sat up straight with almost a physical jolt. He raised his eyes from his binder, almost surprised to see the familiar trappings of his own office. For a while there, with the taste of the bitter dregs of coffee on his tongue, caught up in the analysis of evidence, he was a DA again, putting on this case rather than defending it. The feeling was unexpected and somehow unsettling.

He got up, shaking his head. In front of his desk, he threw a round of darts, then walked over to the window and looked down at Sutter Street. Outside, San Francisco wore its usual workday face after the glitzy and gaudy weekend — street debris kicked up by a good breeze off the bay, an obscure sun fitfully breaching the cloud cover.

He realized that it wasn't just the mnemonic tug of the coffee. The truth was that he was in prosecutor mode. To prove his client's innocence, it inexorably followed he must show that someone else had killed Tim Markham and presumably his whole family, as well. That left him only one mandate — find that person and the evidence to convict.

It was ironic, he knew, that he'd ever become a defense attorney in the first place. He wasn't drawn by nature to stand up for the accused. On the justice versus mercy continuum, he always came down for justice. After he'd gotten out of the marines and Vietnam, he walked a beat as a cop for a few years. Then he'd gone to law school thinking he'd make a career taking bad people to trial and putting them behind bars — that had been his whole orientation, in work and in life. If a previous DA hadn't fired him over office politics, he had little doubt he'd still be down at the hall working with Marlene and for Jackman. And though by now he'd been on the defense side long enough that he had grown used to it, part of him still longed for the purity of prosecution.

The law, as David Freeman was fond of saying, was a complicated and beautiful thing. And, Hardy thought, never more so than in this: while a not-guilty verdict did not always mean your client was factually innocent of committing the crime for which he or she had been charged, on the other hand a guilty verdict meant that he or she was. When Hardy the defense attorney got a client off with a good argument or some legal legerdemain, there was of course some satisfaction that he'd done his job, earned his pay. But only rarely did it compare to the soul-affirming righteousness he had sometimes felt when he'd convicted a truly evil miscreant and removed him or her from society.

He sat back down and took another sip of the cold coffee. His eyes went back down to his binder.

Here were interviews with several nurses at Portola. A quick perusal told him that Bracco and Fisk had done some basic footwork, which might save him some time. He noticed, though, that they didn't seem to have identified anyone who had been present at or about the time Markham had died. He flipped more pages, but found no sign of this essential and fundamental information.

He looked up again, staring angrily at nothing into the space in front of him. His jaw was tight, his eyes hard.

Jackman was keeping his end of their bargain. He had sent him the discovery folders, all right, but they obviously weren't complete. Hardy didn't think this was an accident, but he didn't see Jackman's hand at work withholding his evidence. He saw Glitsky's.

Bracco and Fisk had gotten into the office late in the day because, over Bracco's objections, Fisk insisted that they keep trying to find some kind of lead on the car. So first they'd gone door to door in the neighborhood again, catching a few people who hadn't been home a week ago, although coming away with about the same results. No one had seen the accident or noticed the car speeding away. Next — Fisk was at the wheel today — he'd driven Bracco crazy by making the rounds of his old hit-and-run connections: several body shops on Lombard, Van Ness, in the Mission. He'd put them on notice last week. Now he was following up.

One of them actually had an early-seventies green Corvair in the shop, brought in late yesterday afternoon, damage to the right front bumper and the hood. The owner claimed his brake had released itself on one of the city's famous hills and he hadn't remembered to curb his wheels. The car had rolled twenty feet or so and hit a tree, a branch of which had then fallen on the hood. The owner of the shop, Jim Otis, had been planning to call hit and run sometime today, and certainly before he did any repair work on the vehicle.

But a quick spray with luminol pretty much eliminated the car from contention. Luminol was a nearly foolproof agent for revealing the

327

presence of blood — even trace amounts, even after a washing — and there was none on the Corvair. Still, Fisk dutifully took down the owner's name and address. Before this was over, he vowed, he'd find out if he had an alibi for 6:30 last Tuesday morning.

Now, after lunch and under Glitsky's direction, they were finally on their way back to Portola for more interviews. The lieutenant had reviewed their work from Friday and now wanted to know about the two other doctors who'd been in the ICU last Tuesday. He also wanted the exact chronologies of people coming and going as far as the nurses at the ICU station could remember.

But it wasn't turning out to be as simple as they'd hoped. Different ICU nurses had come on duty with the new week. Of the two that had been on duty when Markham and Lector had died, Rajan Bhutan had transferred to labor and delivery and was in the midst of a traumatic childbirth. Connie Rowe, assigned to general floor duty, was out at lunch.

Asking Fisk if he'd mind holding the fort for a few minutes while he took care of some business, Bracco left his partner to wait for her and went back upstairs. When he got back to the ICU nurses' station, he introduced himself for a second time to the female nurse sitting at the console. When he asked, she explained that her shift partner was in with one of the doctors while he made his rounds. They'd both be back out shortly if he needed to talk to either of them.

But after making sure that the doctor was

neither Cohn nor Waltrip, whom he *did* want to speak to, Bracco told her that what he really needed was a few minutes at a quiet spot — would she mind if he went to sit in the waiting room just down the hallway there?

A middle-aged couple sat miserably holding hands and whispering on one of the couches. Bracco took the upholstered chair near the hallway, where he could see both the entrance to the ICU and the nurses' station. Sure enough, the other nurse emerged with her doctor in a couple of minutes. After a brief conversation in the middle of the hallway, the doctor left the nurse and turned to come this way, while the nurse returned to the station with her partner.

Standing up as the doctor entered the waiting room, Bracco went back into the hallway. One of the nurses — he didn't know which one — still sat at the console, facing away from him, working at a computer terminal. The other was nowhere to be seen.

He crossed the hall and in ten steps was at the door to the ICU. A wired-glass pane afforded a clear view inside the room. He saw nothing but beds. A last look at the typing nurse, a glance toward the waiting room — no one was visible. In an instant he was inside.

He checked his watch and moved. Forcing himself to an almost leisurely pace, he walked the periphery marked by the beds, stopping while he counted to five — the most he could bear — at each one. The entire circuit took him forty-eight seconds.

Again, he checked the door's central window-pane. Then he pushed at it, was back in the hall, and let it close behind him.

At the nurses' station, he cleared his throat and the same woman he'd originally spoken to turned from her work at the computer. "Did your partner come back out yet? I notice that a doctor just came into the waiting room, I was wondering if she'd come out with him?"

The nurse smiled at him. "I think she may have just run to the bathroom for a minute. She ought to be right back." She, too, glanced down the hall to where the doctor had gone. "When she does, it might be a good time for those questions you said you had for us."

"That's what I was just working on back there." He motioned to the waiting room. "As it turns out, I don't think I'm going to need them after all. But thanks for your time. Sorry to have bothered you."

"No problem," she said. "Anytime."

Downstairs, Bracco learned that Connie Rowe had returned from lunch and that she and Inspector Fisk had gone back to the cafeteria where they could talk without too much interruption. By the time he sat down with them, Fisk had started. They sat kitty-corner to one another and the tiny tape recorder was on the table between them. Praying that Fisk had remembered to turn it on, Bracco pulled up his chair.

Q: You know Inspector Bracco? From last week? Ms. Rowe was just telling me about her partner, Rajan is it?

A: Rajan Bhutan.

330

Q: What about him?

A: Well, as I was telling Inspector Fisk, it's nothing really specific. The way the shifts break, I only wind up working with him in the ICU about ten times a year, but it seems as though every time he's on, something bad happens.

Q: Do you mean somebody dies?

A: No, not just that. People are always dying there because they're usually critical when they come in. But I haven't worked a shift with Rajan without incident in at least the last year. I don't mean to speak badly of him, but . . . it's just really creepy. *He's* really creepy, just skulking around, never talking to anybody really.

Q: Do you think he had anything to do with Mr. Markham's death?

A: I don't know about that. That's such a strong accusation. But then when you all came in on Friday and started asking us questions, and you notice he barely said a word? Didn't it seem that way to you? And he knows how the shifts work as well as anybody. And what happened that day. Who was there.

Q: Ms. Rowe, excuse me for butting in, but when Inspector Fisk asked you if you meant that people died in the ICU when Rajan was on, you said 'not just that,' isn't that right? What did you mean by that? Not just what?

A: Not just dying.

Q: But that, too.

A: Yes, but as I say, a week doesn't go by without that. But things — supplies, I mean — they go missing. And he hovers. Do you know what I'm saying? He *lurks,* and he *hovers.* You'll be coming around a corner and he'll suddenly just be there. Standing there. It's very creepy. Nobody can stand him.

Q: Was he there last Tuesday? In the ICU when Mr. Markham died? Is that what you're saying?

A: We were both in there for both the code blues. I know that. Before that, I was at the desk —

Q: Were you at the computer?

A: I think so, it's a little jumbled now, but I think I was placing some orders, but I don't know where he was.

Q: Ms. Rowe, when you got the signal — the code blue, is it? — and you went into the ICU, was he already there?

A: Yes. By Mr. Lector. The other man that died.

Q: Was there anybody else in the room?

A: Just Dr. Kensing.

Q: And where was he?

A: With Rajan. By Mr. Lector. He was the first code blue.

Q: In other words, they were not by Mr. Markham.

A: No. His monitor went off a few seconds later.

At one o'clock, Hardy picked up the phone on

his desk and heard the drawl of the coroner. "Y'all owe me a thousand dollars. I assumed you were in some kind of hurry, seein' as you had the body delivered straight from the wake, so I worked all day yesterday, Sunday, an' brought in my best lab person. Then a couple of hours this morning. Mr. Lector died because his heart stopped beatin' and nothin' more."

"No potassium?"

"Nothin', Diz. I ran all the scans down to the C level. There wasn't so much as a wayward aspirin he shouldn't'a had in him."

"That wasn't exactly what I'd hoped."

"I know that, you made it clear enough. But look at the bright side. No matter what, your client didn't kill Mr. Lector."

This brought a dry chuckle. "Thanks, John. That's eases my mind considerably."

"You're welcome. And Diz?"

"Yo."

"While I do love my work, there don't seem to be no shortage. This here is your wild-goose allotment for the year."

Rajan Bhutan spoke through his hang-dog face with the clipped, sing-song formality of the subcontinent's accent. "The woman is an idiot," he said with resignation in his tone. He was alone in the nurses' lounge with Bracco and Fisk. "I've had nothing but trouble from her from when she began here, because she is lazy and prejudiced against me. And now you tell me she accuses me of killing these gentlemen? This is really intolerable. I will have to speak with her.

And perhaps with the administration."

In his inexperience, Fisk had mentioned that they'd talked to Ms. Rowe and his name had come up. Now of course, Bhutan was angry with Rowe, and wanted to talk about her failings as a nurse and human being, rather than what he had done last Tuesday night. And naturally Bhutan also figured that these same police would repeat everything that he said to his coworkers. It wasn't the best way to approach an interview. It wasn't even the second best way.

Bracco had taken over the lead in the questioning, trying to get back on point. "Are you telling us you were not in the room when the monitors for Markham went off?"

"Yes. For him. I had rushed in for Mr. Lector, who was first."

"And where were you just before then?"

A disgusted look settled on his features. "You may believe this or not, but even Dr. Ross must have seen me as he came out of the waiting room when the first monitor called. I was with one of the gurneys in the hall, right away there. I believe there were two or three of them, backed up. This is intolerable," he repeated.

"So let me get this straight," Bracco prodded. "You're telling us that when the code blue went off for Mr. Lector, there wasn't anybody in the ICU?"

"Except that it wasn't yet a code blue. Dr. Kensing had just gone in again before, then when I got to Mr. Lector's bedside, he had me call it up."

"And then you were all working on Mr. Lector

334

when Mr. Markham's monitors started to do whatever they do?"

"They screech continually. But yes."

"Nobody had just gone near him?"

"Not that I saw, no."

Hardy and Freeman were walking uphill on Sutter Street. The sun had never quite cut through the cloud cover and now the fitful breeze of the morning had freshened into steady wind, as well. It wasn't, all in all, a great day for a stroll, but Freeman had told Hardy that he could only take some time to talk if they could combine it with a shopping trip to Freeman's cigar supplier. He was almost out of them — meaning, Hardy supposed, that he was down to his last dozen or so.

But what else could he do?

"The problem is, I don't really have anybody else," Hardy was saying. "Carla — the jealous wife — might have been a good bet, but she went dead on me."

Freeman clucked. "That is inconvenient."

"And then I really thought I had something with the other guy who'd died at the same time as Markham — Lector. But Strout says no, so now I'm wondering if I should even have Wes Farrell bother to try to get permission for Loring's autopsy."

"Who was there?" Freeman got the door to the Nob Hill Cigar and held it open for Hardy. Immediately, they were both gripped in the thick, humid, fragrant embrace of one of the city's most anachronistic destinations. Freeman, observing the ritual he performed every time he bought his cigars in bulk, didn't so much as glance at the display downstairs, but led the way upstairs. Hardy tagged along. It was pretty much a Victorian men's club, and while of course women were legally permitted, in a dozen or more visits Hardy had never seen one here.

After a few minutes of cigar chitchat with Martin, their host, they found their way to a couple of leather easy chairs with their complimentary snifters of cognac — not for sale, not even legally consumable on the premises, but always offered nonetheless. Martin reappeared in a moment, offered and lit their Cohibas, then retired back downstairs to fill Freeman's order.

Another important element of David's own individualistic ritual was to savor only and not talk until the first ash was ready to fall. Sometimes this could take ten minutes. But Hardy found that today, although he'd come specifically to pick the old man's brain, he was happy to sit and reflect.

The rest of the weekend in Monterey had been sublime. Hardy had always responded to the magic of things nautical, and the aquarium seemed to restore something in his soul, in his connection to his children, his wife. Suddenly he was more than what he did for a living. All the flotsam and jetsam of who he was got stirred, shaken. It woke him up.

In the afternoon, he bought some swim trunks and they'd gone to the beach, explored the tidepools, screamed with joy and madness at the freezing water. They'd eaten splendidly at The

Old House, walked out on the wharf by moon-light, and fed the seals. Back at their hotel, they had managed to upgrade the single room Frannie and the kids had stayed in the night be-fore to a suite, and with the children sleeping soundly behind the connecting door and a little privacy, they'd made love twice — night and morning, like newlyweds.

Up here in the smoking room, Freeman tapped his ash. "So who was there?" he asked. "I believe that's where we were."

Of course he was right. Hardy rarely even mar-veled at it anymore. But he still had the same an-swer as last time, which was a question of his own. "Where, David?"

"At the hospital. You've told me you need people with a motive to have killed Markham, but you don't know of anyone else except your client, so all right, let's assume for the moment that it's not him, although that continues to make me uncomfortable as hell, except still, what you need, even beyond motive, is presence, by which I mean that whoever it was had to be there and that brings us back around full circle."

"I'll give you a dollar if you can diagram that last sentence for me."

Freeman briefly attempted to glare, but the charade didn't hold, so he sipped some cognac and sucked on his cigar. "Occasionally," he said, "the gift of wisdom arrives untidily packed."

When Hardy got back to the office, it was after four o'clock. The alcohol had slowed him down while the nicotine had jolted him up. He went to his windows and flung them both wide open, then got himself a large glass of water and sat down behind his desk. In his absence, he had three phone calls.

The first was from Jeff Elliot, who wanted to know what, if any, progress Hardy had made on the Kensing front. He was working on another Parnassus column and maybe they had some mutually beneficial information they could share.

In the second message, Wes Farrell was calling to let him know that he'd finally persuaded the Lorings to let authorities dig up his mother. Now he was meeting some pretty strong resistance from Strout, with whom he thought Hardy had already cleared it. What was going on?

The third call, at last, was from his client, whom he'd been trying to reach all day. He called him back first and Kensing started off by telling Hardy that he still had the kids after the fight with his wife . . .

"Wait a minute, Eric. Back up. What fight with your wife?"

He explained what had happened in some detail, following up with Glitsky's unexpected visit to his house last night. "I got the impression he thinks I went over there to hurt her. Maybe worse."

Hardy remembered Glitsky's prediction that Kensing would do just that. "But you didn't talk to him again. Please say you didn't."

"No. I didn't let him in. But I thought I'd make myself scarce today."

"Probably a good idea. What'd you do?"

After he'd dropped the kids at their school,

Kensing decided to really take the day off, think a little, get some kind of plan. He'd walked across the Golden Gate Bridge and back, driven downtown and eaten dim sum in Chinatown, taken in a movie, then gone back for the kids at school. He'd also just talked to Ann. She was out of jail and wanted the kids to return to her house, but he didn't feel good about that. What did Hardy think?

"Do you think she's a danger to them?"

"Before Saturday, I would have said no. But I've never seen her like that, and we've had our share of fights, believe me."

"But nothing physical? You're sure?" This was always a critical point to make. It would be very bad if the grand jury discovered that Kensing had ever used any kind of violence on his wife. Better to know now. "You never hit her, Eric? Not even one time?"

"I'd remember. I never hit her, although she's hit me a few times."

Hardy didn't much like that, either, but for Kensing's purposes, it was better than if he'd hit her. "Okay, then. Exactly what happened Saturday?"

"I guess she must have finally convinced herself that I killed Tim."

"That's what I'd concluded, too. Would you like me to talk to her? Do you think she'd talk to me?"

He heard the relief in Kensing's voice. "That'd be great. Either one."

It wasn't really the answer to his question, but it was clearly permission. Hardy felt free to move on. "Eric, can you tell me who was at the hospital with you last Tuesday?"

"Where? You mean in the ICU?"

"Anywhere near it really."

"Sure. I think so. Me, obviously. The nurses." He continued with the litany, which was more substantial than Hardy had realized. That in turn gave him some hope, although it might also mean a lot of work. He hadn't even heard of all of the players yet, and this struck him as unconscionable.

A new wave of anger at Glitsky swept over him. What the hell was he doing? Maybe he had concluded that Jackman's deal with Hardy wasn't his deal, too, but in fact it was. Jackman's deal meant next to nothing without Glitsky's cooperation.

The thought passed, though the anger did not. But Hardy was taking notes through it all. In addition to Carla, Kensing told him, there had been Malachi Ross, Markham's assistant Brendan Driscoll (whom Kensing seemed to dislike), a couple of nurses, and two other doctors, including Judith Cohn. Hardy found himself wondering again how long Eric's relationship with Cohn had been going on. He would have to try and talk to her.

But first, after he'd hung up with Kensing, there was Ann. She answered her telephone. Yes, of course she'd talk to him, she said. Anytime he wanted. She wanted her children back.

It turned out that her house was on his way home. He could be there in twenty minutes.

23

On crutches and with a cast on her foot, Ann Kensing led Hardy into the messy living room. Throwing some dirty kids' clothes to the floor from the couch, she motioned for him to sit on it and then took her spot at the opposite end. Now she'd heard his opening and he could see her wrestling with what to do with it.

"You're his lawyer, Mr. Hardy. What else are you going to say?"

"I could say a whole lot of things, Mrs. Kensing. I could say okay, he did it, but nobody's ever going to be able to prove it. I could say he did it but it was a medical mistake that was unintentional. I could even say he did it but he had a good reason — seeing Mr. Markham lying there under his power rendered him temporarily insane, legally insane. Don't laugh. Juries have bought worse stories. But what I'm here to tell you is that he says he didn't do it at all. I've been a lawyer for a long time. Believe me, I've had clients lie to me more than once. I'm used to it. But the evidence just doesn't prove that your husband did a thing."

"He told me he did it. He even told me how before anybody else knew. How about that?"

Hardy nodded thoughtfully. "He told me about that, too. He was mad at you, insulted that

341

you could even think he could have killed any-body, so he got sarcastic."

"He said he pumped him full of shit."

"Yes he did. But listen, he's a doctor. If he's riffing off the top of his head, just trying to get you going, drugs in the IV is the obvious choice, right?" But he didn't wait for her answer. He wanted to keep her from getting wound up by arguing. Kensing had warned him that when her emotions got her in their grip, she let them carry her where they would — and in her grief over Markham and general rage at the situation, she wasn't likely to be completely rational. Now he leaned in toward her. "What I wanted to talk to you about is how quickly we can get your children back to you."

As he suspected it might, this calmed her slightly — even she understood it wouldn't serve her well to fly off at him. A hand went to her lips as she visibly gathered herself. "I asked Eric if he could bring them back today. He didn't want to do that."

Hardy nodded, all understanding. "He talked to me about that. I asked him to put himself in your shoes. Suppose you were perhaps actually thinking that he'd killed somebody. If that were the case, wouldn't he have fought you to keep you from taking them?" He sat back into the couch, affecting a nonchalance he didn't feel. "If you want my take on this, the problem is that you're both excellent parents. You both have the same instinct, which is to protect your children. This is a good thing, wouldn't you agree?"

"Yes. I think so." Her eyes, rimmed with exhaustion, now shimmered with tears. One drop spilled over onto her cheek and she wiped it away with a weary, automatic swipe. Hardy had the feeling she'd been doing that so much lately that she didn't even notice anymore. "He's never hurt them. I don't really think he would, but then after last week, when I thought . . ." She shook her head.

"When you thought he killed Tim Markham?"

She nodded.

"Mrs. Kensing. Do you really think that? In your heart?"

She chewed at her lower lip. "He could have. Yes. He did hate Tim."

"He hated Tim. I keep hearing that. Did he hate him more than he did two years ago?"

"No, I don't think so."

"Then less?"

"Maybe. I thought he'd gotten used to it."

"Okay. When he hated him the most, did he talk about killing him then? Was he that mad?"

"No. No. Eric wasn't like that. He'd never . . ." She stopped now and looked straight at him, suddenly defensive. "He told me he did."

"Yes he did. He said those words. That's true."

"What was I supposed to think?"

"When did he say all this, Mrs. Kensing? Wasn't it last Tuesday, right after you'd heard that Mr. Markham had died? Right after you accused Eric of killing him?"

She didn't reply.

He kept up the press. "He told me you were in agony. You'd just found out that the man you loved was gone. You were lashing out at the world at the injustice of that, lashing out at him because, maybe, you felt he was safe. Isn't that the way it was?"

He'd never get another chance. In court, in front of a jury, she'd have her story down pat. She'd have been coached over and over again by the prosecution. She'd never embarrass herself by admitting that she might have misunderstood or exaggerated. Indeed, by that time, any doubt would have long since vanished. Even by now, she had already invested a great deal in Eric's confession. Hardy hoped he could lead her to a path by which she could withdraw, if not with her dignity intact, then at least with some grace.

But she couldn't let it go easily. She was pressing her fingers so hard against her mouth that her knuckles were white. Her eyes were closed in concentration, in recollection. "I was just so . . . lost and hurt. I wanted to hurt him, too."

"You mean Eric. So you accused him of killing Tim, knowing it would hurt him, too?"

"Yes." Suddenly she opened her eyes, released a pent-up breath. "Yes. And he said, 'Absolutely.' Absolutely," she repeated.

"And you took that to mean that he admitted the truth of what you were accusing him of, killing Tim?"

"Yes. I suppose so."

"But looking back on it, is that what it sounds like to you now? Is that really what he meant, do you think? That he'd actually done it? Or were you both just snapping at each other in the tension of the moment?" Hardy lowered his voice to the level of intimacy. "Mrs. Kensing, let me ask you to think about something else. After you left the hospital that day and came back here to your life, you had a day or so to get used to this tragedy, isn't that right, before the police came to talk to you?"

"What else could I do? It was the middle of the week. The kids had school. It was just me and them."

"Sure, I understand. But during that time, before you'd heard about the potassium, you had quite a bit of time during which you say you believed Eric had killed Tim. And yet you made no attempt to go to the police yourself?"

The question surprised her, and she hesitated for a moment, perhaps wondering about the why of her answer. "No. I didn't know."

"Why do you think not, if you don't mind?"

"Because I thought . . . I mean, I guess I believed . . . I'd heard Tim died from the accident."

"And you believed that? For two days? Even after Eric had apparently told you he'd killed him? Mrs. Kensing, did you get any sleep in those two days?"

Shaking her head no, she began to sob quietly, but Hardy had to go on. "So when you heard Tim had been killed on purpose, that it hadn't been the accident, what went through your mind?"

"I don't know. When I heard about it . . . it was so unreal. Almost as though he'd died again, a second time."

"And that's when you remembered what Eric had said the first time?"

"Yes."

"But in spite of Eric's apparent confession, you never really seriously considered that Tim had died of anything but the hit-and-run accident?"

"But he said —"

"But you didn't believe him at the time, did you? You didn't believe him because you knew he didn't mean it literally, as a statement of fact. He said it to hurt you, didn't he? It was a sarcastic and hurtful way to call you stupid, wasn't it? That you'd asked such a question."

She looked at him in a kind of panic, forcing him to backpedal slightly. "I'm not trying to put words in your mouth, Mrs. Kensing. I'm just trying to find out what really happened. What you recall now, today."

Hardy waited through the lengthy silence.

"I mean," she said, "if Tim had been killed, that changed everything, didn't it?"

"I agree it changed that it was no longer an accident." He let her live with it for another long moment. "Mrs. Kensing, Ann, I'm not going to lie to you. Your testimony here is critical, and as you said when I first got here, I'm Eric's lawyer. I've got a vested interest in keeping him out of jail." He waited again until she met his eyes. "If in your heart you believe that Eric killed Tim, and meant it when he said he did, I'm not even going to try to talk you out of it. You know what you know. But Eric is among the things that you know best, for better or worse, isn't that right?

And he's been a good father, as you admit; a good doctor. Maybe even by your own estimation, a good man?"

She was nodding, fighting back more tears. "I always thought he was. He is."

And finally, the nub of it. "Do you really believe he *could have* killed Tim? That he actually did that? Because if he didn't, Mrs. Kensing, somebody else did, and that's the person I'd like to find, whoever it might be. And to do that I'm going to need your help."

The real problem with the reunion between Eric and Ann Kensing was that Hardy didn't know that Glitsky had assigned an officer to protect Mrs. Kensing from her husband should he come back to try and kill her again. When Hardy had rung the bell and been admitted to Mrs. Kensing's house an hour before, this officer hadn't molested Hardy in any way, although he had placed a call to Glitsky informing him of the circumstances.

So at 5:35, Glitsky knocked at the door himself. Ann Kensing got up and, thinking it was her husband with her children, she opened it. Hardy, who had remained seated in the living room, jumped up when he heard the voice, but it was too late — Glitsky's foot was already across the threshold. Holding up his badge, he had asked if he could come in, and Ann had seen no reason not to let him.

Hardy, fiercely protective and fuming, stopped when he got to the hallway. "What the hell are you doing here? Are you following me?"

Then, to Ann. "You can ask him to leave. He doesn't have a warrant."

But Glitsky had already won that round. "I'm sorry, but no you can't, ma'am. You let me in. I don't need a warrant."

"So what's your point?" Hardy asked, taking another step toward him. "Just general harassment this time? Just kick all the rules out?"

Glitsky ignored him and spoke to Ann. "I thought you might want some moral support before your husband and this Mr. Hardy double-team you. Has he theatened you in any way?"

"No." She looked back and forth at the two angry men. "Well, just —"

Hardy held out a hand, interrupting. "Ann, please."

"Just what, Mrs. Kensing? Are you saying he has threatened you?"

"No. But he told me some rights that maybe —"

Now Glitsky interrupted. "Is he your lawyer, too? God forbid you haven't let him talk you into that?"

"No, he's . . ."

By now the voices had pitched up. Hardy couldn't resist finishing her thought, which would — he was sure — give him the next round. "She admits the confession was bogus. She's withdrawing it."

Glitsky stood stock-still, rocked by the blow. Although he'd expected something very much like it, the confirmation of the news was a haymaker. His scar flared, his eyes blazed. It took a moment for him to get his senses back. "All

348

right," he said finally, softly. "But both of you are now going to hear me out." And in the most reasonable tone he could muster, he proceeded to give her an earful of angry cop.

Like: "Ms. Kensing, you said that your husband confessed to murder. That's part of the record in this case. If you go changing your story under oath, you might get in very big trouble yourself. Do you understand that?"

Like: "Isn't it obvious to you that Mr. Hardy here is using your own children as bargaining chips so that you'll help him get his client off? Could it be any more transparent?"

Like: "Of course your husband isn't pressing charges against you about what happened Saturday. He's lucky he didn't have them brought against himself. But please be clear on this, I'm asking you. He doesn't decide what charges get filed, the DA does. Try to understand that what he's really doing is trading your *possible* misdemeanor charge against his own *murder* rap."

Like: "You don't have to make this kind of deal. We can in all likelihood have a judge pull a TRO" — a temporary restraining order — "and get your children back with you."

Finally, Hardy had had enough. Glitsky was overdoing it. Besides, it was in his own best interests to rise to her defense. "Actually, the lieutenant's a little off base. There's no judge in the world who would grant a TRO on what's going on here." He turned to Mrs. Kensing. "Unless, it must be said, he issued it against *you*. You're the one with charges pending here, not your husband."

Back at Glitsky, his voice hardened. "And you know the woman's got every right in the world to talk to me, Lieutenant. We need to know exactly what Dr. Kensing said, and if perhaps your inspectors were too eager. Mrs. Kensing got it wrong the first time and, realizing that, would like to get back on some kind of cordial footing with her ex-husband so that they can cooperate, as they always have before, on raising their children. I don't see how you can have any kind of problem with that."

Glitsky's scar seemed to glow red in the dusky light. "You don't? You don't consider what you're doing tampering with this witness?"

"Absolutely not."

"You deny that you're bringing undue influence to bear?"

Hardy bit back his initial response, which prominently featured the vulgarity Glitsky so despised. Instead, he turned again to Mrs. Kensing. "Am I forcing you to do anything?"

"He's not, Lieutenant."

Glitsky believed that like he believed in the Easter Bunny. He wanted to pull Hardy into another room where they could duke out some of their continued differences outside of the presence of this woman, but if he suggested that, he knew it would come across as though he were trying to hide something from her. And he couldn't have that, either. There was no other good option, so he went right ahead with what he had to say.

"Well, I'll tell you what, Counselor. *I'd* call this tampering. I'd call it undue influence, if not outright coercion. Jackman cut you a sweet deal, okay, but that's not carte blanche to sabotage any case we might be building. I think he's going to find you went way over the line with this. To say nothing of this autopsy charade I'm learning about with Strout. And now he tells me you've got Wes Farrell on your team, too, trying to pull the same crap."

"Wes isn't on any team of mine, Lieutenant. He's got his own client and his own problems."

"Yeah, which includes somebody else who died at Portola Hospital? Just surfacing at this moment? You expect me to believe that? It's just a coincidence, is it?"

"I don't expect you'd believe anything I said. But I'm not trying to obstruct this case. I'm trying to see it for what it is and solve it."

Glitsky just about spit it out. "Yeah, well that's *my* job."

Hardy shot it back at him. "Then do it."

"I just tried and Jackman stopped me."

"He did you a favor."

Glitsky snorted scornfully. "You're telling me I got the wrong man? Then how come every time I turn around, you're playing some legal game covering his rear end — cutting your deal with Jackman, muddying the waters with Strout, talking to my witness here. You know what that makes me think? You've got something to hide. That all you're doing is trying to get your client off, and be damned with the law, and be damned with the truth."

"That's not who I am and you know it."

"Yeah, well if the shoe fits . . ." Glitsky turned

to Ann Kensing. "You're making a mistake here," he told her. "If you want to change your mind again, after you've calmed down, you've got my number."

Hardy was in a true high rage now, and he wheeled on them both, his voice laden with disdain. "If you do, make him promise he won't charge you with perjury."

Glitsky glared at him. "You think that's funny?"

"No," Hardy snapped. "I don't think it's funny at all."

While the Kensing children got used to their mother again, the cast on her foot, the bandage on the back of her head, their father stayed away from her. He called out for a pizza delivery and spent the best part of the next half hour picking up around the house — he collected and started two loads of laundry, put every dish and utensil he could find into the dishwasher, ran a sponge mop over the kitchen floor.

Hardy called Frannie to tell her he would be a little late. Yes, sorry, he knew. But he was still shooting to be in time for dinner, which they'd rescheduled over the past weekend for 8:00, instead of 6:30 or 7:00, to better accommodate Hardy's workday. He also took an extra minute and described a bit of his terrible fight with Glitsky. He needed to talk to her; he needed her. And he would definitely be home by 8:00. She could set the clock by it.

Hardy went to the bathroom to throw some water on his face, hoping it would counteract some of the nausea he was feeling, the residue of his argument with Glitsky. He felt as though he'd swallowed a rock. When he returned, the children were devouring pizza in the kitchen, a video of some action flick on and purposely turned up loud.

In the living room, Ann and Eric had taken their respective neutral corners, and now they sat in silence, not even facing each other, waiting for Hardy.

He started to go back to his old spot on the couch with Ann, but decided that this might have the appearance that he was taking sides, so he stayed on his feet and stood by the trash- and ash-filled fireplace. "Both of you are doing the right thing," he began. "I know it's hard." He looked from one of them to the other. Both obviously still seethed. He kept on. "I've been involved with this case for going on a week now and there's far too much I don't know. We need to talk together about it. Who might have killed Mr. Markham."

Ann took it as an opening, and she wasted no time getting to the crux. "All right. I've heard your lawyer tell me you didn't do it, Eric. Here's another chance for you. Why don't you tell me yourself?"

He turned his head to face her, then shook it in disgust and weariness, and brought a flat, dead glance back to her and answered her with no inflection at all. "Fuck you."

"There!" she exploded to Hardy. "See? That's him. That's who he really is."

Kensing came right at her, up out of his chair,

his voice a rasping whisper so the children wouldn't hear. "You don't have a clue who I am anymore. I'm just so tired of your shit. Did I kill Tim for Christ's sake? Fuck that and fuck you again."

"Eric," Hardy began.

But now his client turned on him. "I don't have to listen to this all over again, do I? It won't work with her. You can see for yourself — she's an irrational menace. I'm out of here and I'm taking the kids with me."

"Don't you touch them again!" She might use crutches for her sprained ankle, but Ann could move quickly enough without them when she had to. She was at the entrance into the hallway, blocking Kensing's way, before he'd gone three steps.

Hardy moved too, as fast as he could, getting himself between them. For an instant, he thought he and his client were going to mix it up. "Get out of my way, Diz."

"Not happening," Hardy said. "You going to make me?"

"Don't you make *me*."

"See?" Ann was saying. "This was Saturday! This is what he did then!"

"I didn't do anything on Saturday!" He pointed at her over Hardy's shoulder. "You want to talk about the problem here! You want to talk danger to the kids, you want to talk unstable?" Then he took it directly to her. "You really think I've got it in me to kill somebody? Give me a break, Ann. My whole life is keeping people alive. But you lock me out, raving about maybe

354

I'm here to kill my own children? That's real craziness. That's scary fucking lunacy."

Hardy had to find a wedge to get in or this was over before it started. "Speaking of scared, she was scared, Eric."

"She's got no call to be scared of me. I've never done anything to hurt her. If she doesn't know that . . ." He shifted his focus from Hardy to her, his own anguish now evident in his voice. "What were you thinking, Ann? What's the matter with you?" Finally, a plea. "Would I ever hurt a kid? One of my kids? How could I ever do that?"

Ann was almost panting — taking quick, deep breaths. "When the police told me, I just . . . I was afraid . . . I didn't . . ." Hardy thought she would break again into sobs, but she got hold of herself this time. "I didn't know what to think, Eric. Can't you understand that? I loved Tim, and he was dead. I hadn't slept in two days. I was so scared."

"Of me? How could you be scared of me?"

Now she pleaded for understanding from him. "*I was just scared, okay?* Of everything." Her voice was small. "I didn't want to make another mistake and then, of course, I did."

It was the closest thing to an apology Kensing was going to get. Hardy recognized that and took the moment. "Why don't we sit back down?"

"Did Ross go in?" Hardy asked. "It must have been minutes before the monitors went off."

"He might have. He could have. I just don't know."

355

"Where *were* you then?" Ann's anger hadn't entirely passed. "I thought you were on the floor. It's not that big. How could you not know?"

Kensing kept any defensiveness out of his reply, directed as much to Hardy as to Ann. "We had three patients in the hall. One of them was having problems coming out of the anesthesia, so Rajan — he's one of the nurses — he and I were checking vitals pretty closely. During those minutes, anybody could have walked behind me — I'm sure some people did — and I might not have noticed. An hour before, Brendan Driscoll had just walked all the way in."

"How did that happen?" Hardy asked.

Kensing shrugged. "Nobody stopped him. You'd have to know him. He carries himself with a lot of authority. If any of the nurses would have said anything, he would have just said, 'It's all right, I belong here,' and they probably would have accepted it."

"I hate the little bastard," Ann added. "He actually believed he could order Tim around."

"Did he?" Hardy asked. "Order him around?"

"He tried, especially when it came to his time. Scheduling."

"And how did Tim feel about that?"

"He couldn't live without him," Eric put in, unable to keep some fresh venom out of his voice. "Brendan did about half his work."

"Wrong!" Ann Kensing wasn't going to let Eric slander Tim. "Tim thought big. Brendan was good with details. But Brendan didn't do Tim's work. He took orders . . ."

356

Eric snorted in disagreement.

". . . there's no question who was the leader."

"So there was friction between them?"

"Major," Eric said. "You've got to know Brendan to appreciate him. 'The little engine that could.' "

Hardy came back to Ann. "What else did they fight about? Besides you?"

She hesitated. "I think some of Tim's financial decisions. Tim was more of a risk taker."

"With Parnassus's money?" Hardy's main interest was the murder, but if he could uncover some business dirt that might be helpful to Jackman, he'd be glad to have it.

"Well, I don't know exactly. The last couple of years they've had to run pretty lean . . . and then there were some personnel problems —"

"Me, for example."

Ann shrugged. It was the truth. "Well, yes. Among others."

Kensing amplified. "Brendan wanted Tim to fire me straight out starting three or four years ago. Make an example of me."

"Why? What had you done?"

"General attitude, I think, more than anything. Lack of respect. I kind of took the lead in standing up for the patients over money."

Ann jumped in to qualify that. "Tim would say in resisting the company —"

Hardy cut off the potential argument. "So how did the secretary get involved in all this? He had no real power, did he?"

"How did Rasputin get in?" Eric asked. "He had no real power, either."

357

The dynamic was still eluding Hardy. "But the guy's just a secretary, right?"

For the first time, Ann and Eric shared the same reaction — a shared joke. "Mr. Driscoll," Eric explained, "was an executive assistant. Never, ever, ever a secretary."

"And I hope that's clear," Ann added, a wan smile flickering.

"As to how he got where he did," Eric kept it on point, "as Ann's mentioned, he was the detail guy. Well, you take care of enough details, pretty soon it looks like you run the shop."

Ann started to say something, perhaps defend Markham again, but Eric held out his hand, stopping her. "Look, this is what happens. You get called to the office of the CEO, you're uptight to begin with. So you're waiting outside Markham's office by Brendan's desk, and his attitude tells you that whatever trouble you might have thought you were in, in fact it's worse.

"Then, while you wait and wait, and you do, Brendan the very well-dressed and extremely formal executive assistant basically explains the ground rules. Mr. Markham doesn't like personal confrontation. He prefers to keep meetings short. Within a week, he tells you, you'll receive a written précis of the main points covered and actions you discussed that would be taken. You should then sign this letter to acknowledge its contents and return it to the office.

"The point got made. The guy had developed this just unbelievable array of rules and protocol, all designed to insulate and protect his boss. I mean, he'd write in unsigned postscripts at the bottom of letters, and you'd think they were from Tim."

Suddenly, hearing the specifics, Hardy understood completely. David Freeman's receptionist, Phyllis, was a lesser version of Brendan Driscoll. Hardy had been humorously pressing Freeman to fire her for about five years, but the old man wouldn't hear of it, saying he'd never get his work done without her. And perhaps he believed it. But Hardy had on several occasions seen Phyllis restrict access to Freeman so thoroughly — and with such sincere compassion and sympathy — that associates she didn't like had finally quit the firm over it, thinking all the while it had been Freeman who'd been stiffing them. "And Tim was okay with this?" Hardy asked.

"Actually, no," Ann said. "When he finally started seeing the extent of it. I think it was one of those things that started small, you know, then over time got out of hand."

"Enough to get Driscoll fired?" Hardy asked.

Ann hesitated. She brushed some hair back away from her forehead. "The truth is that Tim felt he was having some kind of midlife breakdown. The business was falling apart around him, then his marriage, his kids, all that. That's why he went back to Carla, to see if he could save something he'd worked years to build, but it's also why he couldn't fire Brendan, though he knew he should. But he couldn't while everything else in his life was in such upheaval. He depended on him too completely."

Hardy didn't know how much of it was true,

how much was a function of Markham's rationalizations to his mistress so that he could appear sensitive and caring. One thing was sure, though — Ann believed it.

"Did Tim talk to him?" Hardy asked. "Give him any kind of warning?"

"Sure. Brendan knew, I think, that Tim had made up his mind to let him go. It was just a question of the timing. Tim couldn't hide that from him if he wanted to, I don't think. If that's what you're asking."

And suddenly, Hardy was thinking that Driscoll was at least some kind of suspect. "How did he feel about Carla?"

"You mean would he kill her? And the kids? What for?"

"That's my question."

She was still thinking about her answer when Kensing had one. "If he felt that Tim was personally dumping him, I could see him wanting to wipe out any trace of him. The whole family."

But this was San Francisco. Hardy had to ask the question. "And you're convinced, Ann, that Tim was completely straight. Sexually. He and Brendan didn't have something else going on?"

"Tim wasn't gay," Ann said, dismissing the idea out of hand. "Promise."

Which, Hardy knew, did not make it a certainty by any means.

Eric spoke up again. "But if Brendan kills Tim, he's unemployed."

"But he's not fired, is he? He's the loyal and hard-working executive assistant up until the very end. He gets another job in fifteen min-

360

utes." Another thought occurred to Hardy, another tack. "When you threw him out of the ICU, where did he go?"

"I don't know. Off the floor, anyway." There must have been very little pleasure in the original situation, but Kensing relished something about the memory of it. "He didn't seem to believe that I could do that to him. Order him out of there. He found out."

"And you're sure he didn't return before the code blue?"

"I don't think he did. I can't say for sure. I told you, I was busy out in the hall."

"But he was definitely still in the hospital, at least."

"Oh yeah. After Tim died . . ." He sighed again. "He didn't take it well. It was pathetic, in fact. Embarrassing."

Hardy checked his watch. He had forty-five minutes before he needed to be home and he didn't want to start something he couldn't finish. But putting these two together was turning out very well, and Ann — as Markham's lover — had access to parts of his psyche that would be unknown to anyone else. "Let me ask you, Ann," he began. "What was in those original memos to Ross that made Tim so mad?"

"Let me guess," Kensing said. "Sinustop?"

Ann nodded. "That's it." She looked at Hardy. "Have you heard of it?"

"It's a new hay fever pill, isn't it?" Hardy had a vague memory. "But there was some problem with it?"

"Not for most people," Kensing said. "Some

361

people, though, developed the unfortunate side effect of death. This was after the reps dumped thousands of samples on us and the directive came down from the corporate office —"

"From Dr. Ross," Ann interrupted. "He made those decisions. Not Tim."

"If you say so." Kensing's look told Hardy he wasn't buying that. "Anyway," he continued, "this stuff was so inexpensive and miraculous that we were strongly urged to prescribe it to all of our patients with any and all allergy symptoms. You know about samples?"

"Not enough," Hardy replied. "Tell me."

"Well, any new drug comes out, their reps go out and try to get doctors to give them to patients for free. The idea, of course, is brand-name recognition. The stuff works, it's on the formulary, we prescribe it. Bingo, a wonder drug is born. But the sample campaign for Sinustop was just unbelievable. Nationwide, they must have given away a billion pills."

"And this was unusual?"

Kensing nodded soberly. "The numbers were unusual, yes."

"So what was the problem between Markham and Ross?" Hardy asked.

Ann looked over at Eric, then back to Hardy. "Tim heard about the first death and got a bad gut feeling. He asked Ross to call back all the samples and take it off the formulary until they could check it out further."

"But he didn't?"

Ann shook her head. "Worse than that, really. He and Tim had had these fights before, but

362

Ross was really superinvested in this one. He tells Tim he's the medical director, he knows this stuff. Tim just runs the business side. Why doesn't he stick to that and keep his nose out of the medicine, which he doesn't know anything about?"

"So they went at it?"

Kensing seemed jolted out of his silence. "Wait a minute. Wait a minute. You're not saying Tim was the good guy here, I hope?"

She faced him with an angry and pitiless look. "What's he supposed to do, Eric? Tell me that."

Hardy didn't want to let any more friction develop. Kensing had enough reasons to hate Markham on his own — he wasn't going to change his mind because maybe Tim had been a better CEO than he'd thought. "So how long had Tim and Ross been together?"

"They were two of the founders." She shrugged. "You could look it up."

"And recently they'd had more than one of these Sinustop–type fights?"

She frowned. "A few. Tim thought Ross's decisions weren't good medicine. He believed we had to keep delivering a good product —"

"Product," Eric said, snorting. "I like that."

Hardy ignored the interruption. "But then with Sinustop, things got worse? What finally happened?"

"Well, Ross got his way. They didn't pull the samples —"

Kensing supplied the ending. "And sixteen other people died around the country. Two of them with Parnassus."

In the telling, Hardy had come to remember the scandal clearly now. But although it had been prominent in the news, he didn't recall that Parnassus had been any part of it, and he said as much.

Ann jumped to Markham's defense. "Tim covered for Ross, that's why."

Kensing was shaking his head. "Not." He turned to Hardy. "Tim released a statement that the two patients who had died had taken samples they'd gotten here from before the first death had been reported — apparently this was true — and that we'd recalled all the samples and taken Sinustop off the formulary at the first indication of any problem. Not true. And if you call that covering for Ross . . ."

"That's what he did," Ann snapped at him.

Hardy jumped in before the smoldering anger in the room could erupt again. "Okay, good," he said. "That's the kind of thing I want you both to keep thinking about." He turned to each of them in turn. But tension remained high.

He was afraid to push his luck any further. Standing, he kept up his patter to keep them from each other. "I'm afraid I've got another appointment. Mrs. Kensing, thanks for your time. We're settled in terms of the kids, right? All good there? Eric, I'd like a few words with you on our way out. I'll wait while you tell your children good night."

"Honey, I'm home!" Ricky Ricardo he wasn't, but for years early in their marriage, Hardy had come through the front door with his dead-on

364

imitation. He'd made it with four minutes to spare by his watch, and considering the ever-escalating demands of the case that had been consuming his hours, he felt he'd done well.

All lanky arms and legs, Rebecca came flying down the hallway. "Daddy! I'm so glad you're home." She jumped at him and knocked him back, but he held on and gave her a spin.

In the dining room, the table was set. Frannie came to the door of the kitchen with her arms crossed over her chest, but she was smiling. "Cutting it close, buster. Very, very close."

"I'll get better, I promise."

They shared a chaste married kiss. Vincent, hanging back by the family room, said, "Gross."

So the two adults made eye contact and suddenly had their arms around each other, making out like teenagers. He picked Frannie all the way up off the ground and she kicked back her heels.

"Gross me out," Vincent shouted.

"C'mon, you guys! Please. Just stop, okay." This was Rebecca, arbiter of social correctness to the whole family.

"I can't help it," Hardy said, finally stopping. "Your mother makes me crazy."

"Kiss me, kiss me, kiss me," Frannie begged.

Hardy complied. The romantic assault drove the two kids to the front of the house, gagging at peak volume. The last kiss turned into a semireal one, and when it ended, Frannie caught her breath for a second, then said, "Oh, that reminds me. Treya called this morning. We talked for nearly an hour."

Hardy was thinking this was swell. The wives were going to referee, and that would end with them all hating one another.

"What about?" he asked.

"She's pregnant."

24

Malachi Ross sat kitty-corner to Marlene Ash at a large table in the Police Commissioner's Hearing Room, facing the members of the grand jury. When Ross had first come in, he took the oath and sat down, declining to remove the jacket to his suit. This had been a mistake. Once the initial opportunity had passed, no other appropriate moment presented itself. He didn't want to seem nervous. Which he was. By now he was sweating heavily.

Rooms in the Hall of Justice were traditionally far too hot or way too cold. Due to the state power crisis, maintenance crews had adjusted each and every one of the thermostats in the building. Now all the rooms that had been too cold were too hot and vice versa. It must have been eighty degrees in the airless chamber.

Ross's original plan was to cooperate fully with the investigation into Tim Markham's death, and to that end his time in the witness chair began amicably enough. For nearly a half hour, this attractive and competent woman walked him through the many years of his and Tim's relationship, the founding of Parnassus, the social contacts shared by the two men. Ms. Ash was looking for the person who had killed Tim. He had expected this sort of background drill, had even mentally prepared himself for it.

He'd just given the grand jury a couple of minutes on the nature of his professional relationship with Mr. Markham. He'd told them that there had been very little friction between the two of them over the course of a dozen years, although of course they'd had their disagreements. But basically, they respected and trusted each other.

Marlene Ash took this moment to stand up and move off a few steps into the center of the room. This was when the focus of the interrogation began to change. "Dr. Ross," she said, turning back to where he sat, "how is Parnassus doing financially right now?"

He took a misdirected shot at some levity. "We're doing about as well as most health organizations in the country, which isn't saying much. But we're still afloat, if that's what you mean."

A frigid smile. "Not quite. I was hoping you could tell us with more specificity. One can be afloat and still sinking at the same time, isn't that right? Wasn't that the entire second half of *Titanic*? Aren't you now the acting CEO of the corporation?"

"Yes." He composed himself, looking down at his linked fingers. When he raised his gaze to the grand jury, the effect of the tragedy he'd endured was apparent. "After last Tuesday, after Tim — Mr. Markham — died, the board appointed me CEO on an interim basis."

"So you're intimately familiar with the company's financial situation, are you not?"

"Well, it's been less than a week. I wouldn't say I've got the handle on it that Mr. Markham had, but I'm reasonably conversant with the numbers, yes. And frankly, have been for some time."

"Then you would know if, in fact, Parnassus is under some financial duress, wouldn't you?"

"Yes."

"Has the company, in fact, considered filing for bankruptcy?"

Understanding that financial pressures at Parnassus would clearly appear to the DA to be a possible motive for Markham's death, Ross had expected his inquisitor to get to this line of questioning sometime, but now that it was here, he felt somewhat unprepared. He ran a couple of fingers over his damp forehead, considered whether he should ask permission to take off his coat, or simply do it. In the end, he did nothing. "It's certainly been discussed. It's an option we've considered."

"Do you know if Mr. Markham had considered it, as well?"

"Yes. The matter has been on the table now for some time."

During the next forty-five minutes, Ash led him on a grueling journey through the Parnassus books, through the intricacies of incomes, copays, expenses, payrolls, premiums, and corporate salaries. The damned woman seemed to know enough to cut through his obfuscation and get to the real nuts and bolts of how the place worked. Ross knew that many other employees had also gotten subpoenas, and figuring that on balance they would tell the truth, he had no choice but to stay close to the facts himself.

"So, Mr. Ross, to your knowledge is Parnassus going bankrupt in the next six months? If not, please explain how you plan to keep the company solvent."

The sheer effrontery of the question made him want to snap back that it was none of her goddamn business, but he realized that he was trapped.

Now began a cat-and-mouse game where he provided as vague and general a version as possible of his plans for Parnassus, from which Ash — calm, collected, and apparently with all the time in the world — pried out details, one by one and piece by piece. He felt as if he were being very slowly ground to sausage.

By the time they finished, the water pitcher in front of him was empty, and he was so wet with perspiration he might well have dumped its contents over his head instead of drinking it. The only good news was that the questions about the formulary had centered on the dollars and cents, details such as how much items cost and the volume of prescriptions. Ash didn't really probe how new drugs got listed in the first place. Ross found it agonizing to wait for that shoe to drop — what if they knew? Or even suspected? Wouldn't they have had to tell him he was under investigation? Would he have to stop and insist on seeing a lawyer?

But these fears remained unrealized. Ash moved along to her own priorities. "So Dr. Ross, to summarize. It is your testimony under oath

370

that you do not expect Parnassus to go bankrupt within the next six months, whether or not the city pays the thirteen-million-dollar bill it has presented."

Ross put on a fresh face for the twenty citizens seated in front of him. He was surprised to see such a focus, an apparent interest, in most of them. They were waiting for his answer, although he had a sense of gathering impatience. But maybe, he realized, that was him. "Well, never say never. Bankruptcy protects the corporation from its creditors, true, and we could indeed use some relief there if the city defaults on its obligation. But with a group like us, when our biggest client is the city and county of San Francisco, it would also negatively impact our credibility, which is not too high as it is. As some of you may know, we've been getting a lot of bad press lately."

"I'm glad you brought that up, Dr. Ross." Ash looked like she meant it. "I was hoping that you could give us some insight on the type of disagreements that must have surfaced at Parnassus in light of, say, the Baby Emily case. I should tell you that the grand jury already has a working knowledge of those events. Maybe you could fill in some of the blank spots? Specifically, Mr. Markham's role and reactions of various staff to it. Please begin with Mr. Markham."

"Are you saying you think his death might be related to Baby Emily or something of that nature?"

"That's what this inquiry is about, Doctor. Mr. Markham's death." She had moved a few steps closer to him and now, standing while he sat, she loomed as somewhat threatening. "Someone introduced a lethal dose of potassium into his IV. As a doctor, would you agree that it is unlikely that this could have been an accident?"

Ross didn't know what kind of answer Ash wanted. He wished they would have allowed him to bring his lawyer into the room. He had to rely now upon the truth, and this made him uneasy. "It's always possible to give an improper dose of any drug. If Mr. Markham's heartbeat had become irregular, I could envision the need to administer a therapeutic dose of potassium. It's also possible, though rare, for a drug's concentration in solution to differ from what's on the label."

He was slightly shocked to find Ash prepared for this. "Of course. Please assume we have the drip bag that held the potassium in this case, and the concentration is correct. Also assume that there is no indication that Mr. Markham's heart, prior to the attack brought on by the overdose, was malfunctioning. So given these assumptions, do you have any explanation for these events other than that this was an intentionally administered overdose?"

Ross wiped sweat from his upper lip. "I guess I don't see any other possibility. Do you mind if I take off my coat?"

"Not at all." In half a minute, he was seated again. Ash hadn't lost her place. "So, Doctor, if Mr. Markham was intentionally overdosed —"

"I didn't say that." Then, amending. "I didn't

realize we'd gotten to there."

At this, Ash turned dramatic. She paused, as though in midthought, and glared down at him. "That's exactly where we are, Doctor. Did you and Mr. Markham have serious disagreements, for example, over policy?"

Ross lifted his chin in controlled outrage. "Are you joking?" he asked her.

"About what?"

"As I take it, you're asking me if some argument about business would have made me want to kill my longtime friend and business partner. I resent the hell out of the question."

"I never asked that question," Ash said. "You made that leap yourself. But having asked it, please answer." She fixed him with a steadfast gaze.

He matched her with one of his own. "No, then, nothing. Nothing that even remotely would have made me consider anything like that." He spoke directly to the jury. "Tim was my friend, a close friend."

Ross forced himself to slow down. A fresh pitcher of water had appeared — maybe it had been there for a while. He poured some into his glass and took a sip. "I need to point out, Ms. Ash, that the medical decision on Baby Emily, though hugely unpopular, wasn't all wrong. Baby Emily did in fact make it to County and to the premature baby unit, where she lived until she was transported back to Portola. I didn't kill her by any means, or even endanger her unnecessarily."

"But how did Mr. Markham react to all this?"

"He was all right with it until it became big news."

"You two did not have words over it?"

"Of course we did, after it blew up on us. He thought I should have consulted him, that I shouldn't have acted only on business considerations." Again, he directed his words to the grand jury. "We had some heated words, that's true. We run a big, complicated business together, and our roles sometimes overlap. We'd been doing this for twelve years." He made some eye contact, decided he'd be damned if he'd even dignify Ash's insinuation with a further denial.

As they'd been sitting down to the Tuesday lunch group at Lou the Greek's, Treya had made apologies for Glitsky's absence. He'd been called away at the last minute to a murder scene in Hunter's Point. Hardy was convinced that this excuse was an outright falsehood.

A murder scene at Hunter's Point indeed, he mused. As though they didn't happen every week. Hardy knew that unless some gangbangers had slaughtered themselves and twenty or thirty other bystanders in a daylight shootout involving children, drugs, the Goodyear blimp, and a sighting of the Zodiac Killer, Glitsky the administrator wouldn't need to be called to a "murder scene in Hunter's Point."

In Hardy's mind, the nature of the excuse had even deeper implications. The mundanity of the explanation, though perfectly plausible on the surface, was in reality so lame that Hardy took it to be a secret yet personal fuck-you message to himself. Murder scene, my ass, he thought. Right up there with "My grandmother died." Or "The dog ate my homework."

Furious at most of them, but especially at him, Abe was avoiding the group today. It probably hadn't helped when he'd gotten the word this morning that Jackman had directed Strout to go ahead with Wes Farrell's request to dig up his clients' mother. Before they'd sat down, Strout told Hardy that he had called Abe as a courtesy to tell him about this decision. He'd endured an angry earful of Glitsky's opinion on the question, then thanked him for it, and said he'd be going ahead on Jackman's approval anyway.

But no one else seemed bothered by his absence. They'd barely gotten settled before the conversation had gotten into full swing. David Freeman had started with a few comments about the Parnassus situation, how prescient they'd all been last week. Before too long, half the table had chimed in with one comment or another. Eventually, they got to Jeff Elliot's first column on Malachi Ross, which led Jeff to ask Marlene Ash if she'd talked to Ross yet and, if so, how he'd fared before the grand jury.

She'd smiled, glanced at Jackman, and sipped her iced tea. "No comment, I'm afraid, even if we're off the record here."

"Ross and Markham were close personal friends is what I hear," Hardy said. "Never a cross word between them." He shot a look at Treya across the table from him. "Kind of like me and Abe."

But Elliot thought he knew where the story lay. "Let me ask you this, Marlene," he began. "Diz thinks they are close personal friends, yet I have heard that they disagreed on just about every decision either one of them made over the past couple of years — Baby Emily, Sinustop, formulary issues, you name it."

Marlene Ash sipped her iced tea. "I can't talk about it, Jeff. It's the grand jury, get it? I'm not even saying who I talked to. You want to think it was Ross, you go ahead."

"It was today, though, right? The grand jury still meets Tuesdays and Thursdays?"

Gina Roake joined in. "Anybody else here for repealing the First Amendment?" But the words were innocent banter, lightly delivered. "She can't talk about it, Jeff. Really. Even to an ace reporter like yourself."

"And far be it from me to try to make her." Elliot shook his head, truly amused at the games these lawyers played, and apparently even took seriously. He flashed a smile around the table. "However, for our own edification, Dr. Ross has a secretary, Joanne, who told me when I called that that's where he was. I don't think she's been let in on the top secret part."

"She talked to you," Roake asked incredulously, "after what you did to her boss last week?"

Elliot nodded soberly. "She might have gotten the impression that I called to apologize or something."

As Freeman and Jackman fell into a more serious discussion about last week's issue — the possibly fraudulent outpatient billings — Hardy leaned over and spoke quietly to Elliot. "How'd you hear about Sinustop?"

"Same way I found out Ross was at the grand jury. I'm a reporter. I ask. You'd be surprised. People talk."

"Not as surprised as you'd think. I've talked to a few people myself. Have you found anything on Kensing's list?"

Elliot gave the high sign and stopped as Lou came around and described today's special, which involved eggplant, tofu, squid, and some kind of sesame oil–based sweet-and-sour sauce. Really good, he promised, maybe even a culinary breakthrough, although those weren't the exact words he used.

When they'd all ordered the special, since there was no other choice, Lou moved to another table, and the buzz resumed at Jackman's. Elliot leaned back toward Hardy. "But about those unexplained deaths? I know one thing is true. It's a definite rumor."

Hardy's face fell. Was Jeff ahead of him on checking out the names on Kensing's list? Maybe he'd discovered that eight of the others had died, like James Lector, of natural causes. "What do you mean?" Hardy asked.

"I said that wrong, I think. Calm down." Elliot put a hand on Hardy's sleeve. "I don't mean it's only a rumor, as in there's no truth to it. What I mean is it's a rumor, a lot of people are talking about it. If I could find a few more items like that, I'd like to patch them all together and get another column, but there's no story there yet.

I've talked to some people at Portola, but no-body has even one small factoid. It sucks."

"What about our friend Ross?"

A shrug. "I did him already, you might recall. And after that, it's pretty much a one-note samba. Ross and Mother Teresa don't share a common worldview, but other than the fact that he's greedy, heartless, and rich, I can't seem to get another column inch out of it."

"I may have something for you. Pay attention."

Hardy then directed his attention across the table. "John." He raised his voice so Strout could hear him. "I almost forgot."

He took an envelope from his pocket and passed it across. "Do me a favor. Next time I give ten-to-one odds on anything, remind me about this one."

As Hardy had intended, this little show engaged everyone's interest. He'd originally planned the move as a way to make his case indirectly to Glitsky. If he could draw the group into a discussion on the Lector autopsy without having to labor over it, Abe might come to see that Hardy's position wasn't entirely self-serving, that it wasn't a lawyer's cheap smoke screen, either, that the idea had merit on its own and had been worth pursuing. Now, though, he realized that he could make a similar impression on Treya and trust that it would get back to Abe through her. For the truth remained — if he couldn't get Glitsky working on his side, he would almost certainly never completely clear his client's name.

Also, though still raw with anger, he wasn't inclined to lose his best friend over his job. He already had sacrificed enough to his career.

To the chorus of questions, Hardy replied that it was merely the payment of a debt of honor. "I felt strongly that James Lector had been killed at Portola, as Tim Markham had been, although maybe not in the exact same way. And I put my money where my mouth was."

Jackman and Freeman disagreed as to whether this was noble or idiotic, but the discussion did give Hardy the opportunity to segue into Wes Farrell's situation with Mrs. Loring, which had been his other intention all along.

Elliot, he noticed, started taking notes.

But Jackman wasn't letting Hardy off without some kind of a warning. They were standing on the corner of Seventh and Bryant just after lunch, waiting for the light. Jackman had held Hardy back under the guise of telling him an off-color joke about Arkansas vasectomies. These were quite common, it seemed, and involved a can of beer, a cherry bomb, and the inability to count to ten without using your fingers. When Hardy finished laughing, he found that they'd hung back enough now to be alone at the curb. Jackman was good with jokes because he never laughed at his own punch lines. No part of him was laughing now. "I did want to make one serious point, Diz, if you can spare another minute."

The switch in tone was abrupt enough to be surprising, and Hardy's expression showed it.

379

"All right," he said. "Of course."

"Due to the nature of our deal, I've been working under an assumption that I've taken to be true, but — Marlene mentioned this to me last night, just before I decided to okay your request for John's second autopsy —"

"That wasn't me, sir. That was Wes Farrell. It's his client."

"Diz." The voice was deep, nearly caressing. Avuncular, Jackman laid a hand that seemed to weigh about thirty pounds on Hardy's shoulder. "Let's not go there."

Hardy thought these were as impressive and effective a few syllables as he'd ever heard. "Sorry," he said, and he meant it.

"As I was saying," Jackman's hand was back in his pocket, they were strolling now in the crosswalk, "I've been working under the assumption that we are sharing our information. We're giving you our discovery, and you in turn are giving us your client's cooperation before the grand jury when he gets there. But beyond that, I would hope you're also giving us — giving Abe, specifically — whatever information you uncover that doesn't implicate your client."

They walked a few steps in silence. Hardy finally spoke. "He's not been in much of a listening mood lately."

"I realize that, but I'd appreciate it if you'd keep trying."

"That's been my intention. But the deal was that my client would talk to the grand jury, not a bunch of cops in a small room with a videotape machine."

"I take your point. But Abe seems to be skating toward the erroneous conclusion that somehow we're all conniving to circumvent due process." They'd reached the steps of the Hall of Justice and stopped walking. Jackman was frowning deeply. "I'm extremely sensitive to this issue. To even the appearance of it."

"Has Abe actually said that?"

"No. But he doesn't like being ordered not to arrest someone."

"With respect, Clarence, that's nothing like what you did. You admitted when we cut the deal that you probably didn't have enough for a conviction, even with the so-called confession. And now he doesn't even have that."

"Which, I need hardly point out, is the latest complaint."

Hardy nodded. "He's in a complaining mood, Clarence. He thinks I saw the opportunity for emotional blackmail and took it. Which, *I* need hardly point out, kind of pisses me off. I didn't and wouldn't do that, and Abe of all people ought to know it."

"Well, one of you big boys is going to have to find a way to settle your differences. And meanwhile, Marlene would probably like to be kept informed of what you've discovered, whether it comes through Abe or not. You've obviously got a few things going on. These autopsies, for example. And as an aside, let me say that as a courtesy, and in keeping with our spirit of mutual cooperation, it might have been appropriate to call them to our attention a bit sooner." He waved off Hardy's apology before it began. "It doesn't matter. That's water under the bridge. But don't forget that I've gone out on a limb here, especially with the chief of homicide, on this call to let Strout go ahead. I'm hoping these . . . unusual exercises have a point, that your client isn't going to do something stupid, or go sideways and refuse to talk at the grand jury. That would make me feel foolish."

"That won't happen, Clarence. But I can't stand here and tell you I've got another suspect who's any better than Kensing. The good news is I have some who aren't much worse."

Jackman took this news mildly. "Then you need to get Abe looking at them."

"That's my fondest dream, Clarence. Honest. Other than Wes Farrell's autopsy paying off."

"With what?"

Hardy's face showed his apprehension. "At this point, Clarence, almost anything."

They said their good-byes and Hardy watched Jackman's back disappear into the building.

A press of humanity was hanging out on the steps, grabbing smokes or snagging last-minute legal advice, or simply ebbing and flowing from the hall itself. A couple of enormous Great Danes were chained to one of the metal banisters. Everyone who passed gave the two dogs a wide berth as they slept on the warm stone — due to the recent death of a young woman by dog mauling, the popularity of man's best friend in the city was at an all-time low. At the far end of the steps, a young Chinese couple was having lunch on either side of a boombox that blared with Asian rap.

The smell of *bao* — those delicious buns of sticky dough and savory barbecued pork — made him suddenly realize how hungry he was. Lou's special today may have broken new culinary ground, but most of the table hadn't evolved to the point where they could appreciate it. Hardy hadn't eaten more than three bites.

When he'd given Jackman enough time to disappear, Hardy went inside himself and rode the elevator to the fourth floor. Glitsky wasn't in his office. Hardy walked out into the hall and punched a number into his cell phone.

Two rings, then the mellifluous tones. "Glitsky."

"How's Hunter's Point?"

"Who's this?"

"Take a stab."

A beat. "What do you want?"

"Five minutes. Where are you really?"

"Department twenty-two."

This was a courtroom on the third floor. If anything at all had been going on in it, Glitsky would have turned off his phone — not to do so would incur the wrath of Judge Leo Chomorro. So the courtroom was dark or in recess and Glitsky was in hiding.

If Hardy was going to accuse Abe of withholding discovery from him — and he was — he was going to do it to his face. The lieutenant sat in the back row, the seat farthest from the center aisle. He looked over briefly at Hardy's entrance, but didn't seem inclined to make an effort to meet him halfway. Which made two of them.

"I just talked to Clarence. He's of a mind that we should cooperate." Hardy's voice echoed in the empty and cavernous space. "I might have mentioned to him that that was a two-way street, but I didn't."

"That was noble of you."

"I was wondering, though, why your inspectors never got around to checking who'd been near the ICU when Markham died. Did you just tell them that Kensing did it, so they didn't need to bother?"

Glitsky's head turned to face him. "What are you talking about?"

"I'm talking about Bracco and the other guy, his partner, what they've been doing this past week." Glitsky folded his arms over his chest and shook his head. Hardy took the nonresponse as a kind of answer. "Because I'm having a hard time understanding why they didn't ask any questions at the hospital where Markham died. Doesn't that strike you as odd? That would seem like a logical place to talk to witnesses, wouldn't you think?"

"What's your point?"

"I believe you told them to go there. That's the first place you would have looked."

"That's right. It turns out that was one of the first places we did go. So again, I ask you, what's your point?"

"The point is there wasn't any sign of that in the complete discovery that you were supposedly giving me. The deal was that I got what you got, remember?"

"You did get it," Glitsky said.

"I didn't get anything on anybody at the hospital. And now you tell me your men were there.

What do you think that looks like?"

Glitsky seemed to be mulling this over. After a second or two, he glanced at Hardy. "Maybe the transcripts haven't been typed up yet."

"Maybe that's it. So where are the tapes without transcripts, since I also have a bunch of those?" But Hardy had been in the practice of criminal law long enough that he'd learned a few tricks used by police to enhance the odds of a successful prosecution. "Maybe," he added pointedly, "maybe you instructed them to forget to run a tape." This was a popular and not uncommon technique, the exercise of which was almost impossible to prove.

"It occurred to me," Hardy went on, "that since you've decided I'm not playing fair, that you might as well do the same thing."

Glitsky's mouth went tight. His scar stood out. Hardy knew he was hitting Glitsky where it hurt the most, but he had to get through to him somehow.

"And as a consequence it took me four days to find out on my own what you already knew," Hardy said.

"And what is that?"

"That there were any number of people with opportunity and maybe even motive to have killed Markham."

But Glitsky wasn't budging. "If you couldn't find it, that's your problem. My inspectors went and asked. They got a complete chronology for the whole day, from Markham's admittance to . . ." Suddenly Glitsky stopped, threw a quick look at Hardy, then stared into some middle distance. His nostrils flared and his lips pursed.

"What?" Hardy asked.

Glitsky's expression suddenly changed. Something he remembered made him draw in a quick breath, then visibly clamp down further.

Hardy waited for a beat. Said, "I'm listening." He waited some more.

Finally, exuding disgust and embarrassment, the lieutenant began to shake his head slowly from side to side. "They forgot to run a tape. It's Bracco and Fisk, you know, their first case. They just didn't follow protocol and . . ." He stopped again, knowing it was hopeless to try and explain further. No one, least of all Hardy, would believe him and, under these conditions, he understood that no one should.

Hardy first reacted as Abe expected he must. "I'd call that self-serving on the face of it," he replied crisply. "How convenient that only just now, at the moment I catch you at it, the explanation comes back to you. And such a handy one at that."

The sarcasm fairly dripped.

"There's only one thing." Hardy took a step toward the door to the courtroom, faced his friend, and spoke from the heart. "The thing is, I know you, Abe. I know who you are and I trust every part of it. If you're telling me that's what happened, then that's what happened. End of story."

"That's what happened." Glitsky couldn't look at him.

"All right. Well, then, maybe somebody could write me up a report on what they found so I'm

386

up to speed." He pushed at the door, but then stopped and turned in midstep. "Oh, and congratulations. Treya called and told Frannie."

Then he was out in the hallway, leaving Glitsky to his demons.

PART THREE

25

Bracco couldn't figure his partner out. Sometimes he was worthless and uninvolved; then he'd get some off-the-wall idea and it would get them someplace.

All day yesterday, they'd been a couple of flat-feet. Walking and talking, walking and talking. The hospital, the coffee group, the Judah Clinic. Ten hours, and then no Glitsky to report to when they'd finally gotten back to homicide. He'd rushed out someplace on some call, evidently in high dudgeon. And they'd gotten the message last time. They could report next morning here at the hall rather than at his house. Although they hadn't been able to do that either, not today. The lieutenant hadn't yet come in by the time they had to leave for their appointment with Kathy West, and that was sometime a little after 10:00.

Now they had all been outside on the patio — sun-dappled, no wind — at this Italian place on Union for over two hours. As far as Bracco could tell, they were having the kind of lunch society folks must have every day, and why weren't all of them fat, he wondered? Then, of course, he realized that Harlen was. But still, two hours for lunch? And it wasn't over yet. Maybe this was how his dad felt, hanging with the mayor.

Bracco had to admit that his partner was doing a hell of a job getting to know Nancy Ross. Of course, he had the entree and help of his aunt Kathy, who was part of their lunch foursome. Even so, Bracco thought that Fisk was handling this interrogation very well. In spite of the tape recorder that now sat in the middle of the table amidst the half-empty coffee cups and tiramisu plates, Nancy — she *was* Nancy by now — seemed to be completely at her ease.

Although Bracco believed she would be equally composed in any situation. She was a thoroughbred, seemingly born to be waited upon, to command, to direct. Though not as physically magnetic as Ann Kensing with her eyes and curvature, Nancy Ross wore a kind of timeless elegance. But she didn't come across as an ice queen by any means. She had a good ready laugh, a naughty turn of phrase. Somehow she'd gotten into a running gag with Kathy West on the word "long" — "My, what long . . . bread sticks they serve here." Or, "Did you notice the long . . . earlobes our waiter has?" — and the two of them had gotten nearly giddy a couple of times.

Fisk was very much at home with her. In some kind of foreign-tailored suit and a bright silk tie, with tasseled cordovan loafers and a cream-colored silky shirt, Fisk had of course taken a good measure of grief in the detail when he'd come in. But Bracco had to admit the guy looked good, like he belonged in these threads, which were cut so well they took thirty pounds off him.

Fisk had asked him to dress nice for lunch, so he'd worn his corduroy sportscoat, a sports shirt with a collar, pressed Dockers. But he felt underdressed, and as a consequence found himself more than a little reluctant to speak — not only because he felt outclassed in a literal way, but because until ten minutes ago, there hadn't even been the pretense of doing any police work. He knew that homicide inspectors didn't punch a clock at the end of the day, but the obverse of that — that he could sometimes take two hours off in the middle of it — made him uncomfortable.

Now it was clear that Fisk had had a plan after all. The anecdotes and chatter were prologue. Nancy Ross by now wanted to help this nice man, this nephew of supervisor Kathy West who also happened to be a policeman, in any way she could.

"I know," she was saying. "Malachi was so nervous this morning. Can you believe this is the first time he's ever testified before a grand jury? He's never even gotten a parking ticket in his whole life, or really talked to any real policemen, working on something this serious. I wish he'd met you sooner, Harlen, and you, too, Darrel. He wouldn't have thought a thing about it."

Fisk tsked sympathetically. "I'm sure he has nothing to worry about. The main reason they wanted to talk to him is to get some kind of day-to-day sense of the pressures at Parnassus. It seems to me that your husband would be the best source of that information now with Mr. Markham gone."

"Oh, he would, that's true. Sometimes I thought he and Tim might as well have had the same job. And now, of course, Malachi has Tim's, although he never would have wanted it in these conditions. This has just been horrible."

"Do you know if he's appointed anybody yet to take over his own old spot?"

She shook her regal head. "No. He's looking but . . . well, to be honest, the basic problem he tells me is that there aren't too many doctors who can make the hard decisions. Malachi's had to learn to live with them over the past few years. They've really taken their toll on him, you know, in spite of the way that awful reporter made him sound."

Again, Fisk clucked sympathetically. As Bracco saw he'd intended, she took it as encouragement to go on. "As though Jeff Elliot, who-ever he is, has any idea of how difficult it is to run a company like Parnassus. What does he think the officers and directors are supposed to work for, minimum wage? I mean, really. He just doesn't know."

"I don't think many people do." Fisk, too, thought this was a sad state of affairs.

"I mean," Nancy went on, "you wouldn't be-lieve the calls to the office the day of that col-umn. I don't know how Malachi stood up to it, how it didn't completely break him, he was so exhausted by then. I mean, the night Tim was killed . . . Oh, never mind."

"It's all right, Nancy. What?"

She sighed. "Just that he was so much trying to do the right thing, as he always does, staying late to talk to that *Mr. Elliot.* He didn't have to do that, you know. But he wanted to try to make him understand, which *Mr. Elliot* obviously wasn't there to do at all. So all that talking and talking till past midnight, when he's exhausted beyond imagining to begin with, and what good did it do him? Still it came out all wrong."

Fisk was in sync with her. "I couldn't believe Elliot mentioned your husband's income in his column. Even if it is supposedly in the public record." He included his partner. "Darrel and I both thought that was pretty low. And as though it's that much money, after all, for the work your husband does."

Kathy West chimed in. "And that's all Malachi does, too. Isn't that right, Nancy? It's not like he's sitting on twenty boards gouging the system."

"Exactly right. That's all we live on. We don't have trusts and inheritances and outside income. Except for a few parties — and without them some important charities would suffer — we live very frugally."

Fisk continued to lead her on. "And half goes to taxes anyway. And then half of what's left on the houses and entertaining. I hear you. I really hear you."

Bracco was trying to do some calculations in his head. Unlike his partner, he did not have any understanding of where 1.2 million dollars could go every year. Even if half — six hundred thousand dollars — went to taxes and then half of that — three hundred thousand dollars more — went to houses (note, plural) and entertaining.

That left another three hundred grand after taxes to squeak by on. That was three times Bracco's gross salary, including overtime. Lots of overtime.

But Fisk had briefed him beforehand that the point of this meeting would be to find out if Ross and his family considered themselves well off or knocking on poverty's door. Astoundingly to Bracco, it was beginning to seem the latter.

"You *do* know, Harlen. I can't tell you how refreshing it is to talk to somebody who understands the numbers. I mean, *a million dollars!* It sounds like so much, doesn't it?" Then, more seriously. "It used to be so much, I suppose, but not anymore."

Fisk appeared to be having a grand old time, laughing at the figure. "I used to believe that I could retire if I had a million dollars. Can you imagine that?"

Nancy laughed at the absurdity of it. "If you only planned to live a year or two after your retirement, maybe. And not that long if you have any household help — I'm not even talking full-time help. And live-in? Forget it. I mean, a maid a few times a week, or the yard man, or kitchen help."

"And don't forget political donations," Kathy West added, half-humorously.

"And the charities, the opera, the donations to the girls' school, which is on top of the twenty-thousand-dollar tuition. It's actually a little terrifying when I stop to think about it."

Bracco almost couldn't bear listening to any more of the litany. In his life, he didn't even have one of the last half dozen expenses they'd mentioned. But he had no idea how to strike the familiar tone Fisk had established, especially when it was about money, and he had to hope his partner was getting to what he had come for.

But Fisk, apparently still sharing Nancy's plight, continued. "What I find so unbelievable," he said, "is that Elliot made it look like your husband was the prince of greed. He should have done another article on real-life expenses. It seems to me that Dr. Ross would be perfectly justified if he just bolted from Parnassus — I'm sure he's in demand — and went somewhere that could pay him what he's worth."

"Actually, he almost did that. He was interviewing last year. Top secret, of course. Even Tim didn't know." Bracco noted that she paused — perhaps she hadn't meant to reveal that. But then she sighed prettily. "I can't tell you how incredibly trying it's been, really only just getting by, if that, year after year after year. No savings, nothing put away for the girls' colleges. And Malachi only staying on at Parnassus out of some sense of duty. And then having everybody suddenly assume we're just fabulously rich. It's just too great an irony."

Fisk volunteered that maybe he could go and talk to Mr. Elliot. "At least try to make him see your side."

"No. Thank you, Harlen, that's very nice, but I don't think it would be wise. He'd only turn it against us somehow. Although I don't know how that could be."

"It couldn't be, is the answer," Kathy West

said. She was patting her hand and reaching for the check. "It'll all blow over, I wouldn't worry, Nancy. The best thing to do with these kinds of articles is forget them."

Fisk neatly palmed the tape recorder and slipped it into his pocket. "I'm sorry we got on this difficult subject," he said. "It's a part of the job I don't much enjoy. But you've been very helpful and the lunch was fantastic."

Nancy Ross also reached for the check. Harlen and his aunt objected, but she overrode them both. Bracco, deeply relieved, stammered out his thanks. He'd caught a glimpse of the figure — $147.88, not including the tip. This was half what Bracco paid his father every month for rent.

Then everybody was standing up and kissing everyone else on both cheeks. Nancy Ross seemed to have completely recovered from the depressing financial talk. For Bracco's part, he shook Nancy's hand and then Kathy's, told them how pleasant it had been, how much he'd enjoyed it. And in a way, he realized, it was true. It had been an intimate glimpse into another, totally separate world that coexisted with his own.

And in that world, Malachi Ross had money trouble.

Wes Farrell got the news about Mrs. Loring from Strout's office about five minutes after he arrived at his office. After thinking about it for a minute, he decided that this wasn't the kind of uplifting information you wanted to immediately share with your client: "Hi, Chuck, it's Wes

Farrell here. Great news. They're digging up your mom's body and cutting it up for science." No. He didn't think so.

It was, however, a good break for him, a cause for celebration, and in the past months there'd been few enough of them. He made a valiant attempt to conduct other business until lunchtime. But once he locked the door and headed back for his house, he suddenly knew that it was going to take more will than he possessed to get him back in his office before a new day had dawned.

He had an artichoke and a can of tuna fish for lunch, then took a half hour power nap in his living room. Now he was outside, accompanying his sixty-five-pound boxer, Bart, on a walk around Buena Vista Park. He sported a pair of threadbare slacks, high-tech tennis shoes, and a sweatshirt that from a distance read BUSH and up close contained the tiny, lowercase fill-in letters _ _ ll _ _ it. Farrell liked to think that hanging in his closet he had perhaps the world's premier collection of bumper-sticker wisdom affixed to shirtwear.

The sun had broken through the cloud cover and the day threatened to grow almost warm. It had been warm only two days before, and no San Francisco native would reasonably expect a reprise so soon. And yet it appeared to be happening. Wonders would never cease.

And among them was the appearance of his beloved, Samantha Duncan. Cute, fit, feisty, and now almost forty, Sam had moved in with Wes over five years ago and both considered the arrangement permanent, although a formal marriage was not in their plans — Wes had been there, done that, and had issues with it, and Sam thought that was fine.

As soon as he'd gotten home, he'd called her where she worked at the Rape Crisis Counseling Center on Haight Street and asked her if she wanted to take some time off and maybe engage in some consensual adult activity — the kind of humor she hated in everyone else in the world, but tolerated in Wes. But she'd been busy and wasn't likely to be able to get away.

But suddenly now here she was, falling in step beside him, taking his hand. He stopped, kissed her, held her against him for a minute. "How'd you get away?"

"Fate. One of the volunteers just decided to come in and work." Bart was pulling at his leash, and they both started walking. She turned to look up at him. "So what happened that it's suddenly a holiday?"

He told her, trying to give her some of the flavor of Hardy's idea, Strout's original reluctance, this morning's turnaround, the immediate and salutary effect it might have on his billings. He could, for the first time in about five years, find himself involved in a high-profile case, get his name in the paper, attract a broader client base.

"Which I've heard you say more than once you don't want to do."

"If I said it, it must be true," he admitted. "But that's the problem. You get a lot of people to start paying you, next thing you know they want you to actually do work for them. It's a hell of a drain on resources."

"But you're going for this anyway?"

"Got to. You've seen what happens when you try to hold your practice to only five or six solid clients at a time, as I have so masterfully done. You find yourself turning into some kind of a legal specialist. You turn in the same motions five times each, except you've changed the names and one or two details. So you cut your work by a fifth and multiply your billings times five. It's just a beautiful license to print money. Fortunately I'm man enough to swallow my principles and bill the shit out of all these people, while still providing excellent service, of course."

"Of course." She dropped his hand. "I have no idea why I like you."

"I'm more fun than everybody else, is why. But I'm even more fun than *that* if I've got spending money. Hence my five-client plan. Except then what sometimes happens, as we've recently seen, is one Supreme Court ruling and the bottom falls out, the money dries up, you leave me, then I probably kill myself. It's horrible, and all because of the Supremes and their picky little decisions."

"Those darn guys," Sam said.

"And two women, don't forget, as I'm sure you never would. Anyway, so I figure this might be good press and a golden opportunity. I can expand the business again, then I can pick and choose great clients who can afford to pay huge fortunes for very little work on my part, and then you and I can go on in our life of meaningless hedonism."

"You *sound* like an awful, awful person. Do you know that?"

"I keep telling you. It's the real me."

"The real you who spent all those nights at your office last summer getting the Mackeys suit included with the others, and then forgot to charge them anything for all that work?"

"I know." Farrell wore a look of chagrin. "I almost fired myself for that. Besides, my real plan was that they'd win the lottery and be so grateful that they'd split it with me. Don't look at me like that — it could still happen."

They'd come around to the grass at the very top of the park. Sam sat, and Wes stretched out on the ground and put his head on her lap. Bart, getting on in years, rested his muzzle on Farrell's stomach.

After a few minutes, Sam stopped combing Wes's hair with her fingers. "I don't understand something," she said.

"No," he said, "you pretty much seem to get everything."

"What you're trying to get is lucky, isn't it?"

"I'm shocked and dismayed that you could think such a thing." He put a finger to his forehead theatrically, spoke as if to himself. "Oh no, wait. I can't be both." Then back to her. "I'm shocked, Sam, that you could think such a thing. I'd never stoop to flattery hoping to coax a carnal favor from you. Our love is too precious and too real."

"I should have worn boots," she replied. "It's a little thick out here."

Wes shrugged. "All right, I'll be serious. What

don't you understand?"

"All this talk about clearing beds. Mrs. Loring even. Dismas Hardy says one possible motive someone might have had for killing her is to get the bed empty. But, so who does that help, if the bed's empty?"

"Then they can put somebody else in it," Wes said.

"Right. That's the part I don't understand. You've got a sick person in a bed, and then that person dies and the next day you've got another sick person in the bed. They're paying the same thing for the same bed, right? So why is it to anyone's advantage to get rid of person A in favor of person B. I just don't see it."

Farrell lifted his head a fraction of an inch. "Bart, you want to tell her? Ow! Those hairs are precious to me."

Wes put his head back in her lap, rubbed a hand over where Sam had pulled. "If you're going to get snippy about it, put simply, here it is. The city contracted with Parnassus to provide all its employees with basic HMO health coverage on what they call a capitated basis."

"Which is?"

"I'm glad you asked. It means that Parnassus gets a set amount every month to provide all the physician and hospital services to city employees who are enrolled in the HMO, which they can do at no cost to them. It comes with the city gig."

"Okay. We've still got that bed."

"I'm getting there, please. So what happens in real life is that Parnassus gets a monthly check from the city. It becomes part of their general

403

operating income. Then, any other set payment, Parnassus starts using it to cover overhead and salaries and so on. So if Parnassus winds up having to provide an expensive service for somebody in the HMO — like chemotherapy or heart surgery — it feels like it's not getting paid for it."

"But everybody agreed up front —"

He wagged a finger. "Not the point. The point is there are other patients, whether they are city employees or not, who have chosen a more expensive provider option. For these folks, Parnassus gets real live money for the services it provides."

"But it gets real money every month from the city, anyway. Right? I'm still not seeing the difference."

"Okay, let's say a city employee enrolled in the HMO spends five days in intensive care. The city doesn't send an extra check. Parnassus gets its hundred and fifty a month and that's all. However, if a person enrolled in a preferred provider program, for example, spends the same five days in the ICU, Parnassus gets about five grand a day. So it can be argued than an HMO city employee in an ICU bed is costing Parnassus maybe as much as five grand per day."

"Per day?"

"Every day, my dear. You don't watch it pretty close, it'll add right on up. So now let's take our own Marjorie Loring, who happens to be a pretty good example of what we're talking about. She was a city employee insured through the Parnassus HMO. So if she happens to defy the odds and hangs on for six months, she's going to cost Portola what? At least a hundred grand, maybe more.

"Now if you were running Portola, would you rather have Marjorie Loring in that bed or someone else who's insured with a preferred provider program that paid a full dollar for every dollar billed, all other things being equal?"

Sam didn't have to think very long. "All other things being equal," she said, "it sounds to me like Dismas Hardy might be on to something."

26

It was getting on to midafternoon and Glitsky couldn't eat another bite of rice cake.

A little-used and semi-enclosed staircase ran along the Hall of Justice on the Seventh Street side, and he took it down to the ground. Out on the corner, he was waiting at the light to cross and go get some peanuts at Lou's, even if they gave him an instant heart attack that felled him at the bar. Suddenly he found himself facing his two new homicide inspectors, coming his way in the crosswalk. Fisk was dressed like a fashion model and even Bracco looked pretty sharp. "Where's the party?" he asked. "You feel like a handful of peanuts?"

Coming from their boss, this wasn't really a social request. The light changed and the three men walked.

The bar at Lou's didn't have any empty stools, so Glitsky stood while he ordered three small bags of cocktail peanuts and a pint of iced tea. Following his nonalcoholic lead, Bracco and Fisk bought cups of acidic coffee, after which they all repaired to a booth and got settled. The lieutenant sat on one side and the two inspectors on the other. Glitsky threw a bag of peanuts at each of them, tore at his own. "So what's got you two boys so duded up?"

Since the lunch with Nancy Ross and Kathy West had been Harlen's idea, Bracco thought he'd let him explain it. He was surprised when the lieutenant seemed to approve. When the narrative ended, Glitsky was nodding. "So we now know what we've always suspected. You can't make too much money, and nobody thinks they got enough. Anything else?"

Bracco decided he needed to speak up. "Couple of things," he said. "One, it might be interesting to compare Ross's tax returns the last few years with what they've spent. Mrs. Ross might not have realized it, but she basically said they were living on more than they were making."

"So am I," Glitsky said. "Who isn't?" He chewed his ice for a moment. "So they've extended themselves on credit cards, so what? And what would that prove anyway? How's it relate to Markham?"

"If Ross was taking money from Parnassus in some way and Markham found out —"

"You mean embezzling? Something like that?"

"I don't know," Bracco admitted.

Glitsky didn't like it. "Anything obvious or proven and he would have fired him on the spot, don't you think?" He drank some more tea, frowning. "My problem with this whole line of thought," he said at last, "is that I've got to go on the assumption that whoever killed Markham in the hospital probably wasn't planning to kill him until he showed up there after the accident. That's why I like Kensing so much. He didn't just have a motive. He had several long-standing motives, where he might see the opportunity and just go, 'At last.'

"On the other hand — just hear me out — if Ross was somehow threatened by Markham to the degree that he actually planned to kill him, doesn't it make more sense to think that he would have done something proactive, like actually try to run him over, for example, rather than just wait for fate to put him in his path? What if it didn't happen? And ten out of ten times it wouldn't."

"If I may, sir?" Harlen said.

Glitsky's face relaxed a degree. "You may."

"They've worked together a long time, Ross and Markham, so there could have been the same buildup of motives that we know about with Kensing, couldn't there? The point we made this afternoon was that Ross needed his job. But something was making him want to leave Parnassus."

This wasn't too conclusive for Glitsky. "He read the writing on the wall. The place was going down. He didn't want to go with it."

"Okay." Fisk's frustration with Glitsky's objections was beginning to show. "But he couldn't get any other jobs. His wife told us he'd gone looking and couldn't get hired anywhere else. Why not? Finally, who benefits most immediately from Markham's death? Dr. Ross, who took over the top job and gets another two hundred grand a year salary, just for starters."

Glitsky upended his peanut bag, threw the last few into his mouth, chewed thoughtfully. "But we don't know that there was in fact any serious — and I mean deadly serious — problems between him and Markham. Do we?"

Downcast, the two inspectors looked at each other, then back across the table. "No, sir," Bracco said. "But it might be fun to keep looking."

"You can look all you want," Glitsky replied. "But as far as I know, the only person we've got in the room when Markham died was Kensing and the nurses who had no personal relationship with Mr. Markham at all. And that pretty severely limits the field, don't you agree? Has that changed?"

"Actually, it might have," Bracco said. "I went back up to the ICU station yesterday while Harlen was waiting for an interview downstairs." He went on to describe his successful entry into intensive care unmolested and apparently unnoticed, and when he finished, Glitsky was frowning.

"What time was this?"

"About the same time Markham died. Early afternoon."

"And what about the nurses' station?"

"One nurse was at it, sitting at the computer."

"How long were you in there?"

Bracco shrugged. "A minute, give or take. I walked around to each bed."

"And nobody else . . ."

"Nobody. I just walked behind the nurse at the computer, opened the door, disappeared. Which means that anybody else could have done the same thing."

Glitsky's face had hardened down to granite. His cell phone rang and he picked it from his belt and growled out his name, then listened intently. The scar between his lips stood out in stark relief. He said, "Are you sure?" In less than a minute, he closed up the phone and stared out over the heads of his inspectors.

The town of Colma, just over San Francisco's border with San Mateo County, has far more dead inhabitants than live ones.

Hardy stood at one of the thousands of gravesites. This one was near the end of a row of headstones, under a redwood tree. With the cemetery's permission, he had planted the tree himself twenty-eight years before.

It was April 16, the day Hardy's son Michael had been born. He'd died seven months later when he fell out of his crib. It probably had been the very first time he'd stood up. Certainly, neither Hardy nor Jane, his wife back then — the marriage was another casualty of the tragedy — had ever seen him get up on his feet. He'd only been crawling a few weeks, it seemed. A couple of film rolls' worth.

So they left the sides down on his crib. Not all the way down. Halfway down. They'd childproofed the house, but neither one of them had ever given a thought to the sides of the crib. Michael wasn't old enough for that yet. But he must have been able to stand all the way up. Otherwise, he would not have been able to pitch over and land wrong.

Hardy wasn't thinking about that now, about that one long-ago moment that had forever modulated the course of his life, who he was, what he had become, into a minor key. He wasn't conscious of any thought at all. He was simply standing here, by his infant son's now-old grave. He had never faced this place before, though he'd always marked the date and had been to Colma many times. He had never before been able to find the courage.

But something had drawn him here today, something he either couldn't define or didn't want to examine too closely. He felt that too many of the important things in his life were slipping away. Maybe he hoped that a gradual slip — unlike an abrupt fall — could be stopped. Lives could be saved.

He had called Frannie and told her where he was going. He could tell the call worried her. Should she meet him there? she'd asked him. Was he all right?

He didn't know the real answer to that, but he told her he was fine. That he loved her. He'd see her tonight, after Vincent's Little League practice, when his normal life resumed.

Downtown, near his office, the day had been threatening to be nice again. Driving out, as far as the Shamrock, he had his windows down. But here, except for his lone redwood, the eucalyptus and the windswept, twisted cypress trees and the thriving endless lawn, it was all grays — everything from the sky down through the air itself. Gray and cold.

He wore his business suit and even with the coat buttoned, it wasn't nearly enough to alleviate the chill. In the groves both close and far, the wind droned with a vibration he felt more than

411

heard. Already in places the cloud cover had gone to ground and wisps of the fitful fog drifted and dissipated into the endless gray.

He had not prayed in thirty years. Perhaps he wasn't praying now. But he went to a knee, then both knees, and remained in that position for several minutes. At last he stood up, took a final look at the name still sharply etched into the marble headstone — Michael Hardy.

Now so unfamiliar, so impossible.

He drew a breath, gathering himself. When he turned to walk back to his car, Glitsky was standing on the asphalt path thirty feet away.

He wore his leather flight jacket. His hands were in its pockets. He took a step forward at the same moment Hardy did. When they had closed the gap, both stopped. "I tried your office," Glitsky said, "then the cell, then Frannie." He hesitated. "You okay?"

He motioned vaguely back behind him. "He would have been twenty-nine today. I thought I owed him a visit."

A gust shuddered by them. Glitsky waited it out. "That's my greatest fear," he said.

"It's a good one."

"I've got my three grown boys, Diz. I beat the odds. Why do I want to do this again?"

Hardy took some time before he answered. "Most of the time it doesn't end up like this, that's why. Most of the time they bury us."

Glitsky was looking somewhere over Hardy's shoulder. "I couldn't put my finger on why I was so . . ." He couldn't get the thought out. "It's, what if they don't bury us? What if it *is* like this?"

"Then you do what you have to do," Hardy replied. "You suppose time goes by, but you're not part of time anymore. And then one day something you eat has flavor again, or maybe the sun feels good on your back. Something. You start again." He shrugged. "You did it with Flo, so you know."

"Yeah, I do know. But the funny thing is, I'm more scared of it now. I'm not good with fear."

"I've noticed that." A ghost of a smile flitted around Hardy's mouth. "I'd actually call that a good sign, especially compared to how you were before you met Treya, that long sleepwalk after Flo died. Now it all matters again, though, doesn't it? And ain't that a bitch?"

"No, it's good, but . . ."

"No 'but' about it, Abe. It's all good." He motioned back toward the gravesite again. "The little guy had something he needed to tell me. I think that was it."

Coming back at Glitsky, he realized that they'd been baring their souls to each other, and that this was, in fact, who they were. Without any need to acknowledge it, both of them knew that their fight, somehow, was over. They might still have serious professional issues between them, but the essential bond was secure.

They started walking together to where they'd parked their cars. "There was something else," Glitsky said. "Why I was trying to get you in the first place."

"What's that?"

"Strout called. Marjorie Loring's autopsy."

"Done already?" This was very fast, but Hardy

413

wasn't really surprised. Jackman had made it clear that it was a high priority.

Glitsky nodded. "You were right. She didn't die of cancer."

A wash of relief ran over Hardy — he'd invested more than he'd realized in these results. "So what was it?" he asked. "Potassium?"

"No. Some muscle relaxers. Pavulon and something chloride. Both of them stop natural breathing. Both would have been administered in the hospital."

"Kensing wasn't anywhere near her, Abe. He was on vacation with his kids in Disneyland. And before you say it, I know this doesn't mean he didn't kill Markham. But it does mean something, doesn't it?"

Glitsky didn't need to go over it. "You and I have to talk. You said you got more of these people?"

Hardy nodded. "Ten more. And that's just Kensing's list. I know at least one nurse that has her own suspicions. She might have some names to go with them, although I'd agree with you that one homicide doesn't mean there are ten of them."

"I didn't say that."

"Yeah, I know. I read your mind. But it does mean there's one of them, and it wasn't Kensing. But it also wasn't potassium, which I kind of wish it was."

Glitsky looked questioningly at him. "Why is that?"

"Because if both Loring and Markham got killed the same way, it would be the same person doing it, wouldn't it?"

"It might at that," Glitsky admitted, "but as far as I'm concerned, this is good enough in terms of me and you." They'd gotten to Glitsky's car. He stopped by the front door. "I think I owe you an apology."

"I agree with you. Was that it?"

A small chuckle. "As good as it gets." But surprisingly, he went a little further. "All I can say is that you don't work with as many defense attorneys as I do. You get a little cynical after a while, even with your friends."

This was the sad truth and Hardy believed it. He could argue that he, Dismas Hardy, Abe's best friend, wasn't just another defense attorney given to pulling unethical tricks out of his hat just to protect his clients. But he knew that in the world of criminal law this in itself would be a rare and suspect guarantee. Hardy had won at least a couple of lesser cases on technicalities that Glitsky in his cop mode would probably consider some form of cheating.

Wes Farrell had gotten his boy off the other day when the arresting officer hadn't made it to the courtroom. For all Hardy knew, Wes had taken the cop out the night before and got him plowed so he'd be too hungover to appear. Beyond that, a true eminence at the defense bar such as David Freeman wouldn't even blush to do exactly what Glitsky had accused Hardy of. Squeeze a witness by bringing her children into play? Get the coroner to dig up half of Colma? Pretend you needed an emergency tooth extraction on the first day of jury selection? If it helped your client, if it even delayed proceedings for any substantial period of time, it was justifiable. Even, arguably, commendable. Ethically required.

"So where do we go from here?" Hardy asked.

Glitsky had no doubt. "Kensing's list. If there's an angel of death at Parnassus, I want to know about it. Meanwhile, Marlene's going ahead with the grand jury. I got another unpleasant surprise about five minutes before Strout called." He told Hardy about Bracco's discovery on the lack of security for the ICU at Portola.

"So anybody could have gone in? Is that what you're saying?"

"Bracco seemed to think so." Glitsky paused. "I don't want to have two potential killers," he said. "I really don't. The idea offends me."

"Me, too, but three's worse," Hardy reminded him.

"Three?"

"Whoever drove the car."

Brendan Driscoll talked most of the afternoon to the grand jury. Obviously, he thought someone who hated him had testified before he did. The prosecutor, Ms. Ash, seemed poisoned against him from the outset. He had been planning to talk about Ross and Kensing and Kensing's damned wife and the others who had made life so difficult at Parnassus.

Instead, she wanted to know all about his personal relationship with Tim, and this made him very nervous. He'd worked very hard to keep it all low-key — of course, they'd had their dis-

416

agreements. When you worked so closely with one individual over a long period of time, there was bound to be some friction. But in general they had been an extremely good team.

But Ash had already heard about the warning memo he'd received from Tim, the personal dressing down he'd endured — Ross must have been the source for that, he thought — and had spent what seemed like a lot of time going over what he'd done at the hospital last Tuesday. Finally, before he could direct her to anyone else who'd had run-ins with Tim, she'd started asking questions about Mr. Markham's correspondence, his own familiarity with it, especially the decision to bill the city for outpatient services.

She was clueless, he thought. He'd rather have her looking at other people than at this business decision, which, so far as Driscoll could tell, had nothing to do with anything except the company's cash flow. But if it distracted her from his own personal issues with Tim, especially during this difficult last month, he supposed he should be happy. He would have preferred to direct her attention to one of his pet enemies, and he tried a couple of times.

". . . the outpatient billing decision was really Mr. Markham's to make, and he was dead set against it. But Dr. Ross . . ."

". . . although during the time you're asking about, Mr. Markham wasn't able to concentrate on his work the way he liked to because Dr. Eric Kensing's wife, Ann, was demanding so much of . . ."

When he couldn't get Ash to bite, he finally

decided he had to leave it.

But Jeff Elliot was a different story. Driscoll had already called the reporter yesterday and made an appointment to talk to him after he was finished with the grand jury. When he got out — quite a bit more shaken than he'd expected to be — he walked to the *Chronicle*'s building, where Elliot was waiting for him.

Now he had a cup of coffee and had finally gotten comfortable on a chair in the little cubicle. He knew who he wanted to vilify, and had printed out Markham's letters both to Kensing and to Ross, as well as over a hundred memos to file. These outlined Tim's ongoing dissatisfaction with both of them on a variety of points. Driscoll was making his pitch that these documents supplied a number of very plausible motives for someone to have killed Tim.

Elliot flipped through the pages without much enthusiasm. "This is good stuff, Brendan, except that it looks like we've got a whole different ball game over there now."

Driscoll straightened himself in the chair. Touching the knot of his tie, he cleared his throat. "What do you mean by that? Over where?"

"Portola. It appears that a lady who died there a few months ago was also poisoned. From what I'm hearing, there may be several more." He filled Driscoll in on most of what he'd learned to that point. "So needless to say, this casts some doubt over whether Mr. Markham was killed for personal reasons. He might have been just the latest in a series of these drug deaths at Portola, in which case the motives anybody might have had to kill him would be pretty irrelevant. Don't you agree?"

"That makes sense, I guess." Driscoll was sitting back in a kind of shock. For three days, he'd been plotting his revenge on Kensing for all the trouble he'd caused, on Ross for firing him. He thought he'd planned perfectly. Certainly he had a great deal of evidence against both of them. If Elliot would go public with any of it, it might force the board and maybe even the police to act.

But he hadn't been able to get his accusations aired either in front of the grand jury or now, here. It wasn't fair. "So what's going to happen now?" he asked. "Don't you want any of this?"

"Of course. This is great stuff." Elliot certainly wasn't faking his enthusiasm. "I just wanted to be straight with you that I might not get to it real soon. But hey, cheer up. Parnassus is going to be news for the rest of the year." The reporter patted the stack of paper. "This will be good bedtime reading."

Brendan had one last question. "So these other deaths at Portola? Do they mean that the police no longer think Eric Kensing might have killed Tim?"

"I think if nothing else it's going to give him a reprieve. Why?"

Driscoll shook his head. "I don't really know. I think I'd just come to believe that he had actually done it. Certainly he had more reason than anybody else. I guess I'll just have to adjust."

Vincent's Little League team, the Tigers, practiced only a few hundred yards from Hardy's house. They'd gotten permission to set up a backstop in an otherwise deserted section of Lincoln Park Golf Course, up against Clement Street. Hardy couldn't commit the time to be the team's manager, but he tried to show up as often as he could and help coach. He'd played ball through high school and his son's love for the game was a source of satisfaction in his own life.

He got back from Colma in time to pitch batting practice. There was no fog here twenty blocks inland. When the team broke down for infield practice, Hardy came off the field and stood next to Abe, who had been watching from behind the backstop. Mitch, the manager, laced one down the third-base line where Vincent snagged it backhand and threw a strike to first. Abe nodded in appreciation. "Your boy's looking pretty good."

Glitsky had called home and told his family to meet him for a barbecue at the Hardys. So after practice, they stopped in at the Safeway and bought tri-tip steaks and some kind of gourmet sausage, prepackaged potato and Caesar salads, sodas, and a six-pack of beer. Vincent pulled a half gallon of cookie dough ice cream out of the freezer. Glitsky held four flavors of bottled iced tea in two four-packs.

Hardy stood behind Glitsky and his son and watched as they loaded their goods onto the conveyor belt. It struck him that Louis XIV — the Sun King himself — probably didn't have this kind of food selection, this kind of weather, that in fact he was living in a kind of golden age and he'd be a fool to forget it. If it sometimes threatened to break his heart, it was a good thing.

He put a hand on Glitsky's shoulder, one on his son's.

"Rebecca Simms? This is Dismas Hardy again."

He thought he heard an intake of breath. Nurse Simms had been straightforward enough last time about not wanting to hear from him again, not wanting any more involvement. He rushed ahead before she could cut him off or hang up. "I know it's a little late, but I thought I owed you a phone call. Have you seen the news on TV?"

"No," she said. "I try not to watch too much TV. I read instead. What news?"

27

Jackman got the word out that he wanted them all in his office before eight o'clock the next morning. What the DA wanted, the DA got. Dead silent, Bracco and Fisk stood against the open door. Wes Farrell and Hardy sat on either end of the couch drinking coffee, while Glitsky was in the outer office with his wife. At a couple of minutes after the hour, Jackman arrived, accompanied by Marlene Ash and John Strout. After greeting everyone cordially, the DA went behind his desk, sat, and gave a sign to Treya. She ushered Glitsky inside and closed the door after him.

Jackman wasted no time on preliminaries. "Diz," he began, "I hear you've got ten more names on this magic list of yours. You'll be giving that to Abe, I presume."

"Yes, sir. Already done. Copies to Dr. Strout. And I spoke to another potential witness last night — a nurse at Portola — who's going to talk to the people she works with. Dr. Kensing only began his list about six months ago. My nurse witness might have more names."

"And that doesn't include what comes out of the woodwork," Marlene Ash put in. "I've got a feeling that everybody who died at Portola is going to seem fishy to somebody."

Jackman nodded in agreement, but he'd considered this. "That's why I'm asking Dr. Strout here to have one of his assistants review what I expect is going to be a flood of requests for exhumations and autopsies. At least that way we'll make sure some doctor might have thought something was wrong about a premature death before we go ahead."

"Good luck with that," Farrell said. "You're talking about these folks overruling the PM their own hospital conducted. You're not going to get a lot of cooperation from doctors who work there. And the administration's going to be worse."

"They'll have to if we order it."

"Sure," Farrell said, "but we can't make doctors and nurses voice suspicions if they don't want to. Or don't have them."

Jackman wasn't worried about it. "Don't get me wrong. I don't want a lot of these requests."

"But we're going to get them, from families if no one else." Ash looked around the room. "We'd better be ready."

"All right." Jackman was ready to move on. "John, why don't you give us a little rundown of your results yesterday, although I think we've all gotten the basic message."

The coroner laid it all out for them. Mrs. Loring had been killed by an overdose of Pavulon and succinylcholine chloride. They were two muscle relaxants that, especially in the case of someone who is already comatose, might mimic a natural death.

"No might about it," Farrell interrupted. "Nobody thought a thing about it until Diz gave me her name and told me I'd be smart to look. I was even planning to sue the hospital over negligent care and didn't have any suspicion she'd been murdered."

Strout went on with his explanation. These drugs were extremely powerful, and always administered in IVs. Beyond that, since Mrs. Loring had been bedridden in the ICU, there was no real possibility that she'd taken pills orally in an effort to end her own life. She wouldn't have had access to them. The conclusion was that Strout was calling this homicide "death at the hands of another." In other words, some degree of murder.

"But no potassium?" Glitsky wanted that nailed down.

"Not any. No."

A silence settled in the room, and Jackman broke it. "It seems to me that the salient point here is not so much the type of drugs that may have been used in these two deaths. And I don't want to speculate ahead of the facts on potential future discoveries we might make. But more than the difference in drugs, the common feature of these two homicides is that somebody seemed to know, or believe, that Portola rubber-stamped their postmortems, when they were done at all, especially in the more obvious cases."

"I checked into that a bit," Strout volunteered. "Seems the cutbacks they've been livin' with have left them very short in this area. Hospital PMs, as a rule, aren't very thorough anyway. These guys were barely goin' through the motions. They don't even have a forensics specialist on staff anymore. Instead, they run only basic scans out to their lab —"

"If they even take it that far," Farrell said.

Strout bobbed his head. "I would agree that it might not always happen."

"So what are the standard scans, John?" Hardy asked.

"It can vary," Strout said, "but basically we're talkin' money and levels of complexity. You've got your A-scan, which is set for alcohol and some of your common drugs — aspirin, cocaine, and so on. Generally, you find a cause or possible cause of death at one level — say you've got toxic levels of cocaethylene, which is cocaine and alcohol, at the A-scan — then you stop looking. But if you want to keep goin', the B-scan's set for a slew of other drugs. Anyway, each level of scan gets more expensive. So if you got a cause of death at the zero-scan level, most folks stop there."

"And that's what you think happened here, with Mrs. Loring?" Jackman asked.

Strout nodded genially. "That's my best guess. Nobody looked too hard. They looked at all, somebody would'a seen 'em."

"Once you got a cause of death, did you stop, too, John?" Marlene asked him. "Or did you take it beyond there?"

"Yes, ma'am, I sure did. She had her chemo agent and some morphine for the pain. I got her records when I called for the body, and she was self-medicatin' with morphine in the hospital. But nowhere near a fatal dose of anythin' else."

"But if she was self-medicating," Farrell asked, "that means she was fairly coherent, doesn't it?"

"It could," Strout agreed. "She knew when she was hurtin', and when it got bad enough, she hit the button for a dose of morphine."

"Which is premeasured, am I right, John?" Ash asked him. "And time-release controlled?"

"Right. No way she overdoses herself, if that's what you're sayin'."

"So she wasn't in any kind of coma?" Hardy had for some reason imagined she was. Somehow the fact of her consciousness made her death all the worse. "You're telling us she was alert and somebody just came in and killed her?"

"I don't know 'bout that, Diz. She might'a been sleepin' at the exact time. But otherwise, in terms of was she in a conscious state? I'd have to say pretty much yeah."

Everyone seemed lost in private thoughts. The DA simply moved his head up and down, up and down. Finally, he stopped. "Mr. Farrell, I want to thank you for coming to this early call. I expect we'll be hearing from you in the near future. I appreciate your cooperation."

It took Farrell a moment to realize that Jackman was telling him to leave. When it clicked in, he was gracious about it, thanking the DA for thinking to invite him, then Strout for his efforts and Hardy again for his.

Strout spoke up, as well. "If you don't need me, Clarence, I got a feelin' I'm lookin' at a busy day, and I'd best get on with it."

After the two men left, Jackman stood and

came around the front of his desk, then boosted himself up onto it. "Diz, we're sharing information with you on Markham and you're the man responsible for bringing Mrs. Loring's attention to all of us. We're grateful to you. But we still expect your client to testify fully before the grand jury. Especially in light of this list he provided for us, which opens its own can of worms." He looked around to Ash and Glitsky, to the two inspectors by the back wall. "If anybody wants Mr. Hardy to step outside, I'm sure he'll understand."

But nobody said a word. Jackman gave it another few seconds, then turned to Glitsky. "All right, Abe, we all know that this throws some kind of a wrench into Markham. How do you propose we proceed?"

When Hardy came in, David Freeman looked up from the no doubt brilliant brief he was writing longhand on his yellow legal pad. "Ah, Mr. Hardy," he said with pleasure. "Come in, come in." He had half of an unlit cigar in his mouth. The top button of his shirt was undone, his tie so loose it was barely attached. Hardy thought it might have been the same tie he'd been wearing yesterday, the same shirt. The shutters were still partway drawn, although it was by now well into the workday. Had Freeman slept here in the office? It wouldn't be the first time, but he decided he wouldn't ask. All in all, he'd rather not know.

"You wanted to see me? If it's about the rent, I'm not paying any more and that's final. In fact, I already pay too much."

Freeman harrumphed. "This Portola woman is your doing, isn't it?"

"Perhaps."

"Which makes you either the unluckiest son of a bitch on the planet, or the dumbest. I'd be curious to know your thoughts when you asked Strout to dig up this poor woman's bones."

"How'd you know it was me? And in actual fact, it wasn't. It was Wes Farrell, although I admit I played a role."

"That charade yesterday at lunch, which perhaps in all the excitement you've forgotten. John Strout mentioned both Mr. Farrell and Mrs. Loring by name, and I happened to notice them again in the newspaper this morning. Front page, if I'm not mistaken."

"And Jeff Elliot's by-line, now that I think of it. I've got to call him and have him buy me lunch or something."

Freeman sat back, took him in. "You're not taking this seriously."

Hardy took an upholstered chair and moved it into Freeman's line of sight, then sat in it. "Yes I am. And with all due respect to your gray hairs, it's neither unlucky nor dumb. I checked to make sure my client was long gone when Mrs. Loring died. He couldn't have killed her."

"No, maybe not her. But maybe she's got nothing to do with Markham."

"Technically true, but not relevant. She's got everything to do with him."

"What, pray? As I understand it, and even Mr. Elliot's article made it quite clear, your Mrs. Loring died of a different overdose, from an entirely different drug, than Mr. Markham. That in itself points to a different hand. *Res ipsa loquitur, n'est-ce pas?* Can it be you don't see this?"

Hardy was getting a bad feeling about Freeman's direction, but he had to admire somebody who could string English, Latin, and French together so fluidly and without apparent forethought. It was something you didn't hear every day. So Hardy had half a grin on when he replied. "Sure, David, I see it. I just don't see the problem."

Freeman came forward, arms and elbows on his desk. He took his cigar from his mouth. "The problem is that it neither proves nor disproves anything about your client in regard to Mr. Markham, and you're pretending that it does. When in fact all it does is bring more pressure to bear on Mr. Jackman to bring an indictment on at least somebody at Portola, and the closest person to hand might in fact turn out to be Dr. Kensing."

Hardy shook his head. "As it turns out, I was just with Clarence. He's not thinking that way at all."

"He will. Give him time."

"I don't think so. He's going to be looking for the person who killed Mrs. Loring, and maybe several other patients at Portola. He's then going to assume that that person killed Markham, as well."

"And why will he do that?"

"Jesus, David. Because it makes sense. Doesn't it just stretch your credibility a little too much to believe that two separate murderers are prowling the halls at Portola?"

Hanging his head, Freeman sighed. "Didn't O.J.'s slow car chase stretch credibility? Didn't Monica's blue dress turning up unwashed stretch credibility? Or the Florida recount — two hundred–some votes out of sixty million. Trust me, Diz, people nowadays are used to a boundless elasticity of credibility. And what I see is that you're sorely tempted to think you've won already, you've gotten Kensing off. I'm telling you that that's not the case. All you've done here is put the magnifying glass on everybody at Portola, and that includes him. You can't ignore that, and from what I'm hearing, that's what you were intending to do."

Hardy glared at the old man. "So what's your suggestion?"

Freeman was glad to give it. "The heat is way up now, Diz. They're going to have to put handcuffs on somebody for something soon, or there's going to be a peasant revolt. They're entirely likely to do your client for Markham, then kind of hint he's good for most, if not all, of the rest, but they just can't prove it." His eyes glinted under the steel wool brows. "You may have given Kensing a defense at trial, but now it's a hell of a lot more likely that he's going to have one."

In fact, Hardy had concluded that Kensing's troubles were pretty much over. In the euphoria of guessing right on Mrs. Loring, then of Glitsky's conversion, he conceded now that he might have gotten carried away with some of the implications of the autopsy's results. Freeman

430

was reminding him that his client was still exposed and vulnerable, and now maybe more than ever. Hardy had better remain vigilant until the whole drama had played out.

"Let me ask you this," the old man said, "what if one of the new batch of autopsies shows potassium again? You think that helps your client?"

"David, he wasn't there for Mrs. Loring. Get it? If he didn't kill her, he didn't kill any of them."

"Not true. Pure wishful thinking. And now you're getting angry, as well you should when you see your logic breaking down. But don't take it out on me." He picked up his cigar and chewed at it thoughtfully. "Listen, I don't want to rain on your parade, I really don't. I admit you've opened a door here and it might lead where you want to go. I hope it does. I hope it's one serial killer who confesses to it all before sundown.

"But think about this. Who supplied the names of the dead people? Kensing. If he was so suspicious so many times, why then didn't he mention some of this sooner? Why did he wait until he was a suspect in Mr. Markham's death? Isn't that a little convenient? And isn't it possible he could have been in collusion with someone else at Portola, maybe one of the nurses, so he needn't have been physically around for every death? You're laughing, but none of these are frivolous questions. Have you considered the possibility that Kensing and one or more of the nurses could have been getting bonuses under the table from Parnassus for clearing the beds of

431

terminally ill long-term patients without adequate insurance? This kind of thing has been known to happen, especially in cash-strapped organizations." He slowed down for a minute, sat back in his chair, and drummed the desktop with his fingers. "I'm not saying any of this is even remotely likely, Diz. But I am concerned. And you should be, too."

Hardy shifted uneasily in his chair. Freeman had been his informal mentor for many years, and though he might sometimes be outrageous, he was never stupid. It was worth hearing him out.

And he had one more point to make. From his intensity, maybe it was the most important of them. "As I understand it, Diz, the ten or so other names on your client's list were all people with a long-term but terminal prognosis. Isn't that the case?"

A nod. "That's why Kensing started noticing them. They died too soon."

"So if that proves to be true, does any further conclusion spring to mind, particularly regarding Markham?"

Hardy saw the problem immediately. "He doesn't fit the profile, either. He wasn't long-term terminal."

"Exactly." Finally, it appeared that Freeman was satisfied. "Now if it turns out that each of the other ten died of this muscle relaxant and not potassium, then Markham had both a different prognosis and died from a different drug than all of them. This, to me, may not be conclusive, but it does provoke its own questions, wouldn't you agree?"

"Such as who killed Markham, and why? Right where we are now." He stood up. "And to think I was feeling good a mere fifteen minutes ago, as though I'd made progress."

"It'll feel that much better when it *is* real, Diz. You watch."

"I'm sure it will, David. I'm sure it will."

He turned to go, but Freeman stopped him again. "There is one way you might be able to use this to help Dr. Kensing, now that I think of it."

"I'm listening."

"If, as you believe, you've got Clarence and Abe excited about the various possibilities raised by your discovery of Mrs. Loring, there might be an opportunity to dig a little deeper into things without arousing any suspicion. Tongues might be looser, pearls might fall."

This was what Hardy had experienced to some degree this morning in Jackman's office, when there had seemed to be a first flush of intuitive belief that maybe Kensing hadn't killed anyone. But Freeman was probably right in saying that it wouldn't last long. If Hardy wanted to take advantage of it, he had to move quickly.

Glitsky wasn't going to send his rookies out alone on this one. He knew that his most senior veteran inspector, Marcel Lanier, had taken the lieutenant's exam in January, passed high on the civil service list, and now craved a chance to show what he could do administratively. He would soon be reassigned out of homicide to his own command and wanted it to be a good one.

This would be his opportunity.

So while Bracco and Fisk got practice writing up search warrants for hospital records, Glitsky left Lanier in charge downtown and drove out to Portola. There he skirted around the phalanx of television news vans huddled in the parking lot and walked no-commenting himself by the knot of reporters in the hospital's lobby.

Outside the administrator's office, the secretary started to tell Glitsky that Mr. Andreotti wasn't seeing reporters individually. He'd be holding a press conference in about a half hour. At this news, the lieutenant produced his badge and wondered if the administrator could spare a few minutes for him right now.

Andreotti came around his desk with a death mask of a smile, grabbing Abe's outstretched hands in a kind of desperate panic. Gaunt, gray, and hollow-eyed, dressed in a gray suit with an electric blue tie, he seemed composed today of equal parts terror and exhaustion. Glitsky didn't suppose he could blame him. In the week since Tim Markham's murder, the hospital's troubles had increased logarithmically, culminating in this morning's bombshell. Not only were Portola's postmortems, as a matter of course, slipshod at best and criminal at worst, but at least one and perhaps as many as ten people had been killed while they lay in their beds in the ICU.

It wasn't yet 10:00 a.m. Harried and distracted, Andreotti had already been on the telephone with *Time* and *Newsweek*, *USA Today*, and *The New York Times*. He'd met with representatives of his nurses' union, of the Parnassus Physicians' Group, and of Parnassus Health itself. The mayor wanted to see him at two o'clock.

He got Glitsky seated, then went around his desk again and sat. "Whatever we can do to facilitate your investigation, Lieutenant," he began, "just let me know. We'll try to cooperate in every way we can. I've told everybody here the same thing. We've got nothing to hide."

"I'm glad to hear that, sir. My staff will be coming by before too long with what's going to look like a substantial shopping list, including search warrants regarding staffing records for the ICU, including the time Mrs. Loring was hospitalized."

"Yes, of course."

"Also, as you may know, there is some speculation that other patients may have been killed here, as well. We've got a list we're working from —"

"Yes. Kensing's, isn't it?"

"Yes, sir, it is."

"All right. You know what you're doing, I suppose, but the word here was . . . that is, I've heard that he was on your department's short list for Mr. Markham's murder?" He phrased it as a question that Glitsky didn't feel compelled to answer. He waited him out. "Anyway," Andreotti finally said, "I guess if it were me, I'd just wonder about any such list supplied by a murder suspect."

Nodding thoughtfully, Glitsky crossed a leg. "Normally, in principle, I would agree with you.

But in this case, the first name came up positive. Mrs. Loring was killed here."

Andreotti said it all but to himself. "Jesus, don't I know it."

"But to backtrack for a minute, you said you'd heard that Dr. Kensing was our prime suspect for Mr. Markham's murder. Was that the common feeling about him around here?"

"Well, no. I mean . . ." Andreotti's eyes shifted to the door, back to Glitsky. "I don't mean to accuse anybody of murder. Dr. Kensing was quite popular here with the medical staff."

"The medical staff?"

"Well, the other doctors and nurses. He's a very good doctor but a bit of an . . . opinionated man. I think many of his colleagues admired his integrity, though he could be difficult to work with. He was not a team player."

"So he didn't get along with the administration?"

"He didn't, no. Nor did he get along with Mr. Markham. It wasn't any secret, you know."

"No. We've heard about that. So he killed Mr. Markham? Is that what you think?"

"Well, he had big problems with the man and he was in the room . . ." Andreotti spread his hands imploringly. "I suppose I've thought about it, though I hate to admit it."

"You're allowed," Glitsky answered, "but I'm not here today about Mr. Markham. I wanted to talk directly to some of the staff, and wonder if you could supply me with some records of who might have been on duty, especially in the ICU, about the time when Mrs. Loring died."

"I'm sure I could find out. Can you give me a couple of minutes?"

It was more like ten, but when Glitsky saw the name Rajan Bhutan, he remembered the name from the transcript he'd read of Bracco's and Fisk's interviews here. He asked Andreotti if Bhutan still worked at the hospital, and if so where he could find him.

Rajan was surprised to be summoned again to talk to the police. They'd been here so often in the last week, talking to everyone. When they'd come to him, what had there been to say? He'd been with Dr. Kensing, treating Mr. Lector, when the screeching had begun on Mr. Markham's monitors. After that it was like it always was during code blue, except twice as busy. He couldn't say who had come into the room, who had gone. He was taking orders from Dr. Kensing, trying to anticipate, all of it going by so fast he remembered none of it really. Although he'd been there, of course.

Entering the lounge, he saw at a glance that this new man was older than the others, and harder. His skin was as dark as Rajan's, but he had blue, very weary eyes. A scar began just above his chin, continued through his lips, cut off under the right nostril. Something about the sight of the man frightened him, and Rajan felt himself begin to shake inside. His palms suddenly felt wet and he wiped them on his uniform. The man watched him walk all the way from the doorway to the table where he sat. He didn't blink once.

Rajan stood before him and tried to smile. He wiped his hands again and extended the right one. "How do you do? You wanted to see me?"

"Have a seat. I want to ask you a couple of questions about Marjorie Loring. Do you remember her?"

Marjorie Loring? he thought. Yes, he remembered her, of course. He tried to remember something about each of his patients, although over the years many had vanished into the mists of his memory. But Marjorie Loring had not been so long ago after all. She was still with him. He could picture her face. She was to have been another of the long-suffering dying, as Chatterjee had been.

But fate had delivered her early.

28

After Freeman's lecture, Hardy wasted no time. Now he was back at the medical examiner's office where, to his complete astonishment, Strout had his feet up on his desk and was watching the closing minutes of some morning talk show on a small television set. Hardy had seen the TV before, but assumed it was inoperable since it must have been used to kill somebody. Strout indicated he should pull up a chair and enjoy the broadcast. The two hosts — a man and a woman — were talking to someone Hardy didn't recognize, about a movie he'd never heard of. The actor was apparently branching into a new field and had just released a CD. He proceeded to sing the eminently forgettable and overproduced hit song from it. When the segment was over, Strout picked up his remote and switched off the television. "I love that guy," he said.

"Who? That singer?"

"No. Regis."

"Regis?"

"Diz, please." Strout didn't believe that Hardy didn't recognize the most ubiquitous face in America. "You ever watch that *Millionaire* show? That's him. You notice the ties I been wearin' this last year? The guy invented a whole line of 'em. My wife tells me I look ten years younger."

"I knew there was something," Hardy said.

"And you know why else I love him? You ever notice how happy he is?"

"Not really, no. I can't say I see too much of Regis myself."

Strout clucked. "You're missin' out." He sighed, then picked up a stiletto from his desk, pushed the button, and clicked the narrow steel blade out into its place. "Now what brings you back here so soon? And I'm hopin' it's not another request like the last couple."

"The last couple got you one headline and a quick thousand dollars."

Strout was cleaning his fingernails with the knife. "Truth of the matter is I been wrastlin' with the idea of givin' you back your money since it turns out you was pretty close to right. That was work worth doin'. After Loring, nobody's gonna call me for doin' the first one — Mr. Lector, I mean."

"Well, you do what you want, John. If you want to give me back the money, I'd take it. But you won it fair and square. While you're deciding, maybe we could talk a minute about Carla Markham."

Strout didn't answer right away. Instead, he closed the knife up, clicked it open again. Closed it, clicked it open. "I was kind of wonderin' when you'd want to talk about her."

"Are you saying there's a reason I should have?"

"No. I'm not necessarily sayin' anything. I ruled on it clear enough, comin' down on murder/suicide equivocal."

440

"But something about it makes you uneasy?"

Strout nodded. "A lot about it makes me uneasy. You get a copy of my report, is that it?"

Hardy nodded. He'd read it for the first time on Sunday night, then again at the office yesterday. It had become a habit for him to read and reread witness testimony and reports, where the truth often lay buried beneath mounds of minutia. "I noticed the gun was fired from below and behind the right ear, going forward."

"That's correct." Strout closed the stiletto again, then stood up and walked over to the floor-to-ceiling bookshelf that lined Hardy's left-hand wall. He boosted a haunch onto the thin counter, pulled an old six-shooter off the first shelf, and spun the cylinder. "I've seen it before."

"How often?"

Strout spun the cylinder again. "Maybe twice."

"In your thirty-year career?"

A nod. "About that. Maybe three times."

Hardy took that in. "So I take it Mrs. Markham was right-handed?"

"Nope. That ain't right, either." Except for an unconscious rocking of a leg, the coroner finally went still. "Plus, you know she'd bit the back of her front lower lip."

"I saw that. Did somebody have a hand over her mouth?"

"Comin' up behind her, you mean? Possible, but by no means conclusive. Just as likely she bit her lip."

Hardy sat a moment. He stared without focus in the direction of the venetian blinds behind

Strout's desk. Dust motes hung in the striped shafts of sunlight. The cylinder spun a few more times. Eventually, he looked up. "So why'd suicide even get mentioned?"

"She had GSR" — gunshot residue — "on her right hand. And I know, I know what you're going to say." Strout held up his hand. "Doesn't prove she fired the gun. The shot that killed her could have put her in the gunshot environment. And you're a hundred percent right. But there's the gun by her hand . . ." Strout wound down, met Hardy's eyes. "I didn't have any forensic reason to rule it out, Diz."

"So somebody might have done a decent job of making it look like a suicide?"

"That's within the realm of the possible, Diz. It surely is. But let me ask you a question. Why do you want her to be murdered?"

"I guess because it's the only place left."

"Except your list, you mean."

Hardy shook his head. "As Mr. Freeman points out, there's no definite correlation between anybody on that list and who killed Tim Markham. But if Carla was killed, I'm betting it had to be the same person who killed her husband."

"But wasn't your client the last one at her house before . . . ?" Strout let that hang.

Hardy sighed. "The theory's not perfect yet, John. I'm working on it."

Armed with their search warrant, Bracco and Fisk approached Donna, the records clerk at Portola. She was about thirty years old, slightly overweight, edgy at first when she found out they were policemen. She wore a small ring in her purple lips and another through her right eyebrow. It was obvious to Fisk that Bracco wasn't going to be comfortable talking to her, so he took point. Somehow, within minutes, they were all friends. She was competent at her job and pulled up and printed out all the Portola personnel and patient records for the relevant days within about a half hour.

After another half hour in one of the conference rooms, they pretty much had what they thought Glitsky wanted. As it turned out, the ICU nurses did rotate on a fairly regular schedule, although throughout the hospital there were more of them than the two inspectors had first been led to believe. In all, on the ten shifts when Kensing's list implied that patients might have died prematurely, nine nurses had spent some time in the intensive care unit. Only two, however, had been on duty for every death shift — Patricia Daly and Rajan Bhutan.

"Except we don't know for sure yet that any of those ten were homicides, do we?" Bracco asked. "All we know is Loring and Markham."

"But we do know Daly wasn't around for Markham, don't we?" Fisk replied. "Although Bhutan was. His partner that shift was — what's her name?"

She was one of the other seven regular ICU nurses, and Bracco had it at his fingertips. "Connie Rowe."

"I don't know how you remember a detail like that. I recognize the name when I hear it but I

443

can't pull it up for the life of me."

"That's all right, Harlen. That's why they put us together. There's stuff you're good at that I'd never think about. Like Donna, for example, just now. Or looking for Loring's shift, which I had completely blown off."

Fisk, warmed by the praise, stood up and stretched. "What's another half hour when we're having this much fun."

They both walked out to records — by now they were old friends with Donna — and told her there was a last shift they had to check. Bracco the detail man remembered the date: November 12th. Marjorie Loring had breathed her last during the swing shift, between 4:00 p.m. and midnight.

Donna's fingers flew over the keyboard, then she looked up at them. "That's weird," she said. "I think every shift you've looked at, there's been this name R. Bhutan, and it's here, too. Are you guys looking specifically for somebody?"

"No, but he just keeps turning up, doesn't he?"

The young woman clicked her black fingernails on the countertop. "What is it about these dates, anyway? Can you tell me?"

Fisk leaned over and theatrically looked both ways, up and down the length of the room. "We could," he said and added the old chestnut, "but then we'd have to kill you."

Donna's eyes grew into saucers for a second, then she giggled and punched the key to print a hard copy of the record. Fisk took the sheet and glanced at it. Connie Rowe again, he noticed, not Patricia Daly. With a meaningful glance, he showed it to his partner, then turned back to the clerk. "Let me ask you something, Donna, if I may. Is there any record of the doctors who came and went during these same shifts that we've been looking at?"

She thought for a moment. "Well, the individual patients would have had their own doctors making rounds. Is that what you mean?"

"Not exactly. I mean all the doctors who had reason to go into the ICU on those days, for whatever reason."

"All of them?"

Fisk shrugged and smiled at her. "I don't know. I'm just asking."

Her tongue worked at the ring in her lip. "They might keep a record at the nurses' station, you could ask, although I don't know why they would. The doctors come and go all the time, you know. I think it would kind of depend on a lot of things."

To Jack Langtry, the crime scene supervisor, the situation was bizarre.

Just before lunch, Marlene Ash invited him down to her office to discuss Carla Markham. When he arrived, another guy was standing by her, leaning over her desk, examining the scene photos. Langtry could smell lawyers a mile away, and this guy was one. And then Ash said by way of explanation, "Mr. Hardy's representing Dr. Kensing. Lieutenant Glitsky and Mr. Jackman have agreed to cooperate with him in exchange for his client's testimony. He'd like to ask you a few questions."

Langtry didn't know what to make of this, but if Marlene Ash was okay with it, then so was he. "Sure, mate," he said. "No worries."

Hardy's eyes were pinned to the color print of Mrs. Markham's body as it lay when Langtry had first seen her on the kitchen floor. The gun was in the top of the picture. Hardy had his finger on it. "Where'd the gun come from?"

"Lower-left drawer in Markham's desk, which was in the office next to the kitchen. At least that's where the registration was, the ammunition and cleaning stuff. We got a picture of it somewhere in that stack."

"I think I've seen it. Twenty-two, right?"

Langtry lifted his own eyes from the picture, looked in Hardy's face, said nothing.

"You got it in evidence, right? How many rounds did it hold?"

"Six, but there were only five spent casings."

Hardy frowned. "So five shots fired?"

Langtry shrugged — how the hell did he know? "Four dead people, one dog, one round each."

"What are you getting at, Diz?"

Hardy turned to Marlene. "I'm thinking somebody else fired the gun the first five times, then put it in her hand and fired again and took the last casing with him —"

"Where'd the slug go?" Langtry asked.

"I don't know. Out the window?"

"Closed."

"Maybe it was open the night before. How about the kids?" Hardy asked. He flipped a few

446

photos to where they began, then he looked up and away for a moment and sucked in a breath. Langtry felt the same way, sickened again at the sight of them.

"What do you want to know?"

"Just what went down."

While Langtry spent the next few minutes outlining the specifics of the crime, Hardy flipped through the pile of photographs. When Langtry was done, he had another line of questioning. "How loud's a twenty-two revolver?"

"Not too. Nothing like a three five seven. Just a flat pop."

"You shoot one in a house at night, you wake everybody up?"

"I don't know. Maybe not."

"All right. Here's another one. Why would Markham have a twenty-two?"

"I don't know that one, mate. Makes no sense for protection. Wouldn't stop any determined bugger, now, would it? Unless the shot was dead-on. Or point-blank, like these here."

"Okay." He flipped through some more pictures. "If you don't mind, Sergeant, and Marlene, I'd like to see the house."

They drove out separately. Langtry met him again at the Markhams' front door, and as he was fiddling with the key, suddenly another man was coming across the lawn from next door, waving at them in a friendly manner. "Excuse me," he said. "I saw you waiting, standing on the stoop here. You should know that nobody . . . nobody lives here anymore."

"Yes, sir, thanks." Langtry had pulled his wallet and badge, and now showed it to the man. "Police. We know all about it. And you are . . . ?"

"The neighbor from over there. Frank Husic." He motioned toward his own home. "Just keeping an eye out."

"We appreciate it. Thank you," Langtry said. "We're taking another look."

"You go ahead then. Sorry to have bothered you."

"No bother."

Now they were inside, in the kitchen. Hardy stood over the chalk outline on the Mexican tiled floor. Warm daylight suffused the room. Through a skylight, the noon sun drew a large and bright rectangle in front of the stove. There was a double-wide window over the sink, a laundry room off the back, well-lit with natural light. A short hallway by the refrigerator — where the dog had been killed — led to a half-glass back door.

Langtry was sitting behind him on a dining room chair that he'd pulled over. Hardy went down to one knee. Rising, he crossed to the sink, undid the latch, and lifted the right-hand window. Stepping sideways, he did the same to the left one, then walked back to the chalk line. "If I'm down here near the ground and put a bullet through either of those windows" — he could have been talking to himself — "I don't hit the house next door. I hit the sky. You want to do me another favor? Stand here in the kitchen a minute."

Langtry did as requested and Hardy went back

out through the dining room. His footsteps fell audibly on the central staircase, then his voice carried as he called down, "Count to ten and then call up to me as loud as you can."

After another minute, Hardy was back in the kitchen. "I heard you, but just barely. I was in Ian's room."

"Which means what?"

"It means nobody wakes up while Carla and the dog get shot. It means the dog's shot to shut him up, which is the only thing that makes sense."

"Then why do the kids get shot?"

"He's afraid he's woken somebody up. Either that or the kids knew he was here when they went to bed. Except the kids are asleep. The gunshots didn't carry up. But it's still too risky. So it's Ian first, and he silences the gun with the pillow. Then the girls. How's that sound?"

Hardy wasn't going to talk to a witness with a cop there. He followed Langtry for a few blocks, then honked a good-bye and drove back to Markham's street, where he pulled up, parked, got back out of his car, and knocked on Frank Husic's door. The gentleman probably assumed, since he'd been next door with Langtry and his badge, that he, too, was a cop. Hardy let him think so.

Husic invited him in and offered him iced tea, which he accepted. They then went out the back door onto a well-constructed redwood deck. Hardy didn't know when he'd last sat amidst such an explosion of well-tended flowers. Husic had planted them around the deck on the ground, in pots on the deck itself and now in late April they were blooming in profusion. But he'd left an open area in the center of the deck, and in that had placed a wrought-iron table, shaded by a large canvas umbrella. Here they sat in comfortable padded chairs.

From the transcripts he'd read, Hardy knew that Husic was a retired dentist, sixty-two years old. He had a ruddy complexion and cropped gray hair. Today he wore faded navy blue slacks, loafers with no socks, a shirt with a button-down collar, two buttons open at the neck. He came across as solicitous, friendly, intelligent. Hardy made a mental note that, should it come to that, Husic would make a terrific witness.

"Yes, I heard the shot," he said. "It's only a stone's throw away over there. I already told this to the police, you know."

Hardy did know this, but one of the frustrations of his discovery in this matter was the ineptness of some of Fisk's and Bracco's interrogations. He wondered if they'd ever heard of the relatively simple concept of asking witnesses where they'd been, what they'd seen or thought, and what they'd been doing at the time of a murder. This, he thought, was not high-concept police work. And Husic's interrogation — just random chat about flowers and investments, almost nothing about the day of Markham's death — had been one of the worst, he thought.

So he had a lot to fill in here. "I realize that," he replied. "In fact, I've read a transcript of that interview, but I've got a slightly different approach. You just now said 'shot.' You only heard one? I thought I noticed you said 'three' somewhere."

Husic sipped his drink thoughtfully, put it down carefully on the table. "They asked that, too, and I'm afraid I don't have a good answer. I believe I told the other officers that I was in bed at the time, pretty tired after the day over at Carla's. It was emotionally draining as hell over there, let me tell you. But if she needed me, I wanted to be available." Lightly slapping his forehead, he made a face. "Which doesn't answer what you asked me, does it? Sorry. You're a dentist, you spend your whole life making conversation with people who can't answer you. It affects your patterns of speech, and here I go again. All right. How many shots did I hear? Distinctly, only one."

Hardy looked across the expanse of lawn to what he knew to be the Markhams' kitchen. He realized they'd left the kitchen windows open when they'd gone.

"I thought it was a backfire or something. I mean, a gunshot is not your first thought in this neighborhood."

"But you may have heard three of them?"

"Well, that's funny, you know. None of them were really loud. In my memory it's three, but when I go back there and try to hear them, it's more like I heard one and remembered two. I'm not making sense, am I? What I mean is, the last one definitely was something — I sat up in bed — but the first two were almost as if I dreamed them, you know how that happens?"

"Sure." Hardy nodded. The siren that turns out to be your alarm clock. But this, he thought, might possibly be the two shots that killed the girls — right there seventy feet away — then the last round through the open kitchen window, which would have been louder. "But you were in bed when you heard them? Do you remember what time it was?"

"Yes, exactly. It was ten forty-two on the clock by my bed. I remember being very frustrated. I don't go to sleep easily since Meg passed — four years ago now — and if I wake up, that's usually it for the night. I'm up. And last Tuesday, with all the strain, I came home from Carla's and had a glass of wine, but barely dozed. Then with the gunshot. . . ."

"You were awake the rest of the night?"

"Until three, anyway. Those are long hours, eleven to three."

Hardy made a sympathetic noise. "I know them pretty well myself. So when did you finally determine that they were gunshots?"

"Oh, not until the next morning." The memory bushwhacked him for a moment. "God, it's just so awful."

"You were close to them, the Markhams?"

He hesitated. "Well, Carla, I'd say so. Tim was a bit of a fish, at least to me." Moving along to happier memories, his face came alive. "But Carla would come over and help with my garden here sometimes. We'd have coffee . . . some nice talks. I can't believe . . ." He hung his head and shook it. When he looked back up, he smiled,

452

but his eyes had a glassy quality.

Hardy let the silence extend another moment. Finally, he asked quietly, "So you didn't go and explore the source of the noise when you heard it?"

"No. After a minute I got up and looked out the window, of course, but everything was still. Just so still."

"Would you mind telling me what you saw, exactly?"

"Well, really nothing unusual at all. Carla's house right there." Husic seemed puzzled by the question. "Just her house."

Not "their" house, Hardy noticed. Just "her."

"But I knew people had been over and if they'd all gone home, I wasn't going to bother her, not that night. Let her sleep, I thought."

"So it was dark?"

Again, puzzlement. "Well . . . no. There were lights on in the kitchen and I remember over the front porch. And then the upstairs hall light was on." He turned and pointed. "That's that middle one, on the top."

"And what did you do then?"

Husic blew out heavily. "I'm sorry, Mr. Hardy, but didn't I already give you all this in my first statement?"

"Maybe not all of it, sir. Could we take five more minutes? I'd really appreciate it."

Another sigh as Husic gave in. "I turned on Letterman. I thought if I could laugh, maybe I could get to sleep. But nothing was going to make me laugh that night. Not even Dave. I was still worried about Carla, couldn't get her out of

453

my mind, actually. What was she going to do now?" Absently, he reached for his drink and stirred the ice in it with his finger. "But I couldn't do anything more that night, you know. I had to wait and let time . . . Anyway, I was still awake, so I came out here — see the little greenhouse back there? — and worked with my bonsais for an hour, maybe two. Then — by now it's two o'clock, thereabouts — I saw the lights were out. So Carla had gone to sleep, at least I thought that at the time, and then suddenly I could, too."

29

The first letter was dated nearly seven years ago.

 Parnassus Medical Group
Embarcadero Center
San Francisco, California

Dear Dr. Kensing:
This letter will document the decisions mutually agreed to by you, the Parnassus Physicians' Group, and the Parnassus Medical Group (collectively, the "Group") pursuant to the disciplinary committee meeting held last week. You have admitted that at various times and in various locations since you commenced employment with the Group, you have taken unspecified quantities of morphine and Vicodin for your personal use. Additionally, you acknowledge that you are an alcoholic whose medical performance while in a diminished mental state due to alcohol consumption has on several occasions fallen below the standard of reasonable medical care.

The Group recognizes your considerable skills as a doctor and communicator and before the recent discoveries memorialized herein, considered you a valuable member of its community. Because of this consideration, after substantial discussion, and over the dissent of the Medical Director, the Group's disciplinary committee decided at this time to issue only this formal letter of reprimand rather than terminate your employment and pursue possible criminal charges against you upon the following conditions: 1) you will immediately and forever desist in the use of all alcohol and all narcotics, except those drugs that may from time to time be prescribed to you by another physician for legitimate medical reasons; 2) you will voluntarily submit to random urine sampling to determine the presence of drugs or alcohol in your system; 3) you will immediately accept the recommendation of the substance abuse counselor and attend and cooperate with any programs recommended by the Group; 4) for the next calendar year, in addition to the regularly scheduled visits with your appointed counselor, you will *daily* attend a so-called 12-step program, approved by the Group, to address your problems with addiction and chemical dependency; 5) after the first year of such counseling, but for the remainder of your service time within the Group, you will attend such 12-step programs as the Group deems necessary, but in no event shall these be scheduled less frequently than once a week.

You freely acknowledge your culpability in

these above matters, and further acknowledge that any breach of the points agreed to above will result in your immediate dismissal from the Group, without appeal, and may result in further criminal and civil charges, as may be appropriate.

Very truly yours,
Timothy G. Markham

Parnassus Medical Group
Embarcadero Center
San Francisco, California

Dear Dr. Kensing:

In view of the fraternal rather than militant approach that I've suggested the Group take in helping you deal with your problems over the past couple of years — and over some high-level objection, I might add — I'd like to personally request that you consider tempering your critical remarks, both to your colleagues and to the press, about our various internal policies regarding the drug formulary. I am not trying to muzzle you or interfere with your right to free speech in any way, but I believe you're aware of the financial difficulties we're encountering in many areas. We'd like to keep the Group solvent so that we can continue providing the best care we can to the greatest number of our subscribers. We're not perfect, of course, but we are trying. If you have specific suggestions for improvement or disagreements with Group policy, I will be happy to discuss them with you at any time.

Sincerely,
Timothy G. Markham

Parnassus Medical Group
Embarcadero Center
San Francisco, California

Dear Dr. Kensing:
It has come to my attention that you intend to appear on the public affairs television program "Bay Area Beat." Let me remind you that the several medical committees on which you sit with the Physicians' Group have confidentiality arrangements with the Health Plan. I will interpret any breach of this confidentiality as grounds for dismissal. As a personal note, you are aware, I am sure, of the critical negotiations we are conducting with the city at this time. I find your public appearances and negative comments about some of the Group's policies to be singularly ungrateful and morally unconscionable, particularly in light of the Group's leniency and compassion toward you in other areas in the past.

Very truly yours,
Malachi Ross
Chief Medical Director and CFO

Parnassus Medical Group
Embarcadero Center
San Francisco, California

Dear Dr. Kensing:
If you don't want to prescribe Sinustop to your allergy patients, of course that is your prerogative and your medical decision. But it is a useful drug, and I have approved its inclusion on the formulary. Your continued efforts to undermine the Group's profitability by questioning my decisions are inappropriate. I have been patient with you long enough on these matters. The next event will have disciplinary repercussions.

Malachi Ross

"Where did you get these?" Hardy asked Jeff Elliot. He flipped through the pages he held, maybe twenty more of them. They were at the counter at Carr's, a nondescript and — due to the new Starbucks around the corner — possibly soon out-of-business coffee shop on Mission by the *Chronicle* building. "Especially this first one. Jesus."

A twinkle shone in Elliot's eyes. "As you know, Diz, I can never reveal a source."

But Hardy didn't have to think very hard to dredge it up. "Driscoll. Markham's secretary."

Elliot's eyebrows went up a fraction of an inch. Hardy knew he would rob Jeff blind at poker.

"Why do you say that?"

"He's come up a few times. He's fired, right, and probably saw that coming in advance. So he emailed his files home in case he wanted some leverage for later. Or just simply to screw somebody for the pure joy of it."

Elliot scratched at his beard. "Without either denying or admitting your guess as to my source, he's a reporter's dream. Vindictive, gossipy, craves attention. He probably gave me five hundred pages."

"All on Kensing?"

"No, no." Elliot laughed at Hardy's panicked response. "No, as far as I can tell, on the whole world at Parnassus."

"Does Marlene Ash know about them?"

"She'd be trying to get them if she did, although of course I couldn't give her any of it, either. I did tell him, though — my source, I mean — that if he wanted to keep any kind of exclusive control over its use, he might want to download it onto discs and put it someplace special, where Marlene or Glitsky wouldn't think to look for it."

"And yet you've got it here."

"I know." Elliot grinned. "Sometimes I like my job."

Hardy picked up his spoon and stirred his coffee. "Anybody could have just typed them, you know. They might not be authentic."

"You're right. Maybe they're not. But somebody would have to type really fast to get all this since last week."

Hardy accepted this. In fact, he had no doubt

461

that the letters were genuine. They'd never be accepted as proof of anything in court — not without hard copies and signatures — but this wasn't the law. This was journalism and Jeff could decide to accept them if his source was credible enough. "So what are you going to do with them?"

This was the crux and they both knew it. Jeff had called Hardy as a courtesy because Hardy was Kensing's lawyer. In view of the intense interest of nearly everything to do with Parnassus since Markham's death, Elliot told him that Kensing's substance abuse problems constituted real news. "On the other hand," he said, "the heat's kind of gone up under the Loring thing. If there's a serial killer at Portola, that's going to trump Kensing every time. I don't really want to run this, Diz — I like the good doctor and it would ruin his day — but if it turns out to be important, I won't have a choice."

"What could make it that important, Jeff?"

"How about if he was high when he was working on Markham in the ICU?"

Hardy had to admit, that would do it. "Has anybody said boo about that?"

"No. But I'll tell you something. If my source actually read most of these pages and thinks about it enough, I predict it's going to come up."

Hardy shook his head, marveling at the capacity for simple meanness in some people. Eric Kensing was only one doctor out of two or three hundred at Parnassus, but he'd unfortunately crossed Driscoll. Perhaps more importantly, he committed the cardinal sin of dissing the boss, with whom Driscoll identified heavily.

But a fresh thought surfaced. Driscoll might have a far better reason to impugn the characters of Kensing or anybody else than wanting to punish them for real or imagined past slights. He might simply want to keep people from looking at him.

"What are you thinking?" Elliot had been watching him.

Hardy covered. "Nothing really, except whether you're going to tell me anything about the other four hundred and ninety-five pages."

"I haven't gotten to them. I can only read so fast. The Kensing letters popped up pretty quick and I thought I owed you."

"As well you did, so now if you do me another favor, I'll owe you, right?"

Elliot considered, nodded. "Maybe. What?"

"If you hear some more rumors from your unnamed source about Kensing's sobriety a week ago Tuesday, don't run the story until you get it confirmed someplace else."

"I don't think the letters are rumors, Diz."

"I didn't say they were. But I've got something that isn't a rumor, either. Maybe we could trade."

When Hardy finally got back to his office at about 3:30, he was both gratified and depressed by the delivery of more discovery on the Markham case from the Hall of Justice. It was nice that Glitsky had moved into a more cooperative mode, but he could do without another six hours of tedious reading material. But he opened the box, pulled out its contents, and placed them in the center of the blotter on his desk. Glancing at his phone, he saw that he had two messages.

"Diz. This is Eric Kensing. Checking in. I'm at home if you need me." Hearing Kensing's voice reminded Hardy of how frustrated he was with his client. Maybe he'd come to terms with his drug and alcohol problems long ago, but how could he possibly convince himself his lawyer didn't need to know about them?

The next voice was Glitsky's. Of course, it being Abe, there was no preamble of any kind. "If you're really there, pick up." A silent three-count pause. "All right, call me." Hardy thinking, What a personality.

He picked up the phone, but didn't call Abe. He called his client. When he finished, Kensing didn't say anything for several seconds. "Eric?"

"I'm here. What was I supposed to do?"

"You were supposed to tell me. How's that?"

"Why?" he asked. "All that's far behind me. That was early career, early family pressure, and a giant mistake. I haven't touched —" He stopped himself abruptly, said simply, "That's not who I am anymore."

Hardy heard the words and believed that they might be technically true. But their truth wasn't his issue. "You're saying you're not an alcoholic? What's the first thing you say at your AA meetings?" Hardy knew the answer: "My name's Eric, and I'm an alcoholic," present tense, a permanent condition of being for those in the program. "Look, this is water under the bridge now, Eric. But Jeff Elliot's got this information and it's the currency he deals in."

A note of panic sounded in Kensing's voice. "He's not going to print this, is he? How did he find it out anyway? Everything about it has been confidential." But Hardy didn't have time to form a reply before Kensing said, "Shit. Driscoll."

"He's upset and taking it out on the world. The point is that the hospital's under siege as it is. If it now comes out that they're making secret deals to hide problems with their doctors . . . there's no question that it's news, Eric."

"Driscoll's trying to take the whole place down with him, isn't he?" A sigh. "And the small shall inherit the earth."

"Let's hope not. Anyway, I made Jeff a deal to keep you out of the limelight a few more days, maybe forever. But I've told him he can't use what I gave him — which means you're still on the burner — until I tell him he can. And that's going to depend on you."

"Okay, whatever it is, I'm in."

"All right." Hardy realized that he'd been gripping the telephone tightly. He relaxed his grip, forced an even tone. "You remember the night Markham died, you went to his house."

"Sure. I never said I didn't."

"I want you to think about what you did when you left. What time was that, by the way?"

"A little before ten, I think. That inspector, Bracco, he saw me drive away. He might have a record of it."

"He might," Hardy conceded. "But he didn't stay around and it's conceivable that you might have come back."

"Well, I didn't. Why would I do that?" He hesitated. "What's this about?"

"It's about Carla's murder. I want to know what you did after you left there."

"What I've always said I did. I drove home and went to sleep."

"I know you've said that, but that doesn't help me. I want you to try and remember if you met somebody in your building, or talked to anybody in the street, or used any of your phones or computer. Anything that could place you away from Markham's house between ten and eleven or, even better, ten and twelve."

Another pause. "I used my cell phone to call the clinic and see if I had messages."

This was good, Hardy thought. There would be a record of the call. They would even be able to pinpoint its point of origin within a several-block radius. "Great. When was that?"

"Right after I left. I don't think I'd gone two blocks."

Wrong answer. Kensing could have made the call, driven around the block, and been back in plenty of time. "Think of something else," Hardy pleaded.

"Why? What's this about?"

He wanted to scream at him to just answer the question — could he give himself an alibi? Instead, he answered, "It's about me talking to a witness who heard the shots, Eric, and placed their time at about a quarter to eleven."

"Which fixes the time of death."

"Yep. Quarter to eleven, she's dead and the lights are on. Two o'clock, they're all off. I figure

466

that whoever killed her waited around a while, then turned off the lights and snuck away."

"Why would anybody wait, though?"

"I don't know. Maybe spent the time looking for something. Maybe covering up. Maybe thought they'd be seen leaving the place after the shots. Your guess is as good as mine, but now we've got a murder and a time, which means you're clear if you can think of anything that —"

"No!" Suddenly, Kensing blurted it out. "Just no, okay? Jesus, I didn't kill anybody, Diz. I'm a doctor. I *save* lives, for Christ's sake. I just didn't do this. Can we leave it?"

Hardy's exasperation boiled over. "Sure we can, Eric. But nobody else on the planet is going to. So you just take your own sweet time and if you remember exactly what you did that night, why don't you call me back? If it isn't too god-damned much trouble."

Hardy slammed down the phone.

30

Brendan Driscoll couldn't believe the emptiness.

He'd gotten up at his regular time, a little bit after 7:00, and made breakfast for himself and Roger. After Roger had gone to the bank, he'd spent a couple more hours with the Parnassus files. But even now they were beginning to lose some of their fascination for him. After all, Jeff Elliot wasn't going to use everything, at least not just yet. Worse, this new situation over at Portola, with the lady they'd found murdered, was going to seem more important to Jeff than any inside information about the business side.

So he'd turned off the computer.

Then, fighting a nagging sense of ennui, he decided to work out at his gym for a couple of hours. When he came home from that, he showered and made a really lovely, well-presented mesclun salad with beets and feta cheese for lunch, which he ate alone on his sunny back patio area. But it didn't cheer him up. Depressed, he called Roger at work, but he was busy with clients and thought he might even be late getting home, which made Brendan edgy. You just never knew, really, and now he didn't have a job. . . .

Well, he was just feeling insecure, and who could blame him? He certainly would never have thought Tim would have considered letting him go, either. People changed. You had to be on your guard, flexible, ready for anything.

The afternoon yawned before him, endless. He put on some music, walked to the back of the house, threw in a load of laundry, washed his lunch dishes. Finally, deciding that it was the house, he was just going stir-crazy, he got dressed, went down to the garage, put the top down on his Miata, and pulled out into the day.

Now he'd been driving for two hours. He'd crossed the Golden Gate Bridge and driven up as far as Novato, then turned and came back, stopping for twenty minutes in Corte Madera for a cappuccino. He spoke to no one and no one seemed to notice him, even in his red convertible. He was alone, alone, alone, crossing the bridge again, the ocean blue and white-flecked below him.

He found himself on Seacliff Drive, turning and pulling up in front of Tim's house. A realty company had already put a sign on the lawn. The sun was behind him, warm on his shoulders. When he could no longer bear sitting in his car, he got out and approached the house, which seemed to shimmer pink in the afternoon light.

On the stoop, he stood and, without really thinking about it, rang the doorbell, listening to the loud chiming. Finally he turned around and sat on the top step. He had no idea how many times he'd looked at his watch today, but now he checked it again.

The sun slipped another degree or two. He didn't move. A Mercedes drove by on the street.

After another segment of time, another car passed, this one throwing newspapers onto some of the driveways, but not the Markhams'. A large crow landed on the walkway down by the sidewalk, hopped a few steps toward him, and cawed loudly.

It was already the longest day of his life, and still hours before the sun would set.

He started to cry.

Glitsky, Bracco, and Fisk met up at the hospital cafeteria and sat at one of the isolated tables, comparing notes.

"I talked a while to Mr. Bhutan," Glitsky said. He had a plain, dry bagel in front of him and a cup of hot water he was turning into tea. "He's an uptight guy and doesn't seem to have many friends, here or anywhere else. But he struck me as more sad than violent. The suffering of patients seems to bother him a lot for someone who works with it all the time."

"Are you saying you think he euthanized some of them?" This was Fisk, who'd reached this conclusion on his own a little earlier.

"Maybe. It's a little early, but he might be worth squeezing as time goes by."

But Fisk was attached to his theory. "He was the only nurse who worked all of Kensing's list, you realize that?"

"Yep. What I don't know, though, is how many of those people were homicides. And were there other homicides, not on Kensing's list, where Bhutan wasn't on duty?"

Some sign passed between the two inspectors,

470

then Bracco admitted that he'd mentioned the same thing a while ago. He was drinking from a can of Diet Coke, and interested in finding more true homicides. "You have any luck with that, Lieutenant?" Bracco asked. "You said you had somebody else with suspicions."

Glitsky nodded. "Another nurse named Rebecca Simms. No names of victims, yet, but she's asking around. I should tell you that she also mentioned Mr. Bhutan by name."

"I like him," Fisk said.

"I got that impression, Harlen. I did, too, for a while, but then I got to talking to him about Tuesday night."

"Tuesday night?"

"When Carla Markham died." Glitsky waited for the words to sink in, then continued. "I'm as fascinated as the next guy with Loring and what we may find with the rest of Kensing's list. But I'll tell you both frankly, I'm having trouble with the leap of faith that we've got related killings."

Bracco repeatedly flicked the side of his soda can. "You mean are Kensing's eleven homicides related to Markham at all?"

"That's it," Glitsky replied. "One thread leads back through these Pavulon deaths and another leads off the potassium, but do the threads meet?" His tea was getting dark enough and he tested it, bit his bagel, chewed thoughtfully, then shook his head from side to side. "I know it's possible. It might even be what we have here. And I'd love 'em somehow to be connected, but I can't seem to make the jump."

"They've got to be," Fisk protested.

471

"Why is that, Harlen?"

"Well, I mean . . . Markham's how we got to here, right?"

"That was my original thought when I first heard about Loring, but now I'm wondering. So maybe you can tell me. Why do they have to be connected? We got any evidence tying them together? We got a similar drug? The same M.O.? Anything? Tell me, I'd love to hear."

Glitsky knew he sounded a little harsh. He was angry with himself, more than anything, with the first of his conjectures brought about by the addition of Loring in the Markham mix. But he'd use Fisk as a surrogate whipping boy — maybe the rookie would come up with something Glitsky hadn't himself considered.

After a moment's reflection, Fisk spoke up. "We do have the same place for the homicides, Lieutenant. The same way the drugs got administered, through the IV, right? That's something."

"Yes it is," Glitsky admitted. He sipped more tea. "But does that in fact really connect Loring and Markham? Same basic M.O. but different poisons? I don't know. The problem is Carla and the kids. I can't believe she's not connected to Markham. I just can't go there."

Bracco had a question. "Okay. How about Bhutan then? You were saying you asked him about Tuesday night."

"I did. Turns out he's got master points in contract bridge and that night he was at a tournament at a hotel in San Jose and spent the night down there. Which, if true and I'm betting it is,

472

eliminates him from Carla, and therefore Markham."

"But not from Loring or any of these others." Fisk finally saw Glitsky's problem.

"Right. It has no necessary bearing on those at all. In fact, if Bhutan did Loring, they almost certainly can't be connected."

And at this truth, they fell silent. Glitsky ate some more bagel. Bracco tipped up his soda. Fisk, deciding he needed some refreshment, pushed his chair back and headed for the snack counter. The two other men watched him go. "So what do you want us to do now, Lieutenant?"

Glitsky knew what Bracco was asking. In an administrative sense, the homicides from the Kensing list weren't going to be part of the Markham homicide investigation any longer — they'd just pretty much established that. The two new inspectors had no claim to the assignment of what might turn out to be a very high-profile serial killer case. "What do you want to do, Darrel?"

Bracco didn't hesitate. "I'd still like to get some kind of a line on Markham."

"And how do you propose to do that? You've been on that case over a week. You got a suspect I don't know about?"

"I got questions I haven't asked, if that's what you mean. I've got a couple of ideas."

"Good. Let's hear one of 'em."

"Let's take the focus off Markham. Nobody saw anything here. But we've still got Carla and as you yourself said, whoever killed her killed her husband, am I right?"

"You might have trouble proving a negative."

"With respect, though, sir, we haven't even looked. You haven't wanted us to." Glitsky knew that Bracco was right, that he'd hamstrung their investigation from the beginning by keeping them away from the true principals, including even Kensing. This had created a vacuum where there should have been basic information — alibis, timetables, opportunities. Bracco was going on. "We've been dicking around for a week now with motives and women's gossip. But if somebody killed Carla, we're looking at a very limited universe of suspects."

"How do you figure that?"

Bracco's eyes were alight with the chase. "First, we forget the nurses here. As I think we've just proven, a connection between any of them and Markham is a fluke. None of the nurses from here killed Carla and her kids, I'd bet a million dollars on that."

"I would, too."

"Okay, so who's that leave? Who else was here last Tuesday?" He ticked them off on his fingers. "Kensing. Driscoll. Ross. Waltrip. Cohn. It's one of them."

"One of who?" Fisk was back with an ice-cream sandwich.

Glitsky was nodding in satisfaction. Darrel was going to be a cop someday.

"What?" Fisk asked again.

Glitsky motioned to Bracco. "Darrel will tell you in a minute, Harlen. Meanwhile, you guys remember Hardy?" Glitsky asked. "Kensing's

474

lawyer? Jackman's office this morning?"

"The guy with Kensing's list," Bracco said.

"Exactly. As you may have noticed, he's got a deal going with Jackman. We've been sending your transcripts and other discovery over to him." At their expressions of disbelief, he nodded. "Don't ask. But in theory we're trading information, so you might want to find out what he knows before you start. Who he's talked to. What they said. He did used to be a cop, and —"

"Who did?" Fisk asked. "Hardy?"

"Long time ago, Harlen. He was my partner, actually. We walked a beat in uniform together." He let them digest that, enjoying their faces. "He's not stupid, and he might have talked to some people already, which would save you time. If you even *think* he's holding back on you, arrest him and bring him to me. Better yet, shoot him and hide the body."

But something wasn't sitting well with Bracco. "So if Hardy's somehow with us, we cross Kensing off?"

Glitsky allowed a hint of a smile. "No, but it wouldn't be the worst thing in the world if Hardy got that impression."

Hardy threw his darts as a form of meditation, "like Sherlock Holmes playing his violin," he'd told Freeman once. But Bracco and Fisk didn't know that. He'd been perusing his new discovery binders for nearly two hours, ever since a few minutes after getting back from his meeting with Jeff Elliot, and when the inspectors had arrived, he had just stood, stretched, decided to throw some darts and let the new facts settle. Both of the inspectors undoubtedly thought he was goofing off at the end of the workday, and he saw no need to disabuse them of that notion. He threw another dart. "What do you want first?"

"The lieutenant said you'd give us whatever you've got," Bracco replied.

"Except that most of what I've got is your stuff. It could get a little tedious." The last shot of the round hit the double 11 and Hardy cracked a quick grin in satisfaction, walked up to the board, and pulled darts. "But okay, here's something you may not know. You remember Frank Husic?"

"The guy next door?"

"Right. He heard the shots at quarter to eleven. He looked next door and the lights were on. They were still on an hour later. Then, two hours after that, somebody had turned them off. And here's a clue — it wasn't Carla."

"I was there at a little before ten." Bracco sat forward stiff-backed on the couch, elbows on knees, hands clasped in front of him. "Does Lieutenant Glitsky know this?"

"I was planning to call him later, so he probably doesn't." He shot a look at Bracco. "What time did you leave there?"

Bracco answered without inflection. "A few minutes after your client, say ten straight up."

"And he was the last visitor?"

"The last car in the street out front, yeah. Plus he told me he was the last one there except the family, and they were turning in."

"After he left," Hardy threw a dart, "did you go up to the house?"

Fisk, idly turning the pages of one of Hardy's magazines, suddenly stopped and looked up at the question.

"No," Bracco replied. "Your guy kind of convinced me that they'd had enough for the day. What did he do after he left?"

"He drove home and went to bed. And, Inspector," Hardy threw again, "he didn't come back."

"Can he prove that?"

"Can you prove he did?"

Fisk cleared his throat, closed his magazine, and dropped it onto the end table. "Mr. Hardy. Darrel. What do you say we keep Kensing out of the mix until he puts himself back in. How's that sound?"

Hardy had gone back to his board and was pulling darts. Now he walked back to his desk, put them down on it, and pulled a chair around. "That's a good idea, Inspector. Dr. Kensing's not going to put himself back in." He met both of their eyes. "I apologize if I'm touchy about my client."

Bracco hadn't moved an inch, but his shoulders settled almost imperceptively. When he spoke, the tone was conciliatory, too. "We've narrowed it down to the five people who'd been around the ICU that morning, excluding the two nurses. Does that fly with you?"

Hardy was somewhat disturbed but not surprised to see Freeman's predictions of the morning come true so quickly. If the nurses were out of consideration for Markham, then Marjorie Loring's death wasn't any part of Kensing anymore, if indeed it ever had been. But, betraying little, he only nodded. "If the nurses have alibis for Tuesday night."

"Both of them do," Bracco said. "Rajan Bhutan was playing bridge in San Jose, although Lieutenant Glitsky says some of the staff think he looks good for Loring. For what it's worth, Harlen and I don't think he looks too bad, either —"

Hardy interrupted. "And he was one of Markham's nurses?"

"Yeah. But with this alibi for Carla. And the other one, Connie Rowe, was home with her family — husband, two kids. She didn't go out."

"Okay."

"So the scenario at Markham's house is that someone came between ten and ten forty-five, and Carla opened the door to whoever it was. Then the kids start going to bed while Carla and X talk a while. At some point, X excuses himself and goes into Markham's office where he keeps his gun."

"Who'd know that?" Hardy asked abruptly. "Not just that he had one but where he kept it?"

"That's a point," Fisk said, "but if X was an acquaintance of Carla's, which it looks like he was, he might have known."

Hardy thought that this was reasonable enough. "Okay. Let's go back to who's left," he said, "besides my client, of course."

Bracco had them on the tip of his tongue. "Driscoll, Ross, Waltrip, Cohn."

Hardy had come across the name Cohn only about an hour before in his reading — the report Bracco and Fisk had written up on what they'd discovered last Friday night but had forgotten to tape. At that time it had leapt off the page at him and brought his heart to his throat. Hearing the name again now, he showed nothing, even let himself chuckle. "You realize I haven't talked to even one of those people. Who are Waltrip and Cohn?"

As far as Hardy knew from the transcripts and reports he'd read, the inspectors hadn't spoken to any of these people, either, although they didn't volunteer that. Instead, Bracco was low-key. "Just some doctors who'd also been in the ICU that day — Kent Waltrip and Judith Cohn."

"But no sign they'd been to Carla's?"

"No," Fisk replied. "We assume they both knew Markham, but other than that, we don't have much on them."

"Their names, is all," Bracco added. "I don't think either of them played any role here, but we kept them in just to be thorough."

Hardy nodded. "So it's Driscoll or Ross?"

It was Bracco's turn to break a small smile. "Under the local rules." Meaning, not including Kensing.

Hardy allowed a friendly nod. "So how are their alibis? Driscoll and Ross?"

Obviously embarrassed, the inspectors exchanged a glance. "We haven't had a chance to talk to them, either."

"Maybe you want to do that," he said gently.

"Meanwhile, just to be thorough, I'll try to get in touch with Waltrip and Cohn."

The second and third names on Kensing's list had been cremated, rather severely limiting the options for further forensic analysis. The fourth name was Shirley Watrous.

She had died on the day after last Christmas. She'd been admitted to the hospital a week before that for acute phlebitis, then suffered a stroke in her bed that left her paralyzed and unable to communicate. Moved to the ICU for observation and further testing, on the fifth day she passed away without ever regaining consciousness. The hospital PM listed the cause of death as cerebral hemorrhage.

This time around, Strout knew exactly what he was looking for — the Pavulon cocktail — and he found it. Mrs. Watrous, too, had been murdered.

Glitsky, Ash, and Jackman were crammed into Marlene's office, having a powwow. Her office mate had checked out at close of business, and Jackman sat at his desk. Glitsky had pulled a chair around and was facing them, straddling it backward.

"Of course," Glitsky was saying, "he's got no idea what he was doing on November twelfth" — he was talking about Rajan Bhutan — "but the day after Christmas, he might remember."

"Is he a Christian?" Marlene asked. "Maybe he doesn't celebrate Christmas."

"Either way, it's a holiday." Jackman turned to

Glitsky. "Abe, he's clean on Carla Markham?"

"He's got maybe twenty people who'll swear where he was when Carla got shot. For me, that clears him on both her and Markham."

Jackman pushed some paper clips around the blotter in front of him. When he spoke, it might have been to himself. "It beggars belief that Kensing could be the source of this problem at Portola when there's no relation to Markham."

Marlene added her own thoughts. "I think it's high time we get him in front of the grand jury, find out what he knows once and for all. Have you ruled him out on Carla, Abe?"

Glitsky almost laughed. "Not close. Far as I'm concerned, he's still the inside track. Matter of fact, I'm dropping by his place on my way home." Glitsky produced a terrifying smile and then a piece of paper from his jacket pocket. "With a search warrant this time."

Marlene got out of her chair. "If you can give me five minutes, I can have a subpoena for you to deliver, too. You mind?"

"Whoa, whoa, whoa," Jackman interjected. "You're both forgetting something. I promised Hardy we'd give Kensing thirty days' grace."

This dampened the room's enthusiasm level for a nanosecond, but only that. Marlene had the answer almost before the objection was out. "That was on Markham's murder, Clarence, when Kensing was our suspect. Rather specifically. There's no way Hardy could object to the grand jury needing to hear about the list Kensing himself provided."

"And as soon as possible." Glitsky turned to

the DA and added formally, "To keep our mutual and cooperative investigations on track."

Jackman considered for a long beat, then finally nodded. "Okay, do it."

31

Dr. Kent Waltrip told Hardy he'd made his morning rounds at the ICU — he had a patient coming out of a bout with spinal meningitis — and he'd finished up at about 10:15, after which he'd gone to the clinic to see his regular patients. He'd worked there all day.

Judith Cohn's office number, too, was listed and Hardy was surprised and happy when he got his second human being in a row to answer the phone at a little past 5:00. He identified himself to the receptionist, explained his relationship to Eric Kensing, then asked if Dr. Cohn would please call him when she got the message.

"I could page her right now," the cooperative voice replied. "If you give me your number I'll just punch it in."

Two minutes later, Hardy was standing by his open window looking down on Sutter Street when his direct line rang. He crossed to the desk in three steps, picked up the phone, and said his name. On the other end of the line, he heard a sharp intake of breath. "Eric's lawyer, right? Is he all right?"

"He's fine. Thanks for getting right back to me. I wondered if I could ask you a few questions?"

"Sure. If they'll help Eric, I'm here."

"Great." Hardy had considered his approach — he didn't want to scare her off — and written a few notes. Now, sitting down, he pulled his pad around. "I'm trying to establish Eric's movements on almost a minute-by-minute basis on the day Tim Markham was killed."

"The police don't still believe he had anything to do with that, do they?"

"I think it's safe to assume that they do, yes."

He heard her sigh deeply. "Don't they know the man at all? Have they ever talked to him?"

"Couple of times, at least."

"Christ, then they're idiots."

"They may be," Hardy said, "but they're *our* idiots. And we have to play with them. I understand you had your own patient or patients in the ICU on that day, as well. Tuesday a week ago."

"Oh, I remember the day well enough. It started bad and kept getting worse. You know how it works with scheduling the ICU and ER, don't you?"

Early on, Kensing had explained the Parnassus idea to maximize efficiency. The doctors at the Judah Clinic, who were part of the Parnassus Physicians' Group as well as usually on the staff at Portola, were responsible for making sure that at least one physician was assigned to the ICU, and at least one to the ER as well, at all times. This duty was on a rotating schedule and its essential purpose, according to Eric, was to eliminate at least one full-time doctor's salary from the payroll. Its other effect was to leave the clinic perennially shorthanded. It was not a popular policy.

"Basically," Hardy replied, "there's a staff physician covering each room."

"Right. In the ICU, only a few of the beds, if any, contain that physicians' personal patients. Except if they get somebody straight out of ER or the OR, or a critical baby, something like that. Anyway, so that morning I had ER downstairs, late to work as it was, when the Markham madness just broke it open —"

"Wait a minute. You were with Markham in the OR? You did the surgery on him?" So, Hardy realized, she had not just floated by the ICU to check a patient — she'd been there at Portola all morning.

"Yeah. He was a mess. I was amazed he survived to get in, much less out. Anyway, I walked in, frazzled at being late to begin with — I'm *never* late —"

"What had happened?" Hardy asked quickly. "With you being late?"

"It was so stupid, I just overslept. Me, Miss Insomnia. I think I must have turned off the alarm when it went off and never really woke up. I guess the only good news is I was well-rested for Markham's arrival. I needed to be, believe me. Although Phil — Dr. Beltramo? He'd just worked ten to six — he didn't appreciate it much."

"So when did you make it up to the ICU finally?"

"I came up with Markham's gurney, when we got him admitted and settled in there, Eric and I. Then I bopped up, I don't know for sure, must have been four or five times before he died.

485

Maybe every forty-five minutes, whenever I got a break. I'd pulled him out, after all. He was my patient." She grew silent for a moment. "I didn't expect him to die. I really didn't."

"He didn't just die, Doctor. Somebody killed him." Hardy was trying to assimilate this unexpected information, which, he had to admit, Cohn was volunteering easily enough. He wasn't picking up any phony sympathy for Markham, any reticence to describe her own actions. "And the police continue to think it might have been Eric. Were you in the ICU when Markham went code blue?"

"No. I was down in the ER. Although I heard it, of course, and came right back up."

"But you didn't notice Eric in, say, the ten or fifteen minutes before?"

"No. The last time I saw him he was in the hallway with Rajan Bhutan. He's a nurse there. They were with a patient on a gurney."

This comported perfectly with everything he'd heard so far about the minutes just before Mr. Lector's monitors started to scream and, as before, it didn't do his client any good, except insofar as it might implicate Cohn herself.

"Let me ask you this, Doctor. Did Eric tell you anything about his visit to Mrs. Markham's later that night?"

"Not really," she said. "I was asleep when he finally got in and then we didn't get any time together for a few days after that. What would there be to say, though? It must have been depressing as hell."

But Hardy had cued on something else. "What

486

did you mean, when he finally got in?"

"Back from Mrs. Markham's, you meant, right?"

"Right. So you were at Eric's place that night?"

A small laugh. "You didn't know that? Whoops, blown our cover, I guess." Then, more seriously. "I thought he could use some company after the day he'd had. I know I could."

Reeling from this latest revelation, Hardy struggled to control his voice. "So what happened? Did you go home from work together?"

Another laugh. "No, no. We've given up trying to plan anything. We're both on call half the time. Our hours get too weird. I just went over there and let myself in. I've got a key."

"Aha," Hardy said, jostling her along.

"But Eric stayed late at Portola, then went to Mrs. Markham's. By the time he got home, I'd finally gotten to sleep."

"The insomnia kick back in?"

"Jesus, with a vengeance, probably because I'd slept in that morning. I've said a million times, if I could change one thing in my life, other than my frizzy hair, it's insomnia."

"Hemingway says he wouldn't trust anybody who's never had it."

"Yeah, well look what happened to him. Insomnia just plain sucks. There's no upside and I ought to know. Can you imagine what it would be like to want to go to sleep, close your eyes, and presto, you're gone? I would call that heaven. I'd sell what's left of my soul for half of that."

"But that wasn't Tuesday night?"

"Jesus." She suddenly sounded tired just thinking about it. "It must have been one o'clock, and I started trying — I'm talking in bed with the lights out — around ten."

"And Eric wasn't home by then?"

"No. He was still at Mrs. Markham's. Evidently it went on pretty late."

Glitsky held the warrant up in front of him. "We're talking now," he said. Marcel Lanier was with him and brushed past in a show of force, getting himself inside the apartment.

"Where do I start, sir?" he asked.

"Back to front, but maybe first the bedroom. I'll be with you in a minute or two."

"What are you looking for?" Kensing had gotten back from a run recently. He still wore his running shoes, shorts, and a tank top. He'd been at his kitchen table, drinking orange juice and ice, when the doorbell had rung. Now he turned at the sound of Lanier rummaging somewhere back in his room. "You can't just come in here and tear things apart."

Glitsky turned the warrant around, pretended to read it, came back to Kensing. "Judge Salter says I can. Oh, and before I forget." He handed him Ash's subpoena, as well.

"What's this?"

"An invitation to talk to the grand jury. Tomorrow, nine thirty."

"You can't do this," Kensing repeated. "This isn't right. Mr. Hardy had a deal with the DA. I'm going to call him."

"Go ahead." Glitsky stepped over the threshold. "He's not allowed in here without our permission when we're conducting a search. He might take something. But you can call him if you want. Then you can both wait until we're done. Take it easy, Doctor. I told you last time you should have let me in when we could have talked in a more comfortable atmosphere. You've really left me no choice."

"What are you looking for?"

Glitsky read from the warrant. "Medical paraphernalia, specifically syringes and prescription drugs —"

"I'm a doctor, Lieutenant. You want, I'll go get all that for you." He turned and wiped sweat from his brow again. "I don't believe this. This is America, right? We do this here?"

"You'd better thank God this is America, Doctor, and that this is how we do it. Anywhere else it wouldn't be so pleasant." Glitsky was reading from the warrant again. "Clothes with splatter or stains consistent with blood —"

"You're going to find that, too. I work with blood every day. It comes inside people."

Glitsky raised his eyes in a baleful expression.

"I want to call Hardy."

"Absolutely. I'd never try to stop you. But he's not coming inside here."

Another thumping noise emanated from the bedroom.

Glitsky raised his voice. "Marcel! Easy! By the book, please. Nice and neat."

The doctor hung his head for a minute, then looked back up. "This is bullshit," he said.

★ ★ ★

Bracco struck out trying to reach either Malachi Ross or Brendan Driscoll. He was in the middle of leaving a message with the latter's answering machine when another call came in on their line and his partner picked it up. "Fisk. Homicide."

"Sergeant Fisk, this is Jamie Rath again, from Carla Markham's coffee group? I'm calling because I've been worrying all day. My daughter said something last night and it got me to thinking that maybe it was something you'd want to ask her about."

"What was it?"

"Well, you know she plays soccer. She's at practice right now, in fact. But she also runs cross-country, so she gets up early every morning and runs down to the greenbelt on Park Presidio and then up to the park and back the same way."

"Okay."

"Well, we were talking about Tim's accident, me just being a bitchy mom trying to remind her how dangerous the streets could be, even when you were paying attention. And she said she didn't need me to remind her. On the same day that Tim had gotten hit, almost the same thing had happened to her, only a couple of blocks away."

Fisk was snapping his fingers at his partner, indicating he ought to pick up the other line.

Mrs. Rath was continuing. "It had scared her silly. She'd just turned off Lake onto Twenty-fifth, coming back home, and was crossing the

490

street. She saw this car coming, but there was a stop sign and she was in the walkway. Then suddenly she heard the tires screech and she looked over and jumped backward and the skid stopped just in time. Lexi was standing there with her hands on the hood, just completely flipped out. She said she yelled something at the driver, to watch where she was going, then slapped at the hood and went back to running. But I didn't have to tell her how dangerous it was. She knew."

"Did she say anything else about the car? What color it was, for example?"

"Oh yeah. It was green, which I guess is what made me think about Tim. Didn't I read that the car that hit him was green?"

Bracco butted in. "What time does your daughter get home from soccer practice, Mrs. Rath?"

Lexi sat between her mom and dad, Doug, on the couch in their living room. She'd been home long enough to have showered and changed into jeans, tennis shoes, and a light sweater. She was a tall and thin fourteen-year-old with braces and reasonably controlled acne. Her long brown hair was still wet. She was holding both of her parents' hands, nervous at being the center of attention, at talking to these policemen who were sitting on upholstered chairs facing her. "It wasn't really that big a deal. I mean," her eyes begged for her mother's understanding, "I had this kind of thing happen before while I've been running. Maybe not this close, but almost. People just space out when they drive, but I know that. So I pay attention when I'm out there."

"I'm sure you do," Fisk responded. "And paying attention the way you do, did you notice anything unusual about the car that almost hit you?"

Lexi threw her eyes up to the ceiling in concentration, looked from Jamie to Doug, back to the inspectors. "I really only saw it out of the corner of my eye. You know, there was a stop sign. I saw it coming up the street and thought it would stop, so I didn't break my stride. I guess she didn't see me until I was right in front of her."

"So it was a woman? The driver?"

"Oh, yeah. I mean, yes, sir. Definitely."

"Was there anybody else in the car?"

"No, just her."

"Did you get a good look at her?"

She nodded yes. "But only for a second."

Bracco had been letting Fisk take the interview. He'd crowed all the way out here about the car, the car, the car. Jamie Rath had called him at the detail, or at least he'd answered the phone. He knew all along that the car would be part of it. Bracco didn't mind — Fisk tended to be good when gentleness was called for. But Bracco thought that sometimes he didn't hit all the notes. "But you *did* get a good look at her for that second, is that true? Do you think you could recognize her again?"

"I don't know about that. Maybe. I don't know."

Doug patted her reassuringly on the leg. "It's

492

okay, hon. You're doing good."

"You *are* doing good, Lexi," Fisk seconded. "What we're asking is maybe we could send an artist out here to try to draw her face as you remember it. Would that be all right with you?"

She shrugged. "I could try, I guess."

Bracco asked her about the time, wanting to narrow it down.

"I know just what time it was because when I stopped, when she almost hit me, and then I started running again, I checked my watch to see how much time I'd lost. It was twenty-five after six."

This perfectly fit the timetable for Markham's accident. "So let me ask you this, Lexi. Would you close your eyes for a minute and just try to visualize everything you can think of about the car or its driver — I know it was only a second — just tell us what you see."

Obediently, she leaned back into the couch, scrunched between her mom and her dad. Closing her eyes, she took a deep breath. "Okay. I was on Lake, just running like, and then I usually turn up Twenty-fifth and cross over, so I got to the corner and there was this car maybe, I don't know, a ways down the street, but coming to the stop sign, so I thought it would stop."

"Was the car speeding, do you think?" Bracco asked.

"I don't know. Probably not, maybe, or I might have noticed it more."

"Okay."

"But then I was off the curb like one step, and I heard the brakes go on, or the skid, you know

493

that sound, whatever it's called. So I turned and she was going to hit me, so I jumped backwards and was facing her. Luckily she stopped just as I was reaching out. You know, in case she hit me."

"All right," Fisk said gently. "So you're leaning on the hood of the car. Is it damaged at all? Crashed in a little?"

"The light, yeah. I guess it would be the front, my left. I remember because I didn't want to cut myself on the broken headlight."

"Front right then, on the car."

"Okay, I guess so." She opened her eyes and seemed to be silently asking her parents if she was doing all right. A couple of nods assured her, and she closed her eyes again, but shook her head uncertainly. "I was kind of shaking then. It was pretty scary. But then I just got really mad and slammed my hands down on the hood again, really hard. I screamed at her."

"Do you remember what you said?"

"You almost killed me. You almost killed me, you idiot. I said it twice, I think. I was really mad and screamed at her."

"Then what?"

"Then she held up her hands, like it wasn't her fault, like she was sorry."

"Lexi," Bracco said with urgency, "what did she look like?"

It was almost comical the way Lexi screwed up her face, but there was no humor at all in the room. "Maybe a little younger than Mom, I think. I can't tell too good about adults' ages. But dark hair, kind of frizzy."

"Any particular hairstyle?"

"No. Just around her face. Frizzy."

"What race was she?"

"Not black. Not Asian. But other than that, I couldn't say."

"How about what she wore? Anything stick out?"

"No. It was only a second." She was showing the first signs of defensiveness. "We just stared at each other."

"Okay, that's good, Lexi," Fisk said. "Thank you so much."

But Bracco wasn't quite done. "Just a couple more things about the car, okay? Would you call it an old car or a new one? How would you describe it, if you can remember."

Again, she closed her eyes. "Not a sports car, but not real big, you know. Kind of like a regular car, maybe, but not a new one, now that I think about it. The paint wasn't new. It just looked older, I guess. Not shiny." Suddenly, she frowned. "The back lights were kind of funny."

"The back lights?" Bracco asked. "How were they funny? How did you see them?"

"I turned right after I started running again. They kind of went out from the middle, almost like they were supposed to make you think of wings, you know?"

"Fins?" Fisk asked.

"Like on Uncle Don's T-Bird," Mrs. Rath volunteered. "You know how they go up in the back. They're called fins."

But she was shaking her head. "No, not just like that. Lower, kind of along the back, where you'd lift up the trunk. Oh, and a bumper sticker."

"You are doing so good, Lexi," Fisk enthused. "This is great. What about the bumper sticker?"

She closed her eyes again, squeezing them tight. But after a minute, she opened them and shook her head. "I don't know what it said. I don't remember. Maybe it wasn't in English."

At the day's last light, the two inspectors made one last stop, at the stop sign at Lake and Twenty-fifth. They had already decided to send a composite artist specialist out to the Raths' to work with Lexi. Fisk had a book at home with front and back views of every car made in America for the past fifty years, and he was planning on bringing that by, as well, to see if Lexi could give them a positive identification on the make and model.

They got out and walked from the stop sign back to the first streetlight. There was no sign of a skid mark, from which Fisk hoped to get something, perhaps a tire size. And then Bracco remembered. "The storm," he said. "We can forget it."

Kensing reached Hardy on his cell. It sounded as though he was in a restaurant somewhere. Jackman had already talked to him. He'd phrased the subpoena as a request. They wanted to proceed with dispatch on investigating Kensing's list, and without his testimony, the grand jury would be left in the dark. Hardy thought cooperation here wouldn't hurt them, and he'd okayed the new deal. But he wasn't nearly as sanguine when Kensing told him about

496

the search warrant. "Glitsky was there tonight? Looking for what?"

"I don't think anything really. I think it was just to scare me, although they did take some of my clothes."

"Why did they do that?"

"They said they were looking for blood. They probably found some."

"Christ on a crutch."

Hardy had meant to turn off his cell phone when he and Frannie had left the house on their weekly date. It was one of their rules, but he'd forgotten and then of course it had rung and he'd answered it, telling her he'd just be a sec. That had been nearly five minutes ago. Once he had Kensing on the line, he wanted to grill him at length about the discrepancy between Judith Cohn's account of Tuesday night, when he hadn't gotten home by at least one o'clock, and his own, which would have put him there by about 10:30.

But they wound up talking about the search, and then about tomorrow's grand jury appearance. Then their waiter came up and gave him the sign and Hardy realized he really ought to hang up. They frowned upon cell phones here. Hardy did, too. Just not at this precise moment.

He squeezed in one more sentence. "But we really need to talk before you get to the grand jury."

If either Glitsky or his inspectors talked to Cohn as Hardy had done, they'd get the message to Marlene Ash and Kensing's appearance tomorrow in front of the grand jury wouldn't be pretty. With his multiple motives and Glitsky's animus, the squishy alibi might just be enough to get him indicted. At least he ought to know his girlfriend's story, or he'd get bushwhacked.

So they were meeting tomorrow at Kensing's at 8:15.

Now Frannie raised her glass of chardonnay, clinked it with his. "That sounded like a pleasant conversation," she said.

Hardy ostentatiously turned off his cell phone, put it in his jacket pocket. "Honest mistake, I swear," he said. "Which is better than the one Kensing made when he talked to Abe, or when he lied about when he got home last Tuesday."

Frannie stopped midsip. "I don't like to hear about clients who lie to you."

"It's not my favorite, either. In fact, as a general rule, I'd put lying in my top ten for what I'm not looking for in a client."

"And Abe just now searched his house?"

Hardy dipped some sourdough bread into a shallow dish of olive oil, pinched sea salt over it all. "I got that impression."

"Last night Abe seemed to think it might not be Kensing after all."

"Right. But last night we were all hot over Mrs. Loring, and we knew for a fact that Eric wasn't around when she was killed, so it looked like he was completely in the clear. But today, unfortunately, it turns out that these other deaths at Portola might have nothing to do with Markham or his wife. Basically, it looks like nobody in the universe that could have killed Mrs.

498

Loring even knew Carla Markham, much less went to her house. In which case, they're unrelated."

"In which case, your client gets back on Abe's list."

"If he ever really left. But you know Abe. He likes to start with a big list, then whittle it down."

"You're saying he's got a lot of other suspects?"

"Sure. It's still early."

"How many?"

"Two, maybe three others."

Frannie whistled softly. "Big list. Anybody else Abe likes as well as Kensing?"

Hardy held his menu and looked down at it, then up at her, grinning. "But enough about the law. I'm going with the sand dabs tonight. There is no fish more succulent than a fresh Pacific Ocean sand dab, and they do them great here. Lemon, butter, capers. Out of this world. You really ought to try them."

32

Kensing was in a business suit, sitting at his kitchen table. He had poured some coffee for both of them, but the cups sat cool and untouched.

Hardy sat between the table and the sink. He had pushed himself back a little so he could cross his legs, and now his ankle rested on its opposite knee. "So you told Glitsky this last night, too?"

"Yeah, of course. Why wouldn't I? It's the truth. Jesus Christ, Diz, why do we keep going back over this? There's nothing to talk about!"

Hardy drew a breath, collected himself, let the breath out. It was possible, he supposed, though doubtful, that Judith had remembered the wrong night. "As a matter of fact, there is, Eric. The reason I can't get over it is that you never told me that Dr. Cohn was here that night, sleeping over. This is hard for me to fathom since she could have corroborated your alibi." His voice grew harsh. "And then we could just leave it. Or is it time to find yourself another lawyer?"

Kensing's eyes did a quick dance, came to rest. "She was asleep when I got home." He paused, scratched his fingernail across the table. "As it turns out, I didn't wake her up. So she wouldn't have known I was there. I wanted to keep her out of it."

Hardy waited to see if Kensing would ask the

obvious question, but when it didn't come, he supplied it. "Aren't you interested in how I found out she'd been here?"

No answer.

"I talked to her and I asked her, how about that? Last night. And she was asleep when you got home, you're right. Although it wasn't ten thirty, was it? It was after one in the morning. Are you going to tell me she's lying?"

Kensing ran a bluff for about five seconds, then all the air left him in a rush. His shoulders sagged, his head hung down. He stood up and walked over to the sink, out of sight behind Hardy, who didn't turn to keep an eye on him and suddenly felt the hair on his neck stand up. A selection of kitchen knives hung off a magnet strip on the wall back there. Kensing could pull one off and slash with it before Hardy could move a muscle.

He whirled.

His client wasn't even facing him, and Hardy felt a moment of something like shame. Kensing was leaning with his hands on both sides of the sink, staring out the window. He finally spoke in a hoarse whisper. "I've been clean and sober for seven years, Diz. Seven years, a day at a time. You know how long that is?" He chuckled bitterly. "The answer is you don't. Nobody does. So last Tuesday, the man who ruined my marriage and took my kids from me shows up in my unit, and three hours later he's dead. Just dead. An act of God as far as I know. Finally some justice, finally something fair. But then between Carla and Driscoll, there's bedlam in the hospital. Then Ann comes to see me and she's raving, talking about me *killing* him, and for a minute I actually wonder if I didn't do all I could to keep him alive."

He stopped, ran water into a glass, drank it off, and wiped his mouth with his hand. "Anyway, somehow I made it through the rest of that day, going over to Carla's, trying to find a place for this . . . this *thing* that had happened. Then that cop, Bracco, outside at Carla's, and more talk as though somebody had done this to Tim. But then I was gone, free from it, driving home at last. I even got all the way here, parked just up the street a ways. I saw the light on and knew Judith was here."

A deep sigh. "Then I walked down to Harry's and had a drink. A double actually. Scotch and soda. Just sitting there savoring it, the most delicious thing I'd tasted in forever. Then another one, drinking to the good Mr. Markham's health, the beauty of it. God, it was so beautiful." He came back to the table and sat. "Then *another* one, this one for all the lost nights and my babies and Annie and all the *shit* I'd taken from her. And a couple more for Parnassus and what my life had turned into, a sham of healing people with minimum care, pretending that I was some paragon of virtue and knowledge. One more because the whole thing's a lie and I'm a fraud. Then the rest because I'm a drunk and a loser and that's all I am. So finally, when I try to order one more, the bartender, God bless him, cuts me off. It's closing time. He'll even give me a lift home if I need it."

"You think he'd remember you?" Hardy asked.

"Without a doubt. But if this gets out, I lose my job. And I won't get another one soon."

Hardy considered it for a while. "You realize this is your alibi for a murder, Eric."

Kensing was adamant. "It can't come out."

A flat gaze of frustration. "Then you better hope Glitsky hasn't talked to Judith."

"If he has, I'll tell him she made a mistake. It wasn't that night."

The rest of the conversation was simpler. It took place in the lobby of the Hall of Justice. Both men had had some time to cool off on their respective rides downtown, although Hardy had come to the unsettling realization that now Judith Cohn had no alibi for the time of Carla's death. But he wasn't going to bring that up to his client, not this morning. He had other, more pressing concerns.

He started the conversation by reminding Kensing that there was no physical evidence tying him either to Markham's death or Carla's. Trials were about evidence. If the prosecutor found herself getting too carried away with motives and possible motives, Hardy told Kensing that he should politely answer the questions. He didn't have to be confrontational. Don't argue. Keep it on point. "And the point, Eric, is to take yourself off the list of viable suspects."

The lecture continued. Hardy once again admonished his client to tell the truth about even the most seemingly damning of situations — between him and Markham, Markham and Ann, him and Parnassus. Tell the whole truth, especially, about his trip to the bar on the night of Carla's death. Eric could believe it or not, but the truth was the best friend of the innocent. And further, protecting the secrets of witnesses was precisely what the grand jury was all about.

"You're telling me they don't leak?"

Hardy hated to admit it, but he did. "No. Everything leaks, Eric, from time to time. But the grand jury really doesn't leak often. If you're low-key and explain the situation, don't call undue attention to it, it will flow right by, after which you're not a suspect anymore." He really needed to drive this home. "Why should the grand jury care if you stopped by for a few drinks at a bar after a stressful day? Okay, you're an alcoholic and not supposed to drink — but murder, not alcoholism, is the crime."

Hardy needed to make him understand this crucial point. They were standing off alone by the wall engraved with the names of slain policemen. It was already after 9:00 and Kensing had to be upstairs by 9:30. The volume in the cavernous lobby was picking up with the increased traffic — cops and lawyers and a steady stream of the public, which sometimes did seem vast and unwashed, especially here. Hardy moved a step closer to his client, into his space, backing him against the wall, locking him in his gaze.

"Listen to me, Eric. You're an intelligent man, but right now you are letting fear and lack of focus hurt you. I don't blame you for being worried. It's a scary time, but don't let it blind you to the way you're going to strike those twenty grand jurors. You're a doctor, an upstanding citizen, a voluntarily cooperative witness in a murder. You can't be a suspect because you simply were not at Carla's when she was shot. You were somewhere else — *where that was specifically* isn't going to matter. Once the jurors hear that, the psychological advantage is all yours. Where you were when you weren't killing Carla Markham won't even be newsworthy enough to leak, no more than what color tie you're wearing. There's really only one person that gives a shit if you went to that bar and had a drink, and that's you. So don't let the prosecutor in there — Marlene Ash — don't let her paint you as a killer. That's not who you are. In truth, and in fact." Hardy actually poked his finger in Kensing's chest. "Get it inside you. Believe it. Act like it."

But his client still wasn't quite with him. "And you're willing to risk my career over it?"

Hardy considered and answered in a level tone. "If you go up there with something to hide, it's going to be all over you like a stink and the jurors will smell it. And when inevitably it comes out, you've committed perjury, which is a felony. Go up there an innocent man, that's how you'll walk out. If they catch you in a lie, and Glitsky will if you give him time, you're probably indicted. Then you've perjured yourself, you're still a drunk, and maybe a murderer to boot. Where's your career then?"

Marlene Ash had a double agenda but there was no doubt at all about which one she was going to pursue first today. She had Abe Glitsky's prime suspect for a murder at the table next to the podium where she stood. While she respected Clarence Jackman's opinion and the deal they'd both made with Hardy, she didn't for a moment believe that one of the staff doctors in the Parnassus Physicians' Group was in possession of any insider knowledge about bogus billing at the corporate level. So she was going for the murder indictment.

Over the past few days, she'd put in long hours going over printouts of computer files supplied by Parnassus, mostly about Kensing, his estranged wife, and their relationship with Tim Markham. It had been anything but pleasant. Without question, the two men had hated each other. Ironically, Marlene thought, and only from reading one side of the correspondence, Kensing seemed to become bolder and more threatening as the relationship between his ex-wife and Markham flowered. Markham appeared to be bending over backward to give Kensing what he wanted — the subtext being that Kensing would expose them.

And now, in spite of her ammunition, Ash couldn't seem to make a hit. She'd had Kensing now for an hour and he'd cordially rebutted each of her assaults with reasonable responses that rang true.

He hadn't been worried about losing his job under Markham (as the correspondence had made clear). The relationship between Markham and his wife was insulation against that. In fact, Markham's death had actually imperiled his employment. He was currently, under Dr. Ross, on administrative leave, proof that in a way Markham had been his reluctant protector, and not a threat at all.

He had once felt rage for Tim Markham and his wife. Certainly. Who wouldn't? But as a matter of fact, he was in a satisfying relationship at the moment. In retrospect, he realized that his wife leaving him had been an opportunity, albeit a painful one. There was no anger anymore. If anything, he was doing better than Ann. The divorce was proceeding amicably. They were sharing visitation.

Ms. Ash was misinformed. There had been no fight last weekend. Ann had had an accident. He had filed no charges against her, and she'd brought none against him. She was hurt and angry and wanted to lash out because Tim Markham had left her the week before. Her rage was understandable; his nonexistent. He took the kids until she was back home. He and Ann had talked for several hours just two days ago. The police had regrettably misunderstood.

Again, Ms. Ash was misinformed. He had never admitted killing Tim Markham. No, of course he hadn't. He wasn't sure what Ann thought she'd heard. She had probably misunderstood. He hadn't wanted to discuss her testimony with her in advance because his lawyer had told him not to.

He readily admitted that the Baby Emily case had exacerbated the already strained relations between him and Parnassus. There he had simply done the right thing, and doing so had angered the money people in his company. This was a recurring theme in medicine everywhere — money versus care. He was a doctor, and made no bones about where he stood on the issue. Did this, he inquired, make him guilty of something?

He had come here voluntarily. He could take the Fifth Amendment, yet did not. He wanted to clear the air, clear his name, so he could get back to his life, his patients.

"All right, then, Dr. Kensing," Marlene Ash said at last. "You were the last person to see Carla Markham alive, were you not?"

"I can't say, ma'am. I'd assume that would be her murderer."

A snicker rippled across the jurors.

"When did you leave the Markham house on the night of Mr. Markham's death?"

"At a little after ten."

"And you told Lieutenant Glitsky you drove straight home, isn't that true?"

"Yes, ma'am. That's what I told the lieutenant." He took in a breath, then came out with it. "But that was not true." He had his hands locked on the table in front of him, and addressed himself to the jurors. "Lieutenant Glitsky interrogated me on this issue. I didn't want to tell him where I'd been. When I talked to my lawyer, he told me that today I would be under oath. He told me my testimony would be protected and you would keep my secret. I'm sorry I lied to the lieutenant, but I didn't go straight home. The truth is, I'm an alcoholic and . . ."

★ ★ ★

Fisk and Bracco had decided that their priority was to collect the facts that they'd been unable to gather previously. To do this most efficiently, they should split up. Bracco had drawn Brendan Driscoll, called him from the Hall of Justice, made an appointment. The suspect seemed enthusiastic.

Driscoll had dressed for the interview — pressed dress slacks, shining wing tips, coat, and tie. When he opened the door, Bracco's first question was if he was going someplace.

The answer surprised him. "Don't I know you?"

"I don't think so, no." He held up his badge. "Inspector Bracco. Homicide."

"Yes, I know. Come in, come in."

They went into the living room, off to the left of the hallway at the front of the duplex. It was a bright space, made more so by the slanting sun through the open windows, the white-on-white motif. Water bubbled soothingly from a Japanese rock sculpture in the corner.

Bracco was suddenly, intensely uneasy. He could not place the other man's face, but there was an unmistakable recognition, a shift in the dynamic between them. Driscoll indicated one of the chairs, then sat kitty-corner all the way back on the couch, almost lounging, one arm out along the top of the cushions. Bracco got out his tape recorder, turned it on, and placed it on the glass tabletop, next to a large, flat tray of raked white sand and smooth stones.

Keeping himself busy with the standard preamble, he finally looked over again at his potential suspect. "I'm going to cut to the chase, Mr. Driscoll. I understand you were at Carla Markham's house in the late afternoon through the evening on the day her husband was killed."

"Yes. That's true."

"Do you remember what you did later that night?"

Obviously the question was unexpected, and resented. "What *I* did? Why?"

"If you could just answer the question."

"Well, I can't just answer the question without a reason. Why would you want to know what I did later that night? I thought you were coming here to talk about Dr. Ross or Dr. Kensing, that maybe Mr. Elliot had come upon something in what I'd given him."

"Jeff Elliot? What did you give him?"

Driscoll had to some degree recovered his aplomb after the insult. "Some of my files from work. Evidence, I would suppose you'd call it. Although the grand jury didn't seem interested when I talked to them."

"You think these files contain evidence relating to Mr. Markham's death?"

"Absolutely. Of course they do. They must."

"And do you still have copies here?"

Driscoll hesitated for an instant, then shook his head. "No. I gave them all to Mr. Elliot."

Bracco didn't believe this for a moment. "And yet you thought I was coming over here to discuss them with you?"

"I thought you must have talked to him."

"No." Bracco met Driscoll's eye. "But maybe I should."

"On second thought, he probably wouldn't show them to you. Sources, you know. But I could call him and get them back, then let you know."

"That might be helpful," Bracco said. "Or we could get a search warrant and go through them ourselves."

Driscoll was shaking his head, supercilious. "You're way late, Sergeant. Ross has erased all the good stuff by now. Everything about him and Tim, anyway."

"But you say you had it and gave it to Jeff Elliot?"

A self-important shrug. "I didn't read it all, but some of it was certainly provocative, if you know what I mean. He was definitely firing Ross, you know?"

"Markham?"

"I'm sure he was taking kickbacks for putting drugs on the formulary. Tim got wise to it, too, after Sinustop. He just needed more proof before he could accuse him directly. But if you read between the lines, you can see it. It was over between them."

Bracco decided not to press anymore with Driscoll the issue of whether he'd kept copies of his files, or what might be contained in them. He'd come here today to talk about the Tuesday night, and he returned to that topic. "I'm still wondering about after you left the Markhams'."

A petulant glare, then a sigh of capitulation. "All right, then, I came home here."

"Thank you. And what time was that?"

511

"I'm not sure. Nine, nine thirty. You have to understand that my world had just fallen apart. I wasn't keeping track of the time very well."

A brusque nod. "Were you alone?"

Brendan brought a hand to his forehead. He closed his eyes for a long moment. "Yes. Roger was working late, which he's been doing all the time recently. But I called him and he was just crunching numbers, no clients at that time, and we could talk. At least we could talk. It had been the worst day, just the worst. I almost went down to his bank just to be with him, but he told me he'd be coming home."

"You called him at his bank after you got home at nine thirty?"

"Yes. I was so upset, just so upset."

"Did you and Roger talk a long while?"

"I don't know. It seemed too short, but you know how that is. I just couldn't tell you how long it was. Honestly."

Ross didn't have any kind of trouble remembering. He told Fisk, "I was talking with Jeff Elliot here in the office until late — I don't know the exact time, maybe nine o'clock, something like that. It had been the day from hell, I'll tell you. Then he finished with me — although he didn't *really* finish with me until he'd written that fucking column — and I realized I'd hit the wall, so I got in my car and went home."

Fisk's young and earnest face clouded over. "So you got home about nine thirty?"

"Yeah, something like that. Is there a problem with that?"

Fisk scratched behind his ear. "Only, sir, that I think your wife said something about you getting home after midnight that night."

Ross gave it some more thought, then let out a humorless chuckle. "No. She's got it mixed up with another night. I've been getting home at midnight so often lately, she probably thinks that's my regular hours. But it wasn't anywhere near there. Maybe ten, tops."

Glitsky had put off taking care of some of his administrative duties as long as he could, but this morning he came in and began. For three hours, he'd been caught up in such minutia as collating the mileage run up by his inspectors on city-issue cars. Now he was chewing on the last dry bit of rice cake and sipping the dregs of his tea, which had attained room temperature. So he was in a suitably cheerful mood when Marlene Ash knocked on his door as she was opening it.

He sat back gratefully, pushed the paperwork aside. "You broke him," he said.

She closed the door quietly, then turned back to him and leaned against the wall, her arms crossed over her chest. "Pending verification of his alibi, which I'd expect in the next few hours, Dr. Kensing is no longer a suspect, at least for Carla's death. And that means Markham's, too, I'd suppose."

Glitsky squinted up at her, shook his head. "He doesn't have an alibi."

"He didn't tell it to you. He wanted the secrecy protection of the grand jury."

"As though I'd tell anybody?"

"He wanted to be sure."

"And you believe it. What was it?"

Ash uncrossed her arms and took one of the folding chairs across from Glitsky's desk. "You know the story of the man in the Old West who was sleeping with his best friend's wife at the time of the murder and got hanged because he wouldn't admit that's where he'd been? It was something like that, except it didn't involve sleeping with anybody."

"He was someplace he shouldn't have been?"

"Close enough, Abe. And about as far as I want to go, even with you. If this gets out later, and it always might, I want to be able to say I never told a soul. I believe it, rock solid. He didn't do it."

Still way back in his chair, Glitsky sat with this new reality for a long beat. "This is one of the few times, Marlene, when I see the value in profanity. You're truly satisfied he couldn't have been at Carla's? Who's going to check this out?"

"Not at ten forty-five, Abe. Unless that time is squishy and I have an investigator out checking now."

But Glitsky had taken Hardy's information, then gone back himself to talk to Frank Husic. He considered that man's testimony to be unimpeachable, and Carla's time of death established. If Kensing hadn't been there at 10:45, he was innocent. He'd give a lot to know precisely where the doctor had been, but knew he wasn't likely to get it from any source, and certainly not from Marlene Ash. "Thanks for the heads-up," he told her. "You got anybody else you like?"

"Not really, Abe. I'm talking to the accountant and maybe a couple of board members this afternoon. I've got to broaden the net and make some progress on the money side or Clarence is going to be unhappy. He's already going to be unhappy that his deal with Dismas got us nothing of any substance."

"It got me something," Glitsky said ruefully. "I didn't arrest him, which is starting to look like a good idea."

This was unarguable, and Marlene went on. "Well, anyway, I've subpoenaed all of their financial records for the past three years and we'll see who can explain them satisfactorily. I'm going to have the grand jury take the fraud issue head-on. Then maybe I'll get back to the murder indictment, but for now my priority . . ."

"What are you guys talking about?"

Bracco and Fisk weren't exactly talking. They'd come back and met at the hall after their respective interviews in the morning. The volume of their conversation out at their desks had pulled the lieutenant out of his office and his meeting with Ash.

"Nothing, sir. Sorry." Darrel Bracco didn't want to fink on his partner, although he was plenty disappointed in him.

"It didn't sound like nothing." Glitsky stood over their combined desk with the stoplight in the middle of it. He was looking down on them, one to the other.

At last, Fisk caved. "Malachi Ross told me

when he went home on the Tuesday night, but it was a different time than his wife had said."

"So Harlen told Ross what she'd said," Bracco finished for him.

"You told him?" Glitsky's voice was flat. Ash had come out and was standing behind him, shaking her head at these Keystones.

Fisk nodded. "She said after midnight and he said ten o'clock. So he just said she was wrong. She'd made a mistake."

"And then, the minute Harlen walked out the door, he called her." Bracco was appalled at his partner's error. "How much you want to bet?"

"Easy, Darrel." Glitsky turned a surprisingly patient eye to Fisk. "Usually when you get contradictory statements from two witnesses, especially if they're closely related, like married, you don't want to tell the one what the other said until you can get them together and confront them with the contradiction. That can be instructive."

"Yes, sir. I got that now. I made a mistake. Do you think he's called his wife?"

"Absolutely," Bracco said.

Ash spoke from behind Glitsky. "Do you have her number? You could call and ask her yourself."

Fisk said he thought he'd try that. While he made the call, Bracco started to tell Glitsky about his interview with Brendan Driscoll. When Ash heard about the correspondence and computer files, she piped in, "What are all these papers? He never mentioned them when he was up before the grand jury."

516

"He told me you didn't ask about them."

"How could I? I didn't know they existed outside of the company computers. What did he do, steal them?"

"I gathered he emailed them to himself before he got fired."

"So he stole them. Are they still at his house?"

"I got that impression, the discs anyway."

Ash turned to Glitsky. "We need that stuff, Abe."

"Jeff Elliot's already got it," Bracco offered.

"Forget it," Glitsky said. "He's a reporter. We'll never see it."

"So we'll go for Driscoll's originals," Ash said. "Where are your warrant forms? You keep 'em up here?"

"You might not even need them," Bracco told her. "Driscoll's just looking for a way that he can disrupt things at Parnassus. He's bitter. He wants to get back at people, especially people who made life hard on Markham."

Ash nodded, but told them to get a warrant anyway. Fisk came back over to the knot of them, dejected. "She didn't admit he called her, but she said she remembered wrong and changed her mind. She was glad I called. She was going to call me." He looked mournfully around him. "Ten o'clock."

"He called her," Bracco snapped.

"It doesn't matter." Glitsky was in a fatalistic frame of mind after Kensing. "The wife wouldn't have testified at trial against her husband anyway. We haven't lost anything. Not like with Kensing."

517

The two inspectors shot glances at each other. "What about Kensing?" Bracco asked.

Again, Ash stepped in. "You can take him off your list. He has an alibi for Carla's murder. I was just telling Abe."

This brought them all to silence, which Bracco broke. "So it's all coming down to Carla?"

Glitsky nodded. "Looks like. Is there anybody left without an alibi? Did you guys talk to Driscoll?"

"I did. This morning," Bracco said. "He might have been talking on the phone."

"To who?"

"His partner, Roger. I was going to check his phone records. It's on my list."

After a moment, Fisk perked up. "I don't know if you've heard, Lieutenant, but we've made some progress on the car."

Hardy should have been elated. After all, his client was no longer a suspect. He'd remained on the fifth floor, eschewing an opportunity to visit with either Glitsky or Jackman, waiting on a bench outside the Police Commissioner's Hearing Room until Kensing had come out. Eric told him how it had gone, which was pretty much exactly as Hardy had predicted.

The two men had walked up to John's for a celebration lunch but it had turned out to be a sober affair, in all senses. Hardy made a few — he thought — subtle attempts to get Eric to open up about his girlfriend. How had Judith Cohn gotten along with Markham? With Ross? With all the Parnassus problems, monetary and otherwise, with which Kensing had such difficulty? What were their plans together, if any?

Eric was reasonably forthcoming. She'd only been on staff at Portola for a year after her residency at USC and internship at Johns Hopkins, then two four-month stints — one in Africa and one in South America — with Médicins Sans Frontières.

"You know, Doctors Without Borders, although she always gives it the French reading, posters in her room and her bumper sticker even. She's proud of her languages, French and Spanish. And she's a fanatic about the organization, really. I think she's got me half-convinced to go over with her next time — it's Nigeria this summer — although God knows there's enough to do here in this country. But if Parnassus does let me go . . . and my kids, I don't know how they'd handle it. Remember when decisions used to be easy?"

After they said good-bye, Hardy stood in the sunshine on Ellis Street, about midway between his office and the *Chronicle* building. It should be over, he knew, but somehow it wasn't. This wasn't the familiar emotional letdown after the conclusion of a trial. There was no conclusion here, not yet.

Someone had murdered Tim Markham and his family. Someone had murdered a succession of patients at Portola.

And he still had his deal with Glitsky. They were sharing their discovery, and he was privy to knowledge that Abe did not share. It rankled and left him feeling somehow in his friend's debt, which was absurd. Hardy had, if anything, done Glitsky a big favor.

But whatever the complications, he knew that he was too involved to quit, even if there was no one left to defend.

It couldn't be the end. It wasn't over.

PART FOUR

33

There was no reason now for Jeff Elliot to use any of the dirt that Driscoll had supplied on Eric Kensing. If he wasn't any longer suspected of killing Markham and his family, then he was a private person with his own private problems, and they were not the stuff of news — at least not the kind of news that made its way into "CityTalk."

Hardy sat in Elliot's cubicle, the stack of paper Driscoll had provided on the rolling table in front of him. He flipped through the pages slowly, one at a time over the course of the afternoon, while Jeff toiled on his next column. It was really a hodgepodge of data. The letters to Kensing that Elliot had shown Hardy the other day, for example, occurred over the course of several months, and were widely separated within the printed documents. Likewise, the memos to Ross and the board on various issues, including Baby Emily and the Lopez boy, occurred in chronological order. Hardy was finding that only a careful reading of all the documents related to any one issue would lead to any real sense of the gravity of the thing over time.

There were at least a hundred memos to file, as well. Formal documentation — probably dictated to Driscoll — of various meetings and decisions. Nothing that struck him as new or important. More interesting to Hardy, although far more cryptic, were the thirty or forty short-hand reminders and comments that Markham had probably typed to himself. It was obvious that he believed he could write in a secure — probably a passworded — document, but that Driscoll had breached that security and gotten access. But try as he might, Hardy couldn't make much out of them.

Markham's early memos to Portola's administration on Lopez were mostly concerned with the facts of the situation. They were about insurance considerations and a litany of medical explanations of specific decisions that might mitigate their liability in the inevitable lawsuit.

Several memos, both to file and to the Physicians' Group, explored the culpability of a Dr. Jadra, who had been the first physician to examine Ramiro Lopez at the clinic. Somehow, Hardy gathered, it was determined that Jadra's actions were not negligent. The boy's fever had been mild on that first visit. The throat infection had not yet progressed to the point where a reasonable diagnostician would necessarily prescribe antibiotics or even order a strep test. Further, Jadra did not note the cut on Ramiro's lip in his file at all, and when questioned about it later, had no memory of it. These Jadra memos struck Hardy as interesting because he could read the obvious subtext: Markham was looking for a scapegoat, and the case against Jadra would not be as clear-cut as that against Cohn. So these

Jadra documents had, to Hardy, an odd, defensive character.

By contrast, when Markham finally recommended that they prepare an 805 on Cohn — which went on her permanent record with the state medical board and the National Practitioner Data Bank — the letter was sharply worded and extremely critical: ". . . Dr. Cohn's inability to recognize the early signs of necrotizing fasciitis and her failure to recommend highly aggressive treatment was surely the primary factor contributing to the patient's death. By the time he was admitted to the ICU, the disease had progressed to the point where even the most active intervention would probably not have been efficacious. We recommend that Portola suspend Dr. Cohn's clinical privileges for thirty days, that you submit an 805 report on this incident, as required, and that you conduct a full enquiry to determine the advisability of Dr. Cohn's continued employ within the Parnassus Physicians' Group."

Hardy knew what Markham was doing here — trying to distance himself and the hospital from Judith's failure to make an early diagnosis. Again, this decision was about insurance, about getting sued, about the money. From Kensing's perspective, though admittedly biased, the real ultimate culprit in this tragedy had been Malachi Ross, pulling the strings and denying the needed care from on high. Instead, the opprobrium was falling most heavily, and solely, on a relatively newly hired, young female staffer. Even if Judith might have done a better job with the early diagnosis, it was clearly unfair to single her out as the reason the boy had died. Many people contributed, as did the corporate culture, and Hardy thought the whole thing stunk.

It did, however, provide a solid motive for Judith to have hated Markham.

He turned the page and stared uncomprehendingly at the next. Something about Ross he was sure. The initials MR. Then "Priv. Invest." But did this refer to a private investment in one of the drug companies with whom Parnassus did business, or to a private investigator that Markham might hire to keep tabs on his medical director? There was simply no way to know.

He went on to the next page.

"I do not remember." Rajan Bhutan shook his head sadly.

Fisk had had a few ideas he wanted to pursue about the car and some other things, so Glitsky had asked Darrel Bracco if he wanted to sit in with him while he talked to Rajan Bhutan, who'd volunteered to come down to the hall in the early afternoon. Nevertheless, Bhutan seemed nervous and reluctant when he showed up punctually for the interview. He asked Glitsky several times if he needed a lawyer, and once if Glitsky was going to arrest him. Glitsky reassured him that he was free to leave at any time. No one was arresting anyone today.

Bhutan told Glitsky he did not like it that people thought he might have killed someone. Glitsky told him they just wanted to clear up some things he'd said before, maybe get a few more facts. But of course (Glitsky reiterated) he was welcome to call an attorney at any point if he wanted to spend the money.

But now with no attorney, Bhutan was saying he didn't remember the day after Christmas. "You don't remember if you worked at all that day?" Bracco was doing bad cop. Glitsky had already made friends with Bhutan in their earlier interview, and preferred to leave things that way.

"I'm sure there is a record of it," Bhutan responded, wanting to be helpful. "You could check with personnel."

"We've already done that, Rajan, and they tell us you were working that day, and it just seems like you would have remembered. Do you know why? Do you remember Shirley Watrous? She died that day. She was murdered on that day."

Glitsky sat at the head of the table, kitty-corner to both of them. He held up a hand, restraining Bracco for Bhutan's benefit. "Do you remember anything specific about Shirley Watrous, Rajan? Was she a difficult patient, something like that?"

Bhutan hung his head, then raised it again with an effort. "I do remember that name. She was, no, not difficult. There really is no one more difficult than another in the intensive care unit. They are all just people who are suffering."

"The suffering bothers you, doesn't it, Rajan?" Bracco was sitting across from him. There was a video camera masked in an air vent mounted in the corner on the ceiling, an unseen tape running under the table.

"Yes. It's why I became a nurse. My wife suffered terribly before she died, and I learned that I could help."

Glitsky poured more water from the pitcher into Bhutan's paper cup. "Did you ever think you could help patients more by putting them out of their misery?"

"No. I have never done that kind of thing. Not one time."

"Never pulled the plug on anyone when it was clear they were going to die? Anything like that?" Glitsky asked gently.

Bhutan sipped from his cup, shook his head. "No. Always, that is the doctor's decision. I am there only to help, not to decide. If I have a question, I ask a doctor." Again, he drank some water. "And I never know when people are going to die, Lieutenant. No one knows that, not even the doctors. No one but God. In these years I have worked at the ICU, I have seen people come in and think they won't make it to the night. But then, a week later they sit up and can go home. It is just what happens."

Bracco jumped all over that. "Well, Shirley Watrous didn't just happen. Something happened to her. Same as with Marjorie Loring. And you were on duty for both of them. What do you have to say about that?"

Glitsky leaned in helpfully. "Maybe they were belligerent, Rajan. They didn't want you poking at them, changing their beds. Maybe they were making it worse for the others in the room."

Bhutan looked from one inspector to the other. "I don't know what to say. What do you want me to say?"

"You are the common denominator on both of the shifts where these women died, Rajan." Bracco thought they were getting close, and his intensity came through. "We've got another nine or ten people who died in the ICU, and you were on for all of them, as well. If you were sitting here where we are, what would you think?"

He brought his hands to the black circles under his eyes. "I would think I must have killed them myself." His eyes sought each of theirs in turn. "But I swear to you, that isn't true."

Bracco threw Glitsky a quick look, then struck in a loud voice. "Are you expecting us to believe you had nothing to do with the deaths of these women? And the others? Who else was there, Rajan? Who else had any chance?"

"I don't know. I don't know, who would do this? There must be a record of who else was there. Some doctor, perhaps. Even a janitor or sometimes a security guard. They come and go, you understand."

Glitsky reached over and touched Bhutan's sleeve. "Do you remember anyone, Rajan?"

Bracco slapped at the table, then stood up, knocking his chair over behind him as he did so. "There's no phantom janitor or doctor, Rajan! There's only you, don't you understand? We have your records. You have been on duty for every death we know of, even Tim Markham's."

"Oh no." Rajan's eyes were wide at the accusation. "I did not kill him."

"But you did kill the other ones?"

"No! I have told you. No."

"Rajan," Glitsky said quietly. "Listen to me.

529

We're not going to go away. We're going to keep on this until we find the proof we need, and we will find it. When you murder ten or more people, I'll tell you for a fact that you've left a trail somewhere, either when you checked out the drugs or someplace else. Maybe you've got vials of it stashed somewhere. Maybe you confided in one of your bridge partners. Or another nurse. Whatever it is, we're going to keep looking until we find it. We're going to ask your friends and the people you work with. It will be very ugly and eventually, after all your efforts to hide it, it will come out anyway. You have to understand that. It will come out."

Bracco: "Or you could just tell us now."

"Do yourself a favor," Glitsky said. "It could all end right now. I know it must be bothering you. I know you need to explain why you had to do this." He stood up, motioned to Bracco. "Let's give him a few minutes alone, Darrel."

Glitsky wasn't going to leave a message at Hardy's conceding his mistake with Kensing. If he'd been wrong, and it looked like he had been — well, he'd been wrong before and would be again. But he wasn't going to give Hardy a tape recording of himself admitting it. His friend would probably run a loop of it and make it a part of the outgoing message on his answering machine. So he'd called once, left his usual, cheery, "Glitsky, call me," and waited.

The callback came at a little after 3:00. "I've got a question," Hardy said.

"Wait! Give me a minute. Fifty-four."

"Good answer. Unfortunately not the right one."

"You weren't going to ask how old I'd be when my child is born?"

"No, but that's an awesome fact. Fifty-four? That's way too old to have new kids. Why, I'm not even fifty-four myself, and my children are nearly grown and out of the house."

"So are mine," Glitsky growled. "So what was your real question?"

"Actually I have two. I had kind of thought we'd agreed on the idea that you'd inform me when you were moving on my client."

"Is that a question?"

"The question is, why'd you choose last night to search his place and not tell me about it first?"

"I won't dignify the second half. As for why we picked yesterday, we wanted to know what we might have with him before he got in front of the grand jury. It would have been embarrassing if he had a floorplan of Markham's home with X's where the bodies were found, and Marlene didn't know about it when she was asking him questions. Know what I mean?"

Hardy did and it made complete sense, as did the lack of warning. If Glitsky had told him in advance when they were searching, Hardy would have gone there first and removed any shred of anything that could have been construed as incriminating. He decided to move on. "The second question is easier. Have you talked to your two cowboys or know where they are now? We were going to get together again and I thought I'd set it up."

"They're out talking to somebody about the hit-and-run vehicle — hey, we don't call them the car police for nothing — but they ought to be back before five. Inspector Fisk has an aversion to overtime, whatever that is. You want to drop by here on your way home, they'll probably be around. I can congratulate you on getting your client off."

"You got the word, did you?"

"Marlene, just before lunch."

"Which leaves you where with the rest of it?"

"Real close."

Hardy chuckled. "Good answer."

"Why do you care, if it's not your case any-more?"

"It's still my case, Abe. I just don't have a cli-ent." A pause. "We had a deal. I may have found out a few things."

Glitsky decided he liked the sound of that. "See you in a couple of hours," he said.

The last time Hardy had just picked up and without any warning decided to pay a call on a working doctor at the Judah Clinic was when he had tried to convince Kensing to talk to him while he was scheduled to see patients. That hadn't worked out so well.

But after two plus hours with Jeff Elliot's doc-uments down in the windowless *Chronicle* base-ment, Hardy couldn't abide the thought of returning to his office. When he told Cohn what his unscheduled visit to the clinic was about, he was confident that even if she was busy, she would see him.

But maybe not. He waited outside with his brain on full speed for a little more than twenty minutes and still she hadn't appeared. He would give her another ten before he went inside again and made a stronger demand. It was the sixth consecutive day of sunshine, and he was going to get as much of it as he could before the June fog slammed the city again.

"Mr. Hardy?"

He squinted up, got to his feet, extended his hand. "Guilty."

Judith Cohn's mouth was set in worry, the cause of which immediately became apparent. The same question she'd asked first thing on the phone yesterday. "Is it Eric? Is he all right?"

"He's fine. In fact, he's better than he's been in a couple of weeks." He explained only that his grand jury testimony had made them decide that he was no longer a suspect. He said nothing about the actual alibi, the stop at Harry's bar. If Kensing wanted to tell her about that, it would be his call.

"So he's clear?"

"Looks like."

"Oh God." She put a hand histrionically over her heart, smiling now broadly at him. "That is such a great relief. I am so glad." Then the smile faded. "But you didn't come here to tell me that, did you?"

"No, I didn't."

Her hand was still on her heart. "What?"

He started at the beginning, his call to her yesterday, which had revealed that she did not have any corroboration for where she had been at 10:45 on that Tuesday night. Then the Lopez case. Her problems with Markham. Oversleeping the morning Markham had been hit. "I'm not saying that I think you've had anything to do with any of this, but the police may not feel the same way if they find out. With very few other people on their radar screens, it's likely that they will. It would be better if you were prepared for their questions."

She'd listened intently and now her face clouded over with dismay. "But I . . . I *was* at Eric's. I never thought I'd have to prove that."

"Did you talk to anyone else, see anybody in the hallway? Do you remember if anybody might have seen you?"

She was continually shaking her head, stunned by this development, how it might play. "And so they'd think . . . I could have killed Mrs. Markham and their children?"

"It would not eliminate you. That's the point. And they're going on the assumption that the same person killed Tim."

"At the hospital?"

"Yes."

For a moment, Hardy thought she might panic. Her eyes locked on his, then combed the street in front of them, as though looking for an avenue of escape. But then, almost as suddenly, the strain bled out of her expressive face. She reached out her hand and placed it on Hardy's sleeve. "Then this would only matter," she said, "if I had been in the ICU within a few minutes or so of Tim's death, right?"

"I don't know exactly. Enough time for the potassium to work."

"So let's even say fifteen minutes outside, and that would be a hell of a long time. That's when I would have had to be there, right?"

"Right. But it was my understanding — you told me last night, in fact — that you were there right after the code blue —"

"I was, but not right before. Right before — a half hour before, at least, maybe more — I was in the ER, putting some stitches in a baby's lip. She dropped her bottle, then fell on it. What a mess. But I had my nurse with me, and the baby's mom. Everybody, in fact. Everybody knew I was there. When they called the code blue, I was just washing up after the stitches and I turned to my nurse and said, 'I've got to go see if that's Mr. Markham.' She'll remember."

When Hardy walked into the homicide detail, it was Old Home Week. Though Bracco and Fisk had not yet arrived, eight out of the fourteen homicide inspectors were at or near their desks. Hardy thought it had to be close to a record for the room. The hazing of the new guys continued, he noticed — a Keystone Kops children's toy, two soft police dolls hanging from a paddy wagon, sat in the middle of their combined desks by the stoplight. While Hardy waited, three separate inspectors pointed out to him that if you squeezed the wagon, it went *"oogah! oogah!"* When he declined to try it for himself, they all seemed disappointed. Adding to the party atmosphere, Jackman had stopped by with Treya at the close of business and, hearing of Hardy's imminent arrival, had decided to wait around. Marlene Ash had finished up with the grand jury for the day. She wanted to get Glitsky's debriefing of Rajan Bhutan, as well as whatever late-breaking news he might have on the still-live Markham suspects, whoever they might be. Glitsky's office couldn't have held the crowd, so everyone had moved over near the first interrogation room, and that's where Hardy joined them.

After taking the expected grief from Jackman about the merits of the deal they'd made about his client, Hardy listened with growing interest as Glitsky went on about the second proven Portola victim, Shirley Watrous, and Rajan Bhutan. The consensus seemed to be that the two series of multiple murders were unrelated, and that Bhutan remained the prime suspect for the people on Kensing's list. They'd talked to him at length this afternoon, and Glitsky had sent two inspectors over to his home shortly after that with a search warrant.

The inspectors sent up a rousing huzzah when the rookies arrived. Glitsky turned and glared at the world in general, then motioned Fisk and Bracco over to talk with the big boys.

Darrel and Harlen, in Hardy's estimation, had accomplished quite a lot in a very short time. Since they'd just arrived from Markham's old neighborhood and their investigations about the car, Glitsky let Fisk expound on that topic, although his skepticism was evident. He proudly showed off to the assemblage a composite sketch of the car's driver. Hardy was glad to note that the woman bore no resemblance to Judith Cohn except for a halo of unkempt dark hair.

As the composite went from hand to hand around the room, Fisk then announced that their witness, a teenage girl named Lexi Rath, had tentatively identified the make and model of the car that had nearly hit her, and presumably hit Tim Markham. It was a Dodge Dart, probably a model from the last year of the sixties or the early seventies. Fisk had already contacted the DMV and discovered that there were only twenty-three such cars registered in all of San Francisco County. When he'd told Motor Vehicles that they were investigating a homicide, they faxed him the names right away. He now had addresses and registered owners for each of the cars, and with luck, by tomorrow he'd have seen most of them.

"Any of the names look familiar, Harlen?" Glitsky asked. "Related to Parnassus or Markham in any way?"

"No, sir."

"Well, good try anyway. If we get the car, that's something all by itself. Keep looking."

Hardy knew Glitsky well enough to see that he was humoring Fisk about his supposed detective work, but he didn't want to ruin his inspector's day, or dampen his enthusiasm. The man had put in a decent amount of effort, and perhaps it still might all lead someplace. Hardy thought a show of interest on his own part wouldn't be out of place. "Could I get a copy of that list, Inspector?"

Fisk looked the question over to Glitsky, who nodded. But it was clear the lieutenant's real area of concern lay elsewhere, in the alibis for the time of Carla's death. "Darrel," he said, turning to Bracco, "did you get anything more on Driscoll?"

"I don't think Harlen was quite done, sir."

His patience straining, Glitsky yielded the floor back to Fisk. "I thought I'd try to make amends for my giveaway to Dr. Ross. So I called my aunt Kathy — Kathy West," he explained to the rest of the room, "and told her what I'd done and what had happened."

"Which was what, Harlen?" Glitsky prompted him, much to Hardy's satisfaction.

He outlined the story briefly — Ross and his wife and his alibi. Then he went on. "I asked her — Aunt Kathy — if she could get in touch with Nancy Ross, just as a friend, and find out if her husband had called her and asked her to change her memory."

"But it doesn't matter. The wife would never testify anyway," Marlene Ash objected, repeating Glitsky's earlier argument.

Jackman added to that. "Your aunt's testimony would be hearsay anyway, and probably inadmissible in any event. Isn't that right, Diz?"

But Hardy was no longer interested in parsing the law. He wanted answers and information. He saw that Fisk had begun to wilt under the heat of the lawyers' questions. He wanted to keep him talking, to find out what had happened. "So what did she say anyway, Inspector? Your aunt."

538

"That Ross had called his wife and told her she was mistaken about that night. He'd been home by ten. She had to remember that. It was important." He looked around the room again. "But Nancy told Aunt Kathy that in fact he hadn't been home by ten, although of course she'd back him up if it was important to Malachi. It was probably some big hush-hush business deal. But she was *sure* that he hadn't gotten home until way after midnight, which is when she'd gone to sleep."

"Still," Glitsky said, "all that means is that he didn't go straight home." Hardy was reminded of Eric Kensing and all the variables on that score. "Is there any sign that he went to Carla's, though? Have you got any evidence or testimony or hint of anything putting him there?"

Fisk's face fell. "No, sir."

Glitsky threw him a bone. "I'm not saying it's not something, Harlen. And it does make up for the morning, okay. Keep on it. Now, Darrel, how about Driscoll?"

"He did make that phone call, all right. I talked to Roger — the roommate — and got the phone bill. Forty-eight minutes, beginning at nine forty-six."

Everybody worked it out in their heads. Glitsky said, "So he couldn't have made it to Carla's?"

Bracco seemed to agree. "He would have had to fly."

It was the bottom of the fourth inning and Hardy was standing in the third base coach's box at Pop Hicks Field in the Presidio. It was a great field in terrific condition in a city starved for playgrounds, but in typical San Francisco fashion, the Little League was probably going to get kicked off it before too long. They might be forced to relocate to a field on Treasure Island, in the middle of the bay. This was because someone had raised the issue that there might be toxins in the dirt. Though none had been found to date, every news story on the issue had pointed out that the Presidio had been a military base for years, after all, and who knew what those military types had dumped where. Probably there was poison everywhere — mustard gas, anthrax, battery acid. Hardy considered it foreordained that they'd shut the field down.

But tonight, it was still a wonderful venue for kids' baseball and Vincent had just opened the Tigers' half of the inning by doubling to the gap in left field — his second double of the night. He was now dancing down the baseline, trying to draw a throw from the pitcher.

Hardy's mind was not as much on the game as it could have been. After the meeting in homicide had broken up and Fisk and Bracco had left, he'd stayed around jawing with Glitsky and Treya, Marlene and Clarence for a few minutes. Marlene seemed to be excited about the prospect of getting her hands on Brendan Driscoll's computer discs, but since Hardy had spent a good portion of the afternoon reviewing those printouts to no avail, he didn't quite share her enthusiasm. He still had copies of Markham's cryptic notes in his briefcase — he thought he'd work on those puzzles over the next few days in his free time.

And in fact, he was doing it now, though still going mostly nowhere.

Clarence, obviously frustrated at the pace of the investigation so far, announced that he had heard from the mayor. His Honor had gotten wind of the second verified homicide from Kensing's list and wasn't much impressed with the DA's subtle approach to Parnassus and its troubles. The HMO was a major contractor with the city and their business practices were seriously suspect. Clarence was now of a mind to go and seize all of its records for the grand jury's perusal and forget about avoiding a possible panic among city workers. People were already beginning to panic — the mayor's office was fielding about fifty calls a day. It was high time to put Parnassus in receivership and turn the grand jury and another team of homicide inspectors concurrently onto this second set of homicides. Whether or not there was any relation between them and the Markham deaths, they were a big deal in their own right.

The mayor was adamant that there had to at least be the appearance of progress — he mentioned creating a special task force if there weren't some results soon. Everybody knew what that would mean. Meddling by amateurs, political deals, compromise, and quite probably no resolution ever. The message was clear: If Jackman wanted to get any credit for fixing this mess, this was his chance and he'd better take it.

The next batter lined a sharp single on one hop

541

to the left fielder and Vincent, running on the hit, was to third base and by him before Hardy got his head back into the game. The throw to home beat his son by fifteen feet. After the play, Mitch, the manager, came down to the end of the dugout. "Diz," he said urgently, "you gotta tell him to hold up on that play. Give him a sign. Come on now. You're coaching. Let's get in the game."

The Tigers won in spite of Hardy's mental error, and the team went for pizza to a place on Clement. The whole family had attended the game and didn't get home until 9:30. Frannie and Rebecca had become *Survivor* fanatics — they'd taped the evening's show and went straight in to watch the replay while Vincent showered, did the last of his homework, made it for the last half of the program. Bedtime rituals consumed another hour, so it was almost midnight when Hardy and Frannie dragged themselves up the stairs to their bedroom.

He came up behind her and put his arms around her as she was brushing her teeth, put his lips against the side of her neck. "I will come straight to bed if you're even remotely alive." They'd been having a decent run of physical contact and he was telling her they could keep the string alive if she wanted, but he knew she was exhausted.

She leaned back into him, managed a goofy smile in the mirror through the toothpaste. "I don't think I am. Aren't you tired?"

"Not really. Evidently I slept during Vinnie's game."

"It wasn't that bad. So what are you going to do?"

"I've got some reading material in my brief-case. Maybe if I blur my eyes just right, I can get it to make some sense."

He was sitting at the desk in the bedroom, five of Driscoll's purloined pages spread out before him. He wasn't completely sure why these five had made his cut — none had more than a couple of lines. But something about each of them had seemed pregnant enough with some kind of hidden meaning to warrant one more round of conjecture.

"See MA re: recom. on SS. Compare MR memo 10/24."

"Talk to MR — address complaints re: hands on at Port. PPG ult."

"Medras/Biosynth/MR."

"Foley. Invest. $$$. Saratoga. DA? Layoff? Disc. w/C."

"See Coz. re: punitive layoffs — MR. Document all. Prep. rpt. to board. Severance?"

And then a little voice said, "Go to sleep. This is not happening." He must have made it to the bed because that's where he was when he woke up.

34

Glitsky kissed his wife good-bye at the front door. "If I'm around for lunch, I'll call."

"If I'm around, I might go out with you." Treya gave him a mock-sad moue. "A year ago the mere thought of lunch with me would have made your morning. You'd have planned your whole day around it."

"I know, but we're married now, and you're pregnant and all. It's pretty natural, the romance going away with all that day-to-day stuff."

She put an arm around his neck and brought her mouth up to his ear. "What was last night, then?"

"Last night?" Glitsky scratched at his scar, pretended to remember. "Last night?"

She swung a hard elbow and caught him in the gut. "Oh, sorry." A smile, then, "Shoot for lunch."

Rubbing his stomach, he closed the door and came back into his kitchen, where Hardy sat at the table. He'd called an hour before and offered to drive Glitsky in to work, though he usually drove in with his wife. But Hardy thought he might have something on Markham, although he didn't know what it was, and maybe Abe, now pulling up his chair, could help.

Hardy drummed his fingers. After twenty seconds, Glitsky said, "You want to stop that?" Then, "Ross looks like he's in some kind of trouble, doesn't he?" A minute later, he pulled one page over in front of him. "This one, maybe, it could be Mike Andreotti."

"New to me," Hardy said.

"The administrator at Portola. He'll talk to you if I ask him to. He's all cooperation with these homicides. I might even go with you. Where'd you get this stuff?"

"Jeff Elliot couldn't make heads or tails of it. He said if I could, I was welcome to it."

"Yeah, but where did it come from originally?"

"It was Markham's, through Driscoll, then through Elliot."

"Not exactly Tinkers to Evers to Chance."

"No, but I'll take it."

"At this point," Glitsky was getting up, "I'll take anything."

If at Glitsky's last meeting with him, Andreotti had been at the edge of physical and nervous exhaustion, now he was the walking dead. He didn't even bother rising from the chair behind his desk, didn't wonder that the new man, something Hardy, wasn't a policeman or a DA or even a reporter. He just didn't have any more energy to expend. He'd been at work all night, dealing with a sick-out of his nurses, scared off either by the rumors or sensing an opportunity for leverage in their struggle for higher wages. He didn't know and really at this point didn't care. The ship was going down anyway, and he saw no way to stop it.

And now these men had a puzzle for him. He got a perverted kick out of that. He was so beat he'd have trouble with the rules of tic-tac-toe, and they wanted him to decipher this puzzle. It was funny, really, if he had the strength to laugh.

"See MA re: recom. on SS. Compare MR memo 10/24."

"No idea," he said.

The other fellow, Hardy, leaned forward slightly. "We believe the MR stands for Malachi Ross. Does that help?"

Glitsky had seen a lot of burnout in his job and read the signs here. He pulled the page around, facing him again. "See Mike Andreotti about his recommendations on SS. Compare with the Malachi Ross memo dated October twenty-fourth. Does that help? What's SS?"

This time, there was no hesitation. "Sinu-stop."

"And what was your recommendation?"

"Well, it wasn't mine. I'm just the administrator, but the PPG recommended —"

"Excuse me," Hardy said. "What's the PPG?"

Andreotti blinked slowly, took a breath, and let it out. "The Parnassus Physicians' Group. Basically, they're the doctors that work here."

"Okay." Glitsky, staying with the program, continued, "And what did they recommend about Sinustop?"

"Just that we'd been inundated with samples, and that perhaps we should make it a policy for a while to go easy on giving the stuff out until more data got collected on it. Which now, in retrospect, was a smart suggestion."

"But you didn't implement it?" Hardy asked.

"No. Ross overrode it. He wrote a long memo justifying the position — I've got it somewhere here. I gather the stuff was medically pretty substandard. I'm not a doctor myself, but some of the senior staffers were appalled that our medical director would put his stamp on anything like that. So as usual, we compromised, and Malachi got what he wanted."

"You don't like him much." Glitsky didn't phrase it as a question.

But Andreotti merely raised his shoulders a centimeter. "People become pricks around money and money's been so tight here for so long . . ." Another shrug. "If it wasn't him, it would be somebody else."

"Only a couple of weeks ago, it was Markham," Hardy reminded him.

"No. It was still Ross. Ross has the passion for money. Markham just wanted to make a profit. There's a difference."

"What's the difference?" Glitsky asked.

"Well, take Sinustop, for example. It didn't have to be any issue at all, but Ross saw it saving us a million bucks a year, right to the bottom line. If there might be some downside, he was willing to risk it if it stemmed the bleeding."

"And Markham wasn't?"

"Sometimes, but nowhere near the way Ross did. You think it was Markham who made the call on Baby Emily? No chance." He pointed at Hardy's page again. "Anyway, I guess that's why he wrote that note to himself. He thought Ross went too far there again."

"What about you, Mr. Andreotti?" Glitsky asked. "What did you think?"

Another weary sigh. "I know this always sounds terrible, but I'm an administrator. I resist the temptation to play doctor. I follow orders."

But Hardy had what he needed, and had already gotten a hint on something else. "If we may, sir," he began, translating the second note as Glitsky had done. "Talk to Ross and address complaints about hands-on at Portola. Parnassus Physicians' Group ult, which must be ultimatum."

"It was." This wasn't any mystery to Andreotti. He actually almost seemed to perk up slightly. "Sometime last year, Ross started coming by the hospital all the time — drop-ins, he called them. Checking up on our physicians' procedures on everything from birthing to surgeries to ER procedures first, making recommendations to save a buck here, a buck there. Later actually advising doctors what they ought to do right while they were treating their patients. Now, when you realize that even the lowliest GP has a self-image just a notch below God's, you can imagine how popular these visits were. Finally, the PPG issued an ultimatum that he had to stop and, mostly, he did. At least enough to satisfy them."

"But not completely?" Hardy wanted to be sure.

"No. But the drop-ins fell off from twenty a month to maybe five and he stopped giving orders disguised as advice."

"Do you have any record of the days he came? The actual dates?" Hardy asked.

Andreotti pondered for a moment. "No, I doubt it. Why would we? He wasn't on staff here, so there'd be no personnel record. He just dropped in. Why?"

"No reason. Just curious." Hardy kept it deliberately vague, pushed the other pages across the desk. "If we could just take one more minute of your time, Mr. Andreotti, does anything else strike you about these?"

The administrator pulled them over and took time now, one by one. "I don't know Medras, but Biosynth is a drug manufacturer. Most of their stuff is low-rent, over-the-counter. They're not real players, but I've heard a rumor they've got something big with the FDA right now." He turned to the next page, looked up. "Foley is Patrick Foley. He's corporate counsel. I don't know who DA is."

Glitsky knew that one. "The district attorney."

A light was coming on in Andreotti's eyes, but he made no comment, turning to the last page. "See Coz. re: punitive layoffs — MR. Document all. Prep. rpt. to board. Severance?"

"Coz is Cozzie Eu. She's the personnel director." He labored over the rest of the note for a few seconds, then slowly he raised his head. "Tim was going to let Ross go, wasn't he?"

Glitsky's mouth was tight. "It's a little early to say, sir. But thanks very much for your time."

As they drove out to the Embarcadero Center and Parnassus Headquarters, the way they decided to phrase it to corporate counsel was that Hardy was an attorney working with the DA. That was true in all its parts if not quite literally. Pat Foley met them at the door, saw them through, then looked back along the hallway in both directions before he closed it. They didn't get a chance to try out their explanation before Foley started talking. "You caught me just as I was going out, but my appointment is just over in Chinatown. Maybe we could talk as we walk."

In five minutes, they were in Portsmouth Square, surrounded by pagodas and tai chi classes, some Asian porn shops, and a line of cars waiting for space in the garage below. High clouds had blown in over the night, and the morning air was chill with a brittle sunlight.

Foley's dome shone even in the faded day. The few hairs that were left were blond, as was the wispy mustache. Thin-shouldered and slightly paunched, he was the picture of what a life behind a desk with tremendous financial pressure could do to a young man — he didn't appear to be much over forty, if that. When he finally sat himself on the concrete lip of one of the park's gardens, he was breathing heavily from the walk.

"Sorry," he said, "I didn't want to talk about it in there. The walls have ears, sometimes."

"Talk about what?" Glitsky asked mildly.

"Well, Susan said you were with homicide. I assume this is about Mr. Markham, or the other Portola deaths. Although I have to say I work almost exclusively with corporate matters. I'm not aware of any information I possess that might be useful to your investigation. If I was, as an officer of the court, of course I would have come forward voluntarily."

Glitsky gave him a flat stare. "Do you talk that way at home?"

Before Foley could react, Hardy stepped in. "Do you really believe your offices are bugged?"

The one-two punch confused him. He couldn't decide which question to answer, so he asked one of his own. "Is this about Mr. Markham then?"

The truth was that neither Hardy nor Glitsky knew precisely what this meeting was going to be about. The telltale initials MR did not even appear in Markham's note. So though they both had their suspicions that Ross was somehow involved, they didn't want to give anything away. "Do you have any idea what the word 'Saratoga' might refer to, Mr. Foley?" Glitsky asked.

"You mean the city down the peninsula, out behind San Jose? I think there's another one in New York, as well, upstate somewhere, I believe. Is that it?"

Hardy and Glitsky fell into a more or less natural double team. Hardy followed up. "Have either of those cities turned up in your corporate work?"

Foley turned to his other inquisitor. He thought a while before he answered. "I can't think of when they would have," he said with a stab at sincere helpfulness. "We don't have any business either place. Maybe a few patients live in the city out here, but that would be about the extent of it."

Glitsky: "So the name hasn't come up recently? Saratoga? Something Mr. Markham might have discussed with you?"

Foley passed a hand over his dome and frowned.

"Maybe not plain Saratoga," Hardy guessed. "A Saratoga something?"

That flicked the switch. "Ah," Foley said. "It's an airplane. Sorry. I think Saratoga and I think Cupertino. I grew up down there, went to Bellarmine. But it's an airplane. It's the one John F. Kennedy Jr. was flying when he went down."

Hardy and Glitsky exchanged a glance, and the lieutenant spoke. "Was the company planning to buy a plane?"

"No, it was Mr. Ross. That's how it was brought to my attention."

"In what way?" Hardy asked.

At this turn in the questioning, Foley actually turned and looked behind him. Wiping some perhaps imaginary sweat from his broad forehead, he tried a smile without much success. "Well, it came to nothing, really."

Glitsky's voice brooked no resistance. "Let us be the judge of that. What happened?"

"One night rather late, I think it was toward the end of last summer, Mr. Markham called to see if I was still working, then asked me to come up to his office. This was a little unusual, not that I was working late, but that he was still there. I remember it was full dark by this time, so it must have been nine or nine thirty. Still, he told me to close the door, as though there might be other people working who could overhear us.

"When I got seated, he said he wanted our talk to be completely confidential, just between the two of us and no one else. He said it was a very difficult subject and he didn't know where he stood, even with his facts, but he wanted to document his actions in case he needed a record of them down the line."

"What did he want to do?" Hardy asked.

"He wasn't even sure of that. Eventually, he came to where he thought he ought to hire a private investigator to look into Mr. Ross's finances."

Glitsky kept up the press. "What made him get to there?"

"Several things, I think, but the immediate one was the Saratoga." Foley was warming to his story, as though relieved that he finally had an opportunity to get it off his chest. "It seems that Mr. Markham and Dr. Ross had been at a party together one night at a medical convention they were both attending in Las Vegas a week or so before. They'd been close friends for years, you know, and evidently they went out together afterward alone for a few drinks, just to catch up on personal stuff. Well, over the course of the next couple of hours, Dr. Ross maybe drank a little too much, but he evidently made quite a point of telling Mr. Markham about the condition of his finances, which wasn't good at all. His personal finances, I mean, exclusive of Parnassus, which was hurting badly enough as it was."

"So Ross cried on Markham's shoulder?" Glitsky asked.

"Essentially, yes. Told him he had no money

left, no savings, his wife was spending it faster than he could earn it. Between the alimony for his first wife and the lifestyle of his second, he was broke. He didn't know what he was going to do."

Hardy had gotten some inkling of this from Bracco and Fisk's report on Nancy, but it was good to hear it from another source. "And what did Markham suggest?"

"The usual, I'd guess. Cutting back somewhere, living within a budget. It wasn't as though Dr. Ross was unemployed. He still had a substantial income and regular cash flow, but that wasn't the point, the point of our meeting that night."

"What was?" Glitsky asked.

Foley had sat on the hard, cold concrete long enough. He stood, brushed off his clothes, checked his watch. "Earlier that afternoon, Mr. Markham's wife had called him — this was between the . . ." Foley decided not to explain something; Hardy assumed it was about Ann Kensing. "Anyway, his wife called and asked if he'd heard the news. Dr. Ross had just traded in his old airplane and bought a brand-new one, a Saratoga. He and his family were taking it to the place at Tahoe that weekend and Markham's wife had called to ask if they wanted to fly up with them, bring the whole family.

" 'You know what a brand-new Saratoga costs, Pat?' he asked me. 'Half a million dollars, give or take, depending on how it's equipped. So,' he goes on, 'I arrange to run into Mal at the cafeteria and tell him I got the word about the plane, but I'm curious,' he goes, 'how are you paying for it?'

"And either Dr. Ross doesn't remember details from when he was drunk, or he figured he could tell his friend and it wouldn't matter, but he smiles and goes something like, 'Cash is king.' "

Now that he'd said it, Foley wore his relief like a badge. Again, he drew a hand over the top of his head. Again, he assayed a smile, a bit more successful than the first. "So that's it," he said. "Mr. Markham wanted my opinion on what we ought to do as a company, how we ought to proceed. He thought there was a chance that Dr. Ross was accepting bribes or taking kickbacks to list drugs on the formulary, but he didn't have any proof. He just couldn't think of any other way Dr. Ross could come up with any part of a half million in cash. He'd already talked to his wife and —"

"Carla?" Glitsky jumped on this sign of communication between them. "I don't remember hearing Markham and his wife got along, even when they were together."

"Oh yeah. They were inseparable for a long time. Before they . . . before all their troubles, they talked about everything. Carla would even come and sit in at board meetings sometimes and she'd know more than some of us did. It pissed off some people, but nobody was going to say anything. And it wasn't like she was a drain on the board's resources. Very direct and opinionated, but smart as hell. Business smart. Put it out there, whatever it was, and let us deal with it."

For Hardy, this cleared up a small mystery. He'd wondered about the note's "Dis./C." and had concluded it must be the personnel person, Cozzie. But now, maybe, C. was Carla. Still, he wanted to bring Foley back to Markham's action. "So what did you both finally decide to do? You said that it all came to nothing in the end anyway."

This was an unpleasant memory. "Well, I told Mr. Markham that if he really thought Dr. Ross was doing something like this, we should probably turn it over to the DA and the tax people and let them take it from there."

"But you didn't do that," Glitsky said. "Why not?"

Foley gave it more time than it was worth. "The simple answer is that Mr. Markham called me off the next day before I could do anything. He said he'd confronted Dr. Ross directly. Their friendship demanded it. Ross told him he should have shared the good news with him when it happened, but the money for the plane had come in unexpectedly from his wife's side of the family. An aunt or somebody had died suddenly and left them a pile."

A morning breeze kicked up a small cloud of dust and car exhaust and they all turned against it. Hardy had his hands in his pockets. He turned to the corporate counsel. "And when you stopped laughing, what did you do then?"

"I didn't do anything. I'd been called off."

"And you believed him? Markham?"

"That wasn't the question."

But Glitsky had no stomach for this patty-cake. "Well, here's one, Mr. Foley. What did you really think? What do you think now?"

The poor man's face had flushed a deep red. Hardy thought his blood pressure might make his ears bleed any minute. And it took nearly ten seconds for him to frame his response. "I have no proof of any wrongdoing, you understand. I'm not accusing anybody of anything. I want to make that clear."

"Just like you didn't accuse anybody of bugging your office?" Hardy asked mildly. "And yet here we are a quarter mile away. We don't care how you justify it. Tell us what you think."

This took less time by far. "Ross had something on Markham, as well. Maybe some shady stuff they both pulled together when we were starting out. I don't know, maybe something even before that. In any case, he threatened to expose Markham, and they got to a stalemate."

"And he heard the original, late-night conversation between you and Markham because the offices are bugged?" Glitsky's scar was tight through his lips.

"That's what I assume."

"How come you haven't swept the place?"

This time, Foley's look conveyed the impossibility of that, especially now if Ross had ordered the bugging and was now running the whole show. "You get on Dr. Ross's wrong side at work, bad things start happening to you," he said. Then added, by way of rationalization, "I've got a family to think about."

There it was again, Hardy thought, that sad and familiar refrain. Today certainly was turning into a day for clichés — first Andreotti just following orders, now Foley and his family. For an instant, the question of what he was made of flitted into Hardy's own consciousness. Why was he here without a client, on the wrong side for a defense attorney, at some threat to his own peace if not his physical safety? He couldn't come up with a ready answer, but he knew one thing — he wasn't going to hide behind his family or his job. He was doing what he had to do, that was what it came down to. It seemed like the right thing. That was enough.

Hardy was still tagging along while Glitsky was trying to get his next warrant signed. Judge Leo Chomorro was the on-call judge reviewing warrants today, and this turned out to be extremely bad luck. He wouldn't sign a warrant to search Ross's house or place of business. A swarthy, brush-cut, square-faced Aztec chieftain, Chomorro had ruined plenty of Hardy's days in the past, and more than a few of Glitsky's. But this wasn't personal, this was the law.

"I'm not putting my hand to one more warrant on this case where probable cause is thin and getting thinner. I've been pressured and finagled and just plain *bullshat* these past few days issuing warrants for everybody and their brother and sister who might have had a motive to kill somebody at Portola Hospital. That doctor you thought did it last week, Lieutenant, you remember? Or that nurse who might have poisoned half the county? And then, last night, Marlene telling me that the secretary had a motive, too?"

558

"That wasn't my office. I —"

Chomorro held up a warning hand. "I don't care. *Probable cause,* Lieutenant. Do these words ring a bell? I don't sign a search warrant, which I might remind you is a tremendous invasion upon the rights of any citizen, unless there is probable cause, which means some real evidence that they were at least in the same time zone in which the crime was committed when it was committed, and left something behind that might prove it."

Glitsky swallowed his pride. "That's what we hope to find with a warrant, Your Honor."

"But you've got to have at least some before you can look for more. Those are the rules, and you know them as well as I do. And if you don't" — Chomorro turned a lightning bolt of a finger toward Hardy — "I'll lay odds your defense attorney friend here is intimately familiar with every single picky little rule of criminal procedure, and I'm sure he'd be glad to bring you up to date. To say nothing of the fact that the named party on this affidavit isn't some schmo with no rights and no lawyer, but the chief executive officer of one of this city's main contractors. You are way off base here, Lieutenant, even asking."

"Your Honor." Against the odds, Hardy thought he would try to help. "Dr. Ross is the answer to the most basic question in a murder investigation: cui bono. Not only does he take over Mr. Markham's salary and position —"

Chomorro didn't quite explode, but close. "Don't you presume to lecture me on the law,

Mr. Hardy or, in this example, some mystery writer's fantasy of what murder cases are all about. I know all about cui bono, and if you're to the point where you believe that a smattering of legal Latin is going to pass for evidence in this jurisdiction, you'd be well advised to get in another line of work. Am I making myself clear? To you both?" He was frankly glaring now, at the end of any semblance of patience. "Find more or no warrant! And that's final!"

"I wish he wasn't a judge." Somehow, magically, the peanuts had reappeared in Glitsky's desk drawer, and Hardy had a small pile of shells going. "I'd kill him dead."

"Don't let him being a judge stop you. It's no worse killing a judge than any other citizen. If your mind's set on it, I say go for it. I'm the head of homicide, after all. I bet I could lose most of the evidence. No, we've done that when we haven't even been trying. Imagine if we worked at it — I could lose *all* of it. And you heard His Honor — no evidence, no warrant. I might not even get to arrest you, although I'd hate to miss that part. Maybe I could arrest you, then have to release you for lack of evidence."

Hardy cracked another shell, popped the nut. "That's the longest consecutive bunch of words you've ever strung together."

"When I was in high school, I did the 'Friends, Romans, Countrymen' speech in *Julius Caesar*. That was way more words."

"But you didn't make them up. There's a difference."

Glitsky shrugged. "Not that much. You'd be surprised."

"You were Mark Antony?"

Another shrug. "It was a liberal school. Then next year, we did *Othello,* and they wouldn't let me do him because he was black."

"Did you point out to them that you were black, too?"

"I thought they might have seen it on their own. But I guess not."

"So you were discriminated against?"

"Must have been. It couldn't have been just somebody else was better for the part."

"Bite your tongue. If you didn't get the part and you were black, then that's why. Go no further. The truth shall set you free. How long have you lived in San Francisco anyway, that I've still got to tell you the rules? I bet even after all this time, you could sue somebody for pain and suffering and get rich. I could write up the papers for you and maybe I could get rich, too. You would have been a great Othello, I bet."

"Freshman year, I didn't get Shylock either, and I'm half-Jewish."

Hardy clucked. "No wonder you became a cop. To fight injustice."

"Well," Glitsky deadpanned, "it was either that or girls liked the uniform."

"Your school did a lot of Shakespeare."

Glitsky slowly savored a peanut. "It was a different era," he said. "The old days."

35

Rajan Bhutan gripped the telephone receiver as if his life depended upon it. He sat at the small square table in his kitchen that he used for eating and reading, for his jigsaw puzzles and bridge games. This evening, the tabletop was bare except for a drinking glass that he'd filled with tap water against the thirst that he knew would threaten to choke off his words when he began to speak.

Since Chatterjee had died, he had been continually downsizing, winnowing out the superficialities most people lived with and even felt they needed. Now the simplicity of his life was monastic.

The two-room studio apartment in which he lived was at the intersection of Cole and Frederick, within walking distance of Portola. It consisted of a tiny, dark bedroom and a slightly larger — though no one would call it large — kitchen. The only entrance to the unit was a single door without an entryway of any kind. The framing itself was flush to the stucco outside and all but invisible. Painted a cracked and peeling red, and seemingly stuck willy-nilly onto the side of the four-story apartment building, the door itself might have been the trompe l'oeil work of a talented artist with a sense of humor. Because of the slope of the street, most of the studio itself was actually below street level, and this made the place perennially cold, dark, and damp.

Rajan didn't mind.

Rent control would keep the place under seven hundred dollars for at least several more years. He had a hot plate for cooking his rice and one-pot curries. The plumbing was actually quite good. There was regular hot water in the kitchen sink and in the walk-in shower. The toilet flushed. The half refrigerator stuffed under the Formica countertop on the windowless front wall held enough vegetables to last a week, sometimes more. A portable space heater helped in the mornings.

Now, as the first ring sounded through the phone, he raised his head to the one window, covered with a yellowing muslin cloth. Outside, it wouldn't be dark for another hour or more, but the shade cast by his own building had already cast the block in dusk. A couple walked by, laughing, and he could make out the silhouettes of their legs as they passed — at this point, the bottom of the window was no more than twenty inches above the sidewalk.

The muscles around his mouth twitched, either with nerves or with something like the sense memory of what smiling had been like. A tiny movement on the Formica counter drew his gaze there — a cockroach crossing the chessboard. For a year now, he'd been enjoying the same game, conducted by mail with Chatterjee's father in Delhi. He thought in another two moves — maybe less than a month — he could force a stalemate, when for a long while it looked as though he'd be checkmated. He believed that a stalemate was far preferable to a defeat — those who disagreed with him, he felt, missed the point.

The phone rang again. He ran his other hand over the various grains of the table, which was his one indulgence. He had always loved woods — he and Chatterjee had done their apartment mostly in teak from the Scandinavian factory stores. Cheap and durable, he had loved the lightness, the feel of it, the grain. They used a sandalwood oil rub that he could still smell sometimes when he meditated.

But he had changed now over the years and this table was something altogether different — it was a game table of some mixed dark hardwoods laid in a herringbone fashion. Each place had a drawer built into the right-hand corner, which players could pull out and rest drinks upon. He hosted his bridge group every four weeks, and the other three men admired the sturdy, utilitarian, practical design.

"Hello. Ross residence."

"Hello. Is Dr. Malachi Ross at home, if you please?"

"May I tell him who's calling?"

"My name is Rajan Bhutan. He may not know me, but please tell him that I am a nurse at Portola Hospital attached to the intensive care unit. He might remember the name. It is most urgent that we speak."

"Just a moment, please."

Another wait. Rajan closed his eyes and tried to will his mind into a calm state. It would not do, not at all, to sound frightened or nervous. He was simply conveying information and an offer. He straightened his back in his chair. Drawing a long and deep breath down into the center of his body, he let it rest there until it became warm and he could release it slowly. He took a sip of water, swallowed, cleared his throat.

"This is Dr. Ross. Who is this again, please?"

"Dr. Ross, I am Rajan Bhutan, from Portola Hospital. Perhaps you remember, I was in the ICU with Dr. Kensing when Mr. Markham died. I am sorry to bother you at home."

"How did you get my home phone number?" he asked. "It's unlisted."

"It can be found if it's needed. If one knows where to look."

After a short silence, Ross sounded slightly cautious. "All right. How can I help you? The maid said it was urgent."

Rajan reached for the water again and drank quickly. "It is that. I need to speak with you frankly. Are you in a place you can talk freely?"

Ross's tone kissed the bounds of aggressiveness. "What's this about?"

"It is something we need to discuss."

"That's what we're doing now but I'm afraid I don't have too much more time. My wife and I are going out in a few minutes. If it can wait —"

"No! I'm sorry, but it cannot. It has to be now or I will speak to the police on my own."

After a short pause, Ross said, "Just a minute." Rajan heard his footsteps retreating, a door closing, the steps coming back. "All right, I'm listening. But make it fast."

565

"As you may know, the police are looking into the deaths now of several patients at the ICU that they are calling homicides."

"Of course I've heard about that. I run the company. I've been monitoring it closely, but that has nothing to do with me personally."

"I'm afraid it has, instead, to do with me, Doctor. The police have talked to me more than once. I am the only nurse who has worked the shifts when several of the deaths have occurred. I think they will decide I have killed these people."

He listened while Ross took a couple of breaths. Then, "If you did, you'll get no sympathy from me."

"No, I would not expect that. No more than you would get it from me if they charged you with killing Mr. Markham or the others."

This time the pause lasted several seconds. "What are you saying?"

"I think you know what I am saying. We would not be talking still if you did not know. I saw you."

"You saw me what? I don't know what you're talking about."

"Please, Doctor, please," Rajan said. He could feel his throat catching, and reached for the water. "We don't need to waste time in denials. We don't have time. Instead, I have a proposal for you."

"You do? How amusing. You've obviously got an agile mind, Mr. Bhutan. So I'd be curious to hear what it was, although your premise is fatally flawed."

"If it is, we shall see. My idea is only this —

566

you may remember the day after Christmas, four months ago, when you did a drop-in at the ICU? Is that still familiar to you? I was on that shift and there was a patient named Shirley Watrous."

"And the police think you killed her? Is that it?"

Rajan ignored the question. "But you were there with me. I keep a daily diary, but also I remember. You and I had a pleasant discussion about working during the holiday season. People don't like it, but it is in many ways preferable to the family obligations and raised expectations. You may remember."

"Maybe I do, but what's your point? Was that the day after Christmas? I don't remember that."

"But you must, you see."

"I'm hanging up now," Ross said.

But he did not, and Rajan went on. "I didn't even realize what you were doing, of course. And then the police told me the names of some of the others. And I realized you'd been there for all of them, and what you'd done.

"I feel like a fool, really. Perhaps I always knew, but how could one in my place ever even suggest that you were doing . . . what you were doing? I, not even a doctor.

"And who was to say it was the wrong thing, to put these people beyond pain, even if I had been sure? No one even questioned the deaths before, so how could I accuse you when everyone else seemed to take these things for granted?"

Rajan's clipped tones were speeding up and he forced himself to slow down. "Then when I saw you with Mr. Markham's IV, I thought again I must have been wrong. I did not want to know. I was too afraid to say anything. Then I was afraid because I had not said anything sooner. But now I am most afraid of all, because I know if I accuse you, you will accuse me. But I was not at the hospital for all these killings, and I know you had to be, because you did them."

He was at the end. He closed his eyes for the strength to finish. "So please, Doctor. Please. You must tell the police I was with you when these people died. You will be my alibi. And, of course, I shall be yours."

"You can't be serious?" Ross's tone was harsh, filled with disbelief and even outrage.

But he was still on the line. Rajan had seen similar bluster among the vanquished during bridge tournaments, and even chess games, when in fact they had known all was lost.

"Your nerve amazes me, Mr. Bhutan. Are you sure that's all you want?"

"No, not quite. I'm afraid I will have to be leaving the country soon. So I will also need to have fifty thousand dollars, please. Tonight. In cash."

Panic was the devil.

Ross had a core belief that it was a characteristic of wisdom not to do desperate acts. His great talent, he sometimes thought, was in recognizing the desperation of others.

Emergency at the office, he told Nancy. Something to do with an audit. Yeah, even Friday night. These people worked all the time. He had to go in, but he'd make it up to her. Tell the Sullivans he was sorry — to make up for the last-minute cancellation of their dinner date, maybe they'd fly them all up to Tahoe next weekend.

In his office, behind the locked door, he was pulling the tenth pitiable little stack of bills out of his safe. This man Bhutan . . . he shook his head, almost smiling at the man's naivete. Fifty thousand dollars for what he knew? That was yet another problem with most people — very few had a clue about value. If it were Ross, it would have been ten times that, and a bargain at the price. But perhaps Bhutan really was being shrewd. If he accused Ross, Ross would indeed accuse him, but that would lead to awkward questions about why he had not spoken up sooner.

Just for a moment, he stood stock-still, trying to remember. He had been alone in the room. He was certain. Bhutan had not come in until he was done. Could he really have seen him from the hall? Seen him without being seen?

Not that it was going to matter. He couldn't take the chance that Bhutan would panic and talk to the police despite being paid. Or *not* panic and decide he needed more money. Or just do something stupid and give them both away.

And if Bhutan was bluffing, if he really hadn't clearly seen Ross at the IV, so much the worse for him. He actually presented an excellent opportunity to resolve this increasingly sticky problem.

The bills would be back in here by tomorrow

morning, although he would miss owning what he called his Bond gun. There was a certain charm in the Walther PPK that his father had chanced upon in a downtown gutter one evening, and had eventually given to him. He loved the secret sense of sin it gave him, the thrill of private power.

Carla had brought it all upon herself. "I know what you've been doing," she told him in the hospital that morning. He was almost certain that she was referring to his second source of income, the kickbacks. But it might have been the other, the patients. He'd had a sense that Tim was closing in on that somehow. Checking his drop-in dates at the hospital. Asking questions he must have thought were subtle.

The accident had thrown Carla into a panic. And under that panic was an insane, inflexible resolve. There was no mistaking the hysterical edge to her control as he'd come up to her in the corridor outside the ICU. Seeing her husband smashed up, intubated, unconscious, had undone her. Ross walked up to her, ready with a comforting hug and some platitudes about bearing up and supporting each other. But her eyes had been wild and desperate as she whirled on him. "Don't you dare insult me with your phony sympathy."

"Carla? What?"

"Whatever happens here, you're finished with us, Mal, with all of this. You think this will free you, don't you? You think this will be the end of it."

He tried again, a comforting hand on her arm.

"Don't touch me! You're not our friend. You're not kidding me anymore. You're not Tim's friend

and you never have been. Do you think he hasn't told me what you've been doing? Well, now I know, and I will not forget. Whatever happens to him — whatever happens! — I promise you, I will take you down. That's what he wanted, that's what he was going to do to save the company from all you've done to destroy it, and if it's the last thing I do, I will see that it happens."

"Carla, please. You're upset. You don't know what you're saying."

But she'd kept on, sealing her own death sentence. "Even if Tim doesn't pull through, I'll owe it to his memory to take it to the board. Even to the police."

After the explicit threat, did she think he wouldn't act? Could she imagine he wouldn't? Unless he acted swiftly, boldly, without mercy, he was done.

Knowing this and what he had to do, Ross first had to disarm her. He took her hands forcefully in both of his. They were eye to eye. "Carla. First let's get through this. Let's get Tim through it. I have made mistakes and I'm sorry for them. But so have we all. I promise you we'll work it out. If I have to leave, so be it. But never say it has anything to do with our friendship. Nothing can touch that. That's forever."

The plan presented itself full-blown. Potassium would leave no trace, and the hospital's PMs were hopelessly shoddy. If the coroner hadn't autopsied Tim — and Ross had never envisioned that — the whole plan would have worked. He realized that if he could make it appear that Carla was distraught enough to kill herself and her family, the police would never

571

even look for a murderer. He would use the gun Tim kept in his home office.

When he got to the house, the upstairs lights were out. He wanted the kids to be asleep so he would not have to see them. He would do that part in the dark. They would feel nothing, suspect nothing. Sleep.

But Carla stood inside the door and at first would not open it to him. "There's nothing to talk about, Mal. We're all exhausted and at the end. We can meet tomorrow."

But he'd worn her down. "Please, Carla. I know Tim must have told you some things, but we were working them out, just like we always have. I loved the man. I need to explain. I need you to under-stand."

"There's nothing to understand."

"Then I need you, at least, to forgive me."

And she'd paused a last time, then unlocked the chain. As he entered, he took the Walther from his pocket and told her they needed to walk quietly to the back of the house.

Now he would do it again. He had experience now. It had to look like suicide. It had to look as though Bhutan, knowing the police were onto him for all the murders at Portola, including Markham's, chose to take the coward's way out. That would close all the investigations.

He also had to make sure no one heard the shot, which he supposed would be louder with the Walther than Tim's .22 had been.

First he would have to distract Bhutan, then use chloroform to put him out. Except it would stay in the system long enough to be detected. Maybe ether? He had ether in his medical bag right here. That would do, as well. And of course he could simply shoot him as though it had been a robbery attempt or something. But a suicide was far preferable. He'd have to consider his options on the drive over, then play the thing by ear.

Bhutan obviously thought the police were coming to get him at any moment. So he wanted fifty thousand dollars tonight. He was desperate and, being desperate, he was doomed to commit foolish acts, to make dangerous decisions.

Just like Tim, for example. He couldn't get over Tim. When they'd both been humping to get the business up and running and there'd been so many opportunities to make hay under the table — much smaller potatoes than now, of course, and much of it in soft currencies and perks — the weekends in Napa or Mexico, the fine wines, the occasional corporate escorts for the convention parties when the wives couldn't make it. Tim had willingly enough succumbed to those temptations, right along with him. But the first hard money payoff had scared him off. This, he thought, was wrong, where to Ross it was no different than what they'd been doing. In fact, it was better.

But Tim always wanted to believe that somewhere inside he was essentially an honest and good person, the fool. Hence all the agony he'd put himself through over wanting to schtup *the admittedly sexy Ann Kensing. Ross couldn't believe that the guy had nearly ruined his life over what should have been at most a playful dalliance. But, no, he'd been "in* love," whatever that meant. *Stupid, stupid*. But not as stupid as letting himself believe that just because Tim had decided not to take anybody's dirty money, Ross was going to do the same thing. Oh sure, Tim had had his little crisis of conscience all those years ago and had come to Ross saying they had to stop — not just because it threatened the health of patients and the company, but because it was wrong. And Ross had pretended to go along. And why not? Why burden the self-righteous idiot? Why split the money with someone who didn't want it? Ross knew the truth was that he wasn't really harming any patients by taking the odious drug money. If Tim was happier living with the fiction that Ross had found the Lord with him, he'd let him enjoy his fantasy.

But then, even while Tim was sleeping around on his wife, he discovered Ross's brilliantly conceived fraudulent billings and could not believe that his longtime partner and medical director still cheated. And took kickbacks. His whining self-righteousness made Ross puke.

What a hypocrite Tim was, coming to Ross in hand-wringing desperation — what should he do? What should he do? It had come to his attention, and so on and so forth. Didn't Ross understand? Tim had asked him. He'd crossed the line where now Tim had to do something, now had to act. And the conflict was ripping him up — Ross had been his friend for so long. Their families, blah blah blah.

But even in the face of this direct threat, Ross remained calm and told Tim that if he felt compelled to accuse him publicly of criminal behavior, that Ross would have no choice but to point the finger back at him. They would both, then, be ruined, *and who would that serve?*

Stalemate.

But he knew that Tim was a time bomb. Eventually he would force the issue again, and again Ross would parry — it was the same with Ann and Carla and Ann again and Carla again. But Ross would not panic. He would calmly wait while Tim vacillated and if something did not change, as it often did, then Ross would eventually have to find a permanent way out, a permanent solution.

And then Tim was suddenly delivered to him, on the edge of death, needing only a push that no one should ever see to send him over.

He kissed Nancy at the door, told the kids to be good. In the circular driveway, he spontaneously decided to take the old Toyota. Bhutan's address was in the Haight and he didn't want to drive one of the good cars, which would only be magnets for the vandals. The old green heap would get him there and attract no attention, and that's what the situation demanded.

Throwing the briefcase onto the seat beside him, he pulled out into the traffic and adjusted the visor against the rays of the sun as it cleared the thin cloud layer above the horizon and sprayed the street in a golden glow.

36

As Ross drove by, the door threw him off at first. What kind of place did this guy live in? If it was just the door and the window down almost at the sidewalk level, the apartment didn't look to be much bigger than a closet. No space to swallow the sound of the shot. Fortunately, there was no lobby. He could simply knock and walk in, take care of his business, then walk out with relative impunity. Nevertheless, his heart was pounding much like when he'd gone to see Carla. This was a necessary business, but he couldn't deny the adrenaline rush.

He finally parked a block and a half down and across the street now in the last minutes of daylight. He tried to envision Rajan Bhutan. He must have met him dozens of times in the hospital, of course, but he hadn't paid too much, if any, attention. If he had any impression of him at all, it was of a quiet man of very slight stature. If so, Ross could subdue him easily if he could maintain an element of surprise.

But what was he going to do about the ether? Rajan the nurse would be intimately familiar with the smell, might pick it up as soon as he opened the door if Ross had already opened the bottle, poured it into the gauze, stuffed it into his jacket pocket. And how would he get behind the man? That seemed crucial.

There was no hurry, he told himself. He'd gotten the call no more than an hour before, then had made noises about fifty thousand dollars being difficult to get ahold of in such a short time. But Bhutan hadn't bought that. Told him to figure some way to get it and then be at his address by nine or he would call the police.

Ross looked at his watch again. It was ten to eight. He had all the time in the world. He held his hands out in front of him and looked at them for a long time. No trace of the shaking that had plagued him afterward with Tim, and then with Carla.

He was actually looking forward to the moment. This last-minute planning even had a little bit of the quality of a game. It was amazing how easily the man had delivered himself up to him. A phone call, then one decisive act, and his problems would be over.

And suddenly as he was sitting there, as he knew it would, as it always did when he really needed it, the solution came to him. He had been trying to be too clever by half. There would be no need for ether, no surprise. As soon as he was inside, he would simply brandish the gun and control events from there. Sit down, Mr. Bhutan. Spread your palm against your temple. A little more distance between the fingers please, so that I can put the end of the barrel right up against the hairline where it ought to be. Thank you. Good-bye.

Smiling to himself, he took the bottle of ether out of his pocket and put it and the gauze back in his medical bag. The gun was in his right pocket, small and concealed. He reached for the brief-case, opened the door, stepped out onto the sidewalk.

The dusk was advancing rapidly now. A light shone inside the low window, but there was no light over the door, which was to the good. He stopped and stood still for a few seconds, then proceeded uphill to Frederick, where his street dead-ended. He crossed to Bhutan's side. Now, on the uphill corner, he could see beyond his car down the hill and in both directions on Freder-ick, the cross street. A few cars were parked up and down both sides of the street, but there wasn't a pedestrian in sight.

He walked past the window once, leaning over to glance inside. It was covered with a cheap cloth he could see through when he got close. And there, waiting alone inside at a table, he saw Bhutan. He remembered him now, a nonentity. He stood another instant at the door, savoring the power.

It was time.

It had been a long hour and then some. Rajan felt himself nearly crying with fear and appre-hension when the knock came at the door. He picked up his water and sipped so he would be able to speak, then put the glass down on the ta-ble, wiped his hands on his pants legs, said, "Come in, please. It's open."

He almost expected Malachi Ross to look somehow different, but it was the same man who'd appeared at the hospital so frequently, over the past couple of years. Tall and thin, controlled and commanding, Ross exuded a quiet, terrible power in the halls of Portola. As soon as he was through the door, Rajan felt that physical force in the room. His bowels roiled within him, and it occurred to him that this might not work. That it had been a mistake. He might not be able to pull it off.

Ross closed the door behind him and took in the tiny room with a dismissive glance. "You live here?"

"There is another room," Rajan replied defensively, indicating his darkened bedroom through the open doorway. "I have simple needs."

"Apparently."

Ross still stood by the door. He held a briefcase and Rajan pointed to it. "Have you brought" — his throat caught — "the money?"

"This?" Holding up the briefcase, the man seemed almost to be enjoying himself, which Rajan could not imagine. "How much was it again?"

He knew that Ross was playing with him, but he didn't know the rules of this game. "Fifty thousand dollars."

"And I'm giving this to you because why? Maybe you could refresh my memory?"

"It does not matter. You know why. That's why you have come here."

"Maybe not, though. Maybe not the reason you think."

Rajan's eyes raked the room's walls. He reached for his water again and drank quickly.

Ross crossed the room in two steps and pulled

a chair out from under the table. "You seem nervous, Rajan. Are you nervous?"

"A little bit, yes."

"It's not quite the same as making threats over the telephone, is it? You and me here together, one on one?" Ross placed the briefcase between them in the middle of the table.

Bhutan tried to answer, but no words came. He tucked his head down quickly and tried to swallow. When he looked up, Ross was holding a gun in his right hand, pointing it at his heart. "Oh dear mother of God," he said under his breath.

Ross still spoke in the same conversational tone. "Do you want to know what I find supremely ironic about this situation? Are you interested? I'd think you would be."

Rajan could only manage a nod. His eyes never left the weapon. Ross continued in almost a playful banter. "Because, you see, what's funny is that you're afraid that the police are going to arrest you for all those poor sick souls at Portola that they think you killed. And you want to run, don't you, because you don't have any defense except to say you didn't do it. Imagine that. I'll be the first to admit that it looks bad for you, and I don't blame you, really. But I'll tell you something. You want to know?"

"Yes. What's that?"

"I think you're going to help the police solve this case, Rajan. In fact, I know it."

"And why is that? I would never tell. What reason would I have to say anything?"

"I'll bet you can figure that out, Rajan. The

answer is that you won't need to say anything. But the great irony is that after tonight, after you kill yourself, everyone will know not only that you killed all those patients — all those poor patients who were costing me thousands of dollars a day — but that you also killed Tim Markham and his family."

"You can take the money back." Rajan's voiced echoed in the tiny space. "A gun! There's no need to use a gun!"

Ross pushed his chair back and started to stand up.

"Don't move! Police! Drop the gun!" Glitsky came out of the darkness and was in the doorway to the bedroom, his weapon extended in both hands before him. "Drop it!"

Ross froze for an instant, turned his head, then slowly lowered his hands to the table. He dropped the gun the last inch to the wood, where it landed with a hollow clunk.

"All right, now, knock it to the floor. All the way."

Ross's eyes never left the weapon that was on him. He still had his hands where he'd let go of the gun over the table and he reached his right hand back as if to swat it onto the floor.

Glitsky saw his move and perhaps misreading it, perhaps lowering his guard for an instant, he let the angle of his own weapon drop a half inch.

Ross moved like the strike of a snake. He grabbed at the briefcase and with a vicious lunge, threw it across the tight space at Glitsky, who fired — a tremendous explosion in the small room — and blew the briefcase open as it hit him, knocking the gun from his hand, spilling the stacks of money onto the floor. Plaster from the back wall rained onto the Formica countertop.

Another explosion and more plaster.

"Don't you move!" Ross had his own gun back in his hands and had fired it at the floor where Glitsky had reached for his own. "Get up, then kick it over here! Now!"

Rajan was huddled in the corner by the refrigerator. Ross glanced over at him and told him to get up, too, then motioned for Glitsky to move out of the doorway to the bedroom and into the kitchen itself. The medical director was breathing heavily, but his eyes were clear and focused. He held a gun in each hand now. His mouth arced in a tight half smile. "You guys stung me," he said. "I'm impressed. Especially you, Rajan, good work." But then the mouth turned into a line of bitter resolve. "But I see what's going to happen here now. You! Cop! You came here to arrest Mr. Bhutan and he decided that he wasn't going without a fight, so it looks like there's going to be a shootout here after all. And sadly, neither of you are going to survive."

Still stuck where he'd been all along, standing behind the wall in the darkened bedroom, Hardy had no choice. There was no way he could predict when Ross might take the first shot at one of the two of them. He had to move first and fast.

The light switches were next to the door and he was right there. He reached up and flicked the switch down, plunging the apartment into total darkness.

And, it seemed, immediately into deafening sound, as well. He dropped to the floor and counted four shots in an impossible succession, running together almost as one within the first heartbeat. Then the sickening and unmistakable crunch of a body ramming into another one and taking the wind out — *"Hnnh!"* — slamming it back into something immovable, and accompanied by the crash of more breakage. Another explosive shot, then a further struggle before a final crash, a hollow thumping sound, and Glitsky's voice, almost unrecognizable, but clearly his, yelling: "Lights, Diz, lights!"

Which he hit just in time for the front door to slam open and Bracco's form to appear in it, gun drawn, hands extended. Turning the light off, and then on, was the signal they'd worked out for reinforcement. Then Bracco was all the way inside the room, Fisk behind him, with his weapon out, as well. Hardy leaned in adrenaline exhaustion against the frame of the doorway into the bedroom.

Rajan Bhutan was still huddled in his corner, crying softly, his head down on his knees. Glitsky, a gun in each hand, had gotten to his feet and was standing unsteadily over the prostrate figure of Malachi Ross, who was bleeding from the nose and mouth.

Turning, Glitsky handed both the weapons, butt end first, to Bracco.

Then he took an awkward half step backward, and stumbled, seeming to lose his balance.

Hardy took a step toward him.

"Abe, are you —"

Glitsky turned to him and opened his mouth to speak, but a trickle of blood was all that came out, tracing the line of his scar before he fell again to the floor.

37

CityTalk

BY JEFFREY ELLIOT

The tragic death of the chief of the San Francisco Homicide Department, Lieutenant Abraham Glitsky, marks a bitter last chapter in the saga of the Parnassus Medical Group and its efforts to remain solvent at no matter what cost to its subscribers and constituency. Glitsky, 53, had been a cop with the city for his entire working life of thirty years. In all that time, half of it spent in the homicide detail, he worked almost ceaselessly in the city's underbelly, interrogating often hostile witnesses, arresting desperate murderers who would not hesitate to kill again. His professional world was filled with violence, drugs, and disregard for civility and even for life. Yet the greatest boast of this deeply humble man was that he had never drawn his gun in anger.

Last night, for the first time, he had to. And it killed him.

He was not working with what the police facetiously call a no-humans-involved case, where everyone involved whether as witness or suspect already has a substantial criminal record. In fact, his killer was a classic white-collar businessman who had been the subject of a recent column in this space — the CEO of Parnassus Health, Dr. Malachi Ross. Glitsky's investigation, which had begun with the death of Tim Markham, Ross's predecessor, in the ICU of Portola Hospital, had grown to encompass the murders of Markham's family, and then, most unexpectedly, numerous other terminally ill patients over the course of a year or more at Portola. Dr. Ross now sits in jail, allegedly the murderer of all of these people, and of Lieutenant Glitsky.

Glitsky was a personal friend of this reporter. He did not drink or swear. He liked football, music, and reading. He had a dry sense of humor and an acerbic wit informed by a wide-ranging intelligence. Beneath a carefully cultivated, somewhat intimidating persona, he was the soul of compassion to the friends and families of victims, a firm yet flexible boss to his colleagues in homicide, and a paragon of honesty and fair-dealing within the legal community. Half-Jewish and half-black, he was well aware of the sting of discrimination, yet it did not color his judgments nor his commitment to due process. He treated everyone the same: fairly. He was justly proud of the way he did his job. He will be sorely missed.

He is survived by his father, Nat; his three sons, Isaac, Jacob, and Orel; his wife, Treya Ghent; and his stepdaughter, Lorraine. Funeral services are —

The phone jarred Elliot from his words.

His weary eyes scanned back a few graphs, realizing that it wasn't nearly enough. It didn't capture the way Glitsky *was*, the essence of him, the force he'd been to those who had known him. He looked at his watch — it was nearly one in the morning. He had another hour until he had to submit this copy instead of the other column he'd written this afternoon. Maybe he could pull the file for an anecdote or two, maybe a picture if they had one of him with something resembling a smile — highly unlikely, he knew — anyway, something to humanize him more. The telephone rang a second time — not picking up wouldn't help, wouldn't change anything one way or the other.

He grabbed at it — Hardy.

"What's the word?" he asked.

On the following Tuesday morning, Hardy sat in the Police Commissioner's Hearing Room, kitty-corner from Marlene Ash's place at the podium. He raised his head and saw the clouds scudding by outside and thought them somehow fitting. It was going to be a cold spring, probably a cold summer. He was going to take a sabbatical for a couple of months after the school year ended, rent an RV with Frannie and the kids, drive all the way to Alaska and back, camping. He was going to fish and hike and take some time, because you never knew how much you were going to have. Things could end abruptly. He needed to think about that, to do something about it.

"I'm sorry. What was the question again?"

"The events that led to Lieutenant Glitsky's presence at Mr. Bhutan's apartment."

"Okay." He spoke directly to the grand jurors assembled before him. "As I've said and as Ms. Ash has explained, I'd been working independently but in a parallel arrangement with the district attorney on elements of the Portola homicides. I had obtained access to some documents that Mr. Markham had written, and following up on those, asked Lieutenant Glitsky to join me. In the course of the morning, we spoke to Mike Andreotti, the administrator at Portola, and then the Parnassus corporate counsel, Patrick Foley.

"Lieutenant Glitsky thought we had enough information to obtain a search warrant for Dr. Ross's house — specifically, he wanted to confiscate his clothing and deliver it to the police lab to check for trace amounts of Mrs. Markham's blood, which — as I understand it — allegedly did turn up on one of his suits. But Glitsky was unable to obtain a warrant with the information we had.

"At that time, Lieutenant Glitsky returned to his duties as chief of homicide. He couldn't lawfully pursue Dr. Ross without more. I was on my own for the rest of the day. During our talk with Mr. Andreotti, I had conceived the notion that Dr. Ross may also have been at Portola and had a hand in the homicides on what we'd been calling Dr. Kensing's list — terminal patients who had unexpectedly died there in the past year or so. Another suspect for those homicides was a nurse at Portola named Rajan Bhutan. Mr. Bhutan appeared to have been the only person with opportunities for these multiple deaths, and with a reason to have killed them — euthanasia. His wife died several years ago after a long illness, and inspectors had noted that for a nurse he appeared suspiciously oversensitive to suffering. The police had interviewed Bhutan, but the lieutenant and I agreed that I should do another interview. Perhaps I would be less threatening since I was not a police officer.

"In any event, I asked Glitsky if I could talk to him and he gave me his permission and Mr. Bhutan's home address and phone number. I went to Bhutan's house after work. As I hoped, he finally voiced suspicions about Dr. Ross. He also admitted to a very great fear that the police would try to blame him for the murders. It became clear that Dr. Ross had been at Portola quite frequently, and at least on several other dates when the homicides were suspected to have occurred.

"At that point, I thought it might be worthwhile to try and force Dr. Ross's hand. Because of some other information we'd gathered, I suspected he had large amounts of cash on hand at his house. I enlisted Mr. Bhutan's aid to pretend to blackmail him, to see if we could lure him out and make him come to us."

Reliving it, Hardy now hung his head, ran a hand over his brow. "In hindsight, this was probably a mistake. I should have simply tape-recorded Mr. Bhutan's original phone call, which would probably have been enough for

Judge Chomorro to sign a search warrant. But I didn't do that. Instead, Mr. Bhutan made the call. When it seemed to work, I called Lieutenant Glitsky, who arrived there with Inspectors Bracco and Fisk within about a half hour.

"I want to add that both Lieutenant Glitsky and the other inspectors were upset with and vehemently opposed to my plan. The lieutenant actually predicted that Dr. Ross, if guilty, would become unpredictable and violent. He was very unwilling to involve a nonprofessional such as Mr. Bhutan in such a situation. Nevertheless, since events had already been set in motion, and since Mr. Bhutan was not only willing but eager to participate, we went ahead. There seemed no way to halt events without ruining whatever chance remained to force Ross's hand.

"So Lieutenant Glitsky and I waited in the darkened bedroom, just off the kitchen, while Inspectors Bracco and Fisk were stationed in their car around the corner with instructions to come running when the lights went on and off."

He shrugged miserably. "The plan seemed reasonable and not excessively risky. But I did not contemplate that Dr. Ross would act so quickly. In fact, had Mr. Bhutan not found a way to mention the gun out loud without giving away our presence, and had Lieutenant Glitsky not acted so quickly, though at great cost to himself, Mr. Bhutan might have been killed."

A week later, after hours, coming out of a client conference in the solarium in Freeman's office, Hardy was surprised by the appearance of

Harlen Fisk, waiting in an awkward stance by Phyllis's receptionist station. The chubby, fresh-faced inspector looked not much older than twenty. He seemed uncomfortable, nearly starting at the sight of Hardy, then bustling over to shake his hand.

"I just wanted to tell you," he said, after they'd gone up to Hardy's office, "that I'm going to be leaving the department. I'm really not cut out to be a cop, not the way Darrel is anyway, or the lieutenant. I don't know if you heard, but Darrel's starting over, in a uniform again, with motorcycles. My aunt's offered to find me something in her office, but I'm not going to go that way. People seem to resent it somehow."

"That's a good call," Hardy said.

"Anyway, I've got some friends with venture capital and they think I'd be valuable to them in some way. I'd like to give something like that a go. Be in business for myself. Be myself, in fact. You know what I mean."

Hardy, with no idea in the world why Fisk was telling him any of this, answered with a neutral smile. "Always a good idea. Is there anything I can do for you?"

"Well, you know," Fisk sighed, "I had hoped that I'd be able to find something on the car that killed Mr. Markham. I know people always were laughing at me, but I really thought for sure there'd be some connection, and I'd show them. But you were the one person who took me seriously, who listened, took a look at my Dodge Dart list, even asked for a copy. I just wanted to let you know I appreciated it."

The kid was going to be a great politician, Hardy thought. Every connection was a chance to make a friend, make an impression, trade a favor. "I thought it might lead somewhere itself, Harlen."

"Well, that's the last thing. I wanted you to know that it didn't. I checked out every one of the twenty-three cars in the city. There were really only twenty. Three were nowhere to be found. I just thought you'd want to know how it ended."

"I appreciate it," Hardy said. "Your new company needs a lawyer, look me up."

"You do business law, too?"

"Sometimes. I'm not proud."

"Okay, well . . ." Fisk stuck out his hand. "Nice to have worked with you." At the door, he turned back one more time. "Nobody blames you, you know. In case you thought they did."

The trail led Hardy to one of the housing projects, apartment house boxes in the Western Addition — three-story blocks of concrete and stucco, once bright and now the color of piss where the graffiti didn't cover it. As he expected, nobody knew nothin'.

But he knew that 1921 Elsi Court, apartment 2D, was the last known address for Luz Lopez, who had been the registered owner of one of Fisk's missing three Dodge Darts. Finally, he convinced one of the neighbor women that he wasn't a cop, that he was in fact with the insurance company and was trying to locate Luz so that he could send her some money. About her child.

She had moved away, the neighbor didn't know where. One morning, maybe three weeks ago, she had just left early and never come back. Though the neighbor thought she had worked at the Osaka Hotel for years. Maybe they had a forwarding address for her.

The car? Yes, it was green. The bumper sticker said, "FINATA."

Hardy did some research on the Net. FINATA had been an agricultural reform movement in El Salvador, where ten percent of the population owned ninety percent of the land. About ten years before, FINATA had been a radical government plan for redistributing the wealth in that country, but its supporters had mostly been killed or driven out.

She'd come here with her son, he reasoned. And then Parnassus had killed him. Markham, as the spokesman for the company, had taken the public responsibility for the boy's death, though Hardy knew it had been Ross.

But to Luz Lopez, Markham had killed her boy.

Powerless, poverty-stricken, and alien, she probably felt she had no recourse to the law. The law would never touch such a powerful man. But she could avenge her baby's death herself. She could run over the greedy, unfeeling, uncaring, smiling bastard.

It was four o'clock, a Saturday afternoon, the second day of June. Outside, the sun shone brightly and a cold north wind blew, but it was warm inside the Shamrock, where Hardy was hosting a private party. The bar was packed to capacity with city workers, cops, lawyers, judges, reporters, assorted well-wishers and their children.

They'd pulled in sawhorses from the back and laid plywood across them to make a long table down the center of the room. There were going to be a few minutes of presents and testimonials, then no agenda except to enjoy. The two guys in wheelchairs were at the head of the table, back by the sofas. Jeff Elliot's was the first gift and he banged on his glass to get the place quieted down. McGuire turned off the jukebox right in the middle of the song Hardy had bought for the occasion — it was the only disco song on the box, Gloria Gaynor's "I Will Survive."

"I think this is only appropriate," Elliot said, handing the flat package across the table.

"What is this?" Glitsky asked.

"It's the page proof of the 'CityTalk' column I was in the middle of writing when it looked good that you were going to die. It's a pack of lies."

"I wasn't ever going to die. I was just resting. It was a fatiguing case."

"Well, you had a lot of us fooled then."

At the shouted requests, Glitsky held the framed page up for the amusement of the crowd and everyone broke into applause.

Hardy, Frannie, and Treya sat around the far end of the table. "The wheelchair is a bit much, don't you think?" Hardy asked. "He was walking fine yesterday at your place."

"He's not supposed to exert himself for another few weeks," Frannie said.

"Doctors orders," Treya added, then whispered, leaning over, "The fool was trying sit-ups last week and ripped open one of the scabs. Sit-ups!"

"How many'd he do?" Hardy asked.

"Dismas!" Frannie, on his case.

"Eight, the fool!"

Hardy shook his head in disgust. "Only eight and he busts his gut." He looked down the table, glad as hell to see his best friend sitting there in whatever condition he might be. "What a wimp."

The trip took Luz thirteen days. It amazed her that after so much time, she could still find the house she'd grown up in. That was because things made sense here, not like in San Francisco. She had turned from the highway and come up through the town. One of the first things she saw gave her some hope. They had rebuilt the building where the newspaper had been, from which they had dragged her father. The last time she'd seen it, it had been a burnt-out shell, but no one seeing it now would ever suspect that.

Then her brother's clinic, Alberto's old clinic. It was still there, in the same place, looking well cared for with the bright flowers planted all around. She didn't remember those, if they had been there when she'd gone. There were a few cars in the lot out in front, people going in to see a doctor they knew. One they could trust.

She felt a sharp stab of regret, but she didn't want to let herself start thinking this way again. She had struggled for months to see that the bitterness was for the most part behind her now, purged in the tears and finally in the taking of that pig's life who had cost her son his. Now, although the loss of Ramiro would never cease to ache in her chest, she could imagine someday coming to a kind of peace with it all.

It all might have been to teach her something she might not have seen on her own. There was only this life and she had squandered a decade of it trying to fit into that foreign place, ignoring her own happiness and trying to make something that would be better for her boy. But what had come of that? Demeaning work, a life she did not enjoy for one day and never would, a boy who never knew the joy of a family, of the love of his father. A pain with no sides.

She was thirty-two years old and a graduate of the university. There was, she knew, work to do here in El Salvador — not only family work, starting over with José perhaps — but work with the people, to make this land theirs. This was where she would make her stand.

Her mother's house had grown young. The banana trees now grew nearly wild over the porch, hiding it in blessed shade. The paint was fresh, the screens fixed tightly to the doors and windows.

She had not called here since she'd left. They would be worried sick. She had just been driving, surviving to get here, through California, Mexico, Guatemala. The borders and *guardia* and men. But she had made it to here now and she stopped the car. After all the breakdowns in San Francisco whenever she really needed it, the car had finally been *fuerte* when it mattered. She pulled to the side of the road. Getting out, stretching, she was aware that she stunk.

She did not care. It didn't matter. She wasn't

in the U.S. anymore.

There was a motor going somewhere in the back and she walked around the house to the sound of it. José — strong, silent, ugly José — had his shirt off working over the generator they still used most of the time for their electricity. After all these years, she still knew his body.

Standing ten feet from him now in the saw grass, she waited in a kind of hysterical suspense. How badly did the scars show on her? Had she changed beyond his recognition, and if he did know who she was, would he still love her? Would she love him?

Suddenly the noise stopped. He straightened up, wiped his forehead with a bandanna, then saw her.

For a long moment, nothing in the world moved. Then his face broke into the smile of his youth. He held out his arms, took a step toward her, and she ran to his embrace.